Accounts of William Gillette

America's Sherlock Holmes

Five Mystery Stories

Flowers Bloom on Broadway

The Case of Slow Service

One Part Suicide

Cash Not Compliments

Fall of the Musketeers

James Michael Walker

Library of Congress and Printing Information.

First Printing December 2017
Second Printing December 2019

Printed in the United States of America

ISBN 978-0-9981121-1-4

Prologue

Charles Frohman was a man who built a multi-million dollar theater syndicate throughout these great United States and Europe from 1880 to his untimely death in 1915. Yet, in his heart my father was a writer, proved by his many journaled accounts of his travels, and adventures with his best friend, William Hooker Gillette.

William was a true genius, aside from being the greatest stage actor in 1900, and the man who brought Sherlock Holmes to the stage he was a set designer, builder, inventor, playwright, and scholar -- just to list a few of his talents. He is one of those rare individuals' who blended high intelligence with life experience to give him an unerring path to the truth. His uncanny reasoning, sharp observation, and leaps of deductions have unraveled many enigmas.

William Gillette's legendary ability to observe finest details and powers of deduction were witnessed by my father Frohman, and faithfully journaled by his hand. There are stacks of these accounts, neatly stacked in separate folders, and were carefully stored in a hidden cedar lined steel box., that I chanced upon in my father's library. I suspect he sequestered these accounts out of respect for his best friend's desire for privacy. William's modesty and wishes for as much privacy as his fame would allow, was well noted by those of us close to him. But now that he's gone…

As an author once said to me 'If it would be written – it should be read.'

Collin Frohman

December 17th

1940

Flowers Bloom On Broadway

October, 1895

PART ONE

"When the stage curtain rises late, it throws off everyone's timing, you idiot! A bad start is worse than a poor finish! I swear to God, if that curtain rise is just one second late, you'll be wishing your mama never took that second glass of grappa from your Pa, you Dag."

"Hold on now! There's no need to bring his mother into this. Or his ancestry! I'm sure there was a perfectly good reason why Roberto Manchella, the best curtain man in the business, was off a tad."

It took a second for my brain to register that someone could be witless enough to open his mouth while I was in mid-tirade! Men fled, women wailed, and children wet themselves when I was irate! I knew I got a bit testy on Opening Day but everyone in the know was smart enough to do their job perfectly and to avoid my attention when the whirlwind was on me.

Roberto, who had just borne the brunt of my latest mad soliloquy, nodded like a loon and sputtered, "Sir! Sir! It was the ropes, Senor Frohman! They were-a hung up on top. Those estupidos who lifted the lights took mi guide ropa with it. It took me a few tries to flip it off!"

"There now! No need to burst a blood vessel." Even from behind me, I knew that familiar voice, but its light sarcastic tone infuriated me so I couldn't focus! I spun around to let my heckler have it with both barrels!

"God's blood, man-"

But, when I looked up at that handsome face, grinning ear to ear insincere fondness, it was like sticking my head in a snowbank. How could you cuss out a mug like that?

As it was, I had to simmer down quickly. It wouldn't do to alienate this man. Besides being America's premier actor, a good friend, and business asset, he was also family of a sort. His wife and mine were second cousins.

"And you really shouldn't blaspheme."

"William Hooker Gillette." I said with a crocodile smile. "What brings you here? Come for the opening, or did you just miss me?" Before he could reply, I added. "And when the hell did I blaspheme?" I jerked my head and we began to walk in the direction of my office.

"Charlie," he replied in a tone one would use with a wayward child. "You should only use our lord's name when in worship or prayer."

I had a wise acre remark to reply with, but one look at him told me he was dead serious. The man had faith running through every bone of body.

This was a side of him I had rarely seen before and I had spent a lot of time with him over the years. We had staged three productions together and each was a tremendous financial success. In that time, aside from amassing quite a pile of money, we had gotten to know each other and had forged a solid friendship. My company had really taken off on the strength of that partnership. This was a man I owed.

"I never really thought of it that way," I said, trying not to sound insincere.

"So, what is so important that it brings you down here on Opening Day?" I asked, to change the subject and tease him a bit. I knew why he was here.

I lit up my face like I just discovered gin, "OH! I know! You came down to see if your new gizmo works, didn't you? It better! Your little brainstorm has cost me some money to put together." I pointed to a board, set just off stage on the wall, which held a row of gleaming new brass valves.

Josh him as I might, but his little invention was the most innovative piece of set design I had ever used. The play was a musical drama, not my first choice of production but it had some snappy numbers and I had a several new, songbird actors I needed to try out. During the opening number, as the leads danced around the stage, they were to pause as she belted out a long note. When this happened, the stage crew would turn the brass valves and a large flower would magically bloom or rather be inflated at their feet. On her last note, as they finished their dance, several more flowers would grow all around them. Corny, but the public loves these effects.

Originally, I was just going to have flowers painted on small canvases and have the prop boys put a tab on the back. Then we would lay them in place and when the girl paused to let it out, she could step on the tab and flip it upright.

That wasn't good enough for William Gillette. When I told him about my ideas a few months back, he loved the concept but hated its enactment. He set out to design inflatable flowers that would appear from the floor of the stage.

William had my wardrobe girls stitch together a few flowers out of colorful light fabric that had their bases sealed around long thin hoses that led to a row of valves that were fed by another single hose. The last hose was hooked into an air compressor I had brought in. If you turned the right valve, the air would flow into a flower and it would inflate steadily until it was upright. Even better, the air pumping in made the flower move as if in a gentle breeze. It was pure genius! Lined in two rows, out of the way at the front of the stage, it had quite the effect.

Feigning indifference, William said nonchalantly, "I suppose I could sit through a demonstration, if you're running the compressor anyways."

"Com'on, you big faker," I chided him as I led him over to the valves, "Pick one and give it a twist."

William studied the markings over the valves and finally gave one a turn. Of course, he picked the finale spot where six flowers were going to pop up.

We stepped back onto the stage to watch. At first nothing happened except it looked like the stage was pulsating.

"Good thought to paint the backs the same color as the floor boards, Charlie. The audience won't even know they are there until they rise."

"If they rise," I teased, but, just to highlight my foolish talk, they suddenly began to rise at a constant rate until all six were swaying on the left corner of the stage. No matter how many times I saw it, I was delighted. There was even a smattering of applause from some of the crew.

William treated it as just another day at the office, though I knew he was very proud with the results.

"I'm glad it works, yet, I actually stopped by your office to see if you were free for lunch and found your secretary in a tizzy! She strongly suggested I take you somewhere and make you eat -- hopefully for an hour or so at least." He smiled, "Looks like I got here in the nick of time."

"William," I said, shocked, "You know I can't go anywhere now! The show starts in three hours. If I leave now-"

"Everything will get done!" He finished for me, then clapped me on the shoulder and laughed. "These people are all professionals! They know what they're doing. You're just the wasp in the bee hive!" He lifted his head and called out in his stage voice, "Am I right Folks? Are you not professionals?"

Between the sparkle in his eyes and chorus of 'Yes sir!', and the head bobbing, I finally caved in.

I looked at my friend and shook my head in resignation, "This better be important, William. You know how I get at Openings."

"Oh, everyone knows!" as he chuckled. "That's why I'm taking you out to lunch. Don't fret so! Everything will be fine."

"From your lips to God's ear!" I said fervently. I learned that expression from my doctor.

"Charlie!" he replied in exasperation.

"What? That's like a prayer!"

He rolled his eyes and shook his head, "But its intention was for personal gain! Thus, not designated as a practical application of the Christian faith and, therefore, not applicable! What was the lesson I just imparted to you?"

I gave him a long look. "That articulation does not belie intelligence?"

He laughed and, hooking my arm with his elbow, he began pulling me towards the door, "You'll think I'm a genius when you hear my idea, old boy. Well, it's more of a concept really."

I was so busy listening to him babble; I forgot to bark any threats on my way out.

PART TWO

I didn't get any more of his 'big idea' before our Rubens arrived. After a few deliberations, we settled on eating at one of our favorite delis, Zach's, just a few blocks from the theater. It was a tiny hole in the wall but it had the greatest sandwiches and soups in town. William and I always chose Zach's whenever we were in the area. It was after the lunch rush so we got one of the four, worn but spotless, tables, and it had a full view of the street outside where we could talk quietly.

"So, tell me your big idea.," I asked around a mouthful of delicious Ruben. I just let the dressing run down my chin as I didn't want to put the sandwich down to wipe it until I got another bite.

William, using a knife and fork, cut away a small part of the behemoth, and replied, "Do you remember that Doyle fellow you introduced me to in Dorchester on our last voyage to England."

"Yeah, I know Artie. Sir Arthur Conan Doyle." I swallowed and took a drink of seltzer to clean may mouth. Each bite was going to be like heaven. A big chomp, slow chew, and let five of God's greatest gifts slowly melt in my mouth.

"I introduced you, remember?"

"You know what I mean, Charlie!" he admonished. "Don't be such a grump when I'm pitching an idea."

"I'm sorry, William. You know how much an Opening Day unsettles me. I want things to go perfect."

"I know you do, Charlie," he said not unsympathetic, "But there is no such thing as perfect." He held up a hand to forestall my retort, "Though I know how hard you try to achieve it. There is always a hitch! It's just the nature of the business. BUT, that's not why I'm buying you lunch!"

'Buying?', I thought to myself, Damn! If I knew he was picking up the tab, I would have gotten a pickle too.

I sighed, "You're right. I'll try to relax. So, what brings Doyle's name to our lunch table?" With that, I took a huge chunk off my sandwich, so I'd be all ears for my friend.

He grinned at my gluttony and sliced another sliver off his. "Do you remember I told you that I was going to ask him if I could bring the Sherlock Holmes character to the stage?" He popped the morsel in his mouth.

He was starting to get my full attention, "Sure, but why would he give up his bread and butter like that?"

"Give it up?" William replied, "He serving it to me on a silver platter! The gist is, Charlie, he told me to do whatever I wanted with him! He said he was sick of writing those stories and he was finished with it! He wrote- and I quote-, 'Cripple him, kill him or marry him off if you like! I care not what you do with my Sherlock Holmes'."

Now, this was starting to smell like money! If Sherlock Holmes was half as popular in the states as it was in England, I'd have to rent some space at Fort Knox to hold the cash. As I looked this man over and saw the enthusiasm in his eyes, I knew he was just the person to pull this coup off. Still, there was no need to look too anxious before we struck a deal.

I raised an eyebrow at him, "Hard to believe that Doyle would toss his revenue away so easily."

He looked like I threw water in his face, then he shrugged, "Are you afraid he'll renege on his offer? I assume he is a man of wealth now and has other non-Sherlock projects he wants to get to."

I nodded noncommittally, "A man of his habits will always need more money, William. Don't matter if you're smoking opium in a chink's basement or using cocaine on an estate, sooner or later you're flat busted."

"You really think so?"

I shrugged, "Doesn't much matter in the long run. You have the letter. It's not like he could come at us for plagiarism or try to cut himself in."

"I'd be willing to give him a small percentage if he demanded one. I suppose it would only be fair. It may even save us some legal fees down the road."

'Right', I chortled to myself, Like any judge in America would rule for some limey hack against William Gillette! Still, William was a straight arrow and there was no need to sully his sense of fair play.

"Let's cross that bridge if we come to it, William."

He grinned, "Then you're interested?"

Infected with his enthusiasm, I countered, "Think you're up for it?"

I took another bite from my sandwich and it nearly dropped back onto the plate as I witnessed the man across from me change into another person completely without lifting so much as a butt cheek off his chair!

William's ears flattened against his head and his eyebrows slowly curled up at the end. Simultaneously, his face grew longer, and his cheek bones rose and became more pronounced under his half closed eyes. Suddenly my lunch partner was gone and some English patrician sat across from me.

"Frohman, old boy!," he said, in an intense, clipped speech, "Aside from the fact that you slept in your office last night, received your permits for the show just this morning, and you felt the need to give multiple demonstrations of curtain handling to Bob prior to my arrival, how was your day so far?"

I was floored. It was all true, but I hadn't seen or talked to him in weeks prior to his walking onto the production this morning. I assumed he may have learned one or two of those facts from someone close to me, but as hard as I racked my brain, I couldn't fathom who he could glean all three facts at the same time. His features returned to normal and he took another forkful with a smirk.

"How'd I do?"

I just shook my head in wonder and swallowed my food. whole.

"I did sleep in my office last night. I finished late and needed an early start this morning, so it made more sense that going all the way home and back again. But I showered and put on a fresh suit today! A new one, in fact. How could you possible tell I didn't sleep in my own bed last night?"

"The very suit you speak of. You have impeccable taste in clothes, Charlie, and that suit is the perfect shade of dark blue for you. You always dress to impress, as they say."

"So, what's the catch?"

"Your handkerchief," he replied with a twinkle in his eye. "A simple plain white linen kerchief would not have been your choice, unless of course, you had no other choice because your selection was unavailable to you."

I looked down and saw his point. I almost went without it because it clashed so, but I can tend to sweat on Opening days, so I tucked it in anyways.

"I'll give you that one, but what about the permits? How did you know I just got them this morning?"

"There is wax clinging to the cuff link on your left sleeve. That particular shade of red the municipality uses on their documents and smudges of ink on your right thumb tells me the ink was fairly new. You wouldn't bother with any correspondence but what would pertain to opening day. Permits were the likely choice.

As for Bob, I noticed when you sat down that there were quite a few scuff marks on the inside of your right shoe. Your left is gleaming with polish, so I inferred that you were showing Bob at what rate you wanted the curtain lowered. Its common practice to feed the rope from under your foot in case your hands slip, leaving the cloth to free fall."

I was flummoxed. It was all dead on and simple when he explained it. Just like Doyle would have wrote it! "Damn, that all seems so obvious."

"Elementary, my dear Frohman, Elementary."

I was hooked, "It's a deal. So, what do you need from me-and how much?"

PART THREE

I chewed and swallowed as we hashed out the details of our next joint venture. It was far more pleasurable dealing with William than most of my business associates because he was honest and fair to a fault which cut down on all the horse trading. By the time I finally wiped my chin and tossed the napkin down we were in agreement how to introduce Sir Conan Doyle's Sherlock Holmes to the public.

I stuck my hand out over the table. "You've got yourself a deal."

"You won't regret this Charlie," he beamed as he took my hand and pumped it once. "I've already outlined the plot and it will have all the key elements, murder, mystery, and the beautiful girl."

"Doyle never wrote women into his stories-unless they were victims or vamps."

"PSHAW!" He replied, "I'm not going to emulate Sherlock Holmes -- I'm going to improve him!"

I would have liked to stay and hear more of his ideas, but the show was going to start in forty-five minutes and I had to make sure everyone had their ducks in a row and collect the box office money before the curtain rose. William paid for lunch as promised and we hustled back to the theater district.

Everyone and everything was in place back stage. William's smug grin grew every time I tried to find fault and there was none. In fact, I noticed most of the crew and actors wore the same look on their face.

I almost picked a few choice words just to wipe off their smug crow feeding smiles, but that would have been petty, so I simply called out above the preproduction hum among the cast and crew.

"Acceptable, people! Nice Job!" Then I smiled to let them know I was proud of them, "Break a leg!"

That brought out a brief round of applause and I turned away. It was time to collect the receipts before I took my seat.

"Where do you want me, Charlie?" William asked. "Should I stay backstage in the shadows or shall I find an empty seat out front, if there is one."

From the noise of the crowd taking their seats, I was hoping there wasn't. Even muffled by the great layers of curtains, it sounded like quite a mass of humanity. A couple of good weeks could really get our new project off to a good start.

"I didn't know you were staying for the show." I patted him on the back. "Sherlock Holmes shall observe from a box tonight." I always took the box, two out from the stage, on the right for Opening Days. I sat back in the shadows so the actors couldn't see me and get nervous-nor the audience. I could be very animated when I watched performances and critical. It wouldn't do to let the audience see me flinch or pound my forehead with a fist whenever someone flubbed a line. William claimed that watching me was far more entertaining than any portrayal he had in his repertoire.

"Just come with me while I collect the receipts and stash them, then we'll head up to the box."

The ticket booth was up one level, so we crossed the stage and walked up a flight of steps to a door that led to a short hallway that ran perpendicular to the street. The box office was grand, gilded in gold with several ticket windows.

My two bully boys, Murphy and Bailey were waiting for me in the hallway outside the door to the box office. They were big Irish thugs and a solid iron chest sat at their feet.

About a year ago, I switched from collecting the money in a satchel to having it lugged around by these street boys. A thief once managed to snatch the bag out of my hands, on my way to the bank. As I chased him I spat out obscenities for I was unable to match the youth's speed. I lost it all!

The next time I collected receipts, I had these bodyguards and a specialty cane that hid a two-shot derringer in the handle. I would never be robbed again!

"We can go in, Boss," Murphy said, "The box office is already closed."

That was great news. That meant the show was sold out. William waggled his eyebrows at me and smiled. I unlocked the doors to find my ticket collector, a girl named Brenda, locking up the shutters. The assistant stage manager, Dave, was also waiting for me to gather the take so he could get back to the show. It was his job to make sure everything the girl took in went into the slot cut into the counter and into the safe directly below it.

"Evening Dave," I greeted him, "Making an honest woman out of Brenda today?" He laughed a bit too hardy at the stupid pun, but I was the boss after all.

Fishing the key out of my vest, I turned to Brenda, who was waiting to be dismissed. "Do I need to frisk you, my dear?" I always flirted with the girls, it makes them feel special.

She gave me a flirty raised eye brow back, "Not for money, Mr. Frohman."

I laughed, "Then you can go. I'm sure your husband is waiting for his supper."

"And the boys too," she replied, turning to retrieve her hat and coat, "Helpless- the lot of them!"

I got down on one knee and opened the cabinet doors that concealed the safe front and the boys slid the chest over within reach. I put the key within the slot but it went in hard, like some part of the mechanism wasn't quite aligned. When I tried to turn it, it wouldn't budge. It was stuck fast. I pressed hard and tried to twist the handle with all my might but both the key and lever were locked into place.

"Is the safe giving you trouble, Charlie?" William asked.

"My key won't work. Damn thing! I'll have to get a locksmith."

"Then why don't you send one of the boys to fetch a locksmith and he can work on it while we watch the show? Your play is almost about to start." William suggested. It went against my grain to leave, but then he added, "You can leave Pat and Mike to watch over the locksmith. They can send word when it's open." He changed his tone to teasing, "And then you can watch all my flowers inflate!"

I laughed, "You're right. It's not going anywhere." Having decided, I went to pull my key out and, to my shock, the lock unexpectedly clicked and then I lifted the lid!

My eyes popped at what I saw inside.

Nothing.

The safe was empty!

PART FOUR

Paralyzed with shock for a moment, my rage quickly overcame my disbelief and I sprang to my feet. Brenda was just about to go out the door when I shouted.

"Stop right there!" Bailey moved to block her way. I turned to Dave, "What the hell is going on?"

Dave quailed at my outburst. Of course, he couldn't see what I had discovered from where he was standing. "Where the hell's my money?" I shouted.

Dave took a few steps to his right and he saw the empty safe. His face went death white and he clutched his chest. "That's impossible! She put it all in the slot! Every penny, Mr. Frohman! I swear on my children's head."

I just glared at the two of them but I could see no sign of guilt on either. They both seemed genuinely baffled. I turned to my Irish mob.

"Murphy- you go get the cops! I want this place surrounded! Bailey- search the room." There weren't many places to hide a pile of currency, but he began to examine the room from top to bottom.

Brenda shook her head violently, "You won't find it anywhere in this room. I put every cent into that safe!"

"You'd better hope I find it woman or you two will be searched buck naked while I tear this room apart!"

William, who I had forgotten was in the room, said gently, "Calm down Charlie. You're scaring the poor woman to death."

I took a deep breath and questioned them. "Anyone else been in this room today?" They both shook their heads. "Anything unusual occur?" Again, they shook their heads.

"We did it the same way we always do." Dave said. "She took their money, gave them a ticket, and put the money in the slot. I watched every transaction. The money went down the slot!" By this time, Bailey had searched the whole room and he shook his head. He found nothing.

I pointed an ominous finger at the two in front of me, "Unless you two can either produce the money or furnish a reasonable explanation, I promise you the cops will take you to the station as soon as they get here. Let's see if a few days in the jug can help you come up with a better story."

I took a step towards them and added in my most menacing voice, "And you'll be lucky if I don't let Murphy and Bailey ask you before they get here! SOMEONE damaged that lock breaking into it! My money went somewhere!"

Tears ran down Brenda's face now and I don't think Dave was far behind her. They both turned to William as a savior when he spoke loudly, "That's quite enough! You will do no such thing, Charlie! You know these two are innocent. They didn't steal your money."

Fact was, he was right. I watched their eyes this whole time and I saw confusion and fear-but no guilt. I knew from the moment we found the money missing that they were as baffled as we were. Still, I was petty enough in my anger to challenge him.

"Then where is it? Could someone please tell me that?" I threw my hands in the air and faced the covered windows to the world outside, "Where's the great Sherlock Holmes when we need him? Hmm?"

"Give me a moment, Frohman."

'Frohman?' I thought, and then I turned slowly to find that stranger from lunch standing not five feet away from me. I could see what he was doing, or rather, who he was portraying, and I should have questioned his motives, but my despair and befuddlement had made my mind a bit fuzzy around the edges. All I could do was nod when he inquired in a clipped patrician tone.

"Might I ask a few questions?"

With a nod and a quick smirk he turned, not to the two inside persons, but to Bailey, who had been holding still waiting for instructions. "What time did you arrive at your post, my good man?"

"Right before the ticket counter opened. Mr. Frohman wants us here in case there's any hickups."

"And was there any? "

"No sir. Pat and I never saw another soul until you and Mr. Frohman showed up."

"And no one came in or out of that room?"

"No sir! That I'm still breathing is proof o' that!"

"I'm sure," he replied in a condescending way of dismissal. He snapped his head at the other two and turned to Brenda, "Madame- when did you make the last deposit in the counter?"

"Ten, maybe fifthteen minutes before you gentlemen arrived,' she answered, looking to Dave for confirmation. He nodded his head as she continued. "Then I stepped away, so Dave could put the rest of my change in the slot and write down the ticket numbers."

"And that's just what I did!" Dave sputtered without prompting, "I put every bit of cash into that slot. I swear, Sir! I heard the coin's drop! I...I don't..." His voice

25

trailed off but my friend had already turned away and focused on me.

"The design of your safe. Does it have a corresponding slot cut into the top plate or is it open?"

I wasn't expecting that question. Perplexed, I answered, "Open. But that's six inches of solid oak sitting on it and it's so snug you couldn't put a razor between the two."

He raised his eyebrows over twinkling orbs and smirked. "In summary- We have a locked door, with two capable men on guard outside. The room is solid concrete with no apertures. Both employees corroborate their procedures. Nothing unusual occurred." Willam paused for dramatics,

"Yet, the money is missing."

We all just stared at him. Hearing him put all the points in a group made it harder to grasp. The enigma was too complex to even comprehend, never mind accept.

"Then the solution is obtainable." He said in all seriousness.

I thought he was losing his wits. "What are you saying?"

"Doyle's Axiom, Frohman. When all other possibilities have been eliminated, whatever remains-no mat"

"No matter how improbable- must be the solution." I finished the quote for him, "I read all his books too."

He laughed, "Then we won't find the answers inside this room. Come along, Frohman. The games afoot!" With that, he dashed out the door.

26

PART FIVE

I didn't have a better way to get my money back, so I told Bailey to join me and told the other two to stay put until Murphy gets back with the cops. I dashed out the door to catch up with William.

"Pull yourself together, Frohman," he said as he straightened his jacket. Without another word, he began to pace down the corridor with measured steps.

I tried to ask him what the hell he was doing, but he waved me off as he concentrated on whatever he was doing. Bailey and I simply followed in confused silence as he counted off his steps.

"Twenty-two", he proclaimed as he came to the door. Without any further explanation, he opened the door and stepped out onto the stair's landing. Rather than go on, he leaned out over the railing and looked down for a minute.

"Come along and bring your man." he instructed as he scampered down the steps. "We shall need some brute strength if I am correct." At the bottom of the steps, he turned to his right and walked past the flight to a wall where scenery props were piled against the wall. The area was used for storage and wasn't well lit. William was almost in the shadows when he came to a sudden stop and held out an arm.

"Stop right there, Gentlemen."

"What is it?" I asked and I could feel my heart pounding in anticipation. I was really starting to enjoy this!

27

"I am not sure yet, Frohman, but I need a moment to examine the area before you and your man obscure any clues that might be lying around."

"Clues? What kind of clues."

"Ha!" he cried out, making us both jump, "Clues such as these!" He turned around, an almost maniacal look in his eyes. "Bailey! Would you be so kind as to fetch a light source? A couple of lanterns would do nicely."

Bailey looked at me and I jerked a thumb at him. He dashed off and quickly returned with two good sized lanterns that cast a strong glow across the floor and up the walls. Bailey handed one to William, who had not uttered a word since he asked for light, and he held the lantern up, high over his head. He swung it back and forth between the props and the general direction of the stage. With the play started, no one noticed us.

"There, Frohman. Do you see?" he asked as he pointed to the floor.

Under the light, I could see two sets of alternating wet spots that started at the scenery and faded as they headed towards the stage area. It clicked in my mind. Footprints!

I shrugged, "So? Someone has wet boots."

William shook his head sadly, "Frohman! You see, but you do not observe! Nor do you deduce. The footprints lead away from the scenery- not to it! The source of the water must be behind the scenery. Perhaps, with the help of your muscular aide, we could move the props aside."

Fortunately, the painted wood slabs were set on a roller to it was easy enough to push it to one side with just Bailey doing the work. To my surprise, there was a narrow door hidden behind it.

"There!" William crowed, pointing at two boot prints whose back halves were hidden by the door. He reached down and dabbed one with a long finger. "Someone has been through here and not long ago."

"Where does that go?" I asked. "I never saw that door before."

"As we are below street level, I would think it an access to the utilities that run below the surface of this street. Many buildings are equipped with these. It makes repairs and inspections easy for the municipality."

"How'd you know it was there?"

"I did not- until now", William replied, as he reached for the door handle. "I considered it a high probability that we would find some type of access in this vicinity."

The door was locked. William raised an eyebrow at me and I shook my head. I didn't even know was there before now, how was I supposed to have a key?

Bailey solved the problem for us. He pulled a six-inch doublebladed boot knife strapped to his ankle and looked to me. I nodded and he stepped up and jammed the blade between the lock and the door jamb. A few quick wiggles and the door popped open like a champagne bottle.

William, his face flushed and eyes ablaze, snatched the lantern from Bailey's hands and went in, staring at the floor like a hunter looking for spoor. I realized then just how much he was enjoying himself. That was alright with me as long as I got my money back which didn't seem likely at this point. I couldn't see how rummaging around a dank tunnel over a few wet prints was going to accomplish that. It was only his intensity, acting like the great detective, that dragged me along this far.

Still, though the curtain had already been raised on my play and the police were on their way, that look of joyous hunger on his face made me hand my lantern to Bailey.

William was just up ahead of us, standing next to a large puddle of water. As we approached, he held up his hand for silence. We all stood rock still but I heard nothing. Nothing but the dead silence.

"There is no need for stealth, I think," William announced and began to walk straight down the center of the tunnel, water sloshing about his ankles.

Bailey shrugged and followed after him, holding the light up as far as possible. Well, maybe William had a closet full of boots and Mike didn't care, but I was dressed for an opening and I wasn't about to soak my best boots in whatever sewage had collected. I fell a bit behind walking slowly and on the upper curves of the pipe to keep my feet dry. William let out a cry and I leapt down to take three steps in the water.

I found my friend standing still with Bailey by his side. He had a look of exaltation and Bailey looked dumbstruck.

The ceiling of the pipe in this place was gone, with rubble in a pile. The exposed wood planks had four solid beams running from the ceiling to floor of the tunnel. But stranger still, was what lay on the floor in front of the supports. A large steel box attached to planks of lumber. It looked just like the safe from the box office with the same key slot.

"Go on Frohman, try your key in it. Twenty-two steps say it will fit."

In a daze, I complied and the key went in easy and turned without a hitch. I pushed the lever down and the door clicked open. I looked up at my friend and stated the obvious,

"This is my safe...but how."

"Quite clever, actually," he replied absently, "A worthy endeavor." Then he snapped out of it and looked at me, "You have to give them credit for imagination- and craftsmanship! Look at those seams!"

He held the light up and I could see a slight color difference in the planks the supports were holding up. Looking down, it dawned on me; the planks were the exact varying lengths that supported the box at our feet."

"Sweet St. Pete!" I snarled, "Those bastards broke through here under the ticket counter and switched the safes! They pulled mine down here and replaced it with another."

"Excellent, Frohman. Though improbable- it was the only solution. Though please express yourself without the blaspheming, if you would. There has been a great amount of preparation put into this caper. Yet, so simple as to be ingenious. They must have loosened the planking under the safe and then wedged it into place with these beams. Then, when the safe was filled, lower it and replace it with a fake.

Which is the one point, I must confess, that hasn't been made clear to me. I can see where it would have been easy enough to take measurements and build an exact replica of the flooring above us, but where could they possibly procure a safe so similar?"

I sighed, "THAT I think I can answer," I replied morosely, "I bought a half dozen of these safes from the same manufacturer. I imagine if we were to check the storage house- we'd find one missing."

"Ah! I suspect you're right, Frohman." He frowned, "But you should not withhold information, although it does shorten the list of suspects. Now we know it must have been an inside job."

"A lot of good a list is going to do me now, inside or out!" I growled, "Those thieving sons of bitches are long gone with my money by now!"

William tapped his chin with a forefinger, "Perhaps not, Frohman. They must have made the switch just minutes before we arrived. While we discovered the crime, checked our surroundings and questioned the employees, they must have been moving the currency and coins. They could not have left here too long before our discovery and that means that the play had probably already started."

I snapped my finger, "And since the only way out is through the theater, they're probably still around."

"I'd wait until the first act ended, then I sneak out when the lights went down." Bailey observed out of nowhere. William and I almost laughed but we knew he was right.

I checked my watch. "Then we have about six minutes." I took off the way we came in. This time, my socks were soaked by the time I reached the back of the stage.

PART SIX

William managed to grab my arm before I went blundering into the milling actors and crew and disrupting the play.

"Slow down, Frohman. Make no overt moves just yet. We don't want to send our quarry into a premature flight. Softly, softly, catchee monkey!"

The three of us milled about the back of the stage staring intently at everyone. I doubted very much that the crooks would be hanging about, my money sticking out of their pockets. I knew all these people and most of the actors had worked for me before and my crews were steady.

Still, I had no problem delaying them after the show. I intended to have the police seal the building and I'd personal see each was grilled and searched before I let them out of my sight.

William nudged me and whispered in my ear, "Do not bother with the cast, Frohman," he said in an offhand way as his eyes scanned the area. "I doubt very much, any of them had the skill or the strength to do such a physical labor! AH! THERE! Who are those men by the balcony prop?"

My eyes followed his gesture until I saw the duo he was referring to. A dead end.

"Can't be those two," I assured him, "They're the Collins boys, Frank and Tom. Work on the props and scenery. Good men and they have been with me for years."

"Perhaps. But today they have wet feet."

Before I even thought of doing it, I was walking towards them, looking down. William was right! Their boots were soaked, little spots of water, puddle around the soles, reflected off the low lighting in the back.

Frank looked up and must have seen something on my face, because he slapped Tom on the chest with the back of his hand and said something to him. The both of them reached over the balustrades of the fake balcony and pulled up large leather tool satchels. Then they turned and headed for the stage exit that led to the seating arena. I had a feeling I knew what was making their bags bulge. "Stop them!" I hissed at Bailey, wishing Murphy was back with the cops already. I could see this turning into a melee and that was the last thing I wanted in the middle of an act, but I decided it was better than being robbed of the day's reciepts.

Bailey got within ten feet of the men's back, with William and me right behind him when Tom suddenly stopped and spun back towards us. Only this time, he had a revolver in his hand.

A few other crew members nearby gasped, but they were all too well trained to cry out during a performance. Bailey skidded to a halt when Tom cocked the pistol and raised it.

"That would be far enough." he warned, "It's not in me heart to plug anyone today, but if ye take one more step, I swear I'll shoot you in the face!" He waved the gun around, "Any if any of you try to follow us,I'll send you home to Jesus!"

As I looked at a man who had worked faithfully for me for years, I felt I had been stabbed in the back. "Why Tom?"

He laughed, "Don't be daft man," he replied jiggling the bag in his hand. With that, he turned and began to run. I wanted to scream in frustration. Not only had I been betrayed, my money was so close I could smell it and I was going to lose it again!

I turned to look for William, but he had already moved off and was fiddling with something in the wings. I looked back to the fleeing crooks when I saw something happen at their feet. One of the flowers had started to rise and, half inflated, caught Tom's foot causing him to stumble sideways towards the edge of the stage. Frank lunged to catch his brother, but he stepped on another semi inflated flower and he crashed into to Tom. Arms and legs pin wheeling, they skidded over the edge and fell into the orchestra pit! As if to cap it off, the stage bunting crashed down over them.

Not seconds later, Murphy came thundering down the aisle with at least a half dozen flatfooted police on his heels. Bailey jumped down and told them quickly what had occurred, while I ran down the steps and tried to explain the situation to the Inspector who headed the squad. When they knew the lay of the land, they tried to grab hold of the struggling crooks when we heard two muffled shots and the bullets ricocheted off the front of the stage. Screams erupted from the audience.

The coppers took no chances after that. They just pulled out their billy clubs and whacked away at the lumps under the curtains until there was no discernible movement. Then they began peel back the layers of material, amidst the groans.

Like a wave, panic had broken out and carried people out of their seats to get jammed up at the exits. Shouting erupted and a few scuffles broke out. I looked up to see William step up to the center edge of the stage.

"Stop! Ladies and Gentlemen! Stop where you are!"

I was amazed how he got his voice to carry over the panic, but most everyone in the hall heard him and recognized him enough to freeze out of simple curiosity.

"Gentlemen and ladies! Please return to your seats and give me your undivided attention for just a moment."

Just like the wave that started it, it seemed to break, and everyone receded back to their places. There was near dead silence as they waited for my friend to continue.

"My name is William Gillette." There was a smattering of applause. He was well known to most theater goers and in his element. "You all came here tonight to see a fabulous play, and so far, you have! I think it's wonderful!" There was a big round of applause. "And we'll get to the rest of it in just a moment, I promise.

For the moment though, I must beg your indulgence while our fine police force wrap up a small matter of some mislaid money." He raised his eyebrows and frowned theatrically, as he pointedly looked down into the orchestra pit. The crowd craned their necks to follow his view as the coppers finally managed to untangle the near unconscious thieves from the curtains and dragged them out a side entrance.

William turned his attention back to the audience. "Well, those gentlemen certainly know why it's 'curtains' for them!" The audience laughed. "I imagine their next play will be the Christmas Pageant at Sing-Sing." They roared with laughter and applauded.

"Now," He turned to the actors behind him, "If everyone is ready to restart the scene?" The actors quickly took their places and nodded.

"Then we shall resume…Enjoy!" As he said the last word, he bowed deeply and disappeared into the right wing.

The Inspector and I went up the stairs and joined William in the wings as the play resumed. To their credit, the actors picked right up where they left off and the audience was watching with rapt attention when Pat and Mike dropped the two recovered satchels at my feet. A quick look confirmed our hopes. I had my money at last.

We answered a few questions for the Inspector then assured him we would be down to the station to press charges after the show. Intermission came, so he took the opportunity to slip out and we watched Roberto and his crew man handle the bunting back onto the stage. He assured me it 'woulda be-a back uppa' before the audience returned. Satisfied everything was back under control, I told Murphy and Bailey to take the bags to my office and sit on them until I get there.

Now that we were alone, I couldn't help but throw my arms around my friend and give him a bear hug. "That was pure genius, William! You fingered them and tripped them up! Holmes himself would bow to you!"

He smiled down at me as I stepped back and said, "So, I take it your satisfied with my audition for my new role?"

I laughed and took him by the arm to head to my office, "Your budget is doubled! I want you hitting the boards by the end of next month."

The Case of Slow Service

Late March, 1897

Will and I stepped out of the cab and, by custom, paused to look at the special menu board, hanging by the simple red door, before we went into our favorite little restaurant. It read:

Osso Bucco
Coq au Vin
Bouillabaisse

"Well, I know what I'm having William," I announced with gusto. "Perfect day for a stew."

William paused in the small foyer and remarked, "Charles, your family would disown you if they knew you were paying Jimmy's prices for food you could get at home for free!"

I laughed. It was true enough. I was arguably one of the most successful theater producers in America, but I came from a long line of fisherman and bay men from the South Fork of Long Island. They would choke on New York City prices for seafood they dragged, netted, and trapped every day. Of course, a true swamp Yankee would balk at the cost of the cab just getting here!

"Yes, well, Gram isn't here to make it for me, so I'll just have to indulge myself."

"Charles Frohman! And William Gillette! Yasoo Filiamos! Welcome my old friends!"

William and I both snapped our heads around at the exuberant greeting, called out loud enough for the entire dining room to hear. There was a momentary lull in the conversation, followed by a slew of head jerking and serendipitous pointing as all eyes fell on us. It was a bit disconcerting, but one had to get used to it if he was going out in public with America's leading man of the stage, William Gillette.

Still, William and I looked at each other and rolled our eyes. We had been on a first name basis for years with Jimmy Woviotis, the owner of the establishment. Jimmy only cried out like that for free advertising. Always working the angles, our Jimmy.

He threw his outstretched arms around me and kissed both my cheeks. "How are you Charlie? It's good to see you." he said in a more sedate voice. He turned to William, who stuck his hand out quickly. He was a bit reserved on intimate greetings.

"And how are you, William?" Wovi asked, taking his hand in both of his. "I heard your last show was a big hit! Bravo!"

"It went well," William said modestly, while gently, but firmly, pulling his hand away. "The public surely has a taste for Sherlock Holmes." He looked around the packed dining room. "You seem to be doing alright yourself, Jimmy. Are you sure you have room for us? I suppose we should start making reservations."

Aghast, Wovi shook his head and cried out, "Never! You and Charles are welcome here any time of the day or night! There will always be a place for you. Now, let me take you to your table, if you will follow me please."

He took us to our favorite booth that was up on a landing in the back with high sides, giving us a modicum of privacy. We asked him if he would join us for a drink before dinner, which was also our custom here. He usually accepted and sat with us, catching up on gossip and whatnot, but today he begged off.

As he hustled off, William said, "That was surprising. Jimmy usually likes to be seen with us." He looked around the room, "Do you think we're losing our public appeal, Charlie?"

"I never had it." I laughed, "Besides, he just busy." I watched the room for a minute and added, "he's short a busboy tonight."

William looked skeptical. "I never know when you're pulling my leg. How could you know that already?"

Still waiting for a waiter to come get our drink order, I decided to engage him. "What? Are we a bit jealous I got one observation up on you?"

William smiled. He loved a challenge. He took another long look around the room and replied, "So, you already know who is the plumber, the Orchestra Leader, and the suffragette is."

I dropped my chin onto my chest and sighed. I should have known better than to bait him. I lifted my head and scanned the room, trying to see what he saw, but to no avail.

He sat across the table from me, that insidious smirk playing on the corners of his mouth. He truly loved his dramatics!

"Alright," I conceded, "Give!"

"The gentleman dining alone against the right wall."

I half twisted in my seat and located the table. It was a deuce with just the single man dining. An older man, he had longish hair and wore spectacles with which he used to read some papers to the right of his plate. Drumming his fingers and turning pages with his right hand, his left forked food into his mouth at a steady pace. He seemed deep in thought. The one oddity I noted was that he had tucked his napkin into his collar for a bib that went below the table line, but he let his drab brown jacket hang over it, exposed to breadcrumbs, spillage, and what not. But not everyone had fashion sense.

"I didn't see a tuba or anything," I said, "Just an old, bored guy-in a bad jacket, dining with friends he doesn't have!"

William laughed and shook his head, "You amaze me, Charlie!" I started to puff up a little and he added, "Everything you see stops at the back of your eyes!

Indeed, he is wearing a rather shabby jacket, considering, yet, from the cut and material of the cuffs protruding-he is more than likely wearing a tuxedo shirt under it. I believe you can even make out the ruby cuff links." I had to strain my eyes a bit, but I could see a glint of red when he put his fork to mouth.

"So, he protects his shirt with a bib because he will need it clean when he dons his tails, tie, and cummerbund later. The uniform of a Maestro.

"Now watch his fingers carefully."

I did what he asked and after a minute or so, I caught on. There was a certain cadence to the finger drumming that had to be more than boredom. After he stopped and turned a page, the rhythm would change up. It was obvious if you were looking for it.

"I'm amazed, William," I said, and I was again. "I would have never noticed the beat to his finger tapping if you hadn't pointed it out."

"Something by Chopin, I believe." he replied. "Now I direct your gaze, discreetly I hope, to the table closest to us, below on the main floor."

I checked it out from the corner of my eye. There was a seemingly well to do couple at the table. The man was unremarkable, could have been mid-level management. The woman was equally as conventional, perhaps dressed a bit better though she looked frumpy all the same. I could see nothing radical about her and I told William so.

"You are mistaking her disarray for Slovenes, Frohman." he countered. I winced at the 'Frohman'. "You will agree that her attire is of the current fashions and she displays the amount of jewelry that a woman of upper income would wear, yet, her hair is windblown beneath the hat and her shoes are muddy. This tells us she has been out of doors for a good part of the day and the wet hem of her dress suggests she was in a grassy area."

"Central Park," It came to me then. "There was one of those suffragette rallies there today!"

William waggled his eyebrows and looked smug.

"But that doesn't mean she was there!" I pointed out. "It's a big city, William; she could have been anywhere doing anything."

Just then a waiter approached their table. He lifted the wine bottle out of the bucket and nodded at the woman's empty glass. He murmured something to the man, but it was the woman who spoke up loudly enough for the surrounding tables to hear.

"Young man! I did not spend the day marching for my rights just to be pandered the first time I sit down! Every woman in here can make her own decisions! Now pour my wine!"

That didn't leave much for an argument. William looked even smugger-if that was possible

"O.K., O.K.! That explains the last two." I took a good look around the room again, but came up empty. "But what about the first? Where do you see a plumber here?"

"Plumber is at the second table from the Kitchen doors. The one that seats two people."

"Deuces, William. We call two tops a 'deuce.'"

"Or two tops," he pointed out with a smirk.

I swept the room until I located the table. There was a man and a woman seated, both dressed nice enough. I looked the man up and down from head to toe and studied his mannerisms, but I could find nothing that indicated his profession. Just another married couple having dinner.

"You sure?" I asked, even knowing I'd get my face rubbed in it over some subtle but obvious point.

"Absolutely," he replied with a straight face. "He did some work for me last month." Then he waggled his eyebrows at me.

He shrugged, "I'm still waiting for an explanation about the missing busboy, Charlie."

I waved it off, "Elementary, my dear William. Elementary. I saw various waiters clearing dishes between courses, pouring water, or bringing rolls to tables, all in this lower right section and all functions outside their purview. The waiters wouldn't be doing any of that if they had their busboy. I know because I washed a few dishes, actually a lot of dishes, when I first came to the city so long ago."

"Really? I didn't know that."

"What? The duties of a busboy or that I had a job dishwashing?

"Both." William said.

"Well, you're just a well of ignorance tonight!" I teased. I was about to dig him a little more when I saw a shadow creep across him. Happy at the thought the waiter had finally arrived, I was disappointed to see Jimmy, the owner, standing next to our table and doubly surprised to see the coat check girl standing by the kitchen doors, holding our coats.

He looked out of whack a bit. His hair was mussed up and his eyes were bouncing around like a marble dropped into a glass jar. Wovi bent at the waist until his head was close to Williams and mine and said in a low voice that no one but us could hear, "Gentlemen, I have a small problem that needs immediate attention. One I thought you might be able to help me with." He looked directly at William. "I understand that you are a man with a distinct talent."

William started to protest, but Wovi ran right over him, "No, No! This is not the time for modesty, William. Something has happened that could ruin me! I'm begging for your help!"

William, for a man of the world, could still be a bit naïve when it came to how things really worked in New York City. "Jimmy, if you have an emergency-you should call the Police!"

"No, no, no, no, no," Wovi whimpered. Then he leaned in even closer, "That would be the end of me. I need discretion, sir. And advice."

My curiosity outweighed my annoyance and even William looked a little put off, but when he looked at me for my advice I nodded. Anything to help Jimmy.

We just started to rise when Wovi took a step back from the table, threw his arms out and smiled like a shark. In a voice loud enough for the booths and tables around us, he declared, "Of course, you may meet the Chef, Gentlemen! I'm sure he'd be delighted to meet William Gillette and Charles Frohman in person, after cooking your favorite dishes all these years!"

I looked at William and he winked at me. Good Old Wovi! Always working the angles. But that's why we liked him so much. There was a straight forward honesty in his hustling. The restaurant was his life and he was its soul. Everything he did was to simply make sure that the show went on. Will and I could admire that sentiment.

Taking one of us in each arm, he marched us purposely to the kitchen doors, where the girl held our coats to us. I looked at Jimmy.

"We going somewhere?"

"The storage rooms."

I nodded. William looked to me and I explained, "There below the kitchen. It can get chilly down there after a while."

Jimmy opened the door to the kitchen and ushered us inside. When he stepped into join us, I was transported back to my youth. The clack of the dishes being racked, the smoke, the heat, and the banter. It never really changed.

William was taking in everything in the focused manner, but Wovi took us both by surprise. Wovi transformed instantly from a happy go lucky, prosperous host into the Simon Legree of the culinary field. With a curt gesture he went right through the middle of the busy kitchen, cracking his whip in every direction.

"You watch how you handle those plates Boy!" He yelled at the dishwasher, "You break one and you don't get paid today!"

He didn't get three steps before he zeroed in on a waiter who was standing at the pick-up window, talking to the cooks as he loaded his arms with plates. Wovi popped him on the back of his head hard enough to get his attention and bellowed, "Quit flapping your gums and get that food out while it's hot!" As he turned away to continue, he added, "And you got money up on fourteen."

I was amused by all this and I think William was too but we both winced when he stepped up to a work table that was manned by a young woman in the process of icing a tray of tiny cakes.

The girl paused and looked up. Wovi ran his seasoned eyes over her work and snarled, "If that's how you ice a petite four, young lady –you might as well go home and start making babies. "

He strode off and she rolled her eyes and bent back to her task. Thankfully we got to the back door of the kitchen before he could accost anyone else. Next to the door was an opening to a stairwell leading down.

Jimmy gave us a little bow and gestured for us to take this path. I stepped in first but stopped on the second step down when I realized no one was behind me. I turned to see William facing off with Jimmy, just inside the doorway.

"Jimmy," William said in a tone that had bristles, "Do you always speak to your help that way?" I winced, knowing I should have seen this coming as William was a practicing Christian- and a chronic do gooder!

Jimmy didn't reply right away. He just reached over and plucked something off the wall that was hanging next to William's shoulder. He took a deep breath and peered up at William over the rim of his glasses.

"William Gillette, I was working in a restaurant since the days you were still taking milk from your mother's breast, so I'll ask you to mind the theater and I shall tend to my restaurant business. Thank you." Yet, when Will's eyes blazed, he added to take the sting out of his words, "You're not a restaurant man, William. Believe me, these people expect me to be hard. They are my children and they want a Father! But they also know if they work hard and remember the house motto, they'll make a decent living."

"House Motto? Since when did you have a house motto?" I asked.

Wovi looked at me and said slowly and distinctly, "You take care of the house- the house will take care of you!"

He turned back to William with a placating smile, "And I feed them something good every shift they work! That's more than they'll get at home or on the streets! After shift meals! These people think I'm a Greek God!"

"Greek God!" I snorted and because all this was getting us no closer to dinner, I added, "You're a God damn Greek! Now tell us what your problem is or feed us already!"

Jimmy recoiled as if he was slapped. Wide eyed and haggard looking, he mumbled his apologies and took the lead again as we headed down the stairs. As he passed me, he clapped me on the shoulders and suddenly chuckled, "God Damn Greek! That is a good one!" I was waiting for admonishment from Will- he hated blaspheming! - but all I got was a sigh as I quickened my pace to catch up with our host.

When we came off the staircase, we were in a hallway with four large wooden doors, each with a huge brass latch. These would be the coolers. We donned our coats at this point.

Jimmy stopped between the second and third doors and said, "I should point this out to you, William. It is very important, I think. These doors are to my coolers. On the opposite side of them, there is a parallel hallway. Each cooler has a back door that opens into it. From that hallway, there is a staircase that goes directly up to the street."

I nodded, "I get it. That's a nice set up, Wovi!"

"The delivery men bring the supplies from the street right down to where you can separate them and put them in the right cooler. Then the staff takes them out this door and up to the kitchen." I gave a low whistle, "I wish we had that where I worked! I remember pulling what the chef wanted out of piles of food and lugging it up two flights of stairs!"

"Thank you, but this is not why I asked you down here. I just wanted to explain to William that each of the doors has a lock on the outside as does the hatch to the sidewalk. There are only two keys. Mine-which is in my pocket and has been all day and my consigner- who only opened them to receive deliveries today and the last was early this afternoon. The only way in or out of here when we're locked up is through the kitchen."

William looked at him curiously, "Why do you feel this is important information for me to have?"

Jimmy put a finger in the air, "Because I read! I've read everything Doyle wrote!!" He turned and continued down the hall. "Come, you will see."

In less than ten steps the hallway ended into a large storage area. One side, on the right, was dry storage for food. Cans, boxes, barrels, and open bins lined wooden shelving. Half of the left was storage for plates and dining room ware, along with a few seasonal decorations. Jimmy was facing the last section, a separate room with a door on which hung a sign- Linen Room. This was ironic for the full bag that lay on the floor next to it. With a sigh, Jimmy picked up the bag, put a key in and opened the door, then bowed us through again. We stepped into a larger room. Ten foot by twenty, with two sides of built in shelving that held clean tablecloths and napkins neatly folded in stacks and two large bins along the other to hold the dirties.

Between them, there was a tablecloth spread out on the floor with an unmistakable shape underneath it.

"Jimmy!" I gasped, "Please tell me there's not a man under that sheet! Especially if he's dead!"

He frowned, "If only I could, Charles. It's Roberto, one of my busboys. Everyone called him Bobby. Bobby four arms."

"That good, huh?" I said. I had heard the comment in my youth. 'Clears a table like he's got four arms.

Wovi smiled sadly, "I think it had more to do with the ladies. Always bragged he had more girls than arms."

"I cannot help you with this, Jimmy." William suddenly spoke up. "You need to call the Police immediately!"

"William, I told you! I can't! I already pay them more than I can afford and if they have this on me, why, they'll double their money! Not to mention what the papers will do to my reputation! I'll be ruined.

"No! No Policia! We must keep this quiet and discreet. Only a few of the staff and now you two even know this happened!"

"So, what the hell do you want us to do?" I asked. "You want us to dump the body?"

His eyes blazed at my sarcasm, but he took a deep breath and went on. "I was hoping William could tell me what happened. That's all I need to know. I can take care of the rest. Please, William? Nothing has been touched since the body was found- I made sure."

Knowing Jimmy, he was probably madder about someone killing his busboy while he was on the clock, but it wasn't our problem.

I turned to tell William as much, but he was already carefully lifting the cloth away from the body. He tossed the sheet into a bin and began to walk slowly around the corpse with that focused concentration that fed him. I realized he was gone. By now, my stomach had stopped growling and started to churn, but I couldn't help but follow William's gaze as he made a slow silent circle around the corpse.

Roberto was laying spread eagled on his back. His face was hard to look at as it was battered with blood at the corners of his mouth. His face was turned towards the floor, his hair splayed out in greasy strands. There was a ghoulish blue tinge to the skin over his cheeks and he was frog eyed, which was understandable when you saw the horrible bruising on his neck and shoulders. It looked like someone throated him with an iron pipe!

There were fainter, but larger bruises on the top of his arms, between his biceps and elbows, and a variety of scrapes and cuts if you looked hard enough, though there was a dozy on his right side.

He was wearing simple black pants and a sleeveless undershirt that was scrunched up to his arm pits and filthy with bits of debris. Everything about him said he had been in a fight and lost. Every aspect of him was either mussed, crooked, or beaten. The one odd note was that he was wearing just one shoe.

William came to a halt, paused for a moment, then reached into his coat and pulled out a slim leather case. He opened it up and, I'll be dammed, lined up in little loops were a variety of small hand tools. He plucked a magnifying glass, a pair of tweezers, and a short pointing stick before he tucked the case away. His eyes bore into Jimmy.

"Who discovered the body and when?"

"Paulus, the other busser on tonight. He brought down some dirty linen about a quarter until eight and found him there."

I checked my watch, "Good Lord, Wovi! That was just twenty-five minutes ago!"

"When someone tells me my busboy is dead in the laundry room, I don't let the moss grow on my feet!"

"The lad's been dead for at least an hour," William intoned.

"Whoa Nelly!" I said, "How do you know that?"

He gave me his most level look, "The skin is room temperature, Frohman. In another hour it will be cool. After that, one needs to measure the rigor mortis to approximate a time of death.

Then he went back to ignoring me. "What time was his shift to start?"

"Six. One of the dishwashers saw him come in the back door and go right downstairs at about quarter until six."

"Did anyone else come in after him?"

"No. Bobby was the last person on the schedule tonight. It was his turn to clean."

"Is this room always locked?"

"Yes. The key hangs on a peg just at the top of the stairs."

"Why keep it locked if the key is accessible to anyone?"

I knew the answer to that, "Keeps the shenanigans down to a minimum. You'd be shocked if you knew half the things a restaurant staff could get up to in a closed room with nobody watching!" Wovi just nodded his head dramatically to back me up.

"Would Roberto have taken the key to use the room for changing into his uniform?"

"Definitely. All the wait staff does. They store their stuff here while they're working and change back afterwards." He pointed to the wall behind us that held a row of pegs with street clothes hanging on them.

"Then was the key in its rightful place when Paulus brought down the dirty linen?"

"Yes, it was. I asked Paulus that very question, and he told me he took the key from the peg and that the door was locked when he brought down the bag and saw Bobby. He threw the bag down and ran to get me."

"What was your first reaction?" William asked.

"Of course, I came right down here and found Bobby just as Paulus said. Then I sent him back to work and locked the door. Next, I came to you Gentlemen."

"And have you heard of anyone else come through the kitchen? A delivery man, or an off -duty employee perhaps. Could someone have laid in wait for him?"

"No. Quan, my pot scrubber, would have noticed. All he does is scrub the pots and watch the kitchen. Besides, there are too many people running in all directions to go

53

unnoticed until service! Half the kitchen is running up and down theses stairs during prep time!"

Even I could see, when you put it all together, the big point. "This means that the killer is up there, cooking your food or serving it!"

"I know that, Charles! That's another reason why I can't call the Cops! They'd shut me down and put everyone to the question. By the time they beat a confession out of somebody, I'd be out of Business!

That's why I need your help. I just need to know who did this so I can find out why. Then I can handle it with just a small disruption."

I got little heated when I realized that Jimmy didn't give a fat rat's behind about his dead busboy. Or justice. He was only concerned about how it may affect his business. Chances are, if the killer was a valued employee, he would simple look the other way and use the information to keep him under the thumb. It was the ruthless Greeks who ran successful restaurants.

"So how do you think William's going to solve this without talking to the staff right away?" I snapped at him, "Because if you think we're going to stay here all night until business dies down just because you're short a busboy, you're sadly mistaken."

"Frohman," William said as he began to walk around the room. "Do not talk on so. I need quiet if I am to concentrate."

I just sighed and let the show unfold. William paused by the bins and then reached over to poke the rim of the box. The wood slat fell away in two pieces. William nodded and moved off to the shelving the victim's head was pointing at. He looked around then dropped to one knee and reached behind the stacked tablecloths to pull out a shoe. It matched the one that was still on Bobby's left foot.

Wovi opened his mouth to ask something, but I caught his eyes and put a finger to my lips. William was best when he was left alone.

He moseyed back over to the body and took a long look. After a long minute, he stepped back and shucked off his overcoat, but then slipping on his gloves. He stepped back and squatted on his haunches next to the head. He stared at the wounds for a moment then, using just one gloved finger, tilted the head back until it was facing the ceiling.

"AH!" William cooed. "This makes more sense. Interesting." He didn't look up but gestured for us to come closer.

"Come look at this, Gentlemen. I believe it is the actual cause of death."

"He wasn't strangled?" I asked as we stepped over. What caught William's attention was a clear puncture mark in the victim's temple, where the hairline began. It was elongated, but twisted on the ends.

"I never thought he died from strangulation, Frohman." He pointed at the victim's Adam's apple. "The larynx does not seem crushed and the bruising, though gruesome to observe, are superficial. They are undoubtedly the result of a struggle rather than an assault."

"You think two were in on this?" Wovi asked. "One held him down and the other stabbed him in the brain?"

"Enough," William barked, tossing up a hand and rising. "Hypothesizes are distractions!" He turned to the door and began his soliloquy.

"Roberto arrived at the restaurant just before his shift, about fifteen minutes before five o'clock. He took the key from the wall and came into this room to change. He was changing his shoes, the left having been tied, but not yet the right as the door opened again. His assailant must have followed him into the room and a struggle ensued. The mark on Roberto's side matches the broken rim of the laundry cart, so we must assume it was quite the blow. In the end, Roberto ended up on his back and his assailant on top, pinning Roberto's arms under his knees."

That made sense to me as the bus boy's shirt was scrunched up to his armpits and littered with filth.

"Having gained the upper hand, the Killer was either striking of choking the victim. Roberto must have fought hard, as his untied shoe flew from his foot as he tried to kick his oppressor off him. The struggle continued until his assailant drove a blade into Roberto's temple. Then the killer locked the door and replaced the key back on the wall before returning to his duties."

He paused to see what effect his dramatics had on us. I was my usual impressed. It wasn't a toughie, but he put it together nicely. Jimmy, on the other hand, wasn't satisfied.

"William," He put his head down, hands on his hips, and peered at my friend over the rim of his spectacles. "That someone has taken my busboy off the schedule permanently, this much I know! Who? Why? That's what I need from you!"

"Hey Jimmy," I spoke up, not liking the way he was pushing, "Isn't there a little saying on the back of your menu? I know because I read it a hundred times. 'Time is the essence of good food preparation. If we make you wait it is to serve you better!' Well, investigations are like that."

"Well said, Frohman!" William agreed. "But if it will bring us any closer to dinner, I will do what I can."

"Thank you, William," Wovi beamed, "If you can tell me who before the crew gets off and scatters across half the city, you shall never pay for another meal in this establishment!" He must have felt my eyes boring into him as he added, "Charles too, of course!"

William never heard the offer as he was already back to examining the body. With his tweezers, he was plucking at wounds and picking specks off the victim's shirt to examine under his glass. It was too gruesome to watch on an empty stomach, so I turned to Jimmy, who had moved around to watch over Will's shoulder.

"So, what are you going to do about the body?"

Jimmy was so engrossed he answered honestly on the first try, "I'll send word to the Clancy Street boys later. They'll make it disappear for a sawbuck." He shrugged, "He's got no family in this country."

The thought saddened me. Poor sod would be stripped and dumped in an alley and lay there until the city morgue got around to picking it up to dump it in some potter's grave. I was still struggling with the morality of the situation when I noticed that William had been busy gathering specimens.

His handkerchief was spread out on Bobby's stomach and Will had lined tiny objects across it. He set one down carefully then went back to continue his search. Before I could ask him what he was doing, he twitched and cried out.

"Ha! The confirmation I sought!" He swiveled his head and addressed Jimmy. "I believe you will recognize this!"

He held the magnifying glass in place but moved off to the side so Jimmy could get a better look. After a minute, Jimmy straightened up with a puzzled look on his face.

"I could swear that was a saffron thread, William."

"And you would be correct," William replied.

"But Bobby must have just put on that shirt. We issue them one per shift. They get them right off the shelf over there."

"Then it did not appear until the fight."

Jimmy was going to ask another question, but William had already turned away. He squatted down again and selected the pointing stick from his tools.

Unexpectedly, and extremely unsettling, he poked the stick into the mortal head wound and pushed it in as far as it would go. He waggled it around the opening, and then pulled it out, measuring the distance from the tip to the bloodline and announced, "The blade was four and one-half inches long and straight tapered to an inch where it fit into the hilt."

"So, what's that got to do with your little collection here?" I asked, gesturing to the cloth on the dead man.

He handed me the glass, "Look for yourself, Frohman. Tell me if you recognize anything."

I took the glass and got to one knee. It took me a minute and a couple squints, but I suddenly realized what I was looking at. They were miniscule bits of things I grew up around on the South Fork of Long Island.

"Seafood. All seafood," I pronounced, "There's mussel, clam, and oyster shell, fish scales, shrimp legs, you name it."

I stood up, to see William's usual smug look of triumph and Jimmy's eyes bugging out of his head. The Greek's face was red as a tomato as he held his fists out, trembling with rage.

"That son of a –"

"Before you accuse anyone," William rode over him to caution, "Look at his hands for signs he has been in a fight."

"Are you joking? Every man in that kitchen has hands like a railroad coolie!"

"Well, then, look for fresh blood stain-" Jimmy gave him another look and opened his mouth to protest, but William talked over him. "The chef using a blunt five-inch knife should not have blood stains on his apron or right cuff."

Jimmy was too tense to speak but he nodded vigorously. He turned to leave, but William stopped him, then grabbed his coat.

"Please let us out through the street entrance, Jimmy. We don't want to spook our quarry. Besides, I need some air."

Jimmy led us through the meat room, past hanging slabs of beef, all manner of fowl and pork, and some dried sausage that made my stomach go past growl straight to howl. Unlocking the back door, we went into a hallway and then up a flight of stairs where Jimmy unlocked the hatchway and let us out onto the street. The main entrance to Jimmy's was to our left and the fence that sealed off the alley to the kitchen's back door was to our right.

"Let us enjoy a cigarette, Frohman, and then we can return to our table and await the outcome."

As we lit up, I was fuming because I still was in the dark, even though Jimmy had obviously pegged the killer. And I was pretty sure that William knew I was still in the dark and it amused the hell out of him. But I was damned if I was going to come out and ask.

Smirking, William said, "I wonder what set this tragedy in motion. The sudden change in atmosphere that brought death upon the scene."

"What are you jabbering about? "I asked, ignoring his melodramatic words, which, I was convinced were just to break my stones.

William laughed, "I was just pointing out that this was a crime of the moment. I don't think the killer planned to kill Roberto."

"From the hole in Bobby's head, I agree!" I countered just to be obstinate. Hunger made me grumpy.

William shrugged, "You never know, Frohman. But I think it more likely a dispute over a woman. What did Jimmy say they called him? Bobby four arms?"

My cigarette was almost finished and I had had it. "Alright Will! Damn it! Who? Who snuffed him?"

William was taken back by my outburst, but he stayed in character.

"Really Frohman!" he sighed. "It is really rather simple. You are aware of all the facts, you just need to put it all together."

"No, I don't," I snapped back. "That's what I keep you around for!"

He laughed at that and my waspish streak was broken. I mulled over everything I had seen in the last few hours, but it was all too jumbled to make any sense. So, I tossed my smoke on the ground, put my hands on my hips, and said, "Look Will. It's nearly eight thirty and I haven't had one drink yet! You know I need a little grease for my gears upstairs to work! So why don't you stop kicking me in the crotch and tell me who killed that poor bastard in there!"

He relented, but he wasn't going to make it quick. "The key to revealing our killer was the fact that Roberto had just put on a clean shirt before he was attacked. You remember that Jimmy told us the shirts came off a shelf in that room?"

"Yea, I remember," I replied. "So, all that gunk you picked off his shirt must have come from whoever he fought with!" Then the thought occurred to me, "And if it was a kitchen worker, he would have been wearing an apron. When he sat on Bobby's chest, his apron would be mashed against the shirt!"

William was nodding encouragement when I was talking, and I made another leap. "Since most of what you took off the shirt was seafood, it must have been one of the cooks or prep people that handle that end! That narrows it down."

William raised his long forefinger. "Do not forget that last ingredient I discovered, Frohman. It points specifically to our man."

I ran the scenario in my head one more time then slapped my forehead when it came to me. "The Saffron! Seafood and saffron equals Boullibase! Who was making the stew tonight?"

"Bravo Frohman!" He clapped his hands together. "I don't even know who that might be, but Jimmy seemed to have a good idea."

"That's why you told him to check his shellfish knife. There're about five inches long and certainly sturdy enough to go through a thin temple bone!"

William tossed his cigarette into the street and looked towards the alley door. "I must confess I am anxious to see how this all plays out. "He watched a moment longer then clapped me on the shoulder, "Come on, Charlie! Let's go back to our table and get you your lubrication."

A loud crash came from the alley and we both turned to see the door to the alley crash open and a stout man, dressed in kitchen whites with a poofy hat burst through. He stopped long enough to see us staring, then he changed direction and started running down the street as fast as his bulk permitted.

Before that could sink in, Wovi staggered out onto the sidewalk screaming at the top of his lungs, "Bennett! Get back here!" He went on for a minute, but the rest was in Greek. I doubt it would have set well with Christian ears in English. When he finally ran down, a minute after the chef was out of sight, he turned to face us, and we could see why he was out of his mind. His entire front was caked and dripping with some type of food. It was obvious how the chef reacted when Wovi confronted him.

William and I looked at each other and he shrugged.

"Ne pas faire, Le Cuisenaire!"

I just looked at him. My French wasn't great.

"Don't piss off the Cook!"

I nodded sagely. "I believe I've changed my mind. I'm going to have the chicken."

One Part Suicide

Early May, 1898

Part One

All I did was brood.

I sat in my pretentious, corner office on the top floor of a building I owned and stared out the floor to ceiling windows that overlooked New York's Central Park. I had money, power, prestige, and all the trappings that went with it.

It was in the middle of the day and I usually begin my walk to my reserved table at the club. Morning head fog began to burn off and a plan began to form when my secretary dropped four scripts on my desk deemed by my staff to be the best chances of theater success.

My name is Charles Frohman, and, in all modesty, I could say, that for a good hunk of the population on either side of the Atlantic, an introduction may be needed, even though I touch their lives almost every day with theatre.

I own and built the largest entertainment company in the world. The Theatre Syndicate encompasses the entire eastern seaboard of the United States, branching out with playhouses in New York, St. Louis, Chicago, Phoenix, and California. Smaller towns and cities contribute to the revenues from their smaller modest sized theaters along with their lesser known actors.

Over the last ten years, I have expanded The Theater Syndicate 'across the pond', as the Limeys say. We have strong roots in London and are expanding into Paris and Berlin by the end of 1910. The new talent from Europe has America excited and we are cashing in! Coupled with our own homespun talent, I had some serious decisions to make about which actors were going to play backup and who takes on the lead roles for this upcoming season, which brought me back to the stack of scripts on my desk. After another half hour of thought, I was nearly drowning in possibilities, when fate chose to throw me a lifeline.

There was a discreet knock on my door and when my secretary poked her head in to announce a visitor. Before she could utter a word, a tall, strikingly confident man, stepped past her and struck a pose just inside the door. He bowed grandly and said,

"Tis but I, the lowly jester. I have come to pay homage to his majesty."

"AH!" I replied, delighted for the first time in weeks. "Lucky for you, I just met the Queen last month, so I know what a royal would say to such a loyal and unannounced subject such as yourself. PISS OFF!"

We both roared with laughter and I was off my chair and around my desk to give him a great bear hug before he took two steps. He tried to hold me at arm's length and said, "Oh, Charlie! How I have missed you. How have you been, my friend?"

It was at that moment I realized how much I had missed him, especially this week. His advice is always sound, and his insight astounding. William Hooker Gillette is still the top drawing actor and my closest friend which I hadn't seen for months.

"Where the hell have you been?" I asked. "I got back from London a month ago and I thought you'd come around before now!"

"I just finished that dreary run of 'The Hounds' again in Baltimore a few weeks ago and I've been settling into my new digs since."

"New Digs? Are you telling me you finally grew tired of living on that big canoe of yours and bought a house!? You're a land lubber now?"

He laughed, "Not really, Charles. I rented a place in Greenport for the time being. I know just what I want to build; I just have to find the right setting. Greenport has a lot of good points."

"Greenport, huh? Why the North Fork of Long Island?"

"Well, for starters, between your family and your wife's, you own most of the South Fork."

"You're exaggerating," I protested. "We don't have much left in Montauk and nothing east of the Hamptons!

Besides, it's mostly beach and flat land. Not fit for crops or cattle!"

He shrugged, "I am not interested in it either, though I am looking for some ocean front property. Anyone in your clan want to part with some?"

"Oh, I'm sure someone would sell you a parcel right on the ocean, my friend." Then I remembered my manners and bade him to take a seat. I settled in across from him and continued, "But only a damn fool builds his home within reach of the Atlantic, home of some of the worst destructive forces in nature, William. There's a reason why we build our homes a half a mile inland, unless you want to see your house blown away in the next hurricane!"

"That's not what I'm building Charlie." he countered. "Just give me some bedrock."

"And there's your problem, Bub. There is none."

And so, we bantered on. Eventually the subject changed from family to friends and to business. As with all true friends, time is irrelevant. After a greeting and the hug, the months apart melted into minutes, which is why I was more than a little ashamed that I had to manipulate events at his expense to see my plan through. Embarrassingly easy as it was.

William had just finished telling me a funny story about one of the performances in Baltimore and commented that he was happy to take some time off.

"And what about you, Charles? Are you going to relax a little as the season winds down?"

It was the perfect opening, and, after a minor moral glitch, I plunged forward.

"I would," I replied in a sour tone, "just as soon as I line up the projects for the next season, which should take me right up to the beginning of the season!"

"What? Why?" William asked. "By Jove, Charlie, you have a bevy of stars to choose from! We may need another civil war just to free all the actors you have under contract!"

I laughed, "That's my problem, William. I have six major talents and a boat load of hopefuls to place and just four scripts worth a damn. I want to mix things up a bit this year. My top people had great runs and I don't want them getting complacent. They need versatility if they're going to stay sharp. I wish I could just get them all in one place for a few days and see how they interact. Then I could get a clear vision where to place them and with whom. Unless, of course," I waggled my eyebrows, "you are willing to tread the boards one more time? You can have any house and stage you want. Then I can just toss those scripts in the sty and let the hams fight over them. I'll even take the week-end off and come see you in Greenport."

"Oh No, my friend, as I told you before you bullied me into going to that pimple on the state of Maryland known as Baltimore-"

"Bullied! That was part of the contract you signed!"

"Easy, Charlie," he laughed. "In any case, I told you before I left for Baltimore, that it would be my last performance for some time. This is the first time in my life that I intend to build a domicile and I intend for it to be my last. Every ounce of creativity I possess, I intend to pour into this project!"

Knowing his flair for dramatics, I had a feeling it would rival, or even surpass those places in New Port RI. The income from his work was about to dry up quickly and he was wise to settle down and enjoy his wealth.

"Well, I'm happy for you, William. I know how you love a new challenge." I added with a wink. "But that still leaves me back where I started. How do I get them all together without making it seem like a summons to a business meeting?"

I held my breath. Everything hinged on his next reaction and when I saw his expression change, I knew, shame on me, he took the bait.

"Perhaps I could help you there, Charlie. You're right, of course, if you ask them for the weekend, they'll put up their guards. But, if I were to invite them for a getaway, to my place in Greenport, perhaps with a tour of the twin forks on the Aunt Polly, and you were just another guest..." He let the thought hang in the air.

"Yes!" I cried, feigning astonishment, "Then they would be much more relaxed, and I'd see them at their basics. That would be perfect! But, gee William, that's an awful lot on you. I couldn't ask that of you! Besides, you think they'd all come?"

"First, you didn't ask, I offered. Secondly, of course they would all come. Barrymore is a dear friend and won't turn me down. Adams and Milland will come just because Ethel is, and they fear being squeezed out. Drew and Gilmore will come because they wouldn't want to be left out of the running for a good part and E.H Southern never refuses a free meal or a drink!"

I laughed, but my astonishment was real this time, "How did you know who I wanted to invite? I never gave you any names!"

He shook his head in mock sadness, "Charlie, Charlie. Don't you think I know who your six top draws are?"

I guess I shouldn't have been that amazed. He's been playing the same character for so long, there was, at times, a thin line between the fictional character and the thespian before me.

"Perhaps you do need a break from playing Holmes. You're turning into him!"

"Elementary, My dear Frohman, Elementary!"

We both laughed, and he went on, "We'll send out the invitations for two weeks from now. That will give me enough time to make all the arrangements. I would like to add one more to the guest list, if you don't mind, Charlie. My understudy in Baltimore is Sheldon Steele. You may even know him, his family is from Montauk. In fact, isn't there some Steele's in Denise's family?"

I shrugged and said nothing. William, being a blue blood from Hartford, Ct., could never understand the clannish morays of our extended families on the South Fork.

"Anyways, he did a good job for me when I lost my voice for a few days and I'd like to give him a little exposure."

I managed to spread my hands expansively and smile, "Of course, anyone 'near family' is welcome."

"Good! Then that's settled."

"Now, have you eaten, or could we grab a bite to eat? I'm famished."

PART TWO

William was always true to his word and set the date for two weeks hence. So, on the appointed day, I found myself disembarking the Long Island Railroad in Greenport, Long Island. Things were progressing nicely, and the only hitch was an unexpected errand.

Just as I was packing to go, my wife informed me that my second son, Collin, was suspended from school for fighting. A trait I secretly found admirable, but Collin had yet to develop any sense of discretion. Often, he fought for the right reasons -- just at the wrong time. However, most importantly, he always won! Still, we had strict rules for discipline and suspension from the academy required a mental tune up deemed to be two weeks with Pop-Pop.

Pop-Pop being my grandfather, was a tough old bird and had been fishing for just about seventy plus years. Seine, trap or hook, he was a farmer of the ocean. Pop-Pop took whatever was in season. It was a seven day a week life, where one set lobster pots or raked for clams and scallops whenever there were a few hours left over after emptying the nets. It was a brutal, monastic way of life, yet he was a master among masters on the bay and all others envied his ability. Pop-Pop toughed out bad weather and filled his boat with the best fish. Local restaurants gladly paid a premium since their customers asked if it was Pop-Pop's catch.

As a lad, any transgression a good cuff upside the head didn't cover, ended in me being hauled off to Amagansett to spend some time with Pop-Pop. Happy to have extra hands, he'd work me like a slave and beat me like one too if he thought I was working too slow or too sloppy. If and when he spoke, it was like Moses reading the Ten Commandments to the heathens.

As I look back on those experiences, I realized that my Grandfather's talent really lay in his philosophy of teach once and pound the lesson in. He was a simple man, yet wiser than most. Between the hard work and his strict rules fortified with beatings, by the end of the first week, you had thought about what sent you there and realized it wasn't worth it. By the end of the second, you made a promise to God you wouldn't make the same mistake twice.

So, I had Collin in tow when I hailed a cab at the station to take us to William's. I was supposed to turn him over to Pop-Pop before I came here, but, seeing my son's pugilistic skills in a different light than my wife's, I let him badger me into staying for the week-end and hob nob with the celebrities. Collin always took an interest in my work and I hoped he would follow me into the business one day. The revised plan was to drop him off Sunday, before I headed back to the city.

"You know," I pointed out to him as we settled into the cab. "Waiting a few days for the axe to fall won't change anything. You may want to reconsider your decision. The sooner you go, the sooner you will be finished."

He shrugged, "Today or Monday, the fish will still be there." he sighed, "Just like Pop-pop and the ocean." Then he gave me that 'devil may care' grin that I loved him for and said, "Though I expect I'll get more sympathy from the ocean!"

I let it go and soon we were pulling alongside the dock where the Aunt Polly was berthed. The Aunt Polly was William's houseboat and frequently, his home since his wife Helen died years ago. One hundred and forty-four feet long and thirty-feet-wide, Aunt Polly was a miniature floating mansion with beautiful state rooms, open decks fore and aft, and a saloon lined with windows on both sides that was a delightful place to have a drink any time of the day. I loved the old girl.

You'd think a craft of this size would need a large crew, but William and his man Ozaki managed her nicely, though they would put me to work if we took an extended trip.

No sooner had I paid the cabbie and Ozaki materialized in front of us. Collin leaped forward with a cry and gave the little Asian a bear hug that reminded me of his childhood. All my children seemed to have this secret bond with Ozaki, one that I am not supposed to know about.

He took the contact with his usual oriental stoicism. When Collin released him, Ozaki simply said something low and serious to my son, then playfully ruffled his hair like he did when Collin was six. Collin beamed as Ozaki turned to face me. We shook hands and bowed simultaneously, as was the compromise of our cultures which we had worked out over the years past.

Ozaki was a wise and talented Asian. A Japper by birth, he was short, lean and had that oriental golden hue. He came into William's service many years ago, shortly after the death of Will's beloved Helen.

More than a man servant or valet, he was a constant companion to William, wearing many hats in his service. Not only did he take care of his needs, he piloted the Aunt Polly, and ran his household with an iron fist whenever William had a need to add temporary help.

William, for his part, considered Ozaki to be family. Yet it seemed to me at times, that William wore Ozaki like a coat, a layer between him and the world. Ozaki was his confidant, chef, maid, boat crew, nurse, and bodyguard. Though he would never admit it, I think William loved the dramatics of having a 'mysterious oriental' by his side. It might seem silly to you, but you'd have to know William. He may have been the most private of men as he only showed the public the persona's he wished them to see.

With his usual efficiency, Ozaki had my bags in route to William's new residence, where I would be staying, and Collin took his own bag as he was berthing on the Aunt Polly. He took us on board and left me on the stern deck, which had tables set up and another long table sagging against the salon bulkhead, piled high with food for our luncheon cruise.

By the time Collin dropped his bag and made his way back, I was looking around the stern deck.

"What are you looking for, father?"

"Just wondering where your Uncle Willie hid the hooch."

"When we find it, could I have one with you, Dad?"

"Of course, that would be great." I replied, watching his eyes light up in surprise and delight. Then I continued, "If you suddenly become responsible, that is," I dropped my voice an octave for emphasis, "And drinking wasn't what landed you here so don't let me see you walk a crooked line or slur one word. Understood?"

He shrugged and flashed that smile again, "Yes, sir. But you don't have to worry, I drank enough last week to last me at least a few months!" Collin looked around, taking in the surroundings when he saw the buffet. "Hey, look at all that food."

"You hungry?"

"Hell yes!" He replied with gusto, but then hesitated and looked around, "But shouldn't we wait for Uncle Willie? Where is he anyways?"

"You know your Uncle, Collin," I said as I heaved myself out of the chair. "We won't see him until he gets to make a grand entrance. Everyone else has to get here first."

We walked over to the table of food and as Collin began to load a plate, I saw a pile of scrubbed, hard shell clams in a bucket of ice. A sturdy shucking knife was conveniently set beside the bucket, so I began to swiftly open a dozen for Collin and I. I'd been shucking clams before I could read, and the shells were literally leaping off the back of my knife and fell back on the ice in a neat pile.

On my fourteenth one, I nearly sliced my palm open when a female voice sounded in my ear.

"Good Lord, Charles, You're a veritable mollusk murdering machine!" She purred, "Whatever did those poor clams do to you?"

Ethel Barrymore. Of course, I'd know her voice anywhere. Ethel had been in England, where she made quite a run before returning to the states. She had never been under contract, but I knew she'd be open to any suggestions I made for her next stint.

Ethel was like a sister to me. Our relationship allowed us to skip the fake kissy-kissy and hug of the show biz people. She was bold and brassy, so we were always very comfortable in each other's company.

"Why nothing, my dear," I quipped back, "It's just business. Nothing personal, I assure you." I finished the clam I was working on and in one motion, scooped another and popped the top off.

"I'd hate to see it if you were mad at them. Are there enough there for a poor out of work actress?"

"Don't worry, Darling," I answered as I shucked a few more in rapid succession, "I'll start you off with a dozen."

"That many?"

I chuckled as I put down the knife and hefted the overflowing plate, "Ethel, I've seen you eat half a cow after a long show!"

She stamped her feet and said petulantly, "Are you calling me a glutton?"

She was beautiful, worldly, and had a voluptuous figure and she knew it. And she knew that I knew it.

"All I'm saying is that you are lucky these aren't oysters young lady or I'd chase you around this tub until you jump overboard and swim for your virtue!"

"OOH!" She giggled, "But I'm already a little wet from looking at your clams!"

That got a laugh from me that got stuck in my throat when I noticed Collin standing just behind me with his jaw on the deck and his face beet red. He had heard every word we said.

Ethel flinched when she saw him, but quickly recovered. "And who do we have here, Mr. Frohman?" She looked at him a little closer and then at me, "Does this handsome strapping lad belong to you?"

"Ethel Barrymore, this is my son, Collin." I smiled and winked at her. "He usually doesn't glow like that."

"Pooh! Charles, don't tease him." She gave him her best smile and held out her hands. "Don't mind us old folk, Collin. Unfortunately, vulgarity comes with age."

To my pride and his credit, Collin handled himself smoothly, "No need to apologize." He said as he took her hand, "Youth holds no judgment."

Ethel clapped her hands in delight and looked at me, clearly impressed. "This one's a chip off the old block!" Then she took Collin by the arm, "Just how old are you?" She asked as she led him to a table, me following with the food.

"I'll be eighteen in two months, Miss Barrymore."

"Are you with us for the weekend?"

"Yes, Ma'am." he answered as he held out a chair for her.

"If you survive this crowd for the next two days, you'll be going on thirty." She said as she sat.

The repartee was cut short as a couple of girls called out from the dock. Ozaki materialized and led Maude Adams and Evelyn Milland on board.

After a brief greeting and an introduction for my son, Ozaki showed them to where they could 'freshen up'. As they walked away, Collin said,

"I remember seeing Miss Milland in one of your shows last year, Dad, and Miss Adams looks familiar, but I can't remember where I've seen her before."

"That's because she probably wasn't wearing a dress when you saw her last," Ethel said with a mischievous smile.

Col's eyes widened but I saved him another red face. "Peter Pan." I explained. "She's had that role for years. She looks quite different dressed as a boy."

Collin nodded and said, "I knew I recognized her. I've seen 'Neverland' a few times." Then he added, "Either way, she looks darn good."

Before we could expound on that or even get a bite to eat, another voice hailed us from the dock. "Ahoy there! I finally found you!"

"Ah! Adonis has arrived," Ethel quipped in a low voice as she raised her arm and waved, "Hello, E.H.! You made it!"

Again, Ozaki showed up to let him on board and the girls joined us as E.H. Southern stepped on board.

This round of reunion was considerably more flamboyant. E. H. was one of the more dashing leading men in my company with a natural flair for the dramatic. Women loved him, and he lavished each girl present with personal attention. It was another fifteen minutes before the newcomers got a plate of food and we arraigned ourselves at the tables.

Ethel and I both picked up a fork and we attacked the clams I shucked earlier, when a horn began blaring off the starboard side. Collin was the first one to the railing but everyone except Ethel and I went to see what the hullabaloo was about.

Ethel sighed and dropped her fork, "These damn things are going to grow their shells back before we get to them," She groused as we rose and joined the others.

We got there just in time to see a launch pull up alongside of the Aunt Polly. I recognized the two men sitting in the back. The pilot shut down the engines and stepped over to grab the side of our boat. John Drew Jr. and Paul Gilmore rose from their bench and snapped to attention, looking up at me. Saluting, they cried out together. "Permission to come aboard, Sir?"

They always were clowns. These two I knew I would keep in separate productions. The last time they were in the same play, my production costs soared. Just from their tomfoolery!

"I'm not the man to ask," I replied, "This isn't my boat! But you are holding up our lunch, so whatever you do -- do it quickly!"

Again, Ozaki was Johnny-on-the-spot and he made his way through us holding a rope boarding ladder, which he hooked on the gunwale and tossed over the side. Drew and Gilmore, both being in fair shape, quickly scaled the rungs and deposited themselves in our midst.

The tower of babel rose as the questions and introductions sprouted out of the eight of us. Fortunately, Southern finally said what I was thinking.

"Folks, Folks!" The voices died off and when he had everyone's attention, announced, "I love the ole ang sine routine as much as the next guy, but we've all had a long trip and I, for one, am famished."

"Here, here!" Ethel spoke out.

"So, I say we find ourselves a drink and try to eat William out of house and boat. Now, where's that little Asian fellow?" E.H. quipped, as he craned his head around dramatically.

"I'm afraid he's indisposed. Getting the ship ready to sail. Perhaps I could be of some assistance?"

There was a moment of stunned silence. I never even saw him come on deck, but there he was, standing behind a rolling beverage cart. The cart had champagne and wine on ice with some bottles of the harder stuff and mixers, along with glasses and a tray of fruit wedges.

"Thank God, you're here." I cried out, grabbing my pocket flask off the table and putting it back in my jacket. "Civilization has arrived!"

I quickly stepped up to the cart and lifted a bottle of wine out of the bucket and said to it, "I thought I never see you! Oh, how I've missed you!"

Then I looked up at my friend as if I just noticed him and said, "Oh! Hi William. When did you get here?"

Amid the laughter, everyone stepped up to greet our host. A heartfelt round of hugs and handshakes ensued. When the hullabaloo subsided, Paul asked William,

"So, now you're peddling your own hooch?" Pointing at William's hand that was resting on the cart handle. Then he looked around and I suddenly realized the same thing.

"No crew, Will? Just you and Ozaki running the boat?"

He shrugged, "It's just an afternoon cruise around the island, Charlie. I thought we'd keep it intimate."

I knew why he did it and I appreciated him even more. The less eyes and ears- the less chance of my choices leaking out and stealing my thunder at the end of the month when I announced this season's schedule and players. Not to mention selling a story to the press about our soirée. They'd work it up to a drunken bash to rival Dionysus!

"So, you sent the servants away, William." Ethel sidled up to him and cooed, "You're going to give a girl sinfull ideas."

William laughed and put his arms around her, "My dearest Ethel, though I might consider myself a man of the world I am fairly certain that any idea I could possibly give you has already crossed that exquisite mind, behind that beautiful face, of yours!"

"Twice or more," I added.

PART THREE

It was some time before we all had drinks and had told each other how wonderful we looked before we got to sit back at the table. Unfortunately, our shellfish were submerged in melted ice by then, so I was relegated to shucking once again. Will joined me, and we made quite a show of my prowess with an oyster knife and Will's catching the discards and arranging the mollusks on plates of fresh ice and lemon wedges to pass around.

E.H., forever the clown, started slurping oysters down and waggling his eyes at the ladies to much laughter.

"Why's he doing that, Uncle Will? What's so funny?" Collin asked. "Dad made a joke about Oysters too."

I was about to tell him to 'never mind', the parent coming out in me, but William answered first.

"It's widely believed that oysters are an aphrodisiac," he said, in his stage voice. He grinned as he noticed everyone had heard him and was looking in our direction. William went on, "and that it greatly enhances male performance!"

Titters and grins broke out as Collin's ears reddened slightly.

"Do you mind?" I asked, acting the aggrieved father, "He doesn't need to know all that yet!"

"Oh, don't be such a fuddy-duddy Charles. The lad's starting college this fall! Columbia no less!"

"How about you, Collin," Mary asked in a coquettish voice , just to further bust my stones, I'm sure. "Are you going to have a few?"

"No, Ma'am," Collin shook his head with a sly smile. He waggled his eyebrows and raised his voice, "I don't need them yet."

As the sound of laughter exploded across the deck, I leaned in closer to William as he whispered, "THAT apple didn't fall far from the tree!"

When everyone's plates were properly laden, William called Ozaki over and said in a voice I could just overhear, "Please tell Sheldon we have already begun to eat and to join us."

Ozaki hurried off and William turned his back to me with a touch of disgust on his face. "I was wondering what had happened to him. I remember you were going to bring him along."

William rolled his eyes, "I'm afraid he might have had the delusion of making a grand entrance. I believe his success in Baltimore has given him a bit of a swollen head."

"A Grand entrance! I wonder where he might have picked up that notion." I teased my friend, who had mastered the art years ago, "And his head can swell as much as it wants- he'll never match this lot for ego! Each of them have a full glass and a plate of food, I doubt they'll even notice his arrival!"

Yet, to give the devil his due, the boy did make quite an entrance after all.

The banter and the eating continued for a while longer. Collin was making quite impression on the ladies with his witty remarks and shy smiles. He had turned into quite the debonair young man while I wasn't looking. Only William and I seemed to notice when the lights in the salon went out. Mostly, I suppose, because when you've spent enough time on a boat, you realize your life may depend on any small changes.

Slowly the double doors of the salon that led to the aft deck where we were seated opened, and a dashing man slowly glided out of the darkness into the soft glow of twilight.

He was a handsome devil with light brown curly locks that rolled off his head to a frame his handsome features. Cobalt blue eyes, straight nose, and a solid, slightly cleft chin that would keep him in leading roles for years to come.

He wore simple white tropical linen pants with a bilious white shirt that cinched his small waist and stretched snug over his broad shoulders. Every woman at the table was thinking 'Dessert has arrived!'. He clicked his patent leather heels together and bowed slightly at the waist, his six-foot frame breaking gracefully, "Ladies and gentlemen, Please, pardon my tardiness. There was a small personal matter that needed my attention."

86

Will and I looked at each other and we both rolled our eyes. Even Ethel was amused, as she leaned over to whisper to us, "He would have matched your entrance William, if only he hadn't talked!"

None the less, she was graceful when William got up to introduce his new protégée to the gang. The men were all cordial and kept their thoughts of seeing a younger version of themselves that would likely push them aside in the future. But the girls were more than welcoming, fawning all over him. Those barracudas liked nothing better than a new piece of bait fish.

The one hitch was Collin. Sheldon greeted him last, sticking out his hand, "Well, hello again! I didn't know there'd be Bonackers on board."

Collin, who was engaged in a conversation with E.H., turned his head slowly and stared at the proffered hand. He stared at it long enough for the conversation to fade as everyone took notice of the tension and Collin's wild eyes.

I didn't know what was happening- but I knew my son and it could get ugly quickly. The last thing I wanted him to do was disrupt the evening, so when he caught my eye, I threw daggers with them and stretched my mouth in a nasty smile as wide as it would go.

He caught my meaning and took Sheldon's hand. "Nice to see you again." With that, he turned back and resumed his conversation with E.H. as if Sheldon was never there. I could tell E.H. was vastly amused by the blatant disrespect.

William, ever the good host, managed to cover Collin's rude behavior by quickly seating Sheldon between two of the ladies at the opposite end of the table and returning to his seat next to me and asked, "What has gotten into Collin? I've never seen him act that way before?"

The last thing I wanted was for this to escalate and draw more attention, so I tried to slough it off.

"Who knows, William?" I answered with a shrug. Though I had a sinking feeling that this could turn into more than rudeness. "I didn't even know they knew each other. Maybe Collin didn't like the way he said 'Bonacker'. Like I said, he's a good kid but he needs some adjustments. Don't worry about it," I added. "Pop will straighten him out."

William wasn't convinced, "Still, Charlie, that wasn't like Collin at all. I've never known him to be rude. Oh, sure, he can be a bit hot headed, but he always used to remember his manners."

Now, if anyone else had spoken to me about my children like that, I would have told them to mind their own business and stop talking, but William was Collin's Godfather and has always treated him as if he was his own. The children in turn adored William and have called him 'Uncle Willy' their entire lives.

"I'll pull Collin aside when we get underway", I said, hoping he would drop the subject and it would soon be forgotten, "I'm sure it's nothing more than just juvenile angst, like I said."

"I'm not so sure, Charlie. Maybe I-"

A horn sounded from the wheelhouse, cutting off Will's words as the Aunt Polly slowly swung away from the dock and into the channel. Luckily, Ethel came to the rescue, before he could take up where he left off.

"Just two roosters in the hen house, William. Just keep them apart and it'll all be fine."

He grunted. "Unless they settle on the same Hen!"

PART FOUR

The luncheon progressed nicely from there. After we had a few drinks and we demolished everything in a shell, Ozaki laid out a small, but extravagant buffet. It was mostly just classics, but he did favor us with some tempura that was a favorite of mine. The good food and conversation made the time fly.

So much so, I was surprised to see that we were in the channel between Shelter Island and North haven. I just happened to look up when I noticed a change in the Aunt Polly's engines. William had noticed too and stood, but quickly sat back down.

"We are just giving way to the Ferry."

I sat up in my seat and could see the Ferry that plied between the island and South Fork just coming away from the dock. Ozaki had cut the speed to let it pass in front of us. That's when I saw Collin approach Sheldon, who was at the bar making himself another drink. There was something in his posture and a look on his face that made me nervous, but I dismissed my concern. Collin would know better than to embarrass me or his uncle William.

As it happened many times before in my parenting, I was wrong. They had spoken for less than five minutes before Collin up and cracked Sheldon across the jaw with a left.

The blow staggered Sheldon and he stumbled backwards a few and caught himself on the edge of the bar cart. He just put his drink on the table and hit my son with a haymaker that drove Collin back into the railings. I thought he was going to go over the side for a minute. Collin recovered quickly, shook his head, and launched himself back at Sheldon with a snarl. The fight was on in earnest.

Collin managed to knock one of the chaffing dishes off the buffet and nearly upset the drink cart but accomplished little else. I'm not sure he even landed a solid blow after the first sucker punch. Sheldon was no fop. He ducked and jabbed, landing a flurry of hits as Collin just flailed away at him. I never saw him fight so poorly.

Will was out of his seat faster, as he wasn't critiquing, and I heaved my bulk up to put a stop to it, but Ozaki was there before both of us. He grabbed Collin by the back of his collar and heaved him backwards up against the railing. Will went to grab his protégée, but Sheldon dropped his hands as soon as the little Jap got between them.

I grabbed Collin by the arm, and I heard Ozaki hiss in Collin's ear before he turned him over to me.

"Where you rearn to fight like that!"

I didn't have time to think about it then because as soon as Ozaki stepped away, Collin tried to lunge past me. If I hadn't kept a firm hold on his arm and step in front of him, I have no doubt he would try to rip Sheldon's neck out. I had never seen such rage in my child.

"Collin!" I barked at him, "Get a hold of yourself!"

He didn't even seem to hear me as he tried to get past me again. When he couldn't get by, he shouted, past swollen lips, "I'll kill you, you son of a bitch!"

He was wearing out my patience. I made a fist and extended my middle knuckle that rapped him solidly in the forehead. "What is ailing you Boy!" I shouted in his face.

This stunned him, and his eyes seemed to focus for a second. I almost thought I was going to get an answer out of him, but his eyes focused on Sheldon and he stepped right back into his rage.

He lunged again, screaming, "You're dead! Dead!" and my patience ran out.

I grabbed his shirt by my right and his crotch with my left and a picked him up and pitched him over the railing into the bay.

All hell broke loose. The women were squealing and shouting and the men, with the exception of Will, who looked more puzzled than anything, were hooting with laughter and calling for Ozaki to turn the boat around as they fumbled around looking for life rings.

Of course, Ozaki wouldn't be able to turn the ship around in this narrow channel and even at a reduced speed, we were moving away from where Collin went in the water. When his head broke the surface, I could see he was back to normal when he shouted to me.

I couldn't hear a thing over the din of the other guests, so I shouted for silence. I moved to the stern so I could hear him.

"Dad," he shouted, treading water. "Throw me a rope!"

"Not this time. Forget it!" I hollered back. A collective gasp came up behind me. "You're not coming back aboard this boat! You get your ass to your Uncle Tom and Sadie's. They can put you up for the night. I'll call Tom in the morning and have him take you to Pop's!" With that, I turned and pushed my way through the gawkers to William, who was watching Collin carefully.

My back was still to the scene as I whispered out of the corner of my mouth, "Is he moving?"

William answered in kind, "Not to worry, Charlie, he's already halfway to the pier."

I let out the breath I was holding, and someone grabbed my arm. It was Mary with a scared, embarrassed look on her face.

"Are you sure about this, Charles?"

"Aaah!," I replied flippantly. "He's less than fifty yards from shore and his Uncle is only a few miles down the main road. The swim might bring some sense back to him."

Despite my bravado, I did glance back at the ferry landing and breathed a sigh of relief as I saw Collin climb out of the water.

"Whatever started it?" Mary asked, wide eyed. "One minute they were talking and the next it was rage!"

"I'm sure it was what Ethel said earlier. Two roosters in the hen house," I hoped she would take that and let it lie but William piped up.

"I don't think so, Charlie. I've never seen Collin act like that. There's more to it than that, I am certain."

He turned to his understudy, who was draining three fingers of something from a glass at the drink cart.

"Sheldon, would you mind stepping into the salon for a moment. Charles, please join us."

He looked at William then at me with great uncertainty. He was sure to be feeling he was on shaky ground. No matter if Collin threw the first punch, it was an embarrassment to us all. In fact, the entire dynamics of the group changed. For a few brief moments, Sheldon was the belle of the ball, but now he was just an understudy who just beat up the boss's kid.

Though, after watching this crowd try to figure out how to react to the situation without stepping on my toes, I was relieved to step into the privacy of the salon. I shut the door behind us and closed the curtain. Turning I found William glaring at his understudy, who was literally quaking. I said nothing, just lit a cigar and waited for William.

"Explain!" was all he said.

Sheldon looked at me, his eyes wide and hair sticking out in all the wrong places. I could see just a trace of blood on one of his front teeth and was secretly pleased Collin had managed to land on good blow. I could also see he was on the verge of panic since he knew my reaction would determine his career, and hence, the rest of his life. I had to nip this in the bud.

"Mr. Frohman! Sir!" he blubbered, "You have to believe me. Once your son hit me …wel…I had to-"

"Defend yourself," I finished for him, "Of course you did! Look, Sheldon, I know my boy's a hot head and way to fast to use his fists. I'm just glad he didn't do anything to mess up that face of yours. I'll need you looking good when you get out on your own and I'm sure that won't be too long from now."

William was looking at me like I had three heads, but it was almost comical to see the relief on Sheldon's face change to a self-assured smugness at my comments.

William was about to pipe up when I said to Sheldon. "Now, I think it best that we put this behind us and carry on with the party. After all, we don't want to spoil your mentor's soiree, do we?"

"Oh, No sir!" He stammered, "We wouldn't want that. Thank you for your kind words and-"

"Not so fast!" William barked. "I want to know what the two of you said to each other that led to blows!"

"Now William," I cut in. The little fop looked ready to faint. "Whatever was said was between the two of them. Not really any of our business."

William just stared at me slack jawed, like I was the village idiot who just quoted Shakespeare. He shook his head in disbelief and turned back to his understudy, "It couldn't have been too personal. You had just met!"

"It wasn't, Sir, I swear! Honest Injun! I was just pouring myself a drink when he walked up to me. "I said 'Collin', right?

"He said, 'Frohman, Collin Frohman.' Then he just glared at me and said, 'You're an Evers, a Montauk Evers. Collin was so serious, I thought it was some kind of joke, so I just laughed and said, 'Well, my uncle is but I was born and raised in Baltimore.' I told him I just came up to Montauk for a visit in the summer. Collin just kept glaring at me, so I said, 'And you're from Amagansett way, right? Then I said, just trying to break the ice, mind you, 'There's a lot of pretty girls in old Amagansett'. That's when he sucker punched me!"

I pursed my lips and winced, "OOOHHH! That puts a cap on it!"

"What? What did I say?" Sheldon nearly wet himself thinking he had fallen from his new-found grace.

I showed him my full set of teeth and patted him on the shoulder, "Nothing wrong, son. You probably didn't know."

"Know what, Charlie? Why would that set Collin off?" Will demanded.

"I should have thought of this before, but, you see, the Evers and the Bennett's - Collin's mother's side - have never had what you would call cordial relations. Wherever there is old blood , there's an old Blood Feud.

Being away from all that so long, I've let it slip my mind but Collin, well, he listens to the old stories and he just enough romantic mixed with fighter to take it seriously. And then, when you mentioned Amagansett girls, well, it was like throwing down the gauntlet."

"I assure you Mr. Frohman that was not my intention! I was just making conversation, like I said, trying to break the ice."

"I know that, son," I assured him. "Best we just put it behind us. Hell, chances are you won't cross paths again for a long time -if ever. Go on back to the party now. We'll join you in a moment."

With that, he scooted out the doors and back onto the deck. I hung back because I could tell by the look on William's face, that he wasn't about to leave it alone. Smoothing his feathers would take more double talk.

"What in the name of Sam Hill was that all about, Charlie?" he demanded. "Why were you so patronizing to the kid who just thumped your son all over the deck?"

"Oh, I was not! Don't exaggerate, Will."

"Ha!" He snorted, "You practically offered him a lead role! Why are you taking his side in all this?"

"Because THAT boy will make me money, my friend, the OTHER just spends it."

"Don't give me that! You never put money before your family in all the time I've known you! And what has gotten into Collin, and don't give me that clannish testosterone theory please! I've known Collin since before he was born, and I know he's not the kind of kid to start trouble like that!"

I almost made a snide remark about how many kids he had raised, but I didn't want to hurt my friend, just turn his questions aside. Will's wife Helen had died before they had any children and he had never remarried. At that point, I think he had resigned himself to being without progeny, but he had instead adopted my children as a surrogate family. He was wonderful to my children - never missed a birthday or a milestone. In turn, my children adored their 'Uncle Will'.

I took the cigar from my mouth and stared at it somberly as I twirled it between my thumb and forefinger.

"Up until recently, I would have agreed with you William, but Collin is having, well, some trouble in transitioning from a boy to a man. Lately, he's been a little out of control. At first it was just little things. Sassing his mother or defying me in little ways. You know, just the usual testing the boundaries of a young man. Then he got, for lack of a better term, belligerent. He openly disobeyed his Mother and fought with his teachers, had a few dust-ups with his brothers, and practically everyone who irritated him. I cracked him a few times and tried to put the fear of God into him, but I couldn't get through to him. Then he got suspended and I knew he had to go to Pops."

I raised my eyes to him, with a doleful expression, "I feel awful William. I failed him as a father. I shouldn't need Pop to take care of my own son! I don't know what got into me, tossing him off the boat like that!"

William, seeing the hung dog look I gave him, did what any true friend would and consoled me.

"Ha! In retrospect," He giggled some more, "It was rather funny. And you knew he was in no danger. That boy can swim like a dolphin and you knew Ozaki and I were watching closely."

I grinned at him sheepishly, "I was counting on it."

We both laughed at that.

"Well," William said, "I didn't realize Collin was going through such a rough patch. It's hard to grow up and I'm sure Pop will have him walking a path to glory in no time." He clapped me on the shoulder, "And I know you love him very much to take such extreme measures. Now, perhaps we'd best get back to our guests."

"Gees Louise," I shook my head as I reached for the door, "This is not going to hurt my reputation as an Ogre -- not after our guest tell this story all over the business!"

"Don't be so hard on yourself, Charlie! Most people just think you're a slave driver. Legend has it that you only turn into an Ogre on Opening day!" William laughed, "On the upside, I doubt they would voice any objections to your assignments after seeing you throw your son over board!

PART FIVE

When we emerged from the saloon, we were just off Mashomack Point, on the far side of the Island. We had a ways to go on our little cruise as we still had to swing out past Montauk and into Gardner's bay before we could head back to Greenport.

Judging by the crew seated around the deck, it was going to be a painful afternoon. They all were studiously making awkward small talk while trying not to directly interact with Sheldon or me. All except for Ethel, that is. That woman had a brass set.

"Well Charles," she purred as she lit a cigarette and leaned back in her chair. "Are you through chumming for the afternoon, or should we change into our swim suits?"

There was a collective gasp, but I just smiled at her and sallied back. "One is enough for the harbor sharks. I'm saving you for the open waters. Maybe we will land a great white."

Now that the subject was broached, E.H. said what was on all their minds, "I can't believe you just tossed him overboard like that!"

I gave him a dramatic pause and, placing my left hand on my hip and pointing at him with my cigar and replied,

"One late fall day, when I was a young man, I was seine fishing with my uncle. We had just closed the end off and were heading to shore. I was cold, wet, and bored. Thinking how much I hated that work, I didn't pay attention and I let the end of the net slip off the dory. A lot of fish swam out over the top before we could snag the net and wrestle it back into the boat.

Next thing I know there is a hand on my collar and one on the seat of my britches and before I could take a deep breath, I hit that frigid water. In full winter dress and wearing big rubber boots, it was no easy task to claw my way to the surface. When I finally did, I saw my Uncle rowing towards the beach.

Furious, I screamed, "Are you trying to drown me?"

Never breaking rhythm with the oars, my uncle shouted back. "No, just drowning your stupidity. Now swim for shore and I'll pray your stupidity can't keep up."

There was polite titter from the crowd, less than I would have expected. It was one of my favorite stories. But I was in no mood to be petty and everyone seemed to relax some. With the exception of Sheldon, who parked his carcass next to the beverage cart and sullenly kept his glass filled. I'm sure he could feel the others apprehension at cozying up to him in my presence. I suppose I could have helped him out by showing the others there was no hard feelings, but at that moment, I had no desire to deal with another young man's attitude.

"Ah," Southern said suddenly, "We've sailed into Gardner's bay. Am I right Charles?"

"Right you are, E.H.. We're just a tad above the Village of Sag harbor."

"Then is this part of Amagansett? Where you grew up, Charles?" Mary asked.

"No, No. That's on the south shore, still a few miles across the island, on the Atlantic side. I suppose this is a part of the East Hampton Township, though I doubt if many care."

"Why's that? I thought everyone cares about land." E.H. put in.

I shrugged, "Because no one is paying or collecting any taxes from it."

"Ha!" Gilmore piped up, the first I'd heard from him all day, "I'm surprised the government isn't making the deer pay!"

There was polite laughter, but it was forced. I began to worry the day was really spoiled. Collin's behavior had cast a pall on the dinner cruise. Thankfully, Ozaki came to the rescue by pushing the saloon doors open wide with an enormous rolling table, sagging under the weight of desserts!

I knew William must have had them made, because I have had Ozaki's desserts before and though fine on taste, were like eating air.

There were cakes, puddings, tarts, and éclairs like you would only hope to find in France.

We all dug in with a vengeance and switched to aperitifs, whose sweet flavors complimented the pastries. Even Sheldon moved his chair into the circle to partake, but William and I noticed that his understudy was drinking more for his dessert.

The conversation began to flow a little better and even an occasional sally was tossed about. It was a relief to see everyone relax and interact again, giving me the chance to do what I came to do this weekend. We were so focused on gorging ourselves that we didn't notice the fog coming in until Ozaki blew a horn.

William, who had stood and went to the railing a few minutes before, turned to announce, "Excuse me, it looks like we may have some weather. Nothing serious, but I think I'll have Ozaki head for home. We won't beat the rain, though. We're still almost two hours from Greenport. We'll have to take it slow on account of this cursed fog. I'm afraid it's going to get damp out here on deck. If you'd like to stay dry, I suggest you retreat to the saloon and I shall join you there."

"Oh My, William," Ethel gasped theatrically, "Adrift upon the high seas, blinded by the fog. What shall we do?"

Paul gave her a squinty eyed look and suggested, "Why don't we tie a rope around your feet and use you for soundings. We wouldn't want to go aground now, would we?"

"Wouldn't work, old boy," she retorted with a toss of her head. "Everyone knows- cream rises."

We laughed and William said as he parted, "I'm sure Ozaki will keep us off the rocks."

Maude Adams looked a little less confidant as she stood and walked to the railing. She peered out into the haze for a moment then turned back to us, "Are you sure we won't get lost in this? I can't see anything around us."

"Maybe you should have brought some of that magic dust, Peter!" Drew joked.

She actually stamped her little foot and snapped, "I'm serious John!"

I shook my head and stood to join her. I spoke for the benefit of everyone, "We're not that far out, Maude. If you could see just a quarter of a mile or more in that direction, you'd be looking at the southeast tip of Shelter Island." Then I pointed to about 2 o'clock to my right, "And Montauk is just up the coast that way. We're not even in the Atlantic now."

Then I jested, "As long as we don't go that way", and I pointed to 11 o'clock?"

"What's that way?" Evelyn asked.

"England."

Ethel dropped her plate on the table and stood up abruptly, "Oh, Hell no! I just escaped from there!" She could be such a clown.

"Don't you fret that, Young Lady," I said, "I assure you that you'll do a season in New York before you go anywhere else."

"I shall hold you to that, Charles. In the meantime, I suggest we take our good host's advice and retire to the saloon. I can just feel that damp cool air leeching the curls from my hair. If I stay out here much longer, I'll look like a drowned cat!"

No one wanted to see that, so we made our way into the Saloon, glasses and plates in hand. Everyone settled into a spot in the spacious room except E.H. and yours truly.

"Charles," E.H. said, over the babble. "Could you tell me where the facilities are?"

"Oh sure," I said back loud enough to catch everyone's attention, "Just go out those double doors and take a right. At the end of the hall, go through to door on the left that leads down. At the bottom, go left and it's the third door on the right. Got that?"

"Got it," he said a little embarrassed by the attention.

As soon as he went through the doors, I whistled, and everyone looked at me.

"Let's have some fun!" I put my fingers to my lips then held it up to indicate they should watch and wait.

I bolted through a door behind me that led down to the engine room. I dashed between the engines and machinery, almost snagging my pants in my haste. I reached a door on the far end that was to a stairwell that led to one of the corridors. I quickly pulled my flask from my jacket and stashed it above a fire extinguisher. Back in my youth an old barfly told me that you knew you were hopeless when you took your hooch into the bathroom with you.

I popped out into the corridor and leapt over to the bathroom door, located next to the master suite -- Will's bedroom -- and just got inside before E.H. opened the door at the bottom of the landing.

I waited until he tried to open the door before I ran the faucet. I chortled to myself, knowing he must have been wondering who could be in the bathroom, because everyone but William and Ozaki were in the saloon and those two were on the Bridge.

He knocked, and I called out, "Just a moment." I could almost see the look on his face, wondering if he was crazy or drunker that he thought.

I opened the door and stepped past him briskly, "All yours!" I said cheerily and headed for the door he just came out of. I could hear sputtering noises coming from outside the head and I was nearly racking with laughter as I came back into the saloon.

Everyone looked up expectantly, but I just shushed them and sat down in an empty chair. I quickly lit my cigar, grabbed a drink off the table, and crossed my legs like I had been planted in that spot when E.H. made his way back. He walked directly over to me, a queer look on his face, but I just looked up, as if I was surprised he was back, "Find it alright?" I was the face of innocence.

He was babbling still as the room erupted in laughter as William came in. He knew right away what was up.

"Oh Charlie. The old beat them to the bathroom trick? Haven't you tired of that yet?"

I laughed, "If it ain't broke, Willie...."

"Well, this time it will cost you the dry cleaners bill, if that grease even comes out."

I looked down and sure enough, there were grease marks on the cuff and calf of my left pant leg. I shook my head, "That's what I get for acting like an adolescent!

E.H. was still standing there still looking like someone hit him between the eyes with a dumb stick. William, in a joking manner, took him by the arm as if he was an invalid and sat him in a chair. Patting him on the shoulder, he said, "There, there, Lad. Don't over think it. He's been pulling that stunt since I've had the Aunt Polly."

"And it never gets old," I quipped, "It always works."

"Well," William countered, "Perhaps to various degrees. I remember the time one of your children had an accident while they were waiting for you to come out."

We all laughed. I scrunched up my face, "Oh yes. The wife was quite annoyed."

"You're lucky she didn't toss you overboard!" Evelynn said.

"I would have happily helped, "E.H. joked, as he took a toothpick from his pocket and stuck it in his mouth. He went on, "But I have to say, you're pretty spry for an older guy."

I smiled and gave Ethel a long slow wink. She snorted.

"Yeah, you big talker," she teased. "But enough of your antics, Charles." She turned her attention to

William, who had taken the chair at the head of the table and lit a cigarette. "I want to hear what our gracious host has been up to. We've all been chatting all afternoon William, but we've yet to hear from you. I take it you're still floating about in this leaky old tub?"

"Madame, Please. My *Aunt Polly* may take on a little less water than she keeps out, but she's hardly a tub."

Maude's eyes widened at that and William laughed, "I'm joking, Maude. I promise we won't sink."

"I'll hold you to that, William. I just bought these shoes for this weekend and I'll be very put out if there ruined by the salt water."

"Heaven forbid! Women and shoes first to the life boats!"

"Seriously, old boy," Gilmore said, when the laughter died down. "Most of us did last season in London. How are things here in the states? I hear you've had a great year."

"Fairly well," William responded modestly. "I've been fortunate the public has responded so well to Sherlock Holmes. They can't seem to get enough."

"I know," Evelyn said. "It's all I ever hear about. You know, I just read the stories this past year and I can't believe Sir Conan Doyle just killed Sherlock off like that!"

"Oh, he's not dead," I shook my head and pointed at William with my cigar, "He's sitting right there. On stage -- or off -- he is the sleuth personified."

"Do tell," Ethel said, "Have a lock on that character, do we?"

William just shrugged in humility. He was never one to brag. "People seem to enjoy him."

"Don't be so damn humble," I chided him, "You ARE Sherlock Holmes. In fact, why don't you show them? Are you up for a little demonstration? Show them your shtick, William."

PART SIX

"Oh, no, no. I'm sure nobody wants to see my act. We're off work today."

No matter what he said, I knew he loved to show off his skills, so I pushed him a little, "No, really William. Give us a short Sherlock improv." I turned to the rest, "Would you like to see the great detective at work, folks?"

They all enthusiastically responded, calling out encouragement for my suggestion until William threw his hands up in mock surrender. "Very well then. Just give me a moment."

He got up and went behind a screen that cut off a corner of the room. After a few moments of rustling, a completely different person stepped out into view. It was William of course, but he now wore a cape and deer stalker cap and had a briar pipe stuck between his teeth. But that was just the obvious changes. Somehow, he seemed taller and a bit gaunter in the face. His eyebrows were arched and lips thinner. Even his ears seemed to stick out more and I could swear his chin had a new cleft.

He glided across the room and pulled his chair back a few feet, so he could see everyone unobstructed. He sat slowly and crossed his legs. Eyelids drooping slightly, looking almost meditative as he steepled his long fingers on his lap. He cast a speculative eye about the room and was about to speak, when I cut in.

"I'll pick the victim, Holmes. We wouldn't want anyone to think you were cheating."

"As you wish, Doctor Watson," he replied in a bored patrician tone.

"Cheat? How's he going to cheat? Cheat who? What is he going to do?" Miss Adams demanded.

"Perfect Maude. You can be first. Please stand up and turn in a slow circle."

She made a face and all eyes were glued to her as she obeyed. When she finished, I bade her to sit and nodded to William.

William's head never came off the back of the chair and his fingers remained locked in a steeple. He merely raised his half-lidded eyes and announced, "You have recently visited your Mother while she was on sabbatical from her missionary work with the Latter-Day Saints."

"You're a Mormon?" Gilmore blurted out.

"I did not say that," William answered for her in a bored tone, "In fact, I believe Miss Adams is leaning towards Catholicism."

Maude jumped up in a snit. I knew her to be an extremely private person and these revelations put her nose out of joint. "How could you know that? And who

111

the hell told you I went to Utah? I never even told my agent!"

William just met her ferocity with a blank stare. "Calm yourself, Madame. Put out your left hand."

Maude just glared at him and tucked the hand away, clearly puzzled by the request and possibly weary about what he might reveal next. She just stared at him for almost a minute as we gaped on in wonder.

Finally, William said, "Very well Madame. It doesn't matter. You have not denied my claims." He looked about the room, "Are there any other comers?"

"Oh, all right," Maude nearly snarled as she thrust her hand out over the table for all to see.

It was a dainty hand wearing three rings, one on each finger, middle, ring, and pinky. The one on the middle finger was a rather ostentatious ruby, surrounded by little diamonds that went from fingernail to knuckle. The pinky sported a simple fish design made of gold. The one on her ring finger, however, was a bit unusual. It appeared to be a silver frog with an oblong piece of blue stone set into its back. I had a feeling it was key to William's observations.

Maude, having seemed to calm herself a bit, either that or her curiosity won over, gestured with her hand on display, "So what do you see, oh mystical detective?"

"The ring in the middle, with the frog motif set with a large turquoise stone is a design used by the Ute tribe of Indians that inhabit the area around Salt Lake City."

Maude still looked weary, "So? That doesn't tell you I got it from my mother. How do you know I didn't just buy it in some shop?"

"Because that particular ring is old as you can see by the wear, not made for trade, and it is a design of the Mountain Ute people. Their lands are not near any settlements and they have little contact with white people.

Except for the missionaries of Joseph Smith. I believe the father of the Mormons has adopted a policy of feeding rather that fighting the natives. I think it is safe to say that the ring was given to your mother for some act of kindness on her part to the tribe's women and passed onto you personally by her."

"So how do you know she gave it to me and not someone else to pass it on to me? Or she could have sent it to me by post!" She countered.

A small smirk creeped onto William's face, "Because, dear lady, it is a fertility ring. Ute tradition calls for it to be passed on from mother to daughter. I dare say she wouldn't entrust such a powerful totem to the Pony Express!"

We all smirked a bit at that and I could see Ethel was biting her tongue with a herculean effort.

It was well known, among the performing community, that Maude was a girl who liked other girls. I'm sure you get my meaning. Maude noticed the stifled mirth among the rest of us and she flushed a bit, but she was too amazed to stay peeved.

"That is incredible, William. You are categorically right. I went to see her last month and she's still bringing 'vittles and the truth of Jehovah' to the Indians." She fell silent for a moment, and then asked, almost sheepishly, in a quiet tone, "And how did you know of my interest in the Catholic faith?"

"As to that, Madame, I must confess to a slight jaunt into conjecture. It was the fish ring on your pinky. Quite plain by the standards of the rest of your ensemble, yet it is the ancient symbol of Christianity. Since it is such a modest piece and not a crucifix or a rosary, I surmised that you may just be trying to get used to the idea before embracing their beliefs."

Maude just looked at him a moment longer, then she curtsied and bowed deeply from the waist. "Bravo, Mr. Holmes, Bravo!"

The dam broke and we all started to clap spontaneously.

"Oh, do me next, William," Evelyn squealed as she leapt up. She held out her arms and twirled in a most graceful manner. Her dress rustled and the pendant she wore bounced off her bosom to open up and expose a small clock. The room went silent as William cast an appraising eye on her.

"This is a bit daunting," he confessed. Evelyn's eyebrows shot up and a big grin crossed her face.

"So, I am an enigma to the great Sherlock, am I?" she asked coyly.

William shrugged. "There is very little data to work with. As you recently bought your entire ensemble and have worn it for the first time today, there has been little time to accrue any clues. Other than the fact that you haven't worn that pendant since you were last in London, and you have a new kitten, and you are not counting the hours today."

Her mouth dropped open. She just stared at William, slack jawed, until Ethel said, "Close your mouth dear, before a seagull poops in it."

Even William chuckled at that, if in a refined manner. He spread his hands and looked at Evelyn as if to say, 'Well, how'd I do?'

She closed her mouth and shook her head. "Right on all counts William," then she added, "but it doesn't count if you don't explain your reasoning. How on earth did you know I've never worn these clothes? Or that I have a new kitten? I named him Bootsie. Now that I really think about it, you are right about the necklace. It's been packed away since I left England until this morning. I put it on because it went well with the dress. I'm not too concerned with the time because I am having a pleasant visit with my friends and peers. I hope it lasts forever."

William nodded his head in recognition of her sentiments. Then he got to business.

"I noticed when we greeted, that your clothes smelled like the tissue paper new dresses are wrapped in and you can see where every crease, fold, and line are crisp and clean. Even a single washing or a day's wear would take much of that away. As for your pendant and your lack of concern over the time ,look at the clock below the center stone."

Evelyn lifted the bauble and turned it to see it clearly." Oh! But it's the wrong time."

"Precisely," William replied. "It is exactly six hours too fast. England's time. I state you were unconcerned about the time, because you didn't bother to set it."

She was awed, "I never even thought about it."

"As for Bootsie, I have been the proud parent of dozens of kittens and know their tiny scratches and gnaw marks on your right hand."

She held her hand out for all of us to see the tiny marks and then bowed to William as Maude had. "Bravo, Mr. Holmes. Bravo"

"Two for Two, old boy," I said. "Now let's see what you can do with Mr. John Drew Jr."

John put his drink down and jumped to his feet. Flinging his arms out wide, he did a slow pirouette on one leg and came to a rest with a regal pose, looking off into the distance. He was quite spry and always confident.

"Careful, Uncle," Ethel teased, "You may sprain something at your age."

"Ha!" John scoffed, "I'm as fit as a fiddle." He looked directly at William, "I'm not prone to give away my secrets." He looked himself once over and proclaimed, "I dare say you won't glean much from this rig."

I had to agree with him. Fit and trim for a man in his late fifties, he wore a simple brown country suit with black patent leather half boots. Besides the wedding ring and a small plain band on his pinky, the only other thing distinguishable was the great hairy patch under his nose that covered his upper lip. William as Sherlock was going to have to dig deep for this one. That thought had barely passed from one side of my head to the other when William spoke,

"You have come from Kyalami, where you have set up residence and intend to spend the better part of this year when you're not working. Your daughter has been for a visit and sent you off this morning. Furthermore, you own a new dog. A rather large one. The third in your family."

Everyone shifted their gaze to John and was not disappointed. He looked at William like he grew a second head. "Well, I'll be damned! It's all true! Do tell!"

Though you thoughtfully wiped your boots before boarding the Aunt Polly, the reddish hued sand caught in the crease between the sole and boot could only have come from the sands of East Hampton- where you keep your summer home. Thus, we have a starting point."

"But I thought you said John came from some place called 'Kyalmi', or something?" Maude put in. Just like her to play the devil's advocate.

"Kyalami," I explained. "It's the name of John's summer home. Zulu for 'my home', I believe."

"Kudos, Charles," Drew said. "I'm flattered you remembered." He turned to William with a slight smirk, "The sand was a good thought, Will, and yes, I did come from Kyalami this morning. When you live amongst the dunes, that damn sand gets into everything. But how on earth did you know I was planning on staying, or about my daughter seeing me off?"

"Let's not forget the dog either," Ethel put in.

William waved his hand dismissively, "The daughter and the hound are one and the same."

Everyone's head snapped back at that and John swelled with indignation, "Excuse me? What kind of observation is that?"

I began to worry that William had taken to his role too deeply. He could be brutally honest and has no compunction to control speaking his mind when he was deep in character.

William seemed to snap out of his trance. He sat up straight, waving his hands about. "That sounded completely different than it was meant." He sputtered.

"As for your residence, you came with no change of clothes, so it is easy to deduce you plan on returning home this evening and East Hampton is a far shorter trip than to the city. The South Fork polo club cuff links you sport tells me that you have joined fully, and you must stay near to fulfill your obligations to your polo team."

John plucked at his sleeves and nodded, but Ethel had the bit between her teeth. "So, he joined a club? That doesn't mean he plans on living out here. Perhaps he'll just play there from time to time. You're just making wild speculations."

William gave her a flat level stare. "Hardly woman."

"No, he's right, Ethel. Only the actual team members get these cufflinks. I'll be playing a lot, so I'll be living out here for a while. It was quite an honor to be chosen."

"No more than you deserve," I added. "I've seen you play, and you are quite the forward."

He nodded to me, pleased with the compliment then went back to William. "O.K., I'll grant you that. So, tell me why my dog and my daughter are the same thing."

"I merely meant that I based my deductions on the same type of observation. Hairs. The long golden strand that is caught between your neck and collar could only have come from your daughter. She must have had it loose to get it caught at that angle when she hugged you good bye and that tells us it was early morning, before she had put it up for the day."

"Ergo, Ethel," I said, "She saw him off." Miss Barrymore just stuck her tongue out at me.

"The addition of the third dog," William went on, "is explained by the coarse, black hair that is stuck under your left armpit. That hair certainly doesn't match the pelts of your pug or terrier and that it can reach as high as your armpit tells me it is big. Most likely an African ridgeback or a breed of that type."

John shook his head and smiled with admiration. "You make it seem like child's play, William, when you explain your reasoning."

119

"Simple observation and deduction, my friend. Anyone could do it."

"Ha! I think I could argue that point, but I won't." He stood slowly until he had every inch of his height then bowed deeply from the waste. "Bravo, Mr. Holmes. Bravo!"

As he sat back down, I noticed that the three-remaining guest, besides myself, were all eye balling each other.

I was about to choose the next subject, but E.H. jumped to his feet and proclaimed, "No need to cast your evil eye, Charlie!" He stepped back to give William a clear view and spun in a circle, arms outstretched. He left his arms out after he came to a rest and threw out his challenge. "Come Sherlock Holmes, I'm an open book! Read the pages back to me!"

"I'm not sure your 'book' should be read anywhere but behind closed doors, yet I think I can give you a fair assessment of your itinerary today. You woke and had breakfast at your hotel- The plaza, then you took the 10:40 out of the city to East Hampton. You hitched a ride out to Kyalami with the ice wagon to ride over with John and Paul, but they had already left so you had to walk back to town where you called for a taxi to take you to the trolley. You must have just made the 2:15 to Riverhead and transferred to the Orient line. Another Taxi brought you to the docks and we can only hope it was worth all that effort. OH! And your marriage has collapsed."

Now, I nearly broke out in laughter at the look on old E.H.'s face. His mouth formed a perfect circle, I swear his eyes glazed over and he looked very much like a man who had been pole axed between the eyes. I didn't need to hear any explanations from Will to know he was dead on the mark again. William followed through anyways.

"The toothpick you took from your pocket was emblazoned with a cartouche that is exclusive to the Plaza Hotel in New York. The small blue stain on your lapel is from some type of jelly or jam and wasn't served on this ship. We all know your fastidious habits, so I'm sure you woke and dressed there before you ate. The 10:40, well, I suppose you could put that off as conjecture, but I know that the only train leaving the city for the Hamptons today, with first class accommodations, was the 10:40 from Penn Station.

"Alright!" E.H. said, with his hands thrown up in mock surrender. I think the bafflement was making him drunker. "I'll give you all that! But the ride out to Paul's? The fact that I was at Paul's? Oh no, my friend, you have a little birdie singing in your ear hidden about somewhere. Or! You're a witch!" and he made a cross with his two forefingers and thrust it in William's direction.

"Nonsense, old Boy," I cut in before William got his Irish up. He was never tolerant of religious humor. "It's all elementary. Isn't that so, Will?"

"Rudimentary would be a better word, I think. The same sand fills your boot soles as Johns and Paul's. Thus, you were there. I recognized the small burn on the back of your jacket hem-"

With great flourish, E.H. twirled out of his jacket and found the mark Will was referring to. "Son of a Bitch! I just bought this suit yesterday. How the hell did that happen?"

"It is the result of prolonged contact with Halite, better known to the public as Rock salt. Commonly used by the Ice men to keep their product stable while delivering and most likely the only conveyance headed out to such a remote local. The rest of my deductions are common sense. You must have made the 2:15 trolley to from Riverhead to Greenport because of the particular scent of seat cleaner that line uses and, of course, it's the only one today. To make that, you would have had to call for a cabbie from Paul's house and went directly."

E.H. slowly sank back into his chair. With a lopsided grin, he asked, "And my marriage?"

William pulled the deerstalker off his head and had the grace to look abashed. "Please, E.H., forget I said anything. I was in character and out of line."

E.H. just stared at him for a moment and laughed. "Don't apologize. I asked for it. I was divorced as of last Monday."

Half of us gave our condolences and the other half congratulated him, giving us all a laugh and breaking the tension.

"But don't tell me you didn't hear that somewhere!" E.H. went on.

William grinned and put his hat back on. "You believe I was told this, yet it happened in Virginia just four days ago? My Baker street boys don't cover that much area!

He took a few puffs off his pipe and shook his head. "Perhaps we should just leave it lay."

E.H. would have none of it. "Actually, I'll eat my words. I left Virginia and came north within an hour of signing the papers. So how did you know?"

William looked at him for a moment then sat back and pulled the pipe from his mouth and we all went to the edges of our seats. "First, you will note that I never specified divorce. Only that your marriage had reached a breaking point." He pointed in E.H.s direction with the pipe stem. "Your ring finger told me that much."

E.H. held his left hand up. "Ah! The missing wedding ring!" He laughed, "You know, I may have had an ulterior motive for leaving my ring off!" He wagged his eyebrows at Maude.

"That would not explain the scrapes on your knuckle and the bruising on the knuckle of your ring finger. These obviously show that the ring was pulled off with quite some force. Either Anger or Despair."

E. H. rose, stepped off to the side of his seat and with right leg back, left leg bent chest against the knee, arms outstretched on his sides, and eyes to the floor. He intoned, "Bravo, Mr. Holmes, Bravo!"

There was no need to introduce the next victim. Only Ethel was left, and everyone's eyes went to her. She did not seem too pleased with the prospect.

Looking directly at our host, who was no more than two feet from her, she said, "I don't wish to be a stick in the mud, but I would hate for such a pleasant evening to be ruined by an insensitive observation. I'm feeling a bit

123

delicate. Perhaps it's this excellent wine you've been serving tonight."

William gazed back at her for a moment and then put his pipe down on the table, reached up and pulled off his deerstalker hat and laid it next to the pipe. He reached over and took one of Ethel's hands.

"I think a woman who had turned down the hand in marriage of a man who will most likely be the most powerful man in his country someday, has more steel in her than ceramic. She would be as strong as she was beautiful and talented."

Ethel's eyes widened like saucers then became slits of radiating anger. I was certain my friend had crossed a line he would never see in front of him again. But Ethel's eyes slowly resumed their natural state and she covered Will's hand with her other and sighed, "Yes, Winnie did ask me to marry him, and yes, I said no. Let's leave it at that please."

The surprise rippled around our circle. Winston Churchill was and up and comer in British politics. He came from an old family. Peerage from antiquity. Problem is - Ethel is not. American women are a bit too real for those English stuffed shirts. Yet, the word that spread from both continents told of a great love affair between the two. The lad was willing to give up quite a lot if he wished to marry Ethel.

She patted William's hand, "And a woman doesn't have to be strong. She just has to be smart enough to see where things don't fit." It was a solemn and touching moment and she added, "Besides, I hate God damn tea!"

Thankfully, William didn't call her on taking the Lord's name in vain. William was death on blasphemy, and his apprentice spared us all from another embarrassing silence.

Sheldon lurched to his feet, knocking the chair he was on over and staggered a few steps in our direction.

Flinging his arms out wide, Sheldon gave William a look of rigorous contempt that only a drunk can achieve and slurred out. "And what of me, my master? What clues are roosting on me?" Sheldon nearly fell over when he dropped his arms.

Like magic, as always, Ozaki appeared next to the drunken boy. William sighed. Laying his pipe in the ashtray between us, he rose and said softly, "Mr. Holmes is retiring for the evening and so shall you, Sheldon."

"What?" He protested, "I want to hear some more of your lodical deduckuns."

William glanced over at us and smiled, "Unfortunately, logic only works on the sensible." He turned back to his protégé, "You're drunk Sheldon and it's time to say good night."

He started up with the usual objections one makes in drink, but I caught his eye and when he focused, I barked,

"Say Good Night, Sheldon!" in my best authoritarian voice. I've found through the years that a sharp command, issued in just the right tone will usually set people hopping before they have a chance to consider.

The boy's eyes flew open and he shut his mouth, gave me an exaggerated salute before lurching towards the back door. He only made three steps before he stumbled and if Ozaki hadn't still had a grip on his arm, he would have kissed the carpet. William leapt forward and caught his other arm and between the two of them, Sheldon remained vertical for the moment. William smoothly switched hands on the bicep he grasped, to address his guests.

"If you'll excuse me a moment, I must make a deposit with the Sandman. I'll be right back." Then, as if by an afterthought, he added, with a twinkle in his eye, "Why don't you tell them their selections, Charlie, while I'm away?"

Everyone's eyes bore into me at once. William had really put me on the spot, and he knew it. It's true we had a running gag of tweaking each other, but this was a bit much. It wasn't exactly malicious, but it was definitely some type of payback. I thought it had to have something to do with the way I treated Collin. I've always suspected that Collin was Will's secret favorite.

Of course, I had already decided who was going to what production, but I still tried to stall and hope the joke fizzled on William,

"What makes you think I could?" I argued weakly.

William laughed, "Because I could!"

Before I could retort, he turned back and said to Ozaki over Sheldon's drooping head, "He can sleep it off in my room. I'll stay at the house tonight."

126

PART SEVEN

When I turned back to the room, all six of them were perched on the edge of their seats, staring at me, waiting for me to utter a sound. There was no way I could bluff my way out of this one. Usually, I would summon them all to my office in another month or so. I always made announcements of the season's assignments that way. I learned early on, that if you told them one by one, then you had to listen to a boatload of petulant whining, back stabbing, or their opinions of my decisions that I neither needed nor wanted.

In a group, their collective egos wouldn't let themselves look like they didn't get exactly what they wanted. They be busy trying to out smug each other and I end up looking like the redeemer! But tonight, I wasn't prepared. We spent the day as equals and now I had to be the boss. I would have to think of some special way to repay William for this one.

"Yes, I've made my choices, but-" I was cut off by the colophony of a half dozen voices speaking to me at once. "BUT!", I roared over the din, "I can't do this right now!"

That shut them up and as soon as their jaws snapped shut, I continued, "Right now, I need to pick up that mess out there" I pointed to the back deck where we ate. We're only about a mile out from the dock and Ozaki and William need to run the boat. I won't leave him to clean up- not after such a great - if eventful- day."

"Ethel, of course, was the first to speak, "Oh Charlie! Don't be such a coot! I'll help you and we'll have it ship shape in no time! But, first, the cat comes out of the bag."

"Christ, Charles!" Paul cut in, "We'll all give you a hand. We're not that spoiled!"

"Not on what you pay us!" E. H. added to laughter.

"Alright! Alright!" I growled in a light tone. "If you really want to know..." That brought on another round of applause and cat calls.

"Then here it is, but you'll have to wait on any further discussions." I knew there would be many with this crowd. "Tonight, you just say thank you. E. H -You're Romeo."

He gave me an exaggerated nod, "Perfect, but only if Julia Marlowe is Juliet. I-"

"You'll sing when I tell you to speak and dance where I tell you dance."

Everyone's eyes flew open wide and they looked to E. H. for his reaction. But in reality, E. H. had drunk enough that my words went right over his head. "What the hell does that mean?" he asked.

I shrugged. "Haven't the foggiest. But any further discussion would be pointless because Julia is playing Juliet. And you're drunk!"

"Then I would like to say that-"

"Thank you. Just say thank you, E H." I rode over him.

He raised his glass in toast and said, "I do thank you. Sir. I am very pleased." He tossed the drink back and grinned from ear to ear.

The dock was getting closer, so I tossed aside any pomp and ceremony and moved on.

"Evelyn, You'll be doing 'The Adventure of Lady Ursula'."

"Oh," she clapped her hands together. Is that a new Sherlock? Will I be working with William?"

"No, something completely different. It's your show. You're the lead." That was all she needed to hear. Even going in blind, she was delighted.

"Oh, Thank You, Charles!"

"Ethel, You're going to try something new on your return to the Colonies. 'Captain Jinks and the Horse Marines'. Lead of course."

Ethel's lips graciously said, 'Thank You', but her eyes told me we weren't through talking about this by a long shot. I was confident she'd be happy with the choice in the end. It's a part I know she could own.

Keeping my rhythm, I pointed at Maude and John, "You two are playing in 'The Masked Ball'."

John beamed with pleasure, but Maude was skeptical at best. We had discussed her sliding away from 'Pan' before she was trapped in it, but she didn't know squat about the play or who was directing. I really thought she was going to buck me, but John came to the rescue.

"Thank you, Charles. I think we'll do well with that." He nudged Maude on the shoulder and when she turned and looked up at him, he urged. "Say 'Thank You', Maude. I read a first draft of the script. It's good and I hear Thompson is going to be the S.M. Trust me, you'll be happy."

"And so will your wife, Johnny!' E. H. sniggled. Some of our faces turned red but we managed not to laugh.

Maude threw him a withering look and then turned to me with a stage smile. "Thank you, Charles."

Happy to get past that obstacle, I was pleased to give my final pronouncement, which I also thought would be the easiest acceptance.

"Paul, 'The King's Musketeers'." Paul loved his swashbuckling roles.

He grinned, then, quick as a flash, he squinted at me in suspicion. "D'Artagnan?"

"Of course. It opens in Phoenix in six months."

"Whoa! Even closer to home! You're a prince, Charlie! Thank you!"

Yeah, Right! I thought to myself. I may be a prince tonight, but I was a 'Greedy skinflint who didn't know the first thing about the theatre' last year when I assigned him a role he didn't want.

Actors Done! I thought to myself.

The cleanup went quickly and efficiently. All the shells and garbage went over the side and the girls took all the glassware and silverware to the galley to wash. They even managed to rope John into drying. The rest of us gathered up the linen and folded the tables and chairs to store them. We gave the deck a sweep then rolled the beverage cart back to the galley to check up on the kitchen crew.

They were just finishing up when we arrived, so I poured us all fresh drinks and we sat at the galley table to toast each other. That's where William found us.

"Good Grief!" he cried out, "Did Charlie domesticate you all with his assignments?"

"And how do you know he gave them? Is Mr. Holmes back?" Evelyn piped up.

William just grinned at her, "You don't have to be a detective to see six pleased and relaxed people at my table, my dear. As my Aunt Polly would say, 'you look as happy as a pig in a walla!"

"Isn't this yacht called the *Aunt Polly*? Did you name it after her?"

"Indeed, I did."

"Was it your Mother's side or your father's?" Paul asked, of all things.

If the odd question startled him, he didn't show it. "A little further from the family tree than that," he replied.

I had to clamp a hand over my mouth to keep from laughing. Further from indeed! Polly was an elderly negro woman who cared for William for almost a year when he had some serious ailment as a young man. When the doctor's and his family had given up hope, Polly nursed William back to health, and he loved her like family until she passed away a few years back. But that was his story to tell.

He saw the mirth in my eyes and turned his attention to me and poked me in the shoulder. "And you didn't need to press my guests into a cleaning crew! Ozaki and I would have gotten it in the morning."

"It's done!" I pointed out, "Just-" I didn't finish but cued the others and, God bless 'em, they were in perfect harmony,

"Say Thank You!"

William looked like he didn't know whether to break a bill or look for spare change while we roared with laughter, but he took it all in stride and good grace.

"All right then, Thank You! I also wanted to announce that we have docked". As if on cue, the engines shut down and the still of the night settled over the ship.

PART EIGHT

As our drinking champion snored the night away in William's Cabin, Paul and E.H. bunked in the second and Maude and Evelyn settled into the third, John was given Osaki's cabin, leaving the Ozaki to sleep as best he could in the wheelhouse. That left William, Ethel and I standing on the dock pulling our coats tighter against the dark chill of the bay as we began heading for William's house.

"I don't suppose you have an automobile nearby, do you William?" Ethel asked, "I don't wish to sound weak, but it's late and I have eaten and drank enough for two!"

"I'm sorry, Ethel, but I doubt if we'll find a cab at this time of night."

"Should we walk into town? There has to be some hacks taking the drunks home." I suggested.

William looked dubious. "Downtown can be a bit rowdy on the weekends. I think taking Ethel there might just be tempting fates."

I could see his point. If two of the most well-known stars of the stage were to show up at this time of night, with a mob of drunken sailors staggering about, Lord knows what might come out of the woodwork!

"How far is your home, William?" Ethel asked.

"Just a few streets that way," William answered as he pointed away from the downtown area. "Perhaps a twenty-minute walk. Yet I hesitate to suggest we walk with a woman of such beauty and two elderly Gentleman!"

Ethel rolled her eyes. "I doubt a little fresh air and exercise will do me any harm." She laughed, "And Charlie here has had enough oysters to fuel him for the trip! If you're game, I say we hoof it!"

"I'm certainly game," William raised his eyebrows at me. "Charlie?"

I shrugged. "Let get a move on and try not attract any unwanted attention." I knew from experience that whenever a celebrity went out in public without an entourage, demented fans seemed to fall from the trees.

"We have our canes Charlie. I'm sure we could defend the young lady's virtue." William said playfully. He really wasn't too far off though. The core of William's cane was a three-foot, razor sharp rapier and the handle of my cane detached to reveal an under-over two shot derringer.

I clicked my tongue, "Well, we may be a tad late for that, but we can sure give her honor a shield."

"Oh, you lugs are so sweet," Ethel said in a mocking tone as she reached into her purse and pulled out a silver barreled sleek pistol which she twirled on her finger like an old west gunslinger.

"My word, Ethel!" William croaked, startled as I was at her adept handling of the weapon, no less her possession of one! "Where did you get that?"

"Why, Grand-dad Barry gave it to me and taught me to use it when I was a little girl," she answered coyly. "He always told me, "There will be adoring fans and there will be abhorring fans. THIS, is for the difference!"

She cocked the hammer to emphasize her point. Then she gently set the hammer back slowly and gave it another twirl before it disappeared back into her purse. We just stared at her for a minute.

"You go on ahead. Call us when the coast is clear," I suggested.

Ethel laughed and grabbed my arm, "Oh come on, you old coot. On the way you can tell me why on earth you would try and stick me in some no name show on my grand debut back in the States!"

I groaned, "All of a sudden I need a drink!"

"Then have one!"

"Don't mind if I do." I countered and reached into my jacket. Not feeling anything but cloth I patted myself down.

William laughed, "Never mind Charlie! I've a fully stocked bar back at the house." and he took my other arm and we started out.

It was a pleasant enough walk. The noise from downtown faded as we walked in the opposite direction along a tree lined street. Ethel chatted non-stop, regaling us with a few funny stories about English Theatre and some juicy gossip about our tight knit society. I added a few tidbits, but William refused to participate. He wasn't much for gossip.

We walked through two intersections before we reached our destination. "Here we are," William announced, coming to a halt and pointing at a rather modest two-story cape on a corner, surrounded by a high hedge. "Home sweet home for the time being anyways."

I looked up the sidewalk and saw a break in the hedges, an archway with a fence, so I headed towards it.

"Not there, Charlie. That's the back entrance. It leads to the kitchen. The front door is around the corner."

Another few steps took us around the corner to where there was an even bigger break in the hedges, with a solid wooden door that reached as high as the plant life it separated. William opened the gate and bowed us in.

A short walkway led to a covered full-length porch that spanned the front of the house. Complete with wicker furniture and throw pillows, it could have sat on any house from Maine to New York. William went in the house first and lights began to come on. Ethel led the way inside and we found ourselves in a small foyer. At a glance, I could see it was a typical New England salt box. Through the door at the end of the hall was the kitchen. To our left was a parlor and beyond that a dining room. The door on our right would lead to another sitting room and the master bedroom. Upstairs there were two bedrooms and a commode. The only difference I could see was another hallway that led off the dining room. I assumed that's where the main bathroom would be. I had been in many houses like this in my youth.

Ethel raised her eyebrows, "It's very…quaint, William."

William laughed. "You mean small. You were expecting Kikoi, perhaps?"

He shrugged, "It's just temporary. I promise you when you are invited to my permanent home, providing Charlie leaves me alone long enough to build one, it will be much different."

We followed him into the parlor, and he flicked a switch. Lights blazed from sconces around the room."

"Oh HO! All the modern conveniences, I see!"

"Not really Charlie. I just had the electric lights installed and added a master bath and some updates upstairs."

"Why bother if you only rent?" Ethel asked. "Why not just stay in a hotel?"

William hesitated a moment then lied smoothly, "Ozaki doesn't do well at hotels."

Well, I guess it wasn't really a bald-faced lie, Ozaki didn't appreciate anyone doing something for William while he was around, but the real reason Will avoided hotels was he valued his privacy more than convenience. In the past, whenever he had an extended stay, people would get used to seeing him and begin to accost him for one reason or another. That's why he preferred to stay on the *Aunt Polly* whenever he could.

"Besides," he went on, more to change the subject, "Winter's coming and I hope to get snowed in this year!"

Ethel grimaced, "Snowed in?"

"You know," I replied sarcastically, "When the snow is so high you can't open your front door and the world just shuts down for a few days?" I sighed, "I suppose you've never had that pleasure in your pampered life."

She snorted, "And why would one wish to be sealed away like a hibernating bear in its den? Do you think most people yearn for that sort of thing?"

I was about to retort but William spoke over me, "If you two wish to discuss philosophy, would you care for a nightcap?"

"First sensible thing you've said since we came inside, William," Ethel replied, "But first, where is the little girl's room?"

William pointed to the door I noticed earlier. "Right through there, at the end of the hall. Charlie and I will get some glasses and ice, if it hasn't melted completely by now. We'll meet you back here."

As she sashayed off, William led us through a door on the opposite side of the dining room and into the kitchen. He headed over to the ice box and announced we were in luck. Taking the pick, he began to chip away with sure firm strokes. "The glasses are in the pantry behind you."

Actually, there were two doors behind me and the first one I opened, on the left, revealed a narrow servant's staircase.

"Your pantry is upstairs?" I teased.

"No, that's the door on the right. Actually, that leads up to the room you're staying in."

I studied the layout quickly and shut the door. "Oh no! You put me in Ozaki's room?" I had visions of paper lanterns and all the furniture being floor level.

"It would be if Ozaki stayed here, but he won't. He prefers to stay aboard the *Aunt Polly*."

I was a bit surprised by that admission; William and his man were very close. Then I realized that was most likely best for both of them. Being in anyone's presence for all twenty-four hours, seven days a week would be nerve wracking.

"Even so," I mockingly protested, "You put ME in the servant's quarters?"

"Well, I couldn't very well have put Ethel there, could I?" He looked at me with a twinkle in his eye as he put the ice chips into a bucket. "Besides, you can have the rest of the night off."

I laughed, "Oh, thank you master."

"After you get the glasses!"

PART NINE

I was certain that sleep would never come this night. The day's events kept flashing in my mind, blocking out the sheep, but I must have dropped off at some point for I was startled back to consciousness by a light rap on my door.

"Yes?" I called out in my confusion. The sky was just starting to lighten, so I did grasp it was in the pre-dawn hour. I heard the doorknob rattle and was grateful I remembered to lock it. I knew the muffled voice that came through the door as an urgent whisper. It was William.

"Charlie! Get dressed and meet me downstairs. I need you to come with me."

"Come where?" I asked groggily from bed as I tossed my legs over the side and sat up.

"Back to the 'POLLY'. There's been an incident. You need to come."

"Meet you in two minutes," I claimed and heard William go down the stairs as I stood up. And I could make good on that time because I was still dressed in the same shirt, pants, socks, and everything beneath them. I thought about changing but I didn't want to take the time. I just reached for my half boots. And as I put on the left one I saw the grease mark on the calf I picked up last night and wondered if it would ever come out not that it had set for eight hours. I almost reconsidered changing again when I found a matching stain on the right leg as I put on that boot! But there was something in William's voice that made me want to hurry. He sounded agitated and that took a serious malfunction to put him in that state.

So, a minute later, I was shrugging into my jacket. I had a feeling it would be chilly this early in the morning, so I put on my coat. Grabbing my hat, I unlocked the door and stepped out into the hall. Before I could step forward, the door at the end of the hall popped open and Ethel stood there.

She wore only a sheer, shimmering silk night gown that was slit down the side from pelvis to floor and a deep neckline. The light shone from directly behind her, outlining her form. Six cups of coffee couldn't have woken me up more!

"What's going on?" she asked, completely at ease with her immodesty.

"I...I don't know," I stammered. "William says something happened on the *Aunt Polly*. We're headed there now."

"Tell him to wait for me," she commanded as she spun away, peeling the night gown off.

She didn't take the time to shut the door. William called up to me and I fled down the stairs. I felt like the altar boy who just looked up the Nun's skirt.

When I reached the bottom step, I found William, with coat and cane, standing behind a cab and staring in the general area where the *Aunt Polly* was berthed. Paul Gilmore was leaning against the hood looking like he would go ass over kettle at any moment. His chin was resting on his chest over loosely crossed arms and he didn't stir when I tossed out "What the hell is going on?"

When William heard my voice, he spun around to face me, "You've got your coat, Charlie. Excellent! We can go." He reached over a squeezed Paul on his bicep. "Paul? Are you coming with us?"

Paul slowly lifted his head and managed to nod. He looked like death warmed over. His clothes were rumpled. No spats. No collar. And his jacket was buttoned wrong. The face that stared back at us was deeply lined and pale. Even his lips were colorless. If he felt half as hung over as he looked, we were going to have to carry him.

"Damn Gilmore, you had better never show up to work looking like that!" I said, trying to make light of his condition.

"Oh, give over, Charlie!" William snapped. "The poor man was roused out of a deep sleep and sent up here to retrieve us!"

I already knew he was worried about something and I could forgive him his rudeness so gave him a flat stare,

"Simmer down, William. Whatever it is we can handle it."

"So, what happened?" I asked Paul, who seemed to have woken up some during our exchange.

He unfolded his arms and stood up straight. A quick shake of his head and he replied, "I dunno, Charles." He tossed his head in William's direction, "His man just shook me out of a deep sleep and sent me here to fetch you two as quickly as possible."

"Three," Ethel called out as she glided down the stairs. She was fully dressed in a new outfit and looking as fresh as a daisy. I don't why I was so surprised she could look so good so fast. The girl has had more costume changes than baths in her life.

She stepped past me and up to the cab to stand in front of the door, waiting for someone to open it. William looked like he was searching for a reason to leave her behind, but before he could protest; she turned her head and cast a steely eye on my friend.

"Well? Are we going to go find out what has your servant in a tizzy, or not?"

Paul opened the door. Ethel climbed in and slid over to the far side of the seat, leaving the rest of us to pile in with our comments left unsaid. As soon as the door was secured, the gears ground loudly and we lurched away from the curb.

Ethel tried to grill Paul, but she got the same response we did. She looked at William, "Any ideas, William? Should we be worried? You know your man better than us, is he prone to melodramatics?"

"Bah!" I scoffed. "Ozaki wouldn't panic if his pants were on fire. He is as solid as a rock!" I turned to William, "But I wonder why he didn't come himself. It isn't like him to involve…" I hesitated, then gestured at Paul, "someone else if there was trouble."

"Exactly," William replied in a grave tone, "There must be something he needs to keep an eye on."

That erroneous statement set the three of us back in our seats, but William simply turned his head away to stare out the window, lost in his thoughts. After last night's demonstration, none of us were going to question him. We rode in silence until we reached the docks.

PART TEN

William flung open the cab's door and was across the dock and up the gangway before the rest of us got out. I paid the man with a hefty tip for the early hour and the three of us hustled after William only to find the aft deck deserted. We went into the salon but that was empty. We stood still and listening hard for a clue as to where William went until a side door opened and we all gasped and jumped.

"Sorry. I didn't mean to startle you." William said. He looked as haggard and somber as I have ever seen him. "I'm afraid I have some terrible news. Sheldon is dead."

Paul and I were stunned speechless, but Ethel inhaled sharply and asked, "How? What happened?"

William turned his baleful eyes on her. We're not quite sure. Could I ask a huge favor of you, Ethel?"

"Of course. Anything."

"Would you mind terribly going to the galley and putting on some coffee for us? Charles and I need to see to this matter, and I think the rest of you should remain as uninvolved as possible. I fear it's going to be a long day."

"Good Lord!" Paul slapped his forehead. "If the papers get wind of this, they'll have a field day considering all the fame that's stuffed into this tub!"

I could see that Ethel had a slew of questions she wanted to ask, but something passed between William and her and she simply replied. "I'd be happy to. Believe it or not, I can make coffee!" Then, to forestall Paul, she tapped him on the chest. "You're with me. I may need your muscles."

"Paul?" William said. "I have a rather large favor to ask of you. Would you wait a half hour or forty-five minutes, then walk up town and discretely inform the town police and ask them to send some men quietly, along with a doctor."

Paul shrugged, "As long as Ethel's coffee is drinkable, I can do that. But why wait? Shouldn't we get someone right away?"

"William Gillette!" Ethel barked. "I hope you are not considering tampering with anything! Our reputations are not worth you going to jail!"

"Ethel, do you really think I would do such a thing?"

"You would if you thought it was the right thing to do."

"Then he'd be doing the right thing," I interjected, my nerves stretched taunt, "So could we get on with it?"

Paul saw the stress on me, so he took Ethel by the arm and led her to the galley. Ethel, diva she is, had to get the last word in.

"Don't let Charlie talk you into anything stupid, William" she called out over her shoulder.

'Too late for that,' I thought to myself. As soon as the door shut behind them, I turned to William. "What is going on? If the kid is dead, what's another hour going to gain us?"

William didn't reply right away. He reached up and put his hands on my shoulders in a comradery way that made my bowels shrivel. I think for the first time in my life, he was at a loss for words. "We must hurry!" was all that he said before he spun and headed for the door to the port gangway. My chest felt tight and beads of sweat formed on my forehead, but I shot out the door after him.

"What the devil are we doing?" I hissed at his back when I caught up to him, but there was no reply until we reached the door that led to his stateroom. Only then, with the doorknob in his hand, did he stop and turn to me. Again, he laid a hand on my shoulder. "Charlie...this is bad. You must brace yourself...but remember you are among friends." And of course, the damn fool went in without another word.

The first thing I saw as William stepped into the room was a privacy screen that made kind of a foyer for the bedroom. Some asian design, painted with cats, of course, that blocked my view of most of the room. But what I did see made me stumble. Besides William, who was looking at me with grave concern and Ozaki, who

148

was holding something at his waist, standing there was the last person I would have expected in this whole crazy situation.

Collin stood there, in dry clothes now, but shoulders slumped, staring at the floor, and looking miserable. When he raised his eyes to me, I saw such pain and anguish that is almost stopped my heart. I wanted nothing more to rush over and throw my arms around him, but I only made it a few steps before I remembered why we were summoned here in the first place. I turned and looked at the bed.

Sheldon was lying there, most of his body covered with sheets and blankets, his head turned away. There was no mistaking the bright red hole with blackened edges, dead center in his ear.

I looked to William in a confused panic and he sighed and looked to Ozaki. I followed his gaze and the little man slowly pulled away the hand that concealed the object he was holding and held it out for me to see clearly. It was a small caliber pistol that I had given to Collin for his last birthday.

The next few minutes are still hazy, and I felt like everything I ever wanted out of life had just turned to dust. A red mist had clouded my eyes but as I finally focused through it. I found Collin's shirt front in my white knuckled fists, slamming into his chest as I shook him back and forth, while I shouted,

"What have you done?!"

He made no move to defend himself, just flopped like a scup at the bottom of the deck. When I finally stopped shaking him, he looked up at me with eyes filled with remorse and a plea for understanding, but there are times when a father can afford ether.

"Did you shoot that man?" I demanded, pointing at the corpse.

After a second, he nodded vigorously. "I had to, Pop! He-."

I wasn't about to let him finish, so I did something I had never done to any of my children before. I slammed my hand into the side of his face.

"Charlie!" William carped from behind me, shocked. I didn't look at him but held up my palm to silence him. Ozaki murmured softly, and I could feel William moving back from me. Ozaki, at least, seemed to understand a parent's rights. Collin's eyes rolled back in his head and a drop of blood formed on his lip, but I had no mercy in me at the moment.

"Are you telling me you came back here and shot this man, just because he whupped you?"

"You don't understand, Pop." He began desperately, "I had to! I should have as soon as I laid eyes on-."

This time I made sure of his silence. I grabbed him by the throat and squeezed his air off. I heard William gasp behind me, and Ozaki hissed a warning, but I held on and snarled at my son. "You will not say one more word! Do not open your mouth again until I ask you a question or there is a damn good lawyer standing next to you! Do you understand? If I hear a peep, I will beat you senseless."

He was a little blue in the face when I released him, but he kept his mouth shut. I was almost relieved to see a bit of defiance creep back into his eyes. He would need his spirit to get through the rest of the day.

I knew then that I would have to do the right thing, but I had no clue as to how and go about it. I just stood there like a lamp and looked from Collin, to the corpse, and then to William. He and Ozaki were in a deep conversation I couldn't hear. When they finished, they looked up and a most awkward silence filled the room. Collin, my poor son, was looking ragged as a street urchin. I started feeling guilty about knocking him around, especially since he probably hadn't slept since his last beating by Sheldon. I just wanted to take him in my arms and hold him like I did when he was a child. Until I looked at the hole in Sheldon's head and then the anger came back. The moron botched everything!

Then, just to put another fly in the ointment, the door on the other side of the room suddenly open and Ethel stepped in, "William?"

Her breath caught in her throat and her eyes snapped wide as she saw Sheldon lying on the bed between us. She was staring straight into his face, but she couldn't see his wound from that angle. She was transfixed for a moment until William said her name. That brought her out of her reverie, but she quickly went back to confusion when she saw Collin.

"How...when did?"

"Ethel," William said loudly to get her attention, "Was there something you need?"

"OH, yes. Well, everyone is up and in the galley. Some are hungry, so I came to ask if you minded if we make ourselves some breakfast." Her eyes flickered to Sheldon again, "Though I may not eat today."

"Yes, of course. I'll send Ozaki down in a minute."

"Don't be silly. Between us we can manage breakfast. You have your hands full enough. Oh! And Paul says he's ready anytime."

"Please tell him to go in a half hour -- no less."

She stood and looked at the four of us, but again, some subtle signal passed between William and her and she kept her questions to herself.

"Then I'll be going back. Will we see you later?"

"I'll come explain everything as soon as I can."

She nodded and went out the door without another word.

We went back to our awful silence until William suggested, "Charlie, perhaps we should send Collin up to the wheelhouse. He can rest on the cot there."

I turned to my son, "Go with Ozaki and remember what I told you. Not a word!"

Collin nodded and Ozaki took him out the door to the gangway. As soon as we were alone, I looked at my friend.

"Thank you, Will. I can't think with him near me. I'm torn between taking his hand and running as far away as we can and grabbing him by the scruff of the neck and beating the hell out of him before turning him in!"

William waved off my rantings. He knew me better. "Bah! Neither of those are good options."

"Then we had better find some others." I said.

He looked thoughtful. "Believe it or not Charlie, I considered just sending everyone home and dumping his body at sea."

I saw a glimmer of hope at that point. It would be the perfect solution for us all, except Sheldon, of course. But I also knew it was too much to ask of his Christianity. After all, Sheldon was his understudy and they had spent a lot of time together these last few months. That was what was going to make this all the harder to make go away.

"But Ethel has seen both the body and Collin; there is no way to keep this a secret." He looked thoughtful. "We should talk to Collin. If we knew why he did it...."

"Why? I'll tell you why," I snapped. Now that my best option was off the table, I began to seethe again. "Because he's a hot head and too smart and too proud for his own good. He couldn't stand being humiliated in front of you and the girls!"

"Or you. Mostly that, I dare say."

He was probably right, so I grunted. I was beginning to feel trapped, so I ranted on, "How the hell did this happen? How'd he get back on board, from North Haven, in the first place?"

William shook his head slowly, "He never left Charlie. He swam to the Island than took the ferry back to Greenport and waited for us to return. His determination is disturbing, Charlie. Not to mention the fact that he brought a pistol with him in the first place."

"He always has that!" I protested. "You know he practices every chance he gets. He won several target tournaments last year!"

"I know, Charlie. I was there, remember? But that's not going to sit well with the police."

Those words struck me like a hammer between the eyes and my world seemed to crumble a bit more. However it played out, my life would be altered, and we'd never be the same family again. Though it wouldn't change the outcome, I had to have it spelt out. I need to know everything before I acted.

"So, he deliberately disobeyed me and came back to Greenport, then waited for us to return so he could sneak aboard and gets his gun from his luggage. What happened next?"

"According to Ozaki, he awoke shortly before dawn because he 'felt' something was wrong. He can be quite dramatic at times. In any case, he was checking the ship when he discovered that Collin's bag was open, and the contents riffled through. He was wondering why someone would pick Collin's to get into when he stepped on a pile of clothes. Some were still damp.

He knew then that Collin must have returned somehow and then he heard a noise on the port gangway. Half way up the ship, he saw an open porthole and went to investigate.

When he neared, he noticed the door was slightly open."

"How is that possible, Will? We locked that door ourselves last night."

"Collin is a clever boy," he replied and pointed at a belt that lay at the base of the wall between the porthole and the door. It was obvious he had put his arm in the open porthole and swung his belt to catch the latch lever on the inside of the cabin's door."

When I nodded my understanding, he went on to finish.

"Ozaki looked in and saw Collin, standing over Sheldon, with his right hand bundled up in thick cloth. He didn't realize what Collin was up to, but he knew it was probably something wrong, so Ozaki went through the door to stop him.

Collin never saw or heard him coming and Ozaki almost had his hands on him when he heard a muffled 'popping' sound. Sheldon's head jumped off the pillow."

It took a lot for him to tell me all this and he looked even more morose.

"Ozaki had no choice but to take him down and disarm him. Then he roused Paul and sent him for us."

"Ozaki should have broken his fool neck!" I groused.

"Charlie! You don't mean that!"

I took a deep breath. "Yes, you're right. But what are we going to do, Will? This can't end any way but badly. Not even you could straighten this out!"

William didn't answer right away as I just stared up at the ceiling, hoping God might show a little mercy. Yet, when I turned back to him, my friend was gone. The man standing before me looked a bit gaunter and his eyebrows bushed up where his eyes narrowed. It was the same man I saw sitting in the salon last night, entertaining his guests.

"We shall see, Frohman. We shall see…"

PART ELEVEN

Considering the circumstances, Sheldon didn't look all the worse for wear as we moved in for a closer examination. His head lay back on the pillows in perfect repose with his arms across his chest. If not for his open bulging eyes and twisted sheets around his legs, you would think he was still sleeping it off. Unfortunately, there was a strong underlying odor as we stood over the body that made me thankfull I hadn't had any breakfast yet. He smelled like stale cologne, drying hair grease, and something rancid I could not quite identify.

William stared intently at the hole in Sheldon's ear for a moment then crossed the room to a dresser, where his famous deerstalker hat rested on a bust of him. He opened a drawer and took out a familiar leather-bound bundle.

I was with him when he bought it out in Long Island a few years back. He laid the kit on the edge of the bed and unrolled it to reveal a variety of tweezers, pointers, and his favorite prop, the magnifying glass. Taking out the glass first, then some other instruments, he began to examine the wound closely. I wasn't sure what he was looking for, but he spent an inordinate amount of time poking around it.

Finally, he stopped mucking about it and stood. He gently pulled Sheldon's head back towards us, then walked around the bed and gave the other side a thorough looking over. Finally, he stood and looked at me.

"The wound would have been instantly fatal, Frohman. The bullet is still lodged in the brain."

"What does that have to do with the price of tea in China?" I snapped, but then something stuck me, "What do you mean 'would' have been fatal? Is there a difference between 'would have' and 'was'?"

"Not to Sheldon to be sure," he replied, then added with a tiny smirk on his mouth, "But it is my hope we can keep master Collin away from a life of wearing prison stripes...or worse."

But before I could dare to hope, to my disgust, he began sniffing around the mouth and cheeks!

"Good Lord man! What are you doing?"

He straightened up and looked down at me, a perplexed look on his face. "Why, looking for the source of that particularly rancid smell in the air. You must smell it yourself Frohman!"

"Everything about this stink's!" I groused, "Why pick one?"

That got his goat and he gave me a hard level look.

"If you have nothing to contribute but gripes, then just be quiet! Your petulance is distracting."

158

Rebuffed, I realized that I was acting childish. William was only trying to help Collin and I knew in my heart that he was the only one who could. If he failed, I would have some hard choices to make.

So, I mumbled an apology and asked him if he had any cigarettes around. He pointed to a table across the room without looking up and I found the Chesterfields. I lit one up and that first drag was like a warm compress on my forehead. Regaining some composure, I turned back to watch William as he went over the scene.

He could make an ant seem like a sloth when he was searching for clues, or data, as he preferred to call it. He started with Sheldon's face and head, peering into his mouth, both nostrils, and peeling back his eyelids. And that was before he got the gloves out of the dresser.

He pulled on a pair of tight white gloves, shrugged off his coat, and pulled his shirt sleeves up to mid forearm. After that, he was like a medical student taking his final exam.

Using his tweezers, scrapers, probes, and ever faithful magnifying glass, he went over every pore on Sheldon's face. He peeled back the lips and examined the teeth. He stuck things deep into the mouth and mumbled the measurements. He scrapped along the upper and lower lips then examined the goo on his stick under the glass. I had to look away a moment as he stuck tweezers up the nostril and drag some solidified fluid out.

Satisfied he had gleaned everything he could from Sheldon's head, he examined his hands next and had me help him put the body in a sitting position so he could look underneath. The body was so cold and stiff.

Arranging him carefully back into his original position, William then began to examine the sheets near the head and even dropped to his knees to peer at something ground level. When he got to his feet, he looked at me with an expression I had seen before. He scraped something off the bed linen and smelled it. He knew something was askew, but he could not quite explain it.

He took a sconce off the wall next to him and motioned me over. "Look in his mouth," He instructed as he held the lamp, so the light reflected directly on Sheldon's face. I've learned not to question William when he is in this mode. So, no matter how much I didn't want to peer into those blood shot bulging eyes staring up at me, I leaned over to look. The first thing I noticed was the darkened skin tone slightly smeared with some dried fluid, and some redness around the mouth and nose, some of which had gone over to a slight bruising. His lips looked distorted, as if he had a chaw in both top and bottom or he was blowing a bugle. The next thing I noted, as I leaned closer, made me snap my head back in revulsion.

The inside of Sheldon's mouth, from the teeth back, was filled with what only could have been vomit. It was not only disgusting in smell, but tiny bubbles were popping along the surface, like champagne. Still, I wasn't surprised with the amount of hooch the boy had put away the night before. Besides, what difference did it make? The only thing the cops would see is the hole in Sheldon's head!

William spun around to dart into the bathroom behind me, leaving me with the question hanging on my tongue.

He was gone for just a moment then he walked slowly back in the room and stated absently, "The drain is still damp and there is a hand towel and a bar of soap missing."

Again, I had no idea why that would be relevant, but I was still a question behind. I waved my hand over Sheldon's face.

"How does any of this change the fact that Colin shot him?"

William struck a pose then, hands behind his back, back straight, and looking down his nose at me. "Are you familiar with the term, Aspiration?"

I just stared at him. "Gee," I replied sarcastically, "I must have missed that class back at East Hampton High." I was in no mood for games.

He ignored my tone and answered his own question, "It is the condition where the victim chokes to death on his own vomit. If Sheldon had the misfortune to suffer an attack, and I am certain he did, that would exonerate Collin from a murder charge."

It took a moment for the idea to sink in, but I felt a resurgence of hope, a light at the end of the tunnel. "Are you saying this 'Aspiration' thing happened before Collin shot him?"

"Oh yes! That is most curious fact about this case Frohman. Sheldon had succumbed long before your son shot him."

I had more than enough faith in my friend and his abilities to believe him whole heartedly, yet I knew a

D.A. wouldn't be as easy to convince so I found myself playing the devil's advocate.

"How could you possible know that?"

He sighed and shook his head. "You are not using logic, Frohman. What did I tell you about the result of the wound Collin inflicted on Sheldon?"

I recounted the conversation in my mind. "That it would have been a quick death. Instantaneous."

He nodded, "Collin put the pistol in his hand and wrapped it and his hand up in his coat to muffle the sound. Then he placed the barrel right up against Sheldon's ear and pulled the trigger. Yet, what is absent on the pillow next to the wound?"

It took me a moment, but I finally opened my eyes. "No blood. There's nothing coming out of his ear! I thought gunshot wounds always bled."

"They do Frohman, if the body is alive and circulating blood. Although, I will say that most of the wound is the powder burns. I believe the bullet traveled straight up the ear canal with minimal damage."

"But still, there should be some type of ichor leaking out, right?"

"Quite so. And what did you just observe in Sheldon's mouth and nostrils?"

"Puke."

"Yes. And so?"

"So, what?" I answered in a surly tone. I hate it when he expects me to be as astute as he is.

He rolled his eyes, "Frohman, a body does not expel vomit after death."

"Where do you get that from? I've heard most people soil themselves when they die. It's a natural occurrence."

He shook his head in disgust and flapped a hand in the air as if to slap the notion away. "That is a loosening of muscles, Frohman! Vomiting is the contraction of muscles. One does not throw up after death has occurred. Once his brain had died, whatever was in his stomach would have remained there!"

I thought that over for a moment then I almost did a jig. I was pretty sure I could get Collin out of any charges the Police slapped on him, as long as it wasn't a murder rap. As long as the doctor signed off on a 'death by natural causes', we were in the clear.

That made sense and I could see where it was heading, but I needed to hear him say it plain and simple, so I said, "So, you're saying that Collin didn't actually kill him and that Sheldon had already died a natural death."

"No, I am not."

My heart sank at first then it froze in my chest.

"I think he was murdered – just that someone else got to him first!"

PART TWELVE

I put my eyebrows up over my hairline. "Mur-der?" I asked, stretching it to two syllables. "A bullet to the brain is murder William. Choking on your own vomit is just dumb luck! So, just what is it?"

He didn't answer right away. He strode over to the table and got himself a smoke. When it was lit, he turned back to me. I'll grant you that the timing would have been a colossal coincidence, but I can see no other solution."

He walked back over to the bed and stared at the scene some more.

Exasperated, I asked, "Are you going to answer my question William, or do I have to wait?"

"What? Oh! Yes. Well, I am certain that Sheldon was dead hours before Collin shot him." He held up a hand to forestall my demands for proof. "We know this because of the lack of bleeding from the wound and a few other minor signs, such as, body temperature and rigidity. If Collin had killed him shortly before dawn, the body would have been warmer and more flexible."

It made sense to me, but I was doubting a Copper would accept some rich actor's estimate of the time of death. "Alright then, assuming you're right, and I pray with a father's love you are, he must have died from that Aspiration thing!"

"Yes and no, Frohman. Aspiration is an extremely rare and can only occur in ideal circumstances. The body will expel toxins but there are natural safeguards that make the experience unpleasant but non-fatal. I think that Sheldon's bout may have had some outside influence." He walked over to the head of the bed, opposite me, and began pointing at areas to coincide with his narrative.

"You see the bruising of the lips and surrounding tissue of the mouth and the inside of his lips that have several small cuts-that bled. These are signs that someone violently clamped a hand over his mouth and nose."

"I hate to break the news to you William, but most people slap a hand over their mouths before they vomit-it's a natural reaction."

"I am aware of that fact, Frohman." he replied coldly. "Yet there is no trace of vomit on Sheldon's hands. No, my friend, Sheldon was gripping something altogether different. Most likely his assailant's arms while trying to tear them away. Now, let me finish. You can see where he thrashed his lower body about as death came upon him, yet his upper body remains in the position we left him in last night. Someone obviously held him down."

He walked over to the side of the bed and motioned me over. He pointed to a small puddle next the head. "That is a small amount of vomit from what he ate and drank yesterday. Much less than he would have expelled naturally."

I had to break my silence, "Because he choked on the rest! Isn't that what you said?"

He shrugged slightly. "It would seem to me, Frohman, that if he could have expelled that much, the rest would have followed unless it was impeded."

Then there is the 'coup de gras'. He reached down and lifted the bed skirt up, so I could see the goo he had examined earlier. "What do you make of that Frohman?"

I bent for a closer look and cautiously sniffed. Any man would know what it was. "It's hair grease."

"Observe Sheldon's hairline," he instructed, and I could see where it had been flattened. Our killer must have put one hand on Sheldon's head to hold him down, and then he wiped it off on the bottom of the bed skirt."

I snorted, "Sheldon would have a lot puke on his other hand, and I don't see any puke..." I let my voice trail off when I remembered, "Which is why there was a towel and a bar of soap missing!"

"Correct Frohman!" he said smugly.

"So then spell it out for me, William. You think an intruder came in, just when Sheldon was starting to get sick, then jumped on him and slapped a hand over his mouth until he choked on his own vomit? What are the odds that your intruder had such great timing?"

"I had considered that the killer waited for his moment, but I cannot help but feel that Ozaki would have discovered someone while he was on watch. No, I believe the person came with murder in his heart and decided he could make it look like a natural death. Whoever it was, he was a quick thinker."

"And who would want to kill him that badly in such a macabre manner?"

I know it seems a bit farfetched, Frohman, but it's the only theory that fits all the facts!" He shrugged, "When all other possibilities are disproved…"

I knew the rest of the line and it was true enough, but,

"That may be all fine and well, but I doubt you can convince a doctor, much less some hick constable that was the case. They are going to see that bullet hole and start looking for someone to shackle!"

I could see it in his eyes that he knew I was right. No matter how right he was, Collin was sure to take the fall. He mulled it over for a minute then took out his pocket watch and checked the time.

Dashing over to the closet, he took out a large valise and brought it over to the bed. I recognized it at once. It was his theatrical make-up kit. Everything he needed to transform himself on stage.

"What are you going to do? Gussy him up or disguise him?"

"Spare me the remarks, Frohman, as I am about to commit a criminal act to spare your son!!" He began pulling various items out and laying them on the bed. "Now keep a close watch! It's magic time!"

I wasn't sure what he was about to do yet I had all my trust in him. I went to the door and peered out. It was empty, so I crossed back over to the door that led to gangway and made sure no one was coming that way. I got quite a start when I opened the door and something furry stepped on my shoe and meowed. It was one of William's many feline members of his family. When I nudged her back out of the doorway, she hissed at me and arched her back. I was about to put the boot to it when William said sharply,

"Do not dare kick my cat, Frohman. In fact, let him in. Miso usually sleeps in here."

I'm not sure how he knew this as he never looked up from his work and the cat wasn't in his line of sight anyways, but I knew William had a special bond with the many creatures he kept.

"You sure you want this red haired she devil in here, Will?"

"He is a cream-colored tabby and I do indeed. He may just be the touch we need."

Whatever that meant, I wasn't about to pursue it any further. I just stepped back, and that cat put its nose in the air and walked pass me like I was a contemptable doorman. I went back to my vigil and glanced over at William every few moments.

He had years of experience at make-up and I had seen him transform himself many times, yet I was still fascinated but how fast and sure his fingers moved. For having been born with a silver spoon in his mouth, he was quite good with his hands.

First, he cleaned the powder burns away and, using swabs carefully cleaned the blood from the ear canal.

Then he used a little wax to build up the torn away areas and smoothed them with a small trowel. Satisfied the ear looked normal, we went through a few bottles until he found the right shade of powder and judiciously applied it around the earlobe.

When he had packed up and returned the case to the closet, I stopped bouncing back and forth between doors and lit another cigarette before inspecting his work.

It was like the wound was never there.

I gave a low whistle. "I'm impressed Will. Do you think it will fool the flat foots?"

He didn't answer me as he stared down at his protégé's face, a pained look on his. Though I knew it for a good cause, I couldn't help but feel a twinge of guilt for how we treated Sheldon's remains. More so on William's part as he had spent much of the last year grooming him. He turned his head slowly to me and said something strange.

"The things I do for love." Then he sighed and placed both his hands on Sheldon's torso. Standing up on his tip toes, he shoved downwards.

I damn near died of shock when the corpse's head bobbed, and vomit bubbled up to overflow his cheeks, a large gob having settled right into the ear William had just repaired.

Will then lifted the arms and placed the hands in closer proximity to the face, making sure to dip the fingers in the bile. Then he turned to me.

"Every magic trick is simple misdirection, Frohman." he declared as he walked into the bathroom to wash his hands.

When he came out, he checked his watch again. "If Paul followed my instructions, the authorities will be here shortly."

Seeing him standing there, calm and assured nearly broke me down. Even with all our years of friendship, I never would have expected him to go so far to protect my son. "William, if Collin walks away from this-I will be indebted to you for the rest of my life! Collin too, for that matter! I...I... don't know what to say really..."

"Then please do not," he said kindly, placing a hand on my shoulder. "Collin is a good boy and will be a better man. Perhaps a bit hasty in his sense of decisiveness, along with the hutzpah to act on it! Collin has a good and righteous soul." He looked me dead in the eyes. "Just like his father."

I wasn't about to ruin that monologue with a reply.

"Frohman, do you see any movement out there?" he asked as he checked the door leading to inside of the ship. There was no one on the gangway.

"Coast is clear," I called out.

"Excellent Frohman," as he headed for my door. "Let us check on Ozaki and your son, then we had best greet our guest and give them forewarning of today's events."

I felt like a doubting Thomas, but I grabbed his arm and asked him once more. "Do you really think we can fool them?" He jerked my chin towards the bed.

He pointed at me, "Remember Frohman---it is all in the misdirection, yet I think our chances are good.

William looked straight down at me with a stern expression. "If we succeed in deceiving the authorities Frohman, it will be our responsibility to find the killer!"

PART THIRTEEN

I grabbed a smoke for the walk and chased after him, "William," I called out, causing him to slow down enough for me to catch up with him. I crooked my head and said in a low voice, "Will, you can't possibly think that one of the five who stayed on board had anything to do with this? Do you?"

"Six! He pointed out. Ozaki was on board also."

I waved that idea right off. "Ozaki wouldn't kill anyone, William, unless you told him to!"

He sighed. "Frohman, when will you learn to look at these problems dispassionately? We cannot rule Ozaki out as a suspect, simply because we are fond of him!"

I opened my mouth to protest, but he rode right over me, in his infuriating lecture tone.

"There are three key components to any murder, Frohman. Means, motive, and opportunity. Ozaki obviously had the opportunity and most likely the means. In fact, if anyone could possibly be patient enough to watch a sleeping man for such an opportunity, Ozaki would be our man!"

"Yes, but why? I assume Ozaki could have done away with him anytime over the last nine months he has been traveling with you!"

He shook his head. "Last night would have been the perfect time for Ozaki to strike. With five others on board, the suspect pool grew more than enough to aid in his concealment."

I couldn't believe what I was hearing. It was like he was trying to put a noose around his man's neck!

"Yet, you are correct, Frohman. What lacks in Ozaki's case is motive. He has had little to no social interaction with Sheldon, probably owing to how I felt about him."

This was news to me. "You didn't like Sheldon?"

William stared out over the harbor. "It has no bearing on the matter, but no, I did not care for him as a person. He was arrogant, boorish, drawn to drink and ambivalent about the Lord. At one time he even tried to treat Ozaki as a servant! I put a quick end to that! No Frohman, Ozaki would have given him a good drubbing if necessary, possibly even slay him openly, but he would not murder Sheldon in his sleep, when he was defenseless."

"Í agree. I would also dare say that, though the other five may have had the means and opportunity, none of them had even met Sheldon before last night. In fact, none of them even knew he would be on board! Hell, I never met the kid until last night! You're screwy if you think any one of them could do what you think was done!"

173

William gave me a long appraising look. "So, you doubt the facts I lay out now, Frohman?"

"No, no," I shook my head, "I've seen this act too many times to doubt you, old friend. I'm just saying your interpretations may be off. I really can't see how someone could have gotten past Ozaki, been in position at the perfect time to murder the poor lad, and then get away cleanly. Even you must admit the odds are long, William. Let's face it, if Collin hadn't mucked up the works, we would have all thought it to be a natural death. I mean, who would want to kill him?"

I know he heard every word I said but you wouldn't know it from the expression on his face. "We shall see, Frohman. We shall see." He started walking again.

"I believe Colin may shed some more light on this matter."

I sighed and chased after him.

The curtains were drawn on the galley, but we could hear raucous laughter and loud voices, so we knew the gang was all in there. We slipped into the next doorway and took the four steps that led into the wheelhouse. The door was locked so William had to knock. It opened just a crack and Ozaki's head appeared. He looked at us and made sure there was no one else before he let us in.

"Is there any sign of the authorities?" William asked his man.

"Nothing yet. Mister Gilmore only left a short time ago. He should be back with the police in twenty minutes or so."

Collin sat in the far pilot's chair, slumped and despondent. When he saw me, he slowly slid down to his feet and stood as if he were a criminal on the docket. William was about to say something to him when he noticed a pile of items on the floor under the panel.

Looking closer, I saw it was a ruck sack. William bent and picked it up, Ozaki staring at him in defiance. William opened the pack to find clothes, food stuffs, and various sundries for traveling. He turned an eye to Ozaki.

"Were you really planning to put Collin on the run? Make him a fugitive?" He asked with anger in his voice.

Ozaki just gave him a steely look and replied. "He will not go to prison."

Never had I been so touched by a simple statement. I knew Ozaki was fond of my children, as they were of him, but I never dreamed he would risk prison himself -- or the wrath of his master -- to protect him at such great lengths. Will was not so moved.

He closed the pack and tossed it hard under the panel. "You presume too much! Why did you not wait for us to discuss this?"

Ozaki just shrugged and replied. "You are too goody-goody."

Even under the circumstances, I had to stifle a laugh. I was afraid William might fly off the handle and make this worse. Now was not the time for feuding between those two.

William just heaved a sigh of resignation and said, "We are fortunate you have not hatched this mad scheme. Our problem may yet go away."

Collin looked up, a glimmer of hope flashing in his eyes. William turned his attention to him. "Do not be overly optimistic, lad. What you did was heinous." Collin dropped his head again. "Yet your father and I will put our best efforts forth for your benefit. To that end, I need some honest answers from you."

I reached out and put a hand on Will's arm. I turned my back to my son and said quietly to William. "Please, let me speak with him first. I'm...I'm feeling bad about the way I treated Collin earlier."

He looked at me strangely but nodded. "Of course, Frohman. Only be quick about it. Our time is short."

I walked over and stood before my child. He lifted his head in stoic defiance. His thoughts were written across his face in bold letters- 'Hit me if you must. I did what I did!'.

I was so proud of him at that moment, but deeply saddened also. So, I just reached out slowly and cupped the back of his head and pulled him closer, so I could kiss him on the forehead. It occurred to me then that I had not done that for many years. Then I whispered, "It's going to be fine now. Your Uncle Will can prove that Sheldon was dead long before you pulled that trigger. With a little luck, we can get you off the hook with the coppers." His eyes widened in surprise and he opened his mouth to speak.

"SSSHH!" I admonished him, "Just listen for now— it's important. When your Uncle ask you why you did it."

"But, Dad!" he finally spoke. "That's what I've been trying to tell you."

I put a finger on his lips. "Doesn't matter now, we can discuss it later! But when he asks you 'Why?' you just tell him you didn't like losing that fight. You got that?"

He was confused but I knew he was listening when he nodded and said, "Don't worry Pop."

I knew then he would be alright. A weight seemed to be lifted off me, now that I was away from the corpse and I knew my son would be protected. I was ready then to see this through. I gave Collin a slow, exaggerated wink, like I used to when he was little, and though it didn't elicit the giggle it used to, I managed to get a weak attempt at a grin, before Will and Ozaki walked over.

"Sorry, Frohman, but our time is running out." Will said.

I ignored him for a moment and looked to Ozaki. It was just a brief nod and a down cast of my eyes, but the little man knew I was putting myself in his debt for his actions on Collin's behalf. I looked up to William, keeping my face neutral. "He's sticking to his story, William."

Anger flashed in his eyes and he looked right over the top of me, "You expect me to believe that you skulked aboard my ship and stuck a revolver in a sleeping man's ear, shooting him in his sleep over your pride?"

"There is no honor in this!" Ozaki butted in. I was surprised to see the effect his words had on my son. They hit him harder than I had earlier, and great tears began to well in his eyes.

My parental instincts kicked in and I snapped, "That's enough you two!" Not that they would listen to me, at any rate, but Collin got his reprieve.

"Enough of what?" a female voice said as we could suddenly hear the gang in the galley more clearly. Ethel's head bobbed up the hatchway. She looked around then realized we were all staring at her in a stunned silence. She turned and pulled the door closed behind her and climbed up the few steps.

"Has something happened, William? Or should I say -- something more?"

"No, No, Miss Barrymore," William answered. "We were just discussing how to handle the Police when they arrived."

She stepped right up to him and placing a hand on his arm, looked up and said. "Don't you think you should talk to the rest of your guests before they get here?"

"She's right, Will," I put in. "This crowd will surely clam up when the cops arrive." We in the show business were not at odds with the police but we generally tried to avoid them. Many of our member's lifestyles were illegal in themselves. I suppose my approving attitude, in itself is a sin, but I have a simple moral code. Anyone who contributes to putting a fanny in a seat is on my good list. Anyone. Period.

William gave me a queer look but turned his charm on Ethel. "They are actors, everyone, dear lady. They will deliver few lines without direction."

She gave him a level look, "Still, William, it would be better to let them have the script changes, don't you think?"

I had no time for their little games, "You haven't told them about Collin?"

She arched her eyes at me, "Charles, I almost married the next prime minister of the United Kingdom and kept it secret! Don't you think I know when to be discreet?" Her eyes flicked over to Collin, "Especially when I am not cognizant of all the facts. Or are you just gut-kicked because a broad could keep her yap shut?"

She caught us all off guard with her last statement and William barked out a sharp laugh.

"If I were you, Frohman, I would simply agree that she is an extraordinary woman and leave it at that." He smiled and bowed slightly to her. "And we shall heed her sound advice." He gestured towards the hatchway. "Lead on MacDuff!"

She turned to head back down the stairs to the galley and Will said to Ozaki, "Stay here and keep a watch for Drew and his escort. Let me know the moment they are in sight." Then he cast a baleful eye on Collin. "You, young Master, shall remain here and stay out of sight. Our conversation is not finished by any means."

He turned and followed Ethel. I brought up the rear thinking I had dodged another bullet.

PART FOURTEEN

They were all seated around the galley's table. Plates with various degrees of breakfast on them, coffee mugs, and a tall bottle of Whiskey in the center. They all cried, "Cheers" as they lifted their mugs in the air then fell into a fit of laughter.

E.H. gave us the once over and cried out, "Well, Boys, I see your already dressed." He arched an eyebrow at me, and I realized how rumpled I looked in my slept. Dressed in pants with the dual grease marks, wearing an unshaven face, and scuffed up shoes. "Have you had any breakfast? Ethel here makes a mean flap jack!"

"Have some Irish coffee with us, Charlie!" Evelyn chirped. There was little more than half her food eaten, and I would guess she was on her third cup.

Maude, however, was neither tipsy nor jocular. She sprang up and pushed past me to square off with William. "What's going on William?"

William just tilted his head but said nothing.

She plowed on. "Don't give me that! We wake up when your little man rounded us up and stuck us in here and told us to wait for you while he scurried off. Then John up and disappears and Ethel gives us breakfast and a bottle, then SHE tells us to stick around until you show up! And where's that understudy of yours, Sheldon?"

"Why are you badgering the man?" Paul admonished from the table as he poured himself another coffee and added a dollop. "You act like we're being held prisoner! Why don't you sit back down and finish your breakfast? Let them have a cup of coffee. I'm sure William will fill us in when he's ready."

Maude turned to give him an earful, I'm sure, but, once again, Ethel stepped in.

"Maude," she said sharply, and when Maude saw the look on Ethel's face, she went silent, "Please, Dear, have a seat. William has something to tell us all."

She stepped back, and Maude obeyed her. All eyes went to William.

"There has been an incident, one that could have an effect on us all." He looked slowly around the table. "Sheldon is dead."

Like a ballet troupe, they all jumped to their feet, questions spilling out in one jumbled din.

"Quiet PLEASE!" I barked in my Boss voice. "Settle down! Let the man speak! We don't have much time until the Cops get here."

They all sat back down, wide eyed but quietly murmuring their condolences with a liberal sprinkling of 'That poor Boy" and such platitudes.

"No problem, Boss. Just tell us what you want us to say." E.H. proclaimed after a moment.

I shook my head, the lie coming easy, "It's nothing like that, Lawrence. It was natural causes."

William gave me a side glance and went on, "Sheldon, as you all witnessed, drank far past the point of good reason last night. As a result, he suffered a bout of Asiration. It was fatal, but there were extenuating circumstances." Of course, he did not say any more for the moment.

"What the hell is that? I've never heard of Aspiration." Paul asked, after an awkward pause.

"He choked on his own vomit," Ethel replied for William in a steady, calm voice. "It happens to some who go to bed dead drunk. They get sick in their sleep and choke on their own vomit."

The stunned silence around the table was broken by Evelyn, "Well, that's an ugly way to go! And such a good-looking man too! But how is that going to affect us, William? We hardly knew the boy!"

I took that one. "Well, my dear, how do you think the papers will react when they hear that a young actor died while attending a party hosted by William Gillette, with the a-list of Broadway's stars? And that young actor had been in a fight with my son?"

"Oh, dear lord!" Maude exclaimed. "It'll be Fatty Arbuckle all over again!"

"Where do you get that from?" E.H. asked. "There certainly wasn't any under-age girls involved and nobody forced him to drown himself in booze! We were all blissfully unaware as we were all passed out until the Ozaki woke us up."

"Oh, I'm sure the rags will take all that into account, E.H." Ethel said in a scathing sarcastic way. She shook her head. "Just imagine the speculation about our hedonistic ways and wild out-of-control parties. They will use this to drag William's name through the mud, and all our names also, I'm sure."

Everyone was quiet while that sunk in. They all looked nervous as they all had seen what bad press could do. This might not ruin their career but once your name has been smeared it's hard to erase the stain.

Paul spoke up, "Look, we all can be as discreet as you need us to, William. In fact, I see no need to mention Collin or the fight. Collin is gone, and it had no bearing on the outcome. If you can get the cops to play it down and the Doctor to keep his mouth shut, this will all blow over in a few weeks."

Everyone at the table added their consent to the suggestion. Warily, I looked to Ethel, the only one of them that knew Collin was still on board, but she put a finger to her lips, and I knew she would hold her tongue. I was deeply moved by their loyalty.

"Thank you, Gilmore." William replied. "If we can keep it out of the papers for a bit, I will release an obituary to the press after we have all gone back to our homes. That should stifle the worst of it."

The rest of the discussion was killed when Ozaki popped is head in the hatchway and informed William that John was back with the cops.

"They are walking up the dock right now."

William went into action, "Meet them on the dock and bring them in through the salon." Ozaki disappeared, and he turned to the rest of the gang. "Frohman and I will take the authorities to Sheldon. If you are asked any questions, please do me a favor and answer with only the facts as you know them."

"But we don't know anything!" Maude exclaimed.

"Precisely! Let us not give them any bones to chew on."

"What about those extenuating circumstances?" Maude pressed. I had to admit, she was sharper than most of the rest, except Ethel maybe, she was the sharpest, but she also knew when to keep her mouth shut. Maude was just plain mule stubborn when she got her back up.

"Let us handle those," I answered for William. "It's complicated and the less you know, the better the chances you won't be dragged into it."

I thought, from the look in her eye, that she wasn't going to let up, but she ran out of time to badger us as John stepped into the Galley ahead of a new herd of folks.

The first man after Paul was easily identifiable as he was donning the complete uniform of the local constabulary, from shiny brass button on the peak of his cap to the gleaming tips of his black leather patent shoes. Rather skinny I thought for a copper but the big side arm and thick black club that hung on his wide leather belt more than made up for his lack of musculature.

The second man was considerably more robust. Taller by six inches and built like Gentleman jack. He was wearing an off the rack daily suit. I imagined he had four others of different colors that he rotated through each week. He was already pulling out a notebook with a meaty paw, exposing the grip of his weapon I assumed hung in a Docker's rig. A thick and neatly trimmed beard hid most of his face but the eyes above it were sharp and intense with focus. It was obvious he was a detective for Greenport.

The third man was also a give-away, carrying a black medical bag with the ease of having done so a long time. That was as far as his professionalism went, because when the Detectives blocked the view of the room, the good Doctor froze in place. His jaw bounced off the deck and his eyes doubled in size behind his spectacles. I had seen this act a thousand times before. The Doctor was a true theater fanatic.

"Oh, My Lord!" he whispered in a hushed tone.

After a moment, Ethel asked in a sweet voice, "Is everything alright, Doctor?"

Thankfully, that snapped him out of it. His mouth went right into high gear.

"Um, Yes, of course. I'm sorry, but I was thrilled enough just to have the opportunity to speak with Mr. Drew on the way over here and I never imagined too see all of you in one place-outside the theater no less! It's quite intoxicating. Brenda Lee, my bride, will be green with envy that I had the fortune to meet all of you. Miss Maude Adams, Miss Evelyn Milland, and the incomparable Miss Ethel Barrymore, along with E.H. Lawrence and Paul Gilmore."

He stumbled when he got to me, "I'm sorry Sir. You I don't recognize. Are you with the theater?"

"The fringe," I replied blandly. "My name is Charles Frohman."

"THE Charles Frohman? The President of the syndicate?"

"That's what they tell me." I said flippantly and gestured to Will, "And this is my associate, William Gillette."

Before the doctor could gather his wits and go on, the Detective stepped up to William. "You are William Gillette, owner of this boat?"

"I am," William stuck out his hand, "And whom am I addressing?"

"Eker. Detective first grade." He answered as he took Will's hand. "The patrolman is officer Audi, and the doctor you requested is Hines. Doctor Peter Hines."

He broke off the handshake and gave the room a hard look, eyes lingering on the half-eaten plates and the mostly empty Whiskey bottle. With four of them still in their night clothes and the doctor acting like he just walked into an after party, I don't think the detective was ready to take us too seriously.

"Well, Mister Gillette," he said, looking my friend in the eye, "Your man told us we were needed and to bring a doctor. But I don't see anyone in distress and no ones in a hurry to tell us why we're here." He gave Will a hard look, "I hope we weren't dragged away from our business on some drunken lark."

William arched an eyebrow at him, I can assure you, Detective first grade Eker, that your presence is justified and needed."

He looked skeptical. "Yeah? Well, unless you have a body lying around somewhere…"

"Excellent deduction. In my cabin. A young man named Sheldon Steele." William said with a straight face and gestured to the door they had just come in. "If you will come this way, please."

The detective got professional in a hurry.

"Audi, get up on dock! No one gets on or off until I say!" The constable hopped out the door and was gone in a flash. I got the feeling that Eker was of the no nonsense type personality. Eker faced the gang and cleared his throat loudly. Everyone's eyes went to him.

"I must ask you all to stay on board until we get this sorted out." There was a bit of narrowing in the eyes and I thought Maude might have another tantrum but once again Ethel took the lead.

"Of course," Ethel spoke for the group. "We'll be happy to co-operate in any way we can. It was a senseless tragedy, but I imagine you will still have a copious amount of procedures you must follow."

Eker nodded sagely, "You have no idea, Madame."

Before we took a step, the Doctor chimed in, "Are you sure he is dead?"

"Doc," I replied, "Even an old stagehand like me knew he was gone the moment I laid eyes on him."

Eker looked at William as if for conformation. William shrugged slightly, "It was obvious. The body-"

Eker held up a hand and cut him off, "If you don't mind, Sir, just show us where. I like my first impressions to be untainted whenever possible."

William arched his eyebrows and gave the cop his most condescending look of approval. "An excellent habit, Detective. Follow me, if you please."

PART FIFTEEN

The Detective frowned a bit at William's left- handed compliment but fell in line as William led us out the door to hallway. The Doctor and I were right on their heels but as soon as the door shut behind me, Eker turned a baleful eye on me.

"You should stay with the others, sir. Mr. Gillette can show us the way and answer any questions, I'm sure." He said it in the same tone you would use to dismiss a hovering waiter at a restaurant. I had no argument to counter his directive. Thankfully, William finally stepped in.

"Perhaps, Detective Eker, he should accompany us. Frohman was with me when we discovered the body and he may be able to provide some small detail that I may have overlooked."

I'm not sure if that swayed him but the Doctor said gruffly, "Com'on Ed! Let's just get to it! I have a patient waiting."

Eker looked at all three of us and shrugged. "Come along then. Please stay back and touch nothing!"

William and Eker started off down the hall and quickly rounded the first corner with their long strides. The Doctor and I fell into place side by side and followed. The Saw bone's concern for his 'patient' seemed to dissipate as he launched into a diatribe about his love for the theater and his admiration for William's work. He was curious at the line up in the galley and was hinting shamelessly, trying to learn the reason for so much talent being on the boat.

For my part, as much as I wanted to tell him to put a sock in it, I needed to keep him distracted so I answered him in vague innuendos. I considered bribing him with season passes, but I didn't want to make him suspicious. I was still mulling it over when we reached the cabin door. William took out his keys, yet before he could open it, the Detective asked,

"Was the door locked last night?"

"No. Sheldon was nearly passed out when we put him in bed and we were offshore, so I saw no need to. I locked the door this morning so none of the guests would wander in here." That may have been the first time I heard William tell a lie.

That seemed to satisfy the copper, so William opened the door and stepped back to let the Detective and Doctor in first. They both stepped through the door and stopped. Eker made a disgusted strangled sound and the doctor cried out, "Jumping Jehoshaphat!"

That was not what I would have expected to hear from two seasoned professionals, so I panicked and followed them in, sliding between the two.

I nearly jumped back when I saw what they did.

The body was lying just as we left it, and since we came in the opposite door than before, the bulging eyes and rictus mouth seemed to be greeting us. There was only one big difference.

One of Will's cat was perched on the corpse's torso, licking up the dried vomit with gusto. If I had my cane with me, I would have shot the beast.

"Millie!" William barked out, as he stepped past us to the bed. He grabbed the cat by the back of its neck and hauled it off. "Bad Cat!"

He set the cat down on the floor and the little varmint had the gaul to hiss at us before it sped away through the open door.

"My apologies, Gentlemen-."

"No need." Eker held up his hand. "My daughters each have one. Filthy creatures."

I winced at that, as William was a cat lover of old, but thankfully he let it pass and Eker began a slow walk around the bed. He jotted a few notes on his pad as he carefully examined the scene. His face showed nothing as he bent in from spot to spot for a closer look at something. I don't think I drew a breath the entire time he was studying.

And not just because of the stakes involved! It was the odor that kept the rest of us back. As the *Aunt Polly's* port side was facing east, the rising sun had been beating on a bank of windows since sunrise and the temperature in the room had risen considerably. Nothing can smell worse that warmed up old stomach contents.

Finally, he straightened up and slowly walked back over to us. "Doctor?"

The doc nodded and walked over to set his bag on the nightstand. He opened it and removed a pair of surgical gloves. Once he had them on, he began his examination.

Pulling back the sheets and blankets to expose the entire body, he then gave the body a cursory once over. Then he looked over his shoulders at the detective.

"Ready?"

Eker nodded and his pencil hovered over his paper. The Doctor began to drone, "Patient is a white male-," He looked to William, who said quickly "Twenty-six".

"Twenty-six years of age. No obvious defects or abnormalities."

He reached into his bag and removed a few items. The first was thermometer, which he placed between Sheldon's toes. The other was a plain, wooden tongue depressor, which he used to probe around the mouth area, obviously reluctant to have any contact with the vomit that covered the lower face and neck. After a minute or so, he checked the thermometer and announced, "I estimate the time of death to be between 11pm and two am." He cocked his head and poked around the mouth some more, actually scooping some of the vomit out of the mouth and letting it run back in. He turned to face us.

"Funny thing is, the vomit's fluidity isn't consistent with the body temperature. "

"What does that mean, Doc?" Eker asked, "In layman's terms."

The Doctor frowned at him. "It means his puke is wetter than it should be, Ed. It should have crusted up by now."

"I'm not surprised," I piped up, "Most of its booze! The boy drank enough to float this boat!"

Eker gave me a sideways glance that was a clear indication he would rather I kept quiet. "What is the significance, Doc? Are you saying he puked up after he was dead?"

"Is that even possible?" William asked in all innocence, despite the fact he already knew the answer.

"No, of course not. Vomiting is a series of contractions." He went on to explain it almost word for word as William had to me earlier.

"An external force then? Perhaps one of my cats jumped on him just the right way?"

The Doctor shook his head. "A cat is too light, Mr. Gillette. You can see by the splatter marks here and here." He pointed to smears on the pillows and sheets a good foot or more from Sheldon's mouth. "That it came up with some steam behind it." He mulled it over for another minute.

"Unless! Unless there was a gas build up in his stomach. A bubble big enough could shift and push its way out, clearing the vomit as it escaped."

William clapped his hands together sharply and cried out, "Brilliant deduction, Doctor! Worthy of Holmes himself! You really should add Detective of medicine to your shingle."

I thought he was laying it on a bit thick, but the Doctor was soaking up the praise like a barfly does his first drink.

The Doctor's chest puffed up and there was a certain swagger in his hands as he proudly said, "Feel free to use it in one of your plays."

Will's eyebrows shot up, "Why, Thank you, Doctor. That is very generous of you."

"How am I to write this up, Doc?"

"Oh, I don't know, Ed. No, wait, I got it! Write-'additional expulsion of stomach contents due to post-mortem discharge of gas'. Got all that?"

Eker scribbled furiously, "Every syllable of that gibberish. This is why the chief hates reading your reports, Doc."

The doctor ignored the remark and, grabbing Sheldon by the knee and the chest, pulled the corpse onto its stomach. The rank odor magnified as fresh bile oozed out his mouth.

The doc reached into his bag and pulled out a large, gleaming pair of shears. Starting at the collar of his shirt, he sliced the cloths in a straight line all the way down until he reached the crotch, right through the belt and all the layers. Then he branched off down both legs, including the socks. Then he folded back the clothes like he was unwrapping a roast from the butcher.

That was my cue. I reached into my jacket to retrieve my flask and I took a heathy slug. Eker was eyeballing me, so I held it in his direction and raised my eyebrows. To my surprise he took the flask.

But instead of taking a drink, he poured a few drops on his fingers and rubbed it on his upper lip. He handed it back to me and turned his attention back to the Doctor's movements.

It took me a minute to figure out what I just saw, then I followed suit. It stung a bit in the nostrils, but the smell of juniper berries was far preferable. I took a deep breath and took my attention back to the proceedings. The doctor was still spitting out little blurbs. 'No this and No that. Patient this, patient that.' I didn't catch most of what he was saying as I was worrying about what he might say before he was done.

The entire back half of the corpse, from his heels to his neck was discolored. Even though I knew it was the pooling blood that caused it, I was astounded how dark his skin had grown. My surprise didn't compare, however to the gruesome shade of white of his front side.

My heart did a skip when the Doctor's hand strayed too close to William's work, as he gently rolled him back to his original position. Even though it was half covered by hair and dried vomit, I was sure the doctor was going to discover our ruse. I began to imagine Eker's hand on the back of my neck. I nearly wet myself when he spoke to me.

"Are you alright, Mr. Frohman? You look a little
…green."

"I'm alright," I answered shakily, "It's just hard to see
someone this young, that you know, in this state."

Eker cocked his head and squinted at me. "I thought
you said you had never met him before last night."

I froze for a moment, but dissimulation came naturally
to me. "Well, yes, this was the first occasion that I had
spent any time with the lad socially. I knew him as
William's understudy, but William's been on the road
for the last half year or so."

Eker gave me a long hard look. "Are you sure there's
nothing you're holding back, Sir? Remember -- this is a
death inquiry. You need to be as forthcoming as
possible."

I had forgotten how hard it was to lie to a good cop. I
was racking my brain for a response when William,
bless him, stole the scene from me.

"I am responsible for Sheldon's death," he cried out,
tears welling in his eyes. I knew this would be a
performance and I prayed it would be one of his best.

Eker and the doctor looked at William in shock. Eker
spoke first.

"What are you saying, sir?"

"I am saying that if there are any charges to be leveled-
they should be heaped upon me! Sheldon was in my
charge! He was a guest on my ship and…." He paused
dramatically to catch his breath and wipe a tear away, "It
was my liquor that I freely provided that caused his

death! I might as well have put a gun to his head! It was my negligence, both as a host and a friend that allowed him to drink such a lethal amount."

Then he dropped his head in his hands and his shoulder shook with grief.

The cop and the detective were stunned by the outburst and I think a little embarrassed by William's break down. The doctor looked like he wanted to go around the bed and give William a hug. The Detective rolled his eyes and sighed.

"Why don't you tell us what happened between last night and now, Mr. Gillette." He suggested. "Or Mr. Frohman can if you're not up to it."

Not raising his head yet, William put out a hand in a pause sign. "No, no. I can do this." He raised his head and proceeded.

I, myself, only listened with a half an ear as he described how he had arranged this weekend on my behalf, hence his invitations to the six actors and his understudy. I was wondering how he would skirt Collin and the fight.

"So that's how you decide who stars in what play, Eh?" The doctor asked, pulling me back to the moment, as he moved closer to me.

"No, not really," I answered. "But I had two girls returning to the states for the season and a slew of new scripts. A reunion of sorts seemed like a good way get a refresher of their personalities, so I could choose a spot for each of them. Fact is, I offered Sheldon here a leading role. It would have been his big break."

"In any case," William went on. "We had a pleasant day, more or less, drifting around the bay during our luncheon. When the weather turned on us, we returned to the dock here and carried on. When the sun fell, we all retired to the salon where we had after dinner drinks and amused ourselves with a game. It was then we realized how stewed Sheldon was. Though he could barely stand or speak, he managed to be belligerent and offensive. Ozaki, my servant, and I, carried him here, to my cabin, and we laid him in bed. He was dead weight by then and starting to snore loudly."

He gave a little grimace, "I left the inside door unlocked so Ozaki could check on him, and went out the door to the gangway, locking it behind me before returning to my guests."

"And did your man check on Sheldon during the night?" Eker cut in.

"I don't think so," William replied after a moment's thought.

"The party broke up shortly afterwards. Miss Milland and Miss Adams shared the other suite and Lawrence and Drew bunked in the crew quarters. Gilmore was given Ozaki's cabin.

Frohman, Miss Barrymore, and I went to my rented home on Front Street where we got some little sleep before Gilmore came and awoke us around five am. Ozaki had taken a cat nap in the wheelhouse and woke with the dawn. Shortly afterwards he checked on Sheldon and found him in this condition, so he sent Gilmore up to the house to fetch us. After I had assessed the situation, I sent John Drew out to ask for your assistance."

A few more shoulder shakes and a quick hand through the hair, then William straightened up and concluded his act.

"So, you can see it was clearly my responsibility. I should have paid more attention to his consumption and I should have never left him alone in that state. Damn my eyes for leaving him here unattended -- to die!" He said violently as a single tear drop ran down his face. His head drooped, and silence filled the cabin.

All we needed was a curtain to drop.

PART SIXTEEN

Had I been in the front row of a playhouse, I would have applauded William's little performance. He both broke the Doctor's concentration and managed to not lie at the same time.

The Detective was not so moved. He must have been a more jaded man as he rolled his eyes again with an expression that shouted, 'Oh Boy!'

The Doctor, however, was more than sympathetic to William.

"Mr. Gillette, you mustn't blame yourself. Please listen as I finish this report. "He turned to the Detective, taking out his watch. "The time is eight o three AM on this date, and I declare this man, Sheldon Steele, dead…by natural causes. Aspiration brought on by alcohol consumption and rich food."

He looked back to William, "Did you catch the distinction, William?"

One corner of William's lips twitch at the use of his Christian name, but he let it pass and replied. "Doctor, I see now that the food he ate could have contributed to his condition, but I fail to see where that absolves me."

"Doctor!" Eker was clearly tired of this conversation, "Is that your final verdict?"

"It is."

"Then we are done here." He flipped his notebook shut and pointed his pencil at William and said bluntly. "You need to get off the cross!"

A double whammy! Blasphemy and belligerence! I wasn't sure how Will was going to take that-especially while he was in role. But William just bobbed an eyebrow and said icily, "I beg your pardon, Detective Eker?"

The big man grimaced but then collected himself. He heaved a sigh and tucked the pencil in a pocket. "Look, Mr. Gillette, I've seen a lot of tragedies due to drink in my line of work and I've learned that you can't make a person who wants to drink, drink in moderation short of doing them bodily harm. I've had to rap many a sot over the head to drag them out of a saloon in my younger years.

That being said, as a disinterested third party, I can tell you that Mr. Steele here was a grown man, doing well for himself, and free to make his own decisions. All the chest beating and gnashing of teeth doesn't change that. Like my old Grandpa used to say, 'The sun rises, the sun sets- everything else is just a bet'. Besides, from what I've learned here today, it was a medical condition. I'm not sure how much he drank is relevant."

"He's right about that," the Doctor put in. "It's a rare occurrence, but any number of factors could have contributed to the cause. You should listen to Ed, he's talking good sense."

William mulled the points over for a moment then looked up with a shy semi smile on his face. "Perhaps you are right, Doctor." He looked at Eker and added, "I suppose I can be a bit dramatic at times."

Eker smiled and almost chuckled, "We are what our professions make us. Which is why I can be a bit blunt at times. My apologies if I offended you in any way."

"Nonsense, Detective. If any are due, they are on my part. It's all a bit overwhelming."

"Then we should wrap this up as quickly and painlessly as possible. Perhaps we could impose on you for a cup of coffee while we finish the report. I would like to get some air."

"Here, Here!" The Doctor agreed.

William was about to offer the services of the galley but I felt I needed to push my luck and minimalize the damage for my friends.

"One moment please, Gentlemen." They all turned to me and I laid it on thick. "Now, I would never even dream of asking you both to do something unethical, but, I must ask you, for the sake of William and the others on board, if there was any possible way to keep this as quiet as possible.

I mean, it wouldn't affect me so much, I'm behind the scenes, but William and the others are some very public figures. If the rags got ahold of this story, well, you can just imagine how they would sensationalize it! As you well know, the innocent truth doesn't sell papers. Innuendo does. There are plenty of hacks out there who would love to make a name for themselves by dragging everyone's reputation through the mud. And their reputations are their livelihood."

"I know what you're saying, Charles. Some of those gossip mongers should be horsewhipped!" The Doctor agreed

"As for myself, I took an oath for patient confidentiality. There is no reason to show my files to anyone but the family --if they come forward and ask."

We all looked at the detective, who didn't look as comfortable as the Doctor. "Since it's a routine death with no charges pending, I really only have to log it in my daily report. I suppose it may fall to the back of the filing cabinet.

I'm not sure what Audi knows, but I'll tell him to clam up about it." He shrugged, "that might keep him quiet for a week or so."

I breathed a sigh of relief, "That would be just fine, Detective. We can release an obituary in a few days and lay it all out then. As long as we break the story and not our rivals, we stand a better chance of people seeing this as the tragic accident it was. I thank you both for your discretion and understanding."

"Think nothing of it," the Doctor waved it away, "Of course, you'll have to convince the undertaker when he gets here."

PART SEVENTEEN

'OH LORD', that doomsday voice shrieked in my head. I had forgotten about what would happen to the body once the cops were gone! While cleaning and prepping the body for burial, the Undertaker was sure to discover William's handiwork! My panic turned to anger, and I glared at William for not foreseeing this complication! He was supposed to be the clever one.

"It won't be necessary to engage the undertaker, Doctor." William replied to my surprise. Of course, he was one step ahead of us. It was everything I could do to keep my jaw off my spats when he said,

"If you will release the body to me, I will see him home to his kin. Once my guests have departed, I shall refuel and provision and be off with the afternoon tide. We can be on Montauk well before the sun goes down."

Now I was really lost. William had told me the boy had no living parents or siblings.

"You sure about that, Mr. Gillette?" the Inspector asked.

"Sheldon was my protégée and a good companion." Will paused, seemingly near to breaking down again. "It would be unfeeling of me to allow his loved ones to be notified by post. It is only right I should take him to his final resting place myself."

Now the Doctor looked uncomfortable. "Well, and I don't mean to be indelicate, but, you can't just leave him like that. Decency aside, there are health issues involved with a deceased body."

"I understand, Doctor." William cut him off smoothly. "My man Ozaki and I will see to his needs. We shall wash him and dress him in his best, and then Ozaki can sew him into a shroud. That should be sufficient for the short journey."

The doctor still looked uncertain but, in the end, his adoration for fame overcame his good sense.

"Then I suppose it will be alright. Don't worry about the paperwork now. You can swing by my office when you are back in town."

"Detective Eker?" William asked.

He shrugged, "As far as I can see, you're as close as what he has to a guardian." William couldn't help but wince at that, "So you can do what you see fit. Besides, it'll save the town some coin so, I'm sure there will be no complaining."

"Thank you both," William replied simply. "Now, shall we retire to the galley? I'm sure my guests are beside themselves with curiosity."

"Or three sheets to the wind!" The Inspector quipped. I believed he was right on that score and I could sympathize. I wanted another pull off my flask!

To our surprise, the galley was empty.

"That's strange," William said, "Perhaps they retired to the saloon."

When we got there, all we found was Ozaki, standing like a toy soldier between two pieces of luggage and Ethel sitting at the desk, pen in hand.

She set the pen down a rose swiftly- but o so gracefully - from the chair and glided over to William. She obviously been back to the house or had her possessions sent to the boat, for she was fully decked in her traveling clothes and jewels.

She stopped just short of pressing her breast up against him and gripped his forearms. She gazed up at him and asked, "Are you alright?"

William, a tender mien on his face, reciprocated her hold. "Dear Ethel, I'm fine. Everything is going to be alright. Where are the others?"

Ethel eased back a half step and laughed. "E.H. made me swear I pass this message along – "Ethel bullied us out on our rumps.""

"Are you sure he said 'rumps?"

"His term was more colorful, and I did hustle them out. I hope you don't hate me for it."

"Of course not," he replied, "I'm sure you had good reason."

"Oh, Thank you." She squeaked as she got on her tip toes to plant a kiss on his cheek. Only I heard what she whispered in his ear. "Out of sight – out of mind!"

She dropped back to the floor and they looked at each other for a long moment. I was about to lose my mind for the tenth time that morning, but I should have had a little more faith in her.

"When they finished off that bottle of whiskey, I told them it was time to take the party elsewhere. I knew the last people you needed hanging around, at a time like this, was a bunch of drunk, out of work actors! The boys went off in their boat and Maude and Evelynn are holding each other up at the head of the dock waiting for me."

She got serious, "Of course, they all gave their condolences and wanted you to know how much they cared. We didn't really know Sheldon, but we all love you. And, we all thank you for your hospitality. It really was a lovely weekend. I'm sorry it had to end so badly." She smiled and straightened up, "Anyways, I tossed the rest out on their ears, but I just had to see you before I left.

"Will you be alright, Dear boy? I could stick around until you get things sorted out, if you wish. I don't mind."

Even I couldn't read her expression, so I know William didn't know what to make of her offer. I really was beginning to wonder about these two.

William just gave her a sad little smile and released his hold on her. "As tempting as that offer sounds, Dear

Girl, I think its best if Charlie and I handle this. We'll be fine."

She gazed up at him for another long moment and nodded, "Then I guess that's it." She tore her eyes off him and looked at me, "Charles, you scallywag, thank you for the shucking." and she added with a twinkle in her eye, "We're all completely happy with our assignments."

I was about to acknowledge her, but she added, "Well, not Everybody. And maybe not completely."

I sighed and began to frame my response when she cut me off yet again by stepping up to me and planting a kiss on my cheek.

"But we'll save that for your office when you are back because I must be off if I'm going to get that covey of sots on the train."

"And we must be off as well." The Inspector said from behind us. He and the doctor walked around us and paused at the door that led to the deck and the stern ramp.

"Oh, if you are leaving also," Ethel purred at the Cop, "Perhaps you gentlemen would escort me to the stand. Might I impose upon you to use your influence to secure us a cab to the station?" She batted her eyes at them!

"Oh, we can do better than that!" The Doctor crowed with delight, "Ed and I came over by automobile, so we could drive you all to the station right away."

She clapped her hands with glee, "Really? Are you sure you wouldn't mind Detective? I'm sure a man of your stature is a busy one."

The Flatfoot, smiled and said graciously, "It's my civic duty Madame ---and a pleasure!"

"Well then," She arched in eyebrow at William and said in a joking voice, "It seems I don't need you at all, Dear boy!"

William laughed, "You never did, Dear Girl, you never did."

She laughed and gave him a sound kiss, then turned around to go. She saw Ozaki standing next to her luggage and looked at her two escorts, "Would you mind, boys?"

Ozaki stepped back from the bags and bowed, arms spread out as if to say, 'Go on! Get the bags, Suckers!'

When her mules were loaded, she took one on each arm and waited for Ozaki to step over and swing both doors open.

"Take good care of him, Ozaki," She said in a soft voice, and then she looked back over her shoulder and gave William a solemn nod. She winked at me and strode out the door, chatting merrily with her two new friends.

William and I followed them out and waited by the railing until they were at the end of the dock where the others waited. There was brief drunken cheer and applause and soon they were piling into the cars. It was finally feeling like it was almost over.

As I heard the cars starting up, I turned with the intention of heading back into the saloon and pouring myself a stiff sherry, when two hands roughly grabbed my shoulders and spun me around.

Will's face was a thundercloud.

"For the love of God, Charlie! Why did you do it?"

PART EIGHTEEN

He released me roughly, almost pushing me backwards. Ozaki moved forward and glided into a position that was between us but off to the side a few paces. He didn't look much the man servant, more of a fox waiting to pounce on a hapless squirrel, as he glared at me.

William raised his head to the sky, as if to question God himself and asked, "Why did I not see it! It was staring me right in the face! Sheldon was my understudy and has been at my side for months now. And yet, the first time I bring him to my home, two members of the same family try to kill him! Its insanity!" He dropped his head and shook it sadly.

"Will-"

"Don't!" He snapped at me as he turned to face me. He wagged a long finger and said, "Don't try to deny it, Charlie. Your pants would have given you away this morning if I weren't so blinded by friendship to see!"

I looked down at my pant legs. I had forgotten about the grease marks on each leg, but as I stared a little longer, I could see the connection and I winced.

"Yes!" cried William. "You got the mark on the left leg because you went through the engine room on your way to the staterooms, but you came back by the hallway. The only way you would have gotten an identical smear on your right leg is if you had come FROM the staterooms back through the engine room.

Which you did after you murdered poor Sheldon in his sleep. You went that way because you needed to avoid Ozaki at all costs and you knew the sounds of the boilers would mask your movements!" Ozaki's lip curled into a rictus as those black beady eyes bore into me.

"You were the only one, besides Ozaki and I on board last night who knew Sheldon would be here and knows this ship well enough to navigate it in the dark!"

William glared at me, hoping, I thought, to vent his anger at my denials but I kept my trap shut. A warm, comforting calm was coming over me. It was clouded somewhat by dread, but I had never felt such serenity at the end of any ordeal I'd been through.

When I didn't respond, opting instead to take a much needed pull off my flask, his eyes narrowed, and he pointed a finger at me in the classic 'J'Accuse!' fashion. He stepped forward, as if to charge and shook his arm vigorously. I had never seen him so agitated and out of sorts.

"And that! The flask! More confirmation, though I failed to see that also! Until now. Last night, as we

214

walked back to the house, you said you left the flask on the *Aunt Polly* and you and Ethel had to forgo until we reached my house. Yet, earlier, in my cabin, you miraculously had it in your possession- though you never left my side! You did not recover it this morning! That was a mistake, Charlie; you should have left it on board last night!"

I couldn't have answered since Will never gave me an opening. He began pacing again, this time with his arms stretched out in front, palms up and fingers curled into claws.

"WHY! Why Charlie! No matter how many possibilities I can conceive, there are none that explain why my oldest and dearest friend would murder my understudy, who he hardly knows! Or why his son, who just met him, would return in the dead of night to shoot him! Its insanity! There is no logical-"

"He RAPED Arianna." I yelled.

William blathered on for a second then stopped dead in his tracks. "What? What did you just say?"

"He raped my little girl."

Though I said it in a soft, calm voice, it seemed to echo across the water in the stillness that followed. In the corner of my eye, I could see Ozaki's face change from stern disapproval to shock. His eyes widened to saucer size and his mouth formed a perfect circle.

"oh ko," he whispered which I think is the Japanese equivalent of 'Jesus, Mary, and Joseph!'

"How...How could that be? He couldn't...have...he wouldn't...what are you saying?" William stammered, looking like he was just pole axed.

His words brought a rising tide of the rage in me that burned away my inner peace, but I managed to keep a calm demeanor. William was by no means naïve, but he was such a good person at his core, he couldn't see the evil that lurked in those he was close to. A fact I had relied on from the start.

With just a tinge of sarcasm in my voice, I gave him all the answers he would ever need, "How? You want to know HOW? Then listen. About a month or so ago, I came home early one day and found no one about. I heard sobbing coming from upstairs, Ari's room, so I went up.

"Her door was ajar but before I could push it open and see what had distressed my daughter so much, I heard her Mother's voice, already trying to sooth her. So, I listened, unobserved, as she told her mother what had happened to her. Last fall, soon after your boy had signed on with you as your understudy, he was visiting some relatives in Montauk. Ari, Collin and most of the kids in town had gone up to the beach for the end of the summer get together the local kids have every year.

"There, she made the acquaintance of your Sheldon Steele - and Collin too it appears- and they spent some time together. Later on, near the end of the day, Sheldon offered to take her out for a sail where they could watch the sunset.

"Now, Ari was raised proper and I don't think she would have put herself in that position, but she thought

216

Sheldon was 'nice' and when he told her he was going to work for you, well, she trusted him as she would have someone who was 'nearly family'. Besides, he was an older man. She was fourteen years old, for Christ's sake!"

William winced and turned a little green in the gills, but I was unrelenting.

"Once he had her alone, far enough from shore, he tried to romance her. Ari was having none of his advances, so he stepped up his campaign."

I halted there, not wanting to verbalize her pain and mine. I had never spoken off what I heard in the hallway that day and would have taken it to my grave if only I had the sense to hire an assassin in the first place!. William was still having a hard time coming to grips with what I was telling him. The evil he was accustomed to were sly and cunning. Bestial behavior was outside his ken.

"What do you mean...'stepped up his campaign'?"

"I mean, William, that once he found he couldn't sweet talk her out of her knickers, he pushed her to the floor, pulled up her skirt, and took out his-"

"Stop! Stop it, Charlie!" he cried in anguish. I saw tears running down his face.

"And when he finished with her," I plowed on, "he told her that if she told anyone, he'd deny it and tell everyone she was just a slut and it was her idea."

"This is more than I can stand! I 'm not sure I can hear any more!"

"Well, you'll just have to, William. You haven't heard it all! My little daughter, Ari is PREGNANT!"

There. That was it. All the cards were on the table now. And I was almost sorry for the way I told him. He staggered back a step and clutched his chest. I was afraid he stopped breathing in the silence that followed, and then he managed to find his voice.

"Oh, Lord! Charlie, you killed the father of your own grandchild."

That's when my dam of serenity broke, and all my loathing spewed forth. I thrust a finger in the general direction of Will's stateroom and snarled,

"That mangy, coward is NOT the father of any of MY scions! He's just a dog who put his seed in the wrong bitch and I was damned if he would have any part in that child's life! None! And I could never have him around as a reminder in my life."

"Charlie." He shook his head, as if to clear it, "We could have found another way. You-"

"Another way!" I barked, "What would you have me do? Marry them? Force my little girl into spending her life with the man that brutalized her? Sit at a table across from Sheldon at Thanksgiving dinner? Christmas? No, I don't think so, my friend. Any other solution would have just caused Ari more pain and THAT I WILL NOT ALLOW!"

PART NINETEEN

No one spoke for a moment. The three of us just stared at each other. Ozaki 's expression was of approval, but William needed another minute to put his thoughts together. When he got a grip, he looked up at me.

"You had obviously planned this encounter with Sheldon. Were you aware of Collin's intentions too? Please tell me you didn't plan this together."

That surprised me. "No! Of course not! I admit I wanted to confront Sheldon and was looking for a way get him face to face, outside of a large crowd, but I hadn't planned to kill him here. My plan was to lure him away from you with a juicy role and dispose of him some other time and place. I just needed to see what kind of person he was, so I could make a plan. Collin was as much of a surprise to me as the rest of you.

"I hadn't even the slightest indication he knew what had happened to his sister, but she must have written to him at college. Probably what got him suspended. You know what a hot head he is when his bloods up!

"Collin didn't even know that Sheldon was going to be here. But when I saw his reaction to Sheldon, I knew he was in the know and he wouldn't let up!"

"That's why you tossed him off the boat! You were protecting him! You were afraid he would kill Sheldon and pay for it."

"Yes. I had to get him away before he yelled out the reason for his rage. I knew he'd never be able to control himself. Sheldon was a dead man the moment Col laid eyes on him. Only, I realized I was the one who had to do it before he or one of his brothers caught up with Sheldon.

What I failed to realize was the depth of Collin's resolve. He always was the stubborn one, but I never in a thousand years thought he would come back to kill Sheldon." I shook my head in disgust, "I should have taken that stupid gun away from him a long time ago!"

William sighed, "You couldn't have known, Charlie. Apparently though, the old saying is true -- the apple DOESN'T fall far from the tree."

I shrugged, "He loves his sister as much as I love my daughter."

"We all love Arianna." William pointed out. Even Ozaki bobbed his head in agreement.

Then he gave me a pointed look, "Are you sure you didn't plan this whole week-end just for the opportunity to kill Sheldon?"

I was crushed and saddened by his doubts about my explanation so far, but I suppose I deserved every bit of it.

"No Will, I honestly hadn't planned on killing him this week-end. I just wanted to see him and perhaps confront him if the situation permitted us a private moment. Although, perhaps, I was hoping he would give me the resolve once I saw him in the flesh.

"But I didn't count on Collin's reaction and when Sheldon got stinking drunk and acted the fool, I decided I needed to settle this. So, last night, after you and Ethel retired, I snuck down the back stairs and made my way back to the Aunt Polly.

It was late, and no one saw me as I walked down to the docks. I figured Ozaki would be in the wheelhouse, so I snuck aboard the Polly by the stern and went down through the engine room, where I picked up my flask- and made my way to your stateroom.

The hallway door was unlocked so I went in and found the son of a bitch snoring away on your bed. I stood over him with my fists clenched, and tried to build the courage to smash his face in.

But before I could strike, he woke. Seeing me standing over him like the wrath of God must have scared him enough to sour all that booze in his gut! I could see his stomach start to heave and I knew he was going to vomit. Before he could let it out, I clamped my hands over his mouth and put my weight behind it. He only struggled a moment before his legs stopped kicking and he went still.

Afterwards, it was just like you said, William. I wiped his hair grease off my hand on the duvet but then I needed to wash them thoroughly, so I used the rest room and wrapped the used soap on a hand towel and tossed it overboard. Then I snuck back out through the engine room, over the stern, and came back to the house."

William nodded, satisfied his theories were correct.

I looked at my friend with despair. "I am so sorry, William. If not for killing Sheldon, for dragging you into it. It was unforgivable to use you like that! To betray your trust as I did. I want you to know, though I wouldn't blame you if you never trusted another word I said, that it was NOT my intention to kill him last night! I don't know just what I was going to do, but I was as surprised as anyone that I was capable of murder. I just kept thinking of my little princess and the hard road before her and I...I" My voice faded as a single tear rolled down my cheek.

I squared my shoulders and wiped my face before announcing, "I'm ready to pay the piper now, my friends. I will turn myself into the Detective and confess."

William glared at me for a moment, and then his expression softened to a more sympathetic vein. He shook his head in disgust. "Don't be a goose, Charlie. The authorities are satisfied, and Lord knows you had good reason for your action. Truth is if I had known what he had done to Arianna, I might have put him down myself. No, Charlie, we shall attend to the last details this evening and put this matter behind us forever. We shall not speak of it again."

"Only," William added, "In the future, please talk to me first. If there is anything I've learned over the years with you is there is nothing we can't fix if we work together! Had the Doctor been a bit less star struck or the Detective more interested, you might have found yourself in hot water, and over your head to boot!"

"Thank you, William. You are the best friend a man could ever have."

I turned to his man, "Ozaki? Can you forgive me?"

Ozaki bowed solemnly. "What you did, you had to for Honor. Sheldon was Baka! There is nothing to forgive." Then he half smiled and added with a twinkle in his eyes, "Only, please to not sneak aboard this boat on my watch! It makes me look bad."

I almost laughed. "I promise, Ozaki, from this day forward I will never board this ship without your permission."

"Then that's settled. Now we must make ready to sail." Will announced. "We still have some unpleasant tasks to perform. Charlie? Why don't you take Collin and go up to the house and collect your things? We shall sail in a few hours.

Collin! For a brief moment I had forgotten he was still on board! I turned around quickly and there he was, standing in the doorway of the salon, and he had heard every word!

My heart seized! My vision blurred! Not a muscle could I move, though every pore on my skin erupted and my breath froze solid in my chest. I felt like the worst father in the world at that moment.

Then my eyes focused on his face. His eyes were full of love and admiration and they shone with tears of pride. He nodded once and then rushed into my arms, hugging me like he did when he was a small child.

We never spoke of that moment, but it, and the forgiveness of my friends, gave me some measure of peace. Enough to know I could face whatever bill the devil deemed was due one day.

And I know he will collect. I firmly believe this. I don't know when or how, but in some fashion, I will pay for the taking another human life. I will try to pay with grace, but I will live in fear of it the rest of my days.

EPILOGUE

The sea was choppy, and it took a little effort to keep our feet firmly on the rolling deck when the Aunt Polly slowed to a near crawl, about three quarters of a mile off the coast of Montauk. Will, Ozaki, and I were standing around a makeshift platform that rested on one end atop the beverage cart on the gangway and the other stuck out over the railing. Sheldon, who Ozaki had sewn into a shroud along with some weights, lay on it. No one spoke as we contemplated the reasons that led us to this point.

Earlier, before we departed, I had intended to have a serious talk with Collin about his actions, but the old 'do as I say and not as I do' spiel rang hollow even in my ears, so I just had him collect his gear, without the gun which I confiscated and threw overboard. I gave him a long fierce hug, and sent him back to his Uncle Toms. I didn't want him to be around for the next act. He promised he'd stay put until William dropped me off in Sag Harbor. I decided to take him to Pop's personally and perhaps do a stint of penance myself until I got my head straight.

A sudden pitch from a bigger wave almost caused the door, that Ozaki rigged as a funeral bier, to slide out of our grip. Ozaki kept looking back and forth to William and me, as if to say 'let's get on with this, and I was looking to William. I thought he would have something to say, if not insistent on the full funeral passage, but he remained silent also. I cocked an eyebrow at him, and he just frowned and shook his head slightly.

That was enough for me, so I stepped around back and lifted the end of the door. Sheldon slid off the board to splash into the Atlantic. Without a word, Ozaki pulled the board back over the railing and went to stow it away, pausing briefly to spit where the body went in.

William and I watched as the corpse slowly sank until it was lost in the dark blue waters of the Atlantic.

Finally, I thought I could speak without breaking down, "William, I am so Sorry"

"Don't Charlie," He interrupted, cutting me off. "You made your decision and you acted on it and, right or wrong, now you have to live with it.

"Sheldon wasn't the worst person I have known to work with, but when I think of what he did and the damage he has done to Arianna's life, I'm sure he deserved his fate." He put a comforting hand on my shoulder. "Justice was served."

"Then why do I feel so bad, William. I never thought it would feel like this!"

He took his hand away and stared out at the vast expanse of water before us.

"Only the totally corrupted or psychotic feel no remorse when they take a life Charlie. There is always a balance. If you take life, you kill something of yourself. Every murder committed is ONE PART SUICIDE."

Cash, Not Compliments

December, 15, 1899

After a week's worth of hard travel by train, boat, and stage, William and I found ourselves on a platform in the sprawling train yards of St. Louis, Missouri. The rail yard abutted the holding pens for beef, still on the hoof, the stench of cattle hung like a pall in the dry heat. I couldn't decide if it was worse than the smell of the fish houses, I grew up around, but I was praying for the conductor to show up and escort us to our compartments. I was looking forward to this leg of our journey from New York on our way to Phoenix. My office girl, Rae, had managed to get us berths on a private train. A very comfortable train. Its owner was A.J. Cooper, who used it infrequently, so he leased it for charters.

It was a small train. Besides the steam engine and a coal carrier, there was a club and dining car, a double length car with four luxurious berths and a lounge area, luggage car, and the caboose. Rae assured me the compartments were more than comfortable and the food excellent. William and I had connecting cabins on the right side; mine snuggled up against the club car. It would be a relaxing finish to a long trek across the continent.

While we stood baking in the sun, they were loading three horses onto the luggage car, which had been turned into a rolling stable, complete with horse stalls and hay strewn floor. Two men carried the saddles up the ramp and disappeared from sight. The conductor was nowhere to be found.

We were still on the platform, watching the porter gather our luggage, awaiting some direction, when the hearse pulled up. Three men and a woman dressed in black disembarked and gathered their belongings. One of the men had a small valise and the widow just a clutch bag. 'Unlike most occasions,' I thought to myself 'You pack light for a funeral.'

A couple of porters came up, pushing a rolling table, and they loaded a coffin, draped with a white cloth and a bouquet of flowers. Along with the widow dutifully trailing behind, they made a solemn procession as they made their way to the back of the train. William and I doffed out hats to show respect as the coffin and its dark escort moved past us. She was swathed in black from hat pin to shoe tip with a veil so thick I couldn't tell you what color she was, much less her age or appearance. She didn't even acknowledge us as she passed by, but she jumped like a frog when the wheel of the dolly hit an uneven board causing the lid to popped up and topple the flowers. Even swaddled as she was, she was as fast as a snake and she snatched the flower crock out of midair!

The conductor came out of the caboose and he went right to the procession and led them around to the back of the train. The deceased must have been big man, or the coffin was made of lead, because it took a massive effort by all the porters and two of the brothers to get it over the handrails. They finally managed to get the coffin and its bier through the rear door and into the caboose. I chaffed at the delay, but I was happy enough to see they were going to store the body in the last car as I didn't relish the thought of sharing a space with the corpse.

When they finally got the coffin inside, William said, "Strange the coffin wasn't sealed."

I shrugged, "Some women want to look at their loved ones and tell them every last way they went wrong one more time."

"Expose him to the elements in this heat, Charlie? It's not sanitary! And where we're going it's even hotter." The look on his face deepened and he said softly, "There was something odd about that parade, if you ask me."

I didn't mind him worrying about catching a disease, but I didn't like that look on his face. I was going to nip this in the bud.

"Don't start Sherlock! We're just here to take a nice train ride, see some old friends, and start a new venture. There's no need for a detective!"

"That wasn't deduction, Charlie. I was just pointing out the obvious."

"That's what you always say and that's how it all starts." I replied, only half joking. "Well, not this trip. Tonight, we settle in, play little cards, have a nice dinner and get a good night's sleep. No haring off on one of your escapades! Understand?"

He just looked down at me and smirked, "My, my, Charlie. That was a bit melodramatic. It was only a harmless observation."

"AH!" I barked at him, pointing a warning finger at his nose. I would have given him an earful, but I was interrupted by the clopping of hooves. The men who got off the hearse with the widow were leading two horses up to the stable car. Both large in stature, one was coal black, and the second gave me goosebumps. It was a motely cold drab grey, with a white tail and mane. We had to wait even longer while the conductor opened the side door to the cattle car and pull a ramp down.

"Odd again," William remarked as we watched the procedure.

"What's odd?" I asked, and then thought better of it. "On second thought, don't answer that. I don't care. And neither should you!" I was determined to keep my night quiet.

"I am not the potter, Charlie," he said cryptically. And because he just couldn't help himself, added, "One would think that the undertaker in Phoenix would have his own team to pull the hearse."

I rolled my eyes, "And maybe they're going to bury the poor bastard themselves. So, what if they bring their own team? That grey one gave me the willies. Looked like death himself would ride her."

He shrugged, "Even if they have the team, they still need a hearse, Frohman."

"You're going to need the hearse if you start up, William. I swear."

A loud crack cut me off as the conductor slammed the sliding door shut. The conductor checked his watch then looked about until he saw us. He hustled right over, gave us his name, Carlton, and signaled the porters to follow us.

"We're honored to have you aboard this trip, Mr. Gillette, Mr. Frohman." He said as we walked us to the steps. "What brings you so far from Broadway?"

William answered, "Well, Charlie here is expanding his empire. I just came to see an old friend in a new production of 'The Three Musketeers'."

"Really now! Must be good for you to travel all this way." he said as he climbed up and opened the door to the car.

Of course, I was hoping he was right as I indeed was here to expand my production company. We had just acquired a new theater in Phoenix, and I wanted to oversee the opening night. I brought William along for moral support of the lead actor, Paul Gilmore, who had recently lost his wife. That, and the fact that William was starting to fall apart without his man servant, Ozaki, who was in Japan for a family visit. The trip had done him a world of good and he was back to his form.

So, of course, he had to stick his nose in.

"I am sorry to see there is a somber note to this trip." William said casually. "Was he a local man?"

"I'm not too sure." the conductor answered. "The names McAdam's. George McAdams. They were a last-minute booking." He looked back over his shoulder, "But you can't really make plans for something like this can you?" He smiled at his wit, "His widow and her brothers are taking him back to Phoenix for burial. I believe they said they are in the shipping business."

"They must do alright," I observed. "This funeral procession must be costing them a pretty penny. I would have shipped him regular railroad."

"Charlie!" William admonished, "Show some respect."

The conductor laughed good naturally, "Oh, that's alright, Mr. Gillette." He looked past William to me, "And you're right, Mr. Frohman, usually it cost them dearly to book a berth, storage, and five livestock."

"Usually?" William said. "Am I seeing a good deed in the making?"

The conductor grinned and lowered his voice to a conspiring whisper, "Well, when I heard from a friend that a woman was grief stricken because she had no way to get her late husband to Phoenix for burial before…well…you know…it's summer… things sour faster, if you know what I mean.

"I felt it my Christian duty to inform the train's owners who graciously offered to transport her and her brothers- along with their horses and the casket" He paused dramatically, "Free of charge!"

William nodded sagely, and then said, "That was a splendid gesture on your part, Sir. I can see a man before me that handles his great authority with heart. I admire that in a man."

"Oh well," he replied, trying to be humble but not quite catching it, "Cast your bread upon the water' and all that."

"Shipping business, eh?" William went on, "I'm surprised they reached out to you, seeing how they must have access to plenty of horses and wagons of their own."

"It's a long hard journey by road, Mr. Gillette. It would take them four times longer."

"Which would not bode well, with the casket not being sealed, I suppose, given, as you pointed out, it is the worst time of year to preserve a cadaver."

The poor man looked uncomfortable with the subject, "I expect she feels the need to talk to him some more before they put him in the ground. You know how woman are."

I gently elbowed William at that.

"I suppose I'll find out when she asks me to open the door." He said, patting a pocket on his waist coat. "Regular, it's my office and storeroom. When I'm not there, I keep it locked tighter than a Chasity belt!" He chuckled at his own wit, and then said seriously, "I learned a long time ago, it doesn't take a bad person to steal, just opportunity! Ah! Here we are." He stopped in front of a door, unusual for a train because it had no number on it or alongside it. I guess they could keep four cabins straight. "It was a pleasure chewing the fat with you gentlemen."

It always amazed me how people opened up to William. Two minutes after meeting him, they were his confidants. I'm not sure if it was his celebrity status or just his manner, but he would have made a great priest.

"This is your berth, Mr. Gillette. Mr. Frohman is next door. Marquis, your steward will be round shortly, after you've settled in and freshened up. You can pull the bell chord for him anytime, except for the hours between four and seven. Dinner will be available during those hours. At that time, Marquis and the other steward will be manning the club car. The boys wear a few different hats. I hope this won't be an inconvenience for you?"

"As long as one of them is manning the bar," I shrugged.

He chuckled again and gave William and me our keys before taking his leave. We each went into our separate rooms, where we took some time to settle in. They were the most spacious berths I had ever seen on a train, though I had been on only a few private lines before. The bed was full sized, an armoire more than held all my luggage and a table with a full bench and two chairs. I even had my own privy!

The windows showed a nice vista of the landscape we passed through, and the glass that separated my sitting area from the hallway had thick curtains for privacy. I was starting to wish this trip was longer than an afternoon and a night.

After a bit, there was a knock on our connecting doors and William joined me in my cabin, just in time to hear a discreet knock on my hall door. William opened it and gestured for the steward to come in.

"Afternoon, Mister Frohman. Mister Gillette. My name is-."

"Marquis, pleased to meet you." I put in, just to try and chummy up with him. I've always had a soft spot for those in the service industry, as that is where I got my beginnings. I was impressed he already knew our names, though I imagine the sharp ones get a heads up on the passenger lists.

He smiled politely, "Sir. I'll be your steward for the trip. If you need anything, just pull the bell chord and I'll be here to attend. Is there anything I could do for you at this moment?"

"Could we start with some ice and a deck of cards and some coffee for my friend?"

"Of course, Sir! Would you like some chips for your card game?"

"Only if you can snack on them."

"Snacks! Even better! I won't be but a moment, if you would excuse me? I'll go see what the Chef has on hand."

I sent him on his way thinking it was going to be a great stretch. William ducked back into his room and returned with a large hand mirror. He opened the metal stand on the back and jammed it into the wainscoting next to the glass panels that separated my compartment from the hallway. He made a few adjustments and pulled back the curtain far enough to expose it. Then he stepped over and sat on the bench across from me, facing the back of the train. He looked at his handiwork and bobbed his head for different angles to get a mirrored view up the hallway.

"William, could you please just tell me what you're doing without my having to ask!" In reality, I knew what he was doing. He pulls this same trick on the *Aunt Polly*, usually when he has guests. By strategically placing mirrors, he could see what was happening around corners or down hallways. Then he could be ready and poised to greet guests or make a grand entrance. What I couldn't understand is why he was doing it now!

"I just like to see who's coming and going," he replied, turning his attention back to me.

"Why? You don't know anybody on this train! You're just being nosy."

"No, I simply like to be cognizant of my surroundings, Charlie."

"You're on a train heading into the dessert, Will! You're surrounded by sand and cactus! Why bother?"

With his patented smug grin, he reached over to open my travel kit. He ignored my flask and pulled out a glass. He wiped out the glass with his handkerchief quickly and set it in front of me. Before I could open my mouth, there was a knock on the door and a voice called out. "Steward, Sir!"

William waggled his eyebrows and called out, "Come in, please!"

A rolling cart came through the door with Marquis pushing it. "Oh, I see I've kept you waiting, Mr. Frohman! Here you are sir." He took a small bowl of ice chips, with a set of tongs and set it next to me. Then he put a coaster under my glass. Straightening up, he waited for me to choose a bottle from the array on his cart. As we were west of the Mississippi, I chose the whiskey

"Shall I pour for you?"

I nodded and he quickly had the amber gold splashing in my glass, which I savored as he served William his coffee. Then he reached back, under the cart's linen and produced a generous sized platter, filled with what my Doctor's people would call 'noshes'. Small pieces of toast and crackers topped with various meats and cheeses, meatballs and chunks of sausage with picks in them and even a small pile of what looked to be chilled gulf shrimp. I was in heaven at last.

He set us up with utensils, napkins, and a few condiments. His hands moved back and forth from the cart to our table like a seasoned card dealer. He finished and looked the scene over quickly and nodded his head.

"Gentlemen. Unless there is something else you need?"

I was about to tip him and send him on his way when William suddenly spoke up, "My friend and I are very sorry to hear about George McAdams. How is the widow holding up?"

Marquis looked uncomfortable. "I wouldn't know, sir. I have not met the lady."

"Well, what I meant was, how did she seem when you introduced yourself?"

The poor man started to squirm. William had to realize his question was crossing the lines of discretion that a steward was held to. "I...I never met the lady, sir. They told me through the door they didn't want to be disturbed."

William nodded, "Grief stricken, I'm sure. And what of our other traveling companions?"

"Others, Sir? Are there more in your party?"

William chortled, "No, no. I was asking who was in the last berth. Your conductor said that you had a full train and there are four compartments, are there not?"

The smile slipped off the steward's face and he replied stonily, "I can't help you there, sir. That side is Wilsons --the other steward. He tends his and I tend mine. I don't know anything about those folks. I'm sure you'll see them at dinner, though."

"Perhaps," William replied, and then lit a cigarette.

"I think you tend your side just fine, Marquis," I pronounced as my eyes charted a course of gluttony through the platter of food. I took out my travel roll and peeled off a twenty to hand the porter. His eyes bugged out of his head, "Thank you, sir!" The bill disappeared into his vest pocket like I might not realize what I gave him.

I pointed at the pocket and shook my head, "That's for the cook," I instructed. Then I pulled out a fifty and laid it in his hand. "That's for you."

You could have tucked his smile into his ears as he sputtered and gushed his gratitude while backing out of the room. The door closed behind him and we could hear him whistling up the corridor.

William shook his head and smiled. "I will never understand your need to be so extravagant. You know, a kind word, just a little praise, is just as good as money and they'll respect you all the more for it."

"Bull dinkers!" I replied, remembering a quote from a Greek restaurant owner we knew,
"It's cash –not compliments!"

I was just pouring my third drink when I got fed up. Until then, it had been an enjoyable few hours. The terrain was flat, and the ride was smooth. The snacks were delicious, and we spent the time playing cards and gossiping about folks in the business. Beating hearts in changing hands fueled most of our conversation.

I noticed that William's attention was waning. I knew this because I was thrashing him soundly and he was generally an excellent card player. Then I noticed his eyes were almost constantly going to the mirror he planted. I couldn't see what he was so absorbed in William had the eyesight of an eagle and all I could make out were blurry movements in the glass and I was feeling left out.

Finally, after waiting more than a minute for him to discard while he fixated on the mirror, I put my fingers in the corners of my mouth and whistled loudly.

Startled, his focus snapped back on me. "What?"

"What is distracting you? You're playing like a blind man paints portrait!"

He had the grace to look a bit embarrassed. "Am I? Sorry." His eyes went back to the mirror, "There's been a lot of activity out there."

He set his cards down and lit a cigarette. "There are some odd things going on aboard this train. There are Pinkerton men sharing a compartment across the hall."

"Jesus Christ!" I spat out then caught myself. William's face went stern and he drew in a long scolding breath. I threw my hands up and quickly went on before he could preach, "Sorry! Excuse me ...I overreacted...I'll say a few Hail Mary's before I go to bed. I thought we agreed we wouldn't get involved in anything on this trip."

He looked at me like I was speaking Chinese. "My word, Charles! Why so melodramatic? You act like all I do is look for trouble, when all I did was made few simple observations."

I already told him what I thought of his 'observations', so I just took a pull off my drink and stared back at him.

"Well, aren't you at least curious as to why two sets of Pinkerton agents are guarding a woman across the aisle from us?" he asked with his most innocent voice.

It was the dog and the bone all over. I sighed and polished off my glass in one long drought. I poured myself another and folded my hands on the table in front of me. "Why do you think they're Pinkies guarding someone?"

"That's the spirit, Frohman," he said with that familiar gleam in his eye. "They are certainly Pinkerton men. Ah! Here comes one now, the senior agent I believe." He got up and cracked the door, before telling me, "Listen carefully."

I held my breath and closed my eyes, amplifying the rapping noises I heard. Two short raps, a pause, and then another rap.

William gently closed the door, "Obviously a signal," he commented as he took his seat.

"I have observed three different men enter or leave that compartment. All are wearing stock boots, suits off the rack, and the new .40 caliber Colts in Docker clutches, along with boot knives and blackjacks. Ruffians of a sort, who could hardly put out the money for these accommodations."

"Or they could just be U. S. Marshalls transporting a prisoner. You know Will, not every lawman wears a ten-gallon hat and has a six-shooter strapped to his thigh!"

He shrugged, looking at me blandly, "Yet I believe they still wear badges to identify themselves Frohman. These men are guarding someone. A woman is in some peril of one sort or another, I'm sure of it!"

"Now there's a Woman?" I asked, putting my head in my hands. "Have you seen this woman?"

"No, but we both heard what the Porter said. He said he 'knew nothing' about those 'folks', so not just men. The fact that he claimed the opposite side was Wilsons responsibility yet he made a call on the funeral party so that tell us he is holding back."

"None of that makes for a damsel in distress," I said sarcastically. "You need to relax. I wish you drank."

"I did not need alcohol to see the other steward deliver a tea service and a set of bath towels, Frohman. Or do you think those ruffians are having tea before they freshen up for dinner?"

I just stared at him. There it was again.

Frohman.

I planted my elbows on the table and put my head in my hands. In a clipped, measured tone, I said. "Please just knock it off, Sherlock! We're only on this train for another sixteen hours, and whatever you THINK might be going on is none of our business. Let's just have a nice dinner and get a good night's sleep and we'll be in Phoenix soon."

He sighed and, to my dismay, looked sadly resigned when he said, "That would delight me also, Frohman. Yet, I fear there is a dangerous convergence in the offing." He went back to staring at his mirror.

I dropped one hand to the table and propped up my chin with the other. "What the hell is wrong with you?"

I was afraid I had offended him, when he didn't reply and just continued to stare at his mirror. I was going to try and jolly him out of his anger, but I realized as I watched him that he had fallen into one of his concentration trances. I could open the window and throw myself out and he wouldn't notice. Something out there had his attention, for sure!

Instead, I reached for a newspaper that was tucked into a rack and plucked out a 'Phoenix Times'. I selected a lemon tart from the dessert plate and perused the rag. The national and International news I skipped, as I had already read it this morning at the hotel. Obituaries too, because I didn't know anyone out there-except ole' George McAdam's and I was living his obituary!

I went right to the Art's pages as I needed to see what kind of competition my opening had around town. All I could find was a couple of exhibitions in the area, but nothing that would steal my thunder. My jaw dropped when I noticed a small column on the Social page. It reported that a *Miss Catherine Cyr was returning to her family on college break for the season and was expected sometime tomorrow. Her father was the wealthiest man in the mid-west with holdings in textile, oil, and the railroads.*

Currently he was embroiled in a clash with union agitators. From the talk I had heard at the club over the last few months, there had been atrocities on both sides. The unionists were constantly bombing, or assassinating Cyr's management and the breakers were giving back mass beatings and even a few hangings. It was an ugly situation and bad for business everywhere.

I scrunched the paper between my hands and smashed it into the table. I didn't even realize I spoke the vulgarity I was thinking, out loud. William looked at me sharply and then straightened out the paper and folded it so the column was displayed.

William read it over quickly and tossed it back on the table. "And do you think that the lady in our mystery cabin is this young woman?"

I shrugged, "Could be. If you're right about the pinkies.

243

"John Cyr's daughter would need to travel in secret and with an several well trained and armed escorts. If those Union vultures got a hold of her, there'd be no end to their mischief or demands!"

"I take it you are not a Union man."

I crossed my arms, "There is no need for them, Will! This is America. If you work hard, you will make a better life for yourself! Simple as that. Unions don't benefit those who do the work, they benefit the Union leaders who live a cushy life off the dues they collect and the money they extort from us!" I was passionate on the subject, but soon realized my words would do nothing to distract William from his snooping.

William gave me his patented smirk and said, "I shall leave the politics to you, Frohman, and my brother George, the esteemed Senator. For myself, I care not one whit. It is the intrigue it generates a spark in my reasoning!"

That was three 'Frohman's' in a row, so whatever he thought, he was thinking like a detective. I had half a mind to jump up and slap him out of it, but past experiences had shown that it was always justified. So, I just decided to just sit back, with dread, and see what developed. I poured another and drank it straight down.

"Well, you don't want to argue about Unions and you obviously aren't in a frame of mind for cards, so what would you like to do now?"

Before he could answer, something in the mirror caught his eye and I noticed three shadows through the curtains cross in front of the hallway windows.

He swung his head back to face me and grinned, "I think we should freshen up, and then proceed to the dining car. You could have a civilized drink and we could get our dinner. What do you say?"

I was hoping to see he was shucking his Sherlock cap and cape and I joked, "Gee, William, I don't know. I just ate all those canapés. And what's wrong with my drink here?"

He laughed, "As if you could not find room for more food and you are going to want the rest of that bottle for a nightcap. That would have been insulting, if not true. I told him I'd meet him in the hall in two minutes.

The dining car was opulent with an oriental rug so thick it curled around the soles of your shoes and left footprints. Rich crushed velvet lined the walls and polished woodwork. Everything was first class from the crystal sconces that lit the room to the gleaming silverware on the tables. There were three tables and a small bar with six seats as fancy as any place in New York. Old man Cyr knew how to spend his money!

The man behind the bar gave us a huge smile. He must have been the fabled Wilson, I presumed, as he served a beer to the lone man at the six-stool bar. The man had a plate of food and a newspaper and must have been one of men William had branded as 'pinkies' for the cheap suit he was wearing.

Two more men were seated at one of the only two tables in the room. They were two of the three we saw get off the hearse, but the widow herself was seated between them. Marquis was just serving their dinners off a cart. He lifted the silver dome off the lady's dish and asked her a question, but her brothers shooed him away before she could speak a word in reply. I hope she got what she ordered!

Marquis made a face and a rude gesture as soon as his back was to them, as he put the lids on his cart. William and I saw the whole thing and I could not help but bark a short laugh. Marquis looked up in horror, his eyes squeezed shut and he grimaced, but Will gave him a big wink when he finally opened his eyes, and he grinned. He pushed the cart to the bar then swept across the room to greet us.

"So, you pulled waiter duty tonight," I observed.

"Yes, Sir. I take off my jacket and put on this long apron and now I'm a different man."

William laughed along with him, "I can empathize, Marquis. I do the same thing nearly every night!"

William looked around the room, then feigned surprise. Stopping in his tracks, he said to Marquis, "Before you seat us, I would like to give the widow my condolences."

"Of course, Sir. I'll wait right here for you."

I was sober enough to wonder what William was up to and just sipped my drink and then followed him blindly over to the table. We approached the widow from her left side, but I was set back on my heels when the two brothers jumped up and barred our way. I could swear that one of them even reached for a side arm that wasn't there.

"What do you Gentlemen want?" One asked brusquely.

William doffed his hat and I followed suit. "Please forgive us if we are forward Gentlemen. My name is William Gillette, and this is my friend, Mr. Frohman. We just wished to extend our condolences to the Widow McAdam's."

Usually, on the rare occasions that William tossed his name out, it was met with a lot of wide-eyed admiration and fawning. I was afraid we'd be invited to sit, and I really didn't want to break bread with such bleak company.

The one who spoke before gave us a flinty stare. "My sister," he gestured towards the seated woman and his hand hit and empty glass. It flipped off the table, but the Widow slapped her legs together and it bounced off her thighs, where she snatched it out of the air. She set it back on the table and her brother went on.

"My sister is indisposed, Gentlemen. She wishes to be undisturbed while she mourns." That was all he said as the widow stared straight ahead as if we weren't there. The thick veil over her face moved with her breath , but not a sound came out.

"We'd be obliged if you would respect our privacy." Said the other.

"Of course," William replied. "Forgive us for the intrusion."

I did a turn around and Will was right on my heels as he walked back to Marquis with as much dignity as we could muster. I was thinking that William might be smarting a little more than me. I'm not sure if he'd ever been so curtly rejected, and never in my presence.

"Don't let it bother you Will," I advised him, "Sometimes trying to be kind is a waste of time."

"Bother me, Frohman? Au contrar'! It was thrilling. Those two minutes gave us three points to ponder. The falling wine glass itself was worth the rudeness!"

I stopped and cocked my head at him. "What are you talking about? The ill-mannered clod knocked the glass over and the sister caught it! Quick hands, but so what?"

He shook his head, "Remember your Twain, Frohman."

Marquis was holding a chair out for me and I decided I needed a drink more than another bit of his cryptic nonsense. Marquis was quick with the drinks and Wilson was a slow pourer. I was content to look about the room, while William engaged Marquis to give him a local geography lesson and, of course, discuss the trains speed and pulling capabilities. Marquis even went as far as to get him a map that showed the railway's path through this barren land. William was always enthusiastic about trains and railroads.

Trying not to be obvious, I watched the funeral table for a bit. Bright white napkins were spread out on their chest to protect their black suits. They tucked away the food like cowboys on the range. Even the Widow. She didn't even bother to lift her veil. she just hung her head over the plate and let the veil hang down, so her gloved hand had a straight shot to propel her fork, which she held like a knife, from the plate to her mouth. I was glad the veil still hid her features as she must have looked like a cow doing double time on cud.

My eyes drifted over to the single man at the bar and, after a few minutes of observation, I decided that William may indeed be right. He was an older man, with a grey moustache that gave him a look of hard authority, and big hands that looked like they could back it up. I noticed his eyes never stopped moving about the room and he kept his torso positioned in a way that would facilitate his reaching for a sidearm. I had used the Pinkerton agency a few times and this guy came right out of the mold.

Marquis went off to check on our dinners and I turned to my friend, "Why that talk with Marquis about the real estate around here? Planning on buying a sand farm or something?"

He ignored my jibe. "I am just familiarizing myself with the area, Frohman. Forewarned is forearmed."

I raised my glass in a toast. "You were right, William. That man at the bar is more than likely a Pinkerton. Or

248

some other form of agent." I set my glass down and leaned forward. "Do you really think their guarding someone?"

"It seems the likeliest scenario, fitting together the facts as we know them. Our porter just left with a cart carrying three dinners. I assume for the other two Pinkerton's and their charge."

Still hoping to head off an incident, I pointed out, "Interesting, but really not any business of ours. We should let them do their job in peace. I'm sure they're up for it."

"One would hope so, Frohman, for I fear that their mettle will be put to the test soon."

"Soon, as in -- we should go back to our compartment and eat there -- soon?"

"As in, you should ask that man at the bar to join us."

I should have never had five drinks before I ate, but that and my curiosity got the better part of me again. "Why would I do that? Especially if he's a Pinkie?"

He rolled his eyes slightly, "The man at the bar is a senior agent."

I didn't bother to ask him how he knew that. He would have just rubbed my face in it, so I waved Wilson over instead. "Could you do me a favor?" I took a card out and handed it to him, "Give this to the gentleman at your bar and ask him to join us. Then bring us a round when you get a chance."

"Of course, Sir!"

I watched the Pinkie look us over while I was talking to the waiter. When the waiter handed him the card, he glanced at it and shoved it into his jacket. He grabbed his beer off the bar and slid off the stool. I was feeling a bit smug as he sauntered over. Nice to see someone outside our business jump when they recognize my name.

William and I both stood to greet him, but it wasn't my hand he took.

"Mr. Gillette! I'm honored. My name is Heinz. Peter Heinz."

He was a handsome man, in a weather-beaten sort of way a man gets in his fifties, of a slightly better than average build and taller than me but shorter than William. His grip was firm, his hands rough and scarred, and his eyes bored right into mine as if he was searching. I found I didn't like his scrutiny.

I wasn't crazy about his accessories either. Besides a round medallion and a wire fish hanging off his watch fob, the only other item of apparel to grace him was a strange necktie. It looked like a bow tie, left loose, and starched like that. I thought it one of those 'cowboy ties' I had seen in magazines and such, but it was much too thick for that.

"Excellent! You know who I am. That should facilitate matters." Will turned and nodded at me. "This is my friend, Charles Frohman. Please sit down."

Peter Heinz seemed hesitant, but he was obviously a fan of Will's and he didn't want to pass up the chance. When we were settled in our seats, he took the last pull off his beer and looked to me, "So, what do you do, Mr. Frohman? And to what do I owe this invitation?"

"I'm a stage producer," I replied. "I invited you over because William here wanted to talk to a Pinkie."

He shook his head and started to rise, "I don't know if this is some kind of joke or how much hooch you've put away, but-."

"Come now Mr. Heinz," William said sharply, causing Heinz to pause in midrise, "You are senior investigator with the Pinkerton Agency. You are based in Baltimore. You fought for the South in the Great War, a sailor.

Gunner's mate. You are recently widowed. My condolences."

Even blurry eyed as I was, I snapped at his reaction. He straightened up and took a step back with his hand going to the inside of his jacket. I could clearly see the letters on the butt of a large caliber pistol in a Docker's clutch rig.

In a low menacing voice, he snarled, "How could you know all that?"

I had heard that so many times before, I couldn't help myself and I laughed out loud. The two of them looked at me like I just broke wind in a tiny room.

"Oh, believe me! He knows! You may as well sit down and have another beer, Heinz. He'll be happy to tell you all about it!" Then I added, under my breath, "and then some!"

Heinz slowly lower his body back into the chair but stayed back from the table and his right hand rested on his left side. He just cocked his head as if to indicate he was listening. Will smiled at his dramatics and nodded.

"That you are a senior Agent is obvious. In the Pinkerton Agency, a good agent dies, quits, or gets promoted."

"Who says I'm one of Alan's boys, in the first place?"

"Do not waste our time, Mr. Heinz! That big pistol you mare flashing in that Docker's Clutch bears Alan Pinkerton's famous EYE logo engraved on the grip. I'm sure your name is somewhere on there also! As all longtime employees are gifted by the company. Now, shall I go on?"

"Please do."

"I noted that you were based in Baltimore because of one of the ornaments on your fob. You are a long-standing Odd Fellow, are you not?"

William spoke to me, but I knew it was for Heinz's benefit, and explained, "Oddfellows, dear Frohman, are a longstanding fraternal order, founded in Baltimore in 1819, with a proud tradition. There are thousands of chapters across the country and more opening every day! When each chapter opens, it issues a commemorative medallion with its number on it. The number on Mr. Heinz's is 1."

Heinz let that sink in as he stared at William, who pretended not to notice. Will just carried on,

"Your tie, or rather the way you tie it, shows your ties to the Confederate Navy and tells us you were more than a swab. That you were a gunner's mate is obvious from the scars on you left hand, the hand you would have held the taper in as you lit the cannon.

Last and I apologize for speaking of such a personal matter, but your ring finger shows signs that you, until recently, wore a wedding ring. Since you display a symbol of the Catholic Church as a sign of your faith, divorce would not be an option, so I presume you lost your wife recently. Again, my condolences."

William sat back all smug and waited for the pinkie to react. After a long pause, he smiled, "You presume too much, Sir."

William was abashed, "Please, forgive my intrusion into such a personal matter. I was only-."

Heinz held up a hand and stopped him mid-sentence, "I left my ring at home, with the old battle axe, in Baltimore to be resized." He laughed and looked at me, "Though I think I like Mr. Gillette's version just as well!"

"Only two for three, William, you're slipping." I couldn't help ribbing him. He was so rarely off on his 'observations'.

"Impressive, none-the-less," Heinz said. He gave Will a long look. "I had heard...whispers among the theatre crowd about your abilities, Mr. Gillette. Your first two conclusions were right on the mark and the third would be an easy mistake for a bachelor. Very sharp indeed, sir."

Before William could reply, the waiter came with our drinks. Of course, no one reached into their pockets, so, I slipped him another bill.

"Showing off aside, is there some sort of point you're trying to make?"

William looked at Heinz intently and said in a low voice, "My little demonstration in deduction was not meant to impress a man of your experience, Mr. Heinz. I merely wanted to be sure you would take me seriously and if you will hear me out, I believe we can nip an unpleasant incident in the bud!"

Alarm whistles going off in my head, I put my drink down and hissed, "What the hell are you going on about, William? That's the third or fourth time you forecasted doom. I'm about to go lock myself in my privy!"

William gave me a long level look and countered, "This is serious, Frohman. I need you to be quiet and be patient."

He could tell by my face that I wasn't happy about it, but he knew I would back him all the way. It was fish or cut bait time again. Heinz was looking pole axed and he turned to me for an explanation. "Why, exactly, did you invite me over?"

I shrugged and leaned in closer to say softly, "Probably something to do with the woman you three are guarding." Abrupt, I'll give you, but William was the wily one. "Miss Cyr -- if I'm not mistaken."

Heinz began to sputter, "I don't know what or how you know...never mind --you know." He glared at us. "You gentlemen have put me in a difficult position."

He looked so put out I wasn't sure whether he was going to draw on us or just give us a warning to mind our own business at that point, but Marquis came with a fresh beer for him. Heinz was a professional, I'll give you that. He managed to get control of himself and he asked calmly, "And just what sort of 'unpleasant incident' have you conjured up in your mind, sir?"

William didn't care for that kind of flippant tone. "I imagine from whatever you are being paid to guard against. Kidnapping comes to the front of my mind, though I suppose assassination cannot be ruled out. Come now, Heinz. Save your sarcasm and snide tone and hear me out!"

Now it was Heinz's turn. "Listen here, Gillette-."

"Nooo, Nooo," I crooned, cutting him off. He turned his head to look at me and I locked eyes with him. "I advise you to heed his advice, Heinz. When William says it's going to rain, a smart man pulls out his goulashes."

Heinz just stared at me for a moment, but I guess I was convincing enough because he stayed in his seat. We all fell silent for a bit as Marquis brought over our dinner. He even brought me a back-up drink, bless his heart. As soon as he was out of earshot, Heinz quietly asked William.

"Just who do you think is going to attempt something like that against three armed men and a train going at full bore in the dead of the night? Indians? The widow and her unarmed brothers? Or should I be slapping iron on you boys? Mr. Gillette, there is nothing that could happen between here and Phoenix. Not tonight." He chortled and took another long pull on his beer. "Maybe in one of your plays, but not in real life!"

I had to take my eyes off the beautiful mixed grill on the plate before me and look up at that. I knew that was just the kind of remark that set William off. I could see him drawing breath to reply, but a commotion on the other side of the room staved off the reply. The Widow and her party were getting up to leave.

As soon as the bigger brother was on his feet, he snapped his fingers at Marquis's back and barked, "You Boy! Go find the conductor and tell him my sister wishes to see her husband before we retire."

Marquis stiffened visibly, but he had a smile on his kisser when he turned around and nodded. He immediately headed for the door and went out, gritting his teeth.

William's eyes flickered from them, to the Pinkie, and then to his plate as he said quietly, "I suggest you observe them as they leave, Senior Agent Heinz. It may be your last chance." He shrugged, "I have made my offer to assist and you can do what you will with it."

I thought that a bit dramatic, even for my friend, but it struck a chord with Heinz. He nodded and turned in his seat, making a show of stretching his legs. William kept his eyes on his dinner as they walked past our table to the door. Single file, the widow between her brothers, they never looked left or right. I tried to look as if I wasn't, but Heinz was openly watching them, his eyes going up and down each one.

To me, they looked a bit motely. The black suits the men wore, obviously bought when their brother-in-law died, they were so ill fitting. The smaller man's neck was bulging over his collar so much; I wondered how he could even swallow. They compounded the sloppy attire by wearing worn, dirty, cowboy boots with them.

The widow was also a tad unkempt, but that was understandable in her state. Her skirt, her bodice, and even her gloves weren't lined up at the seams. She was so shrouded in lace and veil; she looked more like a leper than a grieving wife.

I felt bad for her as she tried to keep pace with her brothers, taking mincing steps while they strode along. At one point, just as she passed us by, she stumbled on the flowing skirt and I caught a glimpse of one unadorned ear. It was good to know there was really some flesh under all that.

Marquis came back just as they reached the door, causing them to pause for a moment as he sidled past and stepped back into the car. He stepped aside and made a gesture towards the hallway. "The conductor is waiting for you in the rear, Sir."

The barest of nods was all he received before they marched out. Marquis shut the door behind them and grimaced.

"Did anything strike you as odd?" William asked Heinz.

Heinz snorted, "I find this whole scenario odd." He shook his head and took another swig. "If it will ease your mind, Mr. Gillette, know that I already looked them folks over before you and Frohman even got here.

I'll admit they're a bit rough around the edges. No doubt, in my mind, that they'd be riding coach on a regular line. They are socially ill mannered as you witnessed at their table and they eat like they just got out of prison." Heinz took a breath.

"But the only oddity that comes to mind is the boots they wore."

William brightened right up, "AH! Yes, the boots. What are your thoughts."

He shrugged, "Nothing really. I just noticed how deep their spurs had worn into the heels. They spend a lot of time in the saddle. Though I suppose owning shipping businesses would be natural for a couple of saddle tramps."

William looked a bit deflated. "Did you not wonder why they changed into working boots before dinner? They were not wearing them when they arrived on this train."

I took that one, "Because they are comfortable to them, Will. Store bought shoes, like the ones they most likely bought with the suits; take a long time to break in."

"Then tell me Frohman, where did they get the boots from? They had but one small valise between them and no other luggage we saw."

He was absolutely right but it made no sense in my fuddled state. "They must have had them somewhere!"

"Precisely Frohman! A trojan horse, perhaps?"

I was lost then so I just speared a hunk of meat off my plate and stuffed it in my mouth. Better to chew that sound stupid.

William turned back to Heinz. "Aside from the boots, I take it you overlooked the lack of earrings and the Widow's bodice buttoned up the right side---."

"LEFT!" I cried out, around a mouthful, happy to correct William for once. I swallowed. "The woman's buttons were on the left, William."

He beamed at me, "Frohman! You are on quite the streak tonight. Bravo!"

Heinz was not amused, "Bad choices in footwear and a lack of social graces don't make them desperados, Mr. Gillette." He shook his head sadly, "I think you are just

257

letting your imagination run a little wild." He held up his hands in a 'hold up' manner. "It's more than understandable, seeing how you make your living."

William slapped his silverware down on the table hard enough to make his plate jump. He ripped the napkin from his collar and stood. Heinz jumped up to face him. I sighed and rose also.

"You still refuse to see," Will said stonily, "I am warning you now sir. Beware the Trojan Horse! In thirty minutes or so, this train will slow when it climbs the foothills. It would be the ideal place to make one's escape."

Of course, he didn't elaborate. Instead, he cried out, "Marquis, stop a moment, if you would be so kind?"

We turned to see Marquis with a cart he got in the kitchen and was about to clear the rest of the plates from the Widow's table.

William walked over to him. "Could you just give us a moment before you clear? There is something my friend needs to see."

He was perplexed but he just nodded and stepped back. Everyone in the room was staring at us as we got up and joined William. Will picked up the chairs and set them aside then he reached out with his long arms and carefully picked the table up and carried it back a few feet.

"Could you raise the lights please?" Marquis quickly adjusted three nearby sconces which bathed the floor with light.

Heinz got down on one knee and looked carefully, running his hand lightly over the rugs surface. The plush carpet had three distinct sets of boot prints. Even if I had been sober, that wouldn't have made sense. Our Pinkerton had the same reaction.

Heinz leapt to his feet. He stared off into space for a moment then he saw the light.

William and Heinz exchanged looks.

"Damn it!" Heinz snarled and bolted out the door.

"Heinz!" William cried after him, but the agent was already halfway down the sleeper car.

"Quickly Frohman, after him. We may not have a moment to lose."

"No!" I said forcibly. "I'm not taking another step until I know what you've gotten us into this time!" I snarled as I held up a warning finger. "And don't you dare answer my questions with another question! Tell me straight or leave me to my drinking!"

William grimaced and snarled a reply, "Oh, very well, Frohman. The reason there are no marks from a lady's shoe is there is no lady! Under all that black material is another man!"

"What? But why?" I stopped, as I had an idea, "My word! Then they must be the kidnappers you've been warning about! The funeral was just a ruse to get on the train!"

"Exactly! I am sure that, when we reach the point in the line where the train slows on its uphill leg, they will attempt to kidnap Miss Cyr and disembark the train. If they know the country, I imagine they could avoid capture for a very long time."

"But they only brought two horses," I pointed out." There are four of them- and the girl when they make their move."

"You are forgetting the three horses the Pinkertons brought along."

I was skeptical, "How would they know there would be enough horses to steal? They got here after the Pinkies."

He snorted, "Perhaps our Conductor is not as charitable as we were led to believe -- or trustworthy."

It was still hard to put it all together in my head, "O.K., so they have enough mounts. What about the saddles and supplies? Or for that matter-weapons? Those pinkies aren't about to give her up without a fight." I let the thought trail off as I remembered something William had said just a short while before. "The Trojan Horse! The casket! If there's no widow -- then there's no body!

They must have smuggled everything they needed in the empty casket! That's why it wasn't sealed and so damned heavy!"

"Bravo, Frohman, correct on all counts! Now we need to plan our next move."

"Next move? I'll tell you what our next move is -- we go back to our cabin and lock ourselves in until we reach Phoenix! We're not about to face down four armed outlaws. Are you insane?"

"No, but I am not naïve either! Do you really think they will leave any witnesses alive?" He bolted for the door before I could answer.

I must have had enough liquid courage, because I followed him out like a senseless puppy dog.

We burst into the sleeper car and found the hallway empty, but the far door that led to the cattle car was swinging free. William, a few steps ahead of me suddenly stopped and rapped on the first left cabin door. Two knocks. Pause. Another.

The door swung open and found a startled man, who quick as a snake, drew two pistols, one pointed at Will's and one at my face! A cringing young woman leaned forward in a chair and poked her head around her protector's hip. Her eyes went wide and, luckily before anyone pulled a trigger, squealed, "William Gillette!"

Her guardians were taken back by her outburst and William used the void to snap out a quick warning.

"Heinz sent us. There is an imminent danger. Guard her well while Heinz checks in with your other man!" Abruptly, he started back down the hallway, leaving both guns trained on me. I tipped my hat to the young lady and ran after him.

The Pinkerton stepped out into the hallway and looked about, calling out to our backs, "What danger? And who the hell are you?"

William didn't even turn around, "Get back inside and do your duty!"

We almost made it to the open door on the other end, when William stopped suddenly and peered at the corner of the window of the next cabin down- the one the widow's party was in. I nearly bowled into him as he pointed to a smear on the inside of the glass. I stepped up for a closer look and recognized it immediately. It was blood.

William knocked on the door and I nearly wet myself, thinking what we would do if they answered. But there was no movement inside and William threw his shoulder against it. Luckily, the locks were made for privacy and not security as it popped open.

The first thing we saw when we stepped into the compartment was a man sprawled out on the table. He was lying flat, with both arms outstretched at his sides and his calves hanging off the edge closest to the door. He looked like a crucifix that fell over. Only all the blood was on his neck and chest. Somebody had slit Conductor Carlton's throat. The booze started churning in my stomach.

"What the hell is going on, Will?"

He pointed to the dead conductor's vest pocket and I saw the lining was pulled out. Someone had taken his keys. "Apparently, there is no honor among thieves. We must warn Heinz! They must already be in the caboose!"

"What we must do is report this to someone and then barricade ourselves in our compartments until we reach civilization!" Someone had to be the voice of reason, "That man is dead, Will! He was murdered in cold blood!"

"There is no time! We must go warn Heinz," and to my utter desperation, he turned and sped out of the room.

He was already to the cattle car before I managed to step out into the rushing air between cars. Even with the handrails and grated walkway, it was unnerving to cross from one car to another on a speeding train while you are bouncing up and down and being jostled from side to side. You can see the rails rushing underneath in perfect timing. The fading light wasn't helping either. I finally managed to open the door to the stable car.

"Shut the door and get down Frohman!" I heard William hiss from the dim recesses. I did as he instructed. Heinz was with him and they were both on one knee over an inert figure. I got close enough to see it was the other Pinkerton man in the club car and he, too had a slit throat!

"Oh, God damn it!" I said slowly. I could feel William bristle, but he was smart enough to keep his mouth shut this once. Suddenly, the door I just came in swung open behind us and there, silhouetted in the dusk stood Marquis.

"Who's there? Here now, what are you gentlemen doing?" It was apparent he hadn't noticed the body on the floor behind us.

Heinz dropped his head in disgust and William grabbed me by the arm, "Don't let him leave, Frohman. We may need his expertise!"

"Marquis, it's me, Charles Frohman. Mr. Gillette and Mr. Heinz are here too. There is a problem and we need your help!"

"Help with what, Mr. Frohman?"

"Just shut the door and come over please." Now I would see what my fifty would buy me, "And stay low. You mustn't be seen."

I was pleased to see him do exactly what I asked but it took a bit more to keep him from jack rabbiting when he got close enough to see the body.

With his black pants and jacket, white shirt and gloves, and a natural blackface he looked just like a thousand vaudeville acts I have seen. His eyes were as wide as coffee saucers and his nose flared out.

"Lord! What has happened?"

I had to grab him by the forearm to keep him from getting up and bolting, and he calmed down quickly. "Gentlemen, I should go and get the conductor, shouldn't I?"

I snorted, "Fat lot of good that'll do you."

"What do you mean by that?" Heinz demanded. I just stared back at him, not wanting to speak out of turn and say too much. Heinz switched to William, "What does he mean by that? What the hell is happening exactly, Gillette? What do you have to do with all this?"

William opened his mouth to reply, but I rode right in, "If I have this straight, we don't have time for one of Will's explanations, so listen up. Someone caught wind of your plans to escort the wealthy young lady home to Phoenix and they set the whole funeral up as a red herring to get themselves on the train. Only, the widow is no woman, see? He's another one of the gang, dressed like a widow. They filled the casket with supplies and guns and when the train is in the right place, they plan to kill us all and take the girl off the train." Marquis gasp with wide eyes. I continued.

"Their plan was simple. They would use their harmless appearance to surprise the Pinkertons and grab the girl, killing anyone who got in their way. Having already saddled the horses, they could just pull the emergency stop and just ride off into the foothills. It would be a long time before anyone got back out here to set a pursuit." I paused and then added. "We don't know exactly why they killed the conductor."

"He's dead?"

"I'm afraid so, Marquis," William said, "We found him in the widow's compartment. He was killed the same way as this man. The conductor, because he knew who they really were and the agent because he became suspicious and followed them.

The widow's outfit would allow him to get close, and it had to be close because your man didn't even go for his weapon." He pointed at the pistol that still sat snugly in its holster.

"I imagine by now there arming themselves in the caboose and when they are ready, they'll head back toward us!"

Heinz pulled out his pistol, then reached down and took the dead man's also. "Are either of you gentlemen armed?"

"I do not think a gun fight is our best option," William observed, and I could have kissed him for that, "I would prefer a more simple solution."

"Better be quick about it then. Those three will be back real fast, and heavily armed. We're the only ones

264

between them and their horses. That is, if the horses don't get us first!"

It was then I noticed the agitation in the animals. The scent of blood and the frenzied movements by had them in a lather. I was surprised that I hadn't noticed the danger earlier, but perhaps my years backstage had taught me to tune out most of the mayhem around me. Their bucking and rearing had started to break the wood of thier stalls and soon they would be running amok. I was petrified at what five berserk beasts would do to us in this confined space. "Maybe you should shoot the horses first!" I suggested to the Pinkie.

The man just shook his head in disgust at me and flattened himself against the front of the rear most stall and raised both pistols like he was about to have a duel.

William ignored the whole conversation, so deep in thought he could have been a statue. Suddenly, he came back to us.

He took Marquis by the arm and pulled him close enough to whisper a question I couldn't quite catch. Nor could I hear the answer over the whinnying of the horses. He took the map Marquis had given him earlier, out of his jacket and they consulted it for a moment. Whatever the request, Marquis did not look confident, but and nodded his head. "Best to drop your trash as you go," he stated, as he started crawling forward.

He scurried forward to the door that led to the caboose, William right behind him. Crouching to stay out of sight, William took one of the weapons from the agent and then flattened himself against the wall next to the door. Marquis slowly straightened until he could see out the window, then looked down and nodded to my friend. The glass from the window blew inward at the same time we heard the report of a rifle.

By the grace of God, neither William or the porter were hurt. Will froze in his place, gun held in both hands and ready for the assault. Marquis was crawling back towards us and Heinz raised himself up enough to empty his pistol through the window at the caboose. This gave Marquis the time to grab a rope off the stall's post and scoot over to a side window in the car. He opened the window and stuck his head and one arm, with the rope, out the window. He ducked his head back in called over his shoulder, "Mr. Frohman! Hold my legs!"

Without waiting for a reaction from me, me began to wiggle the top half of his body out the opening. I barely managed to grab both his ankles as they lifted off the floor. Then the fireworks really started!

It sounded like firecrackers going off and chunks of wood began to fly off the frames of the stalls. It sounded like a dozen one pond bees were flying past us at light speed! I didn't even know if Will or the agent had fired back as I was too concentrated on holding Marquis's legs and watching holes suddenly appear in the wood planking around me. After what seemed an eternity, Marquis began to sidle back into the car. I feared for his exposure while he tried to expedite himself, so I leaned back and used my considerable weight to yank him through. He dropped the few feet to the floor, spread-eagled. I ended up flat on my bottom. I heard a large crack and something flew past my eyes so close, if I had blinked it would have shaved my eyelashes off!

Marquis got to his feet quickly and looped the rope he still had in his hand around one of the posts. "Got it!" He screamed.

Before I could ask, "Got what?" William hollered, "Brace yourselves!"

Our situation went from grave to chaotic in a heartbeat.

It felt as if the hand of God slapped the side of our car. One side rose sharply in the air and we all tumbled towards the low side. Me and the horses, anyways, and I was screaming louder than them! There was screech of twisting metal and a loud snap, then the car righted itself. We bounced and swayed so hard, I thought we were surely about to derail, but after a moment we smoothed out and continued on our merry way.

There was dead silence. Even the horses had quieted and they just stood, heads down and trembling. Just like I was.

Marquis got to his feet first and he pulled me up. I looked over to see Heinz peering out the back window. My first instinct was to pull him away before the fool got his head blown off, but one look at Will calmed me. He was still crouched against the wall, with sunlight streaming through the holes in the wall all around him. He gave me a smirk before he stood and handed the pistol to Heinz. He stood next to the Pinkerton and looked out also. I stepped up to see and almost laughed in relief.

Fading in the distance, I saw the caboose, derailed and lying on its side, off the tracks. The frame looked nearly collapsed, the windows blown out, and debris was scattered all around. Our would-be assassins were most likely dead or injured and they were miles from nowhere. Finally feeling safe, I nearly had a seizure when then train lurched, and I bumped into the backs of the two men. Someone had put on the brakes.

William turned and pushed me gently aside. "Marquis, please tell the engineer to keep going. Full speed. There is town about twenty minutes up the line. We can sort this out there."

After Marquis left us, William and Heinz walked over to the rope that was still hanging out the window. Heinz reeled it in, and I saw that it was looped on the other end around a shaft of some sort.

"What the hell is that?" I asked.

"Isn't it obvious?" Heinz asked me, in that same tone William always used. I ignored him and looked to my friend, who just gave me that smug smirk.

I turned on my heels and stomped off to find a drink.

Irritated, because I had just been nearly shot multiple times and couldn't get the courtesy of an explanation, I stormed straight through the sleeping car and had opened the opposite door that led to the club car before I heard the door to one of the berths slam open and a clicking noise. I was closing the door to the club car behind me when I realized the sounds I heard behind me came from the remaining Pinkerton man, stepping into the hall behind me and cocking his pistol. I realize he must have been more than panicked by the gunshots and flailing about, so, I wasn't about to stick my head back in that car. He could come in and shoot me over a drink if he had to.

The car was empty. Wilson, wisely, had deserted his post at some point. The room was in shambles. A table was tipped over, the artwork hung askew, and a lot of the stock was broken on the tiles behind the bar. Luckily, I found a bottle of sipping whiskey that had survived and cleared a space on the bar. A few drinks later, my heart was just starting to slow down when William and Heinz made their way in, the other pinkie and a young lady in tow.

"AH! Mr. Frohman. Mr. Gillette said we'd find you here." Heinz greeted me.

"Mr. Gillette is often right about things." I deadpanned. "Too often!"

William had the grace to look abashed as he stepped up to me and clasped my shoulders with both hands. "I am so grateful you are alright. You are, aren't you, Charlie?"

I was embarrassed by the moisture in his eyes. "I'm fine, Will. No holes in me but the originals." He started to smile and I snapped at him in mock outrage, "But this is why I keep telling you to mind your own business! We could have had a pleasant trip if you could just stop …noticing things!"

Will didn't know how to answer that, but the young lady pulled his bacon out of the fire. "Then what would have become of me, Mr. Frohman?"

I looked past William to see a beautiful girl looking up at me with big blue eyes. I slid off the stool smoothly and bowed to her slightly. "Miss Cyr, of course, our sole concern was for your welfare."

That rolled a few eyes, even hers, but I smoothed it over by offering everyone a drink. Even William accepted. Heinz found some more unbroken glasses, I grabbed the bottle, and soon we were toasting each other around a table.

"So chief," The still unnamed Pinkerton said, once he had downed is drink, "Fill me in. I have a feeling I'm gonna be writing out a long report about this…assignment!"

Heinz sighed ad dropped his head on his chest. "Don't remind me about the reports!" He looked up and squinted at William. "I think it might be better to hear it from Mr. Gillette. Take some notes. He may have looked relaxed, but I noticed he sat where he could see both doors and he folded back his jacket to expose the butt of his pistol. Understandable.

I thought I'd rather listen to the sound of the ice in my glass rather than sit through another of William's performances, but he was in high form and soon I was as rapt to his voice as Miss Cyr was next to me. He laid out his observations and deductions in a modest, yet melodramatic fashion that had us glued to our seats as the pinkie scribbled furiously. William had just reached he point where Marquis had come into the horse car when, as if on cue, the door from the front of the train opened and he rushed into the room in a frenzy. His eyes widened but he visibly relaxed when he saw us all seated and drinking.

"The engineer sent me to check on you all." he smiled when we assured him that we were good. "Then, can I get you anything?" No one had a request. "Then I'll be seeing to the horses." He gave us a little bow and went out the door to the sleeping car.

The interruption seemed to take a little wind out of Will's sails, so I had to prompt him to take up the narrative again.

"So, what did you cook up with Marquis?" I asked. "How did we lose the caboose?"

William came out of his reverie. "Oh! That! After determining that our odds were slim that we would survive a charge by the outlaws and there was no possibility we could uncouple the car without taking gun fire, I remembered a spur we were coming up on –"

"Spur? Whatever is a 'spur'?" Miss Cyr asked.

"It's a set of tracks that branch out from a mainline." Heinz explained.

William waited patiently for them to cease their interruptions and he continued. "Knowing Marquis was a former cowboy-"

"Whoa," I cried. "Hold the fort! How did you know he used to be a cowboy?"

William snapped his mouth shut, frowned, then shook his head in disgust. "Really, Frohman! The rolling gait? The rope callouses on his palm's? His tan?"

"Just get on with it! " I groused.

Will snorted and went on. "I knew there would be a switching station ahead, so, I instructed Marquis to rope the lever. The tracks must have changed just as the Caboose passed over and therefore was derailed. We owe that man our life."

I was stunned. If the coupling hadn't snapped and released us, we'd have been spread out across that sandy waste this very moment! When I thought of how we nearly went off the tracks ourselves, I could have slapped that smug look off his face!

"You idiot! You could have killed us all!"

He answered with that damn smirk. "Exhilarating, is it not?"

A bit later, Marquis came back into the car and walked over to our table. Before he could ask, Heinz said, "That was a hell of a toss, cowboy." He stuck out his hand and shook Marquis's. "Thank you."

His man added his gratitude, as did I. The young girl thanked him. We all turned to Will, who hadn't spoken yet.

He slowly stood and reached deep into his pocket. He pulled out a wad of money and slapped it in Marquis's hand, gold money clip and all. William looked him in the eye. "If you ever need anything, just bring that clip back to me and I will help you in any way I can."

Someone from the front of the train called for him and Marquis just nodded before he hurried out the door.

We were all staring at William as he sat back down. He shrugged.

"As you stated earlier, Frohman. It is Cash – not compliments!"

Fall of the Musketeers

December 16, 1899

PART ONE

It was November, in the year 1899, when a man walked into my office as I was discussing a business trip arrangement with my secretary. He was on the tall side, a bit gaunt and robust in his movements as he shut the door behind him and tossed his hat and cane onto the bench along the wall.

"Hello Charlie", he greeted, as he took a few long strides to reach my desk. He was a step from the back of one of the two wing backed chairs that faced my desk when he added, "I was looking for your secretary, but she wasn't at her desk."

My hands were folded on my desk and I unfurled my fingers to indicate the other chair. "That's because she's sitting here, writing down my instructions."

Rae leaned forward, and he noticed her at last, "Oh! Hello, Miss Geisling! I didn't see you sitting there." Without as much as a 'May I?' he sat down in the opposite chair and crossed his legs, making himself at home. We just stared at him as he pulled out a worn leather case and prepped a smoke, oblivious to our looks. In fact, he seemed a bit oblivious to everything. I hadn't seen my friend for a few weeks, however, I had never seen him act this way before.

William Hooker Gillette was free to act anyway he wanted, at least in this building. As America's premier actor and the man responsible for the Sherlock Holmes phenomenon, his theater presence brought huge amounts of cash into my coffers. Indeed, he could do as he damned well liked! But there was something decidedly odd about him today.

The William I knew would never have barged into my office in the middle of the day. It simply wasn't in his nature. He was courteous to a fault and could have taught classes at a school of etiquette. And to flop himself down while I was giving dictation was way over his line.

Then there was his appearance. Though not averse to getting his hands dirty when he was not on stage, he was usually more fastidious when calling on someone. A lifetime of donning costumes inspires most to look their best when out in public. Today William looked just a hair over shabby. His tie was loose and crooked, his shoes were dull, and the creases below his knees were nonexistent. His hair was kissing his collar and his jaw had not felt the caress of a sharp steel blade for days. William's Japanese servant, Ozaki, kept William looking sharp and would never let him wonder about looking like this. Ozaki came from a wealthy family and his brother was a mayor and responsible for shipping hundreds of cherry seedlings to Washington D.C. Ozaki's visit to Japan was leaving William to fend for himself, and it showed. I leaned back in my chair and steeped my fingers under my chin in parody of his most famous portrayal and with a smirk asked, "How long has Ozaki been gone?"

William had been lighting his cigarette and he coughed up a great ball of smoke, looking impressed with me. He laughed and asked "Are you trying to turn the tables on me, Charlie? Ozaki has been gone three weeks so far. He went home to Japan to visit his family. He won't be home for another six or so. However did you deduce that?"

I grinned from ear to ear, having waited for some time to give the reply, "Elementary, my dear William. Elementary" But I didn't elaborate. Sweet revenge for all the times he left me in the dark.

William ran a hand across his jaw and plucked at his clothes. "It's really starting to show, isn't it?" he asked with a frown.

I took pity on him. "Only to those who really know you, William. But in another few weeks I doubt you'll get past my doorman."

Any other time, I would have brought him to my home. Denise and the children, Micheal, Collin, and little Adrianna adored him, and I could see that he was properly taken cared for. Funny how in some way's wealth makes us invalids. I grew up washing my own clothes and now I don't even know how to contact my tailor or where he keeps his shop. My secretary, Rae, takes care of everything. He comes to my office.

But as luck would have it, I was about to take a long trip out west to oversee an opening of a new theater my syndicate contracted with, so that option was off the table. There was only one solution left.

"Rae- please double the arrangements." I pointed at the tablet she was writing on.

"Double sir?" she asked, "I don't understand."

"Easy. Just take all the tickets and accommodations and double them. Make them for two. Mr. Gillette will be joining me on this jaunt."

"Jaunt? What jaunt?" William blurted out. At least I had his attention now.

"William," I said giving him a stern look. "If you're going to come in at the middle of my dictation-"

"Oh! My lord! I didn't… did I?" he blurted out with a look of horror on his face, "Charlie. Miss Geisling. Please excuse me. I don't know what I was thinking."

He stubbed out his fag and made to get up. I put up a hand to stop him.

"Sit down William. We're all through anyhow. Rae needs to get hopping." I turned and looked at Rae, who stared back indignantly. "What are you still doing here?"

"I am just trying to come up with a plan to best suit your needs, Mr. Frohman. My original arrangements took quite some time to complete and you are due to leave in two days." She smiled at me sweetly, like you smile at your great grandfather who can't remember your name.

This was one of those times it was great to be a boss. "That's why I pay you the big money, my dear. Now skedaddle!"

She rolled her eyes and turned for the door. She only paused long enough to look down at my friend and give him a sultry smile. "It was nice to see you again Mr. Gillette."

William flashed a smile at her, "The pleasure was mine, Miss Geisling."

They smiled at each other long enough, so I cleared my throat. Not that I minded a little flirting, you see. I know women love the attention and need it. A happy girl is a productive girl. Hell, I do it myself when I think it's called for. I made a shooing gesture and sent her on her way. Rae gave me the stink eye over her shoulder and sashayed out like she was walking into the 21 club. I let her get almost to the door before I called out, "Book a private car. Less stops the better. And be damn sure the rooms have separate lavatories!" I turned to William, with a wink and added, loud enough for Rae to hear, "I hate smelling another man's business!" With a strangled noise, Rae went through the door, pulling it shut behind her with considerable force. "I expect you'll agree with me once we hit the dry dessert."

I thought that might get at least a chuckle out of him, but he just stared back at me with a perplexed expression. "Are you talking about a trip into the desert?"

I loved the turnaround and was going to play it for all it was worth.

"Paul Gilmore."

He flinched at the name. "Yes, I heard about that. His poor wife died in childbirth. Left the poor man with twins, I understand."

I shook my head. "Left them with Cooper. The old man is going to raise them."

One of those real-life tragedies that was worse than anything ever written for the stage. Paul Gilmore, a driven and gifted actor, marries the daughter of A.A. Cooper; the wagon maker of fame and one of the richest men in America. The happy couple conceives just a year after they were married. What should have been a fairy tale went south when she dies after giving birth to twins.

"Paul ended up giving the children into his father in law's care and hitting the boards once more."

"You don't say. I'm a bit surprised that Paul would give up his children like that. I have always thought of him as a man with mettle."

I shrugged. "Think about it, William. Paul is a middle-aged man with no experience raising children and no roots to speak of. Suddenly he's left with not one, but twin children and no woman to raise them. On the other hand, A.A. Cooper is one of the richest men in America. He can give those children the best education, childhoods filled with treasured memories, and guide them to a bright and wealthy future. Personally, I think he made the right sacrifice."

"I suppose you're right. It must have been daunting for Paul. Wait! Just a minute!" William caught himself. "What has this got to do with a trip?

"Paul is headlining the Syndicate's opening production in a theater we contracted with in Phoenix, Arizona."

"Headlining? It's only been three months since he lost his wife! Isn't that a bit soon?" he blurted out, but before I could answer, William went on, "Arizona! I can't just up and traipse off to Arizona with you."

"Why not? Ozaki won't be back for weeks, and you aren't taking the Aunt Polly anywhere while he's gone. Since you quit working-."

"Hiatus, Charlie. I'm just on a hiatus."

"Whatever you call it, I need to go and make sure the first play in this new venue doesn't get fouled up! Since you're not busy for the foreseeable future, you might as well come along. Between the two of us we might be able to keep it on track."

He frowned at me then gave me his trademark smirk, "You don't fool me, Charlie. You just want to support Paul. You're an old softie when it comes to your stable."

'Stable' is how he referred to my actors under contract. It's true, I always thought of my people like my children, abet, children with big allowances. I shrugged, "He's been through a lot. A few familiar faces would do him wonders."

"What is the name of the play you are you putting on?"

"The Three Musketeers."

He looked skeptical, "That old horse? Don't you think that's a bit tired for a grand opening? Though, it is a role Paul takes to. People do love him as a swashbuckler..."

I just let him rattle on, smiling inside because I knew I'd have company for this trip.

PART TWO

Phoenix was a large city, and more spread out than the Big Apple. Still, besides the dust and glaring sun, it had its own charms. I was particularly impressed with the open spaces as we rounded a corner and the Cabbie said over his shoulder, "That's the Grand Patton there, gentlemen."

The building he pointed to sat on the corner of intersecting streets, yet there were no buildings either behind it or to its sides. Its unobstructed position enhanced the magnificent brocade tenfold. Bright brick and stone, it was flanked by twin towers on each side and set with three rows of gleaming glass bay windows. The name --Grand Patton Opera House -- fanned out between the second and third floors in great gold letters.

On the street level, there were two sets of doors for admittance and two ticket booths on each side to expedite ticket sales. With over a thousand seats, that would make a difference especially in bad weather. Folks who wait less time in lines, receive the show in a much better frame of mind and tend to be less critical. I made a mental note to put safeguards in place to ensure that one side couldn't skim and blame it on the other.

The only point that marred the appearance was a separate shop that occupied the ground floor on the left side. A pharmacy no less. Last thing I wanted was paying customers to have to watch sickly dregs plod between them on show nights!

I forgot all about it when the building began to light up as the sun dipped lower in the horizon. As the streetlights began to flicker on, one by one, the flood lights on the building snapped large swaths of light into the dusk and lights began to come on in each window. It looked even better by gas light.

When I realized how close to dark it was, I looked at my watch and found we had a little over an hour before the show started. So, when we pulled abreast of the stage door on the side of the building with the empty lot, I paid the cabbie and instructed him to drop our bags off at our hotel and went up the few steps to the landing.

When I pulled the door open, light, sound and smell washed across us like a familiar wave. Stepping inside, I stopped to take it all in. Scenery men rolled huge painted wood walls across the stage and lighting crews adjusted their lamps as players and crew danced the preshow waltz. It was a hundred balls of chaos that, when put in a semblance of order, would make the magic we sold.

"Gentlemen, I believe you're in the wrong place. The entrance is on the front of the building. Only cast and crew are allowed back here."

"No, I'm pretty sure we're right where we want to be," I said, amused. I couldn't blame the man for doing his job, you'd be surprised how many gentlemen try to get back stage, usually to try and lure an actress into an intimate dinner or some such tomfoolery. "I'm Charles Frohman and this gentleman is William Gillette."

Surprisingly, neither name made an impression and he never took his eyes off us as he reached over with a long arm and plucked a clipboard off the podium. He made a show of perusing all three pages then tossed it back on the table and glared at us with squinty eyes.

"I never seen you before and you don't work here, so I'm going to ask you Gentlemen to leave."

William seemed amused at his attitude, but I was starting to get my back up, "Now listen here-."

"No" he replied in a menacing voice as he pulled a sap out of his back pocket and started tapping it on his thigh, "You had better listen and turn around. Get your asses out that door before I throw you out!"

Now I was mad enough to spit blood, but William looked at him with something akin to pity in his eyes and said to the door man, "Perhaps you need someone else to check that list for you?" Though it was said calmly, it was a gauntlet none the less and our antagonist stopped slapping his thigh and smacked the sap squarely in his fist. The knuckles on the handle were white, a sure sign he was about to swing it.

Thank the angels because just then I saw a flash of red not twenty feet away and I cried out, "Salmon!"

A slightly built man in a rumpled suit broke off his instructions to some gaffers and looked our way. He sported a shock of red hair and a beard. His skin was the color of fresh cream and the two spots of blush on his cheeks from exertion made him look like a left-over Christmas decoration. Yet he was the best damned stage manager in the business.

Kevin Salmon had been with me for years and always did a bang-up job. For the past few years, I had sent him all across the country as he was my first choice to see our opening productions got off on the right foot. His uncanny ability to identify a problem and solve it quickly would serve me well at that moment. Within seconds of looking over, his eyes popped out of his skull and he half ran over, coming up behind the doorman.

As soon as Kevin was abreast of the guardsman, Salmon reached over and snatched the sap right out of the man's hand! Shocked, he turned, looking ready to kill whoever took his toy away, but Salmon never gave him the chance. Toe to toe, he raised the sap over his head and shook it in the doorman's face.

"What the Sam Hill is going on here?!" he roared, "Are you threatening these men?"

"I...I...I asked them to leave, politely at first, but they refused!" He stammered a reply.

"And why the hell didn't you let them in? They're on the list."

"Well... you see Sir...I didn't-."

"That's because he can't read, Kevin." William in an almost melancholy voice, "Your doorman is illiterate."

Salmon looked back at his man, "Tell me that's not true or explain to me why I wrote out three pages of a guest list for a dummy!"

The man seemed to deflate with a hang dog expression as he replied meekly, "I... I thought I could recognize some letters... and I really needed the work...but, no I can't read sir." His voice faded away and he hung his head low.

Kevin folded his arms across his chest and sighed, "Well, lad, you are certainly going out in style. It's not often a man threatens the great actor, William Gillette and the owner of this Company, Charles Frohman in the same breath!"

Even I felt a little bad for the guy then, but William was stricken. He had such a soft heart for the brute, I knew he would suffer for causing the man's loss of income. So, even though I knew I was stepping on toes, I stepped in.

"Hold up a minute, Kevin," I interrupted. I looked at the doorman, "What's your name, son?"

"Winston, Sir. Jimmy Winston."

I looked him over and clicked my tongue. "Well, Winston. I've found it to be bad omen to fire someone on opening night, so I have no choice but to transfer you to the gaffer crew for your continued employment. Learn how to read and you can have this position back. If you can't read that list in six months, you're out on your keister. Agreed?"

"Yes sir! Absolutely I do! I can learn my letters, sir. I will." He stuck out his hand to shake, but I ignored it and simply pointed in a 'GO' gesture.

Salmon stepped up then, obviously not pleased with my interference, or me for that matter, and stuck his face in Winslow's, abet on his tippy toes. "Six months to the day! Now go find Roberto.

Winston scurried off with his gallows' reprieve and William clasped me on the shoulder, "That was a kind act!"

"Ah, Chad dap!" I retorted in my best Bronx accent, "I had no choice, I already invested six bucks on that lug? Who else could fill that jacket?" and then another thought occurred to me, "And how did you know he couldn't read?"

"The list. The guest list he checked so carefully, page by page, Charlie. They're always in alphabetical order to search time – With the best readers it would take minutes to find a name."

"Wait a minute," I interjected, "How did you know they were in alphabetical order?" I thought I really had him for once in my life.

Salmon snorted with muffled laughter, "Because you ordered us to write them up that way! Three years ago!

Said you didn't want to see the list written out all 'Willy Nilly'."

"Oh Thee, the mighty, set high upon the mount..." William quoted in a soft voice, his lips quivering with laughter.

"Again -- Chad dap! And what does that have to do with it?"

He smiled and shook his head, "Frohman. Gillette. F! G! Those letters are right next to each other and more than likely on the first page. Your new gaffer could not have possibly missed both our names and there was little likely hood that he would need to check all three pages. It was plain as day he was illiterate."

I was getting used to his little displays of deduction and I was more amused than amazed, but Salmon let out a long low whistle and said. "I've heard about you, Mr. Gillette. That's spiffy."

William just shrugged and smiled, modest to a fault. I put out my hand to Salmon.

"Thanks for the rescue, Kevin. How are you?"

"Fine, Sir, sorry about all that. I hired him for his size- not his brains. Its slim pickings out here in the land of sand and sun."

I didn't want to hear any excuses and I didn't want to dwell on it. I could feel the pre-show tension in the air, and I wanted to move on. "It's done. Is everything ready to go on tonight?"

He nodded his head. "There are a few things I need to go over with you in my office."

"Before we talk business," William cut in, "Could we have a few minutes to look up an old friend?"

"Ah! Paul, of course. That's no problem, I can meet you at my office in twenty minutes. Paul is in the back area where the dressing rooms are and most likely around Mary's room." He smirked and without further ado, bolted away calling out orders as he charged ahead.

Standing there, back to taking in the ambiance, William looked at me and said out of the corner of his mouth, "Mary? His poor wife's dead less than three months! And you were worried about his acting?"

I shrugged, then, just to poke at his puritan morality, I winked at him "We all grieve in our own fashion, William."

PART THREE

We strolled slowly, each of us receiving greetings and respect from the company, many of whom William or I had worked with over the years. Thankfully, everyone was busy at their assigned tasks, so we weren't hindered as we watched the production come together for the opening curtain. Afterwards we'd be mobbed by the star struck and the suck ups!

Everything seemed to be in movement, and I saw each move as a single thread being woven into a tapestry. It looked like a collection of separate productions, yet it all worked towards a common goal. You see the same thing in restaurant kitchens just before the gourmet plates are placed under the warmer.

I picked up on a few minor missteps among the various crews, but I held my tongue. Had I been stage manager there would have been screaming, cursing and head slaps until everything was in line, but I needed to let Salmon deal with the details. I had undermined him once already and the last thing I wanted to do was barge in and yank the rug out from under his feet. I had very different plans for young Salmon. I was really here to count the money and with twelve hundred seats for six nights a week, that was a lot of Moola!

William, on the other hand, couldn't help himself. He told the lighting crew they needed to drop the front floods by a foot and a half, then explained to the prop crew why the scenery had to be organized a certain way, and even stopped one of the extras and told her to remind wardrobe that 16th century aristocrat women didn't wear dress boots!

What made me step back and chuckle was how fast they all jumped to comply! Even though William had no official involvement in the production and no authority over anyone here, everyone obeyed him without questions. His reputation and accomplishments made him the top dog and what he spoke was Gospel behind the curtains. When he finally took a long last look around, he seemed satisfied. So, I had to break his stones a little.

"Everything good William? Are we ready?"

"I think so, Charlie," he replied absently as he pulled his watch out. "They should have enough time to make the changes if they get right to it. I'm not too sure-."

He broke off when he saw that I was near laughter. "Are you bucking for Salmon's job?" I asked.

His eyes went wide, "Oh My!" he said, "Have I overstepped my bounds? I wouldn't want Kevin to think I was interfering!"

"William, you were dead on with your suggestions. If Salmon's smart enough he'll thank you for your actions. If not, he'll learn the hard way like we did. Honestly, have you seen anything else that needs last minute fixing?"

"Nothing that we can change, Charlie," he said wistfully, "But I have seen signs of no less than nine romances among the crews. There must be something in this dry dessert air."

"Or their drinking the cactus juice," I quipped, as I scanned the stage. I saw lots of interaction but no displays of public affection. Yet, I knew Will was right. Theater people have a more than open attitude towards romance. The romances tended to rise and fall with the productions and locations and I had no qualms as long as it was consensual and discreet as possible for a community that was hungry for theater gossip. But you did need to keep an eye on somebody who were making monkey business with somebody else' somebody! Those things tended to explode at just the wrong time.

I gave him the eye, "Anything that looks like it might be trouble?" I asked.

William shrugged and chuckled, "It was just some quick observations, not an analysis. You know how these things go. Courtship and romance are different in our business."

"For us upon the boards, Love is naught but beating hearts in changing hands", I quoted.

William stopped dead in his tracks, "Why, Charles Frohman! That was quite profound. Who wrote that?"

"I did when I was a kid. You like it? You can have it. Use it in your next play."

"I may have it crocheted on a pillow."

PART FOUR

Finally, we made our way down to the dressing rooms. After finding Paul's empty, we wound up knocking on a door that bore the name Christine 'Mary' Corbet. After a few moments of frantic movement inside the room, the door opened a crack and a familiar face squeezed out.

"William! Charles!" he squealed, "You made it!" The door opened just enough for him to slip out sideways and he closed it behind him.

Paul Gilmore looked better in real life than his show posters. Six feet of good proportion, wavy brown hair and hazel eyes. Coupled with a modicum of talent, he had been a staple of plays featuring swashbuckling heroes. Despite all his recent tragedies, he looked just as hale as ever.

His greeting was followed by the usual hand shaking and back thumping that faded into an awkward silence because William and I didn't know where to begin addressing our sympathies and Paul's loss of words most likely had something to do with the swath of bright red lipstick on his left earlobe. Thankfully, a voice cried out from inside and broke the spell.

"Paul? Who is it? Who's out there?"

Paul turned his head to the door and called back, "Two old friends I'd like you to meet!"

William and I suppressed our smirks while William pulled out a handkerchief and wiped the red lipstick from his ear, "Old indeed, I'd say."

Paul laughed as he opened the door and introduced us to Christine.

Her dressing room was well lit with a large dressing table with mirror, a couch and a few overstuffed chairs. They were very nice accommodations for a leading lady. Christine hadn't worked in one of my productions before and Paul insisted on her in his letters. She was a looker and if she could act at all, I was sure she'd get by. Paul introduced us, and she fawned over us for a bit.

"It is an honor to finally meet you, Mr. Frohman. Paul has told me all about you."

"Bored you to tears, I imagine," I joked.

"Oh, no, I find successful men fascinating." She turned her charms on William, "And Mr. Gillette, it's so good to see you again! I worked on one of your shows once, though I doubt you'd remember. It was a small part a long time ago."

"It was 'Secret Service', back in 97'. You played Esmerelda, the serving girl." William replied.

"My Gracious! You do remember. But how? I was all done over in black face!" She looked at me and smiled, "I was a very convincing negress."

"It was your palms," William teased graciously. "A man does not forget a set of palms like yours so easily."

We all laughed, and William pointed to a great bouquet of Roses on her dressing table, "But it seems I'm not your only admirer."

"Oh, those," she gushed. "Aren't they lovely?" She put her nose in them and inhaled deeply, a dreamy countenance coming over her face, then giving Paul a sideways look that made him wince. "And I don't even know who they're from! Only this quaint little card." She held it up and read in a stage voice, "On or off the boards…You are my Countess! Isn't that precious?" Paul was rolling his eyes by that point.

Amused as I was by the underplay, the curtain was due to rise shortly so I cut it short. "Well, I can't compete with flowers and poetry, but would you care to join us for dinner after the show?"

She was delighted, "Oh, they're full of thorns anyways! I'd be delighted! Will Paul be joining us also?" She added with a sly smile. We laughed again as Paul pantomimed indignation.

"Well, I will leave you gentlemen to catch up. I must be off to wardrobe" she said as she looked at Paul, then nodded to William and me, "Until later." With that she swished out of the room. Before the door shut, I caught a flash of white and blue below the very red face of another of the musketeers watching Miss Corbet sashay away. I just rolled my eyes and put it out of my mind.

When the door closed behind her, we looked to Paul, who wore a sheepish grin and was at a loss for words.

"What about you Paul?" I asked to break the ice. "You have a few minutes before pre-curtain?"

"Oh sure," he said looking up. "I can't believe you came all this way. I'm…well, it means a lot to me, Charles…William." His voice, choked with emotion trailed off and his eyes misted over. I knew what he was feeling, and I was glad that we made the trip. Cards and letters were fine but sometimes you just had to show up.

"No need to get all sentimental, Gilmore!" I said gruffly, "I'm just here to count the money and you better bring it in! I want to see some justification for the inflated salary I pay you!"

That made him laugh and it broke the maudlin tone. "Ha! I should be an usher for what you pay me!"

Then he looked at the clock on Mary's dressing room table. "I've got just enough time for a smoke."

"Sounds good." I said.

"Great! Got one for me?"

I took one out and lit it for him. He took a deep drag and blew it out in contentment. "Thanks...that's good. I've been dying for one since this morning!"

I didn't like to hear that. I wanted my stars content. "If you need some tobacco, why didn't you just send one of the gaffers for some? There's a pharmacy right next door for Pete's sake!"

"It's not that, Charles. I have plenty back in my stall." He stood and raised his hands up, "It's these damn tights the wardrobe crew squeezed us into! Not a pocket anywhere. I can't carry a toothpick!"

He was right. The main characters all wore those skin-tight whites made of cotton. Put on a tabard, a hat with a big feather, and a pair of high boots and you were a musketeer. Other costumes would slip right over them. But they did leave little room to tote anything. In fact, they were pretty much indecent, and I doubt you could walk down Main Street in them without getting pitched in the hoosegow. I looked to see why William was so quiet when I saw him staring intently at Mary's roses.

"What the hell are you looking at, William?"

Still looking at the glass vase, he replied. "I'm no longer 'looking', Charlie. I'm thinking."

I sighed and shook my head. With a wink at Paul, I asked, "Thinking what?"

He straightened up and, winking at Paul, turned to look at me, "I'm thinking that if you are here to count the money, perhaps you'd better keep an eye on those expensive rose bushes along the east wall. If I'm not mistaken, Miss Corbet's bouquet, which sits so grandly on her table, came from there!"

"OH Really!" Paul crowed, "I can't wait to tell Chris!"

It was trivial, I know, but it irked me none the less. I hated getting pinched for anything! "You sure?"

"They are, as Mary pointed out, full of thorns. Even the poorest flower girl on the foggy streets of London would strip the thorns and dead growth for a better-looking stem. Neither has been done to these and the cuts where they were taken from the bush are ragged, as if an old pen or pocketknife was used, not a pair of clippers as a florist would. Coupled with the fresh, robust aroma they emit, I would say that's exactly where they came from."

Paul laughed and clapped his hands. "I believe you are correct, Mr. Holmes. Oh William, still doing your Sherlock thing I see!"

"Hardly. That's just common sense."

Paul laughed again and snuffed out his cigarette. "Well, you'll have to wait for dinner to explain the difference to me. I've got to be in place shortly." Then he gave me a smirk as he got up, "That is, if I'm invited, Charles."

"Of course, you are!" I replied, as he headed for the door, "We wouldn't have traveled a thousand miles and not let you buy us dinner!"

"Then hope I get a nice Opening Day bonus!" He cried out, not missing a beat opening the door, "Or you'll be eating bean burritos over at Mabel's Roadhouse!"

William gave him the theater's blessing before he could get out the door, "Break a leg, Paul!" Paul smiled and waved a salute as he disappeared.

When the door shut behind him, William and I looked at each other. William barked a laugh that was a scoff all in itself. "I repeat. And you were worried about him?"

I put my palms up. "What can I say? Pau does seem to have bounced back smartly. I was surprised he wanted to get back to work so soon and never mind the rest!"

"I'm not, Charlie. Not really. Paul is a stage rat. Acting is all he knows and all he wants to know. He loves it with all his soul, and it shows in his stage craft. He'd be happy to go out there every night if he could. He'll leave the business feet first- mark my words."

I shrugged, "Let's hope he finishes this run first," I quipped then looked at my watch, "We better get over to Salmon's office if we're going to get to our seats in time."

PART FIVE

Kevin was pacing about his office when we arrived.

"Oh Good! You're here. Everything's on the table," he pointed to my left. Sitting neatly side by side on the table was a director's script, burglar's lamp, and an ocular in a leather tube.

The props were all for me. It has been a long-standing practice of mine to follow a new play with the script to better help me critique the show. Even though I would have a private box, the small lamp kept the light from distracting the actors. My wife has long refused to attend a play with me while I winced, gagged, and growled my way through it. William was more tolerant and would add a comment of his own from time to time.

"I just have one quick matter to discuss before you go," Salmon announced.

"I don't care," I replied. William looked at me with curiosity.

Stunned, Salmon looked at me to see if I was joshing him as usual. "Beg your pardon?"

I looked back at him blandly. "I don't give a fat rat's ass, Kevin. Whatever it is, you deal with it!"

Now I had William's full attention. I had been planning this little surprise since before we got on the train in New York, excluding even William from my intentions. Besides the money, being the boss was lonely and had very few ups and I wanted to enjoy this moment. Salmon didn't know whether to walk away or slap me, but he tried once again.

"I would if I was able to Charles but if this is a budget matter and I need the producer's input."

"Stop!" I barked, "Just stop! Then it's an easy fix! As of this moment you own 28% of this show! You can list yourself a Co-producer and all the privileges and headaches that go with it. If you need more money, take it out of the overage fund. Just remember it's YOUR money too now! Deal?" Salmon's jaw dropped to the floor and William smiled slowly when he saw what I just did. He nodded to me sagely. We both knew that Kevin had earned it. His face flushed the color of his red hair, but his eyes lit up as he realized how much better his life just got financially and professionally.

When Kevin didn't answer right away, I got swept up in the moment, "Holding out, Eh? Then I'll sweeten the pot. Fifty percent after 6 weeks. Seventy- if you're still running in three months. Better?" I stuck my hand out across his desk.

The moment had all the desired effects. I felt contentment for giving someone deserving a big hand up

"I don't know what to say," he said as he took my hand, "But thanks. That is very generous."

"Bah! You've earned it, Kevin." I took out my flask and we sealed the deal with a quick pull each. William added his congratulations but declined the hooch, looking at his watch instead.

Salmon took the hint and pulled his out also. "Twenty-two minutes until the curtain rises, Gentlemen. I guess I'd better get out there and show my face. Charles, all your things are here." he gestured to the table and sighed. "Bear in mind it's been a difficult set up for everybody! New show, new venue, and we're a long way from home."

William looked at me strangely as I walked over and started collecting my gear and said "Kev! I'm here to help you as much as possible, son. I'll maybe have a few observations, that's all."

Salmon snorted and looked to William, "The last time he gave us his 'observations', our wardrobe mistress- sweet old gal- started drinking as soon as he left! It took us months to dry her out!" He looked back at me, "In fact, she came out here with us."

There was more to the story than that, but Kevin didn't have the time for us to stand around jawboning, so I headed for the door.

"Then she better get slippers on those frog ladies," I warned him walking away. Then I added over my shoulder at the door, "Or have another bottle handy!"

William insisted we go back out and enter the theater as if we were ordinary rubes. This would mean checking in at the ticket booth and I groused about going through all that rig a ma role. But it was only whining for show. I knew what William was doing and I appreciated the gesture.

We went out the door we came in and traverse the short alley. As soon as we rounded the corner onto the street we were blocked by a large mob, waiting to get their tickets. I was about to suggest we go back in and just make our way to the box in peace, but he was already in motion.

Like a slow-moving comet blazing across the heavens, he sashayed his way into the thick of the crowd. With a smile plastered on his face, he began an impromptu meet and greet. Though he had not preformed out here in the mid-west in many years, he was instantly recognized and revered. It wasn't every day the public had a chance to rub elbows with a star of his renown, yet he made each one he slipped past feel like he was happier to meet them. He patted backs, gave hugs, and signed a few autographs while edging his way to the window and with me stuck to his heels.

Before you knew it, I spoke to the girl in the booth and she handed us our passes tout-suite. I thanked her and nodded to William who began to make his way towards the doors on the left. Someone, a young lady perhaps, called out, "Enjoy the show, Mr. Gillette."

William paused and turned to the crowd as the doorman opened up for us, "I'm sure I shall," he called back, "Paul is a dear friend and an absolute joy to behold on stage. I'm sure you're going to love it!"

They applauded! I gave him a moment to bask in the adoration, and then I pulled him inside. The door clicked shut and the racket dimmed considerably.

The foyer was as grand as any other theater in the country. Patton had tossed around some serious money and the results were magnificent. From the plush red carpet to the crown molding, the workmanship was flawless. Straight ahead of us lay the entrance to the grand lobby, which had two bars for the intermission thirst and the entrance to the main level. Two sets of stairs on either side bracketed the entrance. One set led to the balcony seats and the others led to the private boxes. That was where we were headed at a quick pace. I didn't want to get caught up with another bevy of admirers when they opened the doors to the public.

I shook my head and chuckled, "The old 'Star of Gillette' routine-gets them every time."

"Oh, Charlie, don't be so cynical. I depend on those folks for my bread and butter."

'And the silver plate you eat from', I thought to myself, but I just replied, "This from a man who almost never grants interviews and sleeps on a houseboat so no one can find him!"

He opened his mouth to protest but I stopped him. "Just kidding William and I thank you. Every one of those guests out there already loves the show because you want them to! Attendance will go up thirty percent this week just because everyone will come to see if you're still hanging around."

"Don't blow smoke, old Chum!" He laughed then put on a calculating expression. "Twenty-five percent is more realistic!"

That banter continued until we reached the top of the stairs where we were met by the usher who worked the private boxes on this side of the theater. He took us directly to the second box and opened the door for us. A deep rumbling calliope of murmured voices filled the air as the last notes of the orchestra warming up faded into the rafters. As the door shut behind us, William strolled up to the railing and looked out over the folk who were filling the empty seats. Someone below saw him and shouted up a greeting. Again, there was a smattering of applause as he waved down to them.

The whole time he was doing his Caesar routine, I was setting up the small lamp, my script, and pre-focusing my opera glasses. I was ready to go when the lights dimmed and the first few bars of the overture began to rise from the pit. William took his seat and smirked at my arrangements.

"I remember when you could read that script in the dark, keep a hawk's eye on the stage, and pick out every pretty girl in the crowd!"

"Shush! Let me concentrate." I retorted. It took me a moment, but I got the lamp adjusted and the script positioned below it. The 'Burglar's lamp was a nifty devise William suggested to me years ago after attending our first opener together. I had a hurricane lamp, set for low light, on the floor of our box and was constantly fiddling with it to read the script. The lamp I had now was basically a small lantern with shuttered sides. With a low wick and just enough of an opening, the perfect amount of light would illuminate the script for me and shield light from the rest of the house. That way I could follow the script as it was acted out and note any differences or missteps. I could really give a crap about the actual story line! It was how they portrayed it that put the food on my table.

The curtain was about to rise.

PART SIX

By the time intermission was looming, I had to admit that everything was moving along nicely. The cast seemed comfortable with each other and well-rehearsed. The orchestra was right on cue and on key. Paul carried out his role with abundant panache' and the rest of the cast filled out the scenes with real teamwork. There were a few missed marks, some lousy positioning, and a few flubs on the script but nothing the audience would notice.

Of course, when intermission came, that wouldn't stop me from heading backstage to address as many of the small issues as I could before the second half began.

"I think tonight I shall forego observing you pass out tongue lashings like a proud new father does cigars!" William said with a sly smile and a wink. "Instead, I shall join the crowd downstairs and see if I can't find a pretty girl to pass the time with!"

I laughed and clapped him on the shoulder. "You do that but be careful! These western gals are bound to be rougher than the genteel fairer ones you're used to. You get too friendly and you're bound to have a shot gun in your back and a ring on your finger before I can save you!"

We split up and I left him to go spread his charisma like the Johnny Appleseed of charm. He did love an audience and the intermission crowd would be thrilled to rub elbows with the famous William Gillette.

As I watched him walk jauntily down the stairs, tipping his hat and mouthing hellos, I realized he was back to his old self. I was satisfied that this trip was turning out to be a bigger success than I had hoped for!

When I reached the backstage, I found that Kevin was about to address most of the salient points I wanted to make. As I stood off to one side in the shadows of the curtains, he dashed about. Snapping instructions at everyone in his path and calling up adjustments to the lighting crew. He jested to the scenery crew, prodded the extras, and still found enough grace to pat a few on the back. Kevin Salmon was every bit as good as I was at his age. So, I contented myself with greeting a few of the veterans of my productions and taking pulls off my flask. When Salmon did notice me from across the stage, he came right over but rolling his eyes, so I just told him it was going great and strolled off, leaving him to his work.

I thought about joining William out front but decided, in the end, to run down the usher and order a drink. By the time I had reached my seat and shed my hat and cane, the waiter arrived with my double Manhattan. I sat back in quiet contemplation of the script and by the time the cherry started bouncing off my nose as I sipped, I had decided that life was grand. I told William as much immediately as he returned.

"How many have you had?" he laughed as he took his seat. He looked a bit mauled over, but he was flushed and smiling.

As a general life rule, I never answered questions like that, so I bent the conversation, "The big fight scene's next! Man, I love watching Paul swing that blade around."

"I won't argue there. He is the best in the business for sword fights."

The first strains of the introduction wafted up from far below and the lights dimmed. A hush fell over the crowd that deepened as the curtain began to rise. William and I both leaned forward in anticipation.

In this scene, set on a country road in France, D'Artagnan and the other musketeers were on their way back to Paris after stealing back the Queen's necklace from Buckingham and thwarting the Cardinal's plans.

They stumble on a patrol of the Cardinal's men, who were sent to stop them from reaching the capitol. Then the action heated up!

From the right-hand side of the stage, a voice called out in military fashion, abet with a slight French accent, "Company -- Dismount!"

There came the sound of creaking leather and jangling equipment and even a horse's whinny. Again, a voice cried out, still hidden from our sight. "Company...Form up! Company March!"

A line of soldiers walked onto the stage abreast of each other. They wore pointed hats and goatees, while garbed in deep crimson period uniforms; right down to the red capes with the white fleur di lis stitched into them. The audience nearly hissed and you could almost feel the venom in the air.

Suddenly, laughing and joking amongst themselves, D'Artagnan led the other three Musketeers onto the stage from the left side. He sees the soldiers and stops dead in his tracks. He stops speaking in mid-sentence and holds up his hand. Across the stage, the leader of the patrol made a similar motion as he lurched to a stop.

Then the nightmare began!

According to the script, the Captain of the guards was supposed to draw their firearms and challenge the Musketeers to surrender, where on D'Artagnan was to reply with a witty remark and pull his sword. The soldiers would fire, hitting nothing of course, and the two sides would close in on each other for swordplay.

I was watching this scene intently, focusing on the guardsmen. The Captain ordered them to draw their weapons and in unison, they put their left legs out and pointed their muskets across the stage.

I looked down and checked the script quickly. Now Paul would dodge the bullets, draw his sword, and fight five of the guardsmen, leaving one each for the other Musketeers. Corny, I know but the audience loved that sort of thing.

None of that happened. Before one line was muttered, the ham playing the Captain screamed 'FIRE!" and shot his gun!

The Idiot jumped his cue! My eyes snapped back up to the stage and I rose out of my seat! You could see the confusion on the rest of the soldiers, and they followed suit and joined in on the carnage. Eight more shots rang out, almost making one sound they were so close together.

I can't say I saw the bullet's impact as I was watching the guards with my eyes bugging out of my head in disbelief. I swear I heard the sound of wet meat when they struck! Across the stage, the Musketeers screamed, not on cue, but in pain.

My eyes snapped across the stage from the horrified looks on the guard's faces to what could only be described as a real-life battle scene. Paul was thrashing around the stage, blood spurting from several places on his leg, while another actor, a minor player named Lewis

Monroe, playing Porthos, clutched his hand and screamed like a stuck pig. One of the other two Musketeers, Athos, was also down, slumped against the scenery panel and clutching his side. Artimis stood stock still and wore a look of fear filled with astonishment seemingly uninjured. All of us had the same thought in our heads.

There was live ammo in those Muskets!

PART SEVEN

A single piercing scream sounded from the audience and the flood gates of panic opened! Within a split second, half the onlookers were screaming and shouting while others were rushing the exits. To my shame I admit, all that railed in my head was the damage and expense this would cost me, today and in the future.

William, though, kept his sanity. "Paul!" he cried in genuine concern as he dashed out into the hallway. That word and deed snapped me back into the moment. I was on his heels as he took the private stairs down to the backstage.

Coming out of the quiet stairway to the backstage was like dropping from still water right into the rapids. It was absolute pandemonium. Between the crying, yelling, and the sound of the curtain coming down, I couldn't hear myself think! Ripped from their perfectly planned routine, no one knew what to do next. People were either running around like beheaded chicken or huddled into little groups, wailing and gnashing their teeth. I couldn't believe my eyes when I saw Salmon pull that blackjack he confiscated earlier and brandish it at a group of men, screaming and waving fists at a terrified crew member pinned against the wall with obvious ill intent. The mob decided it wasn't intent enough to face a whack from Salmon.

William grabbed me by the arm and pulled me in close, "See to your people, Frohman! I need to speak with Salmon immediately. I looked at him sharply, but I saw the change was on him, so I left him to it and rushed to Paul. There was a tight ring around him, so I had to holler and push my way through.

Paul was lying in a near fetal position. Mary was at his side cradling his lolling head, while an older man was pulling tight a piece of rope wrapped high around Paul's wounded thigh. Paul's body spasmed with pain as he appeared to lose consciousness. The rest of the leg was soaked with blood as was the front of Julia's dress and the man's arms.

"Somebody, get a doctor!" I screamed, loud enough to dwarf the tremulous din. "Check the audience!"

"We tried, Sir, but no one even looked back!"

"Then call the nearest hospital!"

"I already did, Sir!" I heard a voice say and turned to see the lug who delayed our entrance. "The hospital is sending over an ambulance!"

One bullet had hit just above the knee and while we learned later that he had been struck twice more in the same leg. Worse, when the old man finished with the leg, he cut the straps of his tabard and pulled it aside to uncover not less than four more wounds! I turned my head away, eyes filling up. Surely, my friend was a goner!

The other victim, Monroe, was being tended to also, by some of the more level-headed cast. Someone had cut the sleeve off his shirt to put a tourniquet on his forearm and one of the girls was gently wrapping a white cloth around his hand. I stepped over and put a hand on his shoulder,

"Steady man," and I told him, "I'm sure an ambulance will be here shortly. We'll get you off to the hospital and they'll fix you up." I gave him my open flask and he took a grateful pull. He swallowed, took another and handed it back to me. When he did, I notice a series of long scratches along the back of his hand and on his forearm. They looked painful enough, but nothing compared to the hand torn apart by a bullet. The cloth was already soaked with blood.

He stared at me with glazed, sunken eyes, "God damn amateurs!" he muttered just loud enough for me to hear. "Can't anyone follow a script?" I thought he was going into shock. The girl finished wrapping his hand and he clutched it to his chest, rocking back and forth slightly, yet glaring at Paul, who had passed out with Mary sobbing over him.

William joined me just before they led Monroe away to find a place to lay him down before the ambulance came. I looked over and saw a crowd around the man who played Athos, but William put a hand on my arm before I could go over.

He shook his head sadly and I saw someone covered Athos's face with a cloth. I was filled with despair at the thought that someone had died. Of the thousands of accidents and mishaps I have seen in this business, no one had ever lost their life on one of my productions. I might have broken down myself if the medical people hadn't arrived just then.

They were quick and efficient. A doctor swooped in with three stretchers and the wounded and dead were loaded and hustled away.

Monroe was strapped in and about to be on his way, when a young pipsqueak ran up.

"Hold up! Excuse me Mr. Monroe. Mr. Brodnicki wants me to take the pistol back to the prop room. I already have your sword."

Monroe glared at him with an expression between contempt and confusion.

"My What?"

"The pistol Sir. Mr. Brodnicki –."

He never finished because Monroe ripped the flintlock from beneath his cloak and flung it right at the boy's face. We all flinched at the malicious act.

The kid had good hands and he caught it just before it smashed his nose.

Everyone froze at the violence of the act, but the boy kept his cool and slowly lowered the gun to his side and squeaked out, "And your scabbard too."

Monroe rose up slightly, his face a rictus of painful rage. He turned his head up at the medic, "Get me to a doctor-NOW!"

They started off and the boy had the nerve to reach out and try to grab the gurney. I put a restraining hand on his arm, "Let it go, Kid. We'll get it later."

"But…But my boss – Mr. Brodnicki and his boss Mr. Salmon both told me to get it!

"I'll deal with them." I assured him. "Just tell them I said it was OK."

The kid gave me a haughty look and asked my name.

"I'm Charles Frohman. And who might you be?"

His face went white. "Nobody, sir." And he scurried over to a handcart and began to pull it away as fast as he could.

I grabbed the doctor's arm before he followed them out. "Make sure they get the best of everything! Whatever they need! I'll be down later to check on them."

Now that the wounded were gone and some of the urgency of the situation abated, I took a long look around at the cast and crew. As it often does, despair turned into anger, then rage.

"How could this have happened?" I lamented, looking at William.

"I am sure the popular explanation would be that someone misloaded the weapons, Frohman."

Before I could make a sarcastic remark, Kevin came running over to us.

"All set, William," Salmon reported, "I've got all the exits covered and everyone I could think who was on or backstage is accounted for. All the men who fired a shot are in my office under a watchful eye and the muskets and pistols are back in props."

William looked at me, "I hope I have not overstepped, Frohman. I took the liberty of having Salmon collect the firearms, detain everyone and post guards at the exits. I thought it prudent until we can figure out what happened here."

"What are you talking about? We know what happened! Some idiot doesn't know the difference between a blanks and real McCoy bullets!"

"Or perhaps someone does," he replied reasonably. "Taking into account-."

Now, I wasn't about to let him turn this into another of his little capers, although I never seem to have a choice. "Why do you want to go fishing about? It was obviously a screw up in props! What we –."

"Charles!" Salmon interrupted me, "We should listen to William. I think the matter bears some considering. If who loaded the guns was the man I think it was, I'd bet my life he didn't make a green horn mistake like that!

"I was down here and…well…I can't put my finger on it but there was something wrong with the…the whole scene"

My first reaction was to peel his hide for bucking me like that, but I realized that he had even more to lose than I did. His first production and it folded before it made it through one show.

William chimed in, "We must eliminate all other possibilities-."

"Oh, don't start with that!" I snapped, cutting him off. "What we need to do is find the prop crew and wring someone's neck!"

"That would be B.J." Salmon supplied.

"Brodnicki?" I snarled.

William cut in harshly. "Let us find Bernard and hear whatever explanation he has to offer."

"Don't you want to talk to the men who pulled the triggers first?" Salmon asked.

"No. Sequester them in your office and do not let them change! Keep them supervised and don't let them have contact with anyone until we have talked to them."

"Why are you waiting?" I asked. I'll admit I was jumpy, but I could feel the tension in the air. Everyone had time to digest what just happened and the mutterings grew louder by the minute. "You got time to sweat them? You can't possibly believe that all eight men planned this mayhem!"

William gave us a long look, "I grant you that scenario seems unlikely, but it needs to be explored. We need to gather as much information as we can before we question those men. One or more of them may hold the key."

I thought it was a bunch of hooey, but I've learned not to argue with William. I closed one eye and tilted my head at him, as we followed Salmon across the stage, "You really think there's something more than criminal stupidity in this mess?"

He didn't answer, and I didn't expect one. His face wore that expression of intense concentration that pinched his face and made his ears stick out. Without looking at me, his eyes sweeping our surroundings like there was a little artist sketching the scenes in his head for further reference, he said, "Did you notice those scratches on Monroe's hands and arms?"

"As a matter of fact, I did. They were the least of his injuries. I think he lost a chunk of his palm." When William didn't comment further, I asked, "So what about them? Probably got them when he went down."

"No, they were hours old, not minutes. None were bleeding, but they had already formed a scab. A distinctive pattern gotten in a familiar way."

I sighed in my head. At these times, he could be a frustrating man. He just didn't think like a normal person, even if he was always right.

"And just what does that have to do with being shot?" I asked. "If he already had them before he was shot -- Why does it matter?"

"HOW he got them is what matters, Frohman. Every bit of information is another piece of the puzzle." He replied as he walked along. He turned his head and looked down at me. "You would find significance in detail if you would only pay closer attention." Of course, he didn't elaborate.

I could hear a double Manhatten calling me from somewhere.

PART EIGHT

It took some extra time for us to get back to the prop room as we were beseeched every step of the way by players and crew alike. Everyone wanted to know what happened and why they couldn't leave. You'd think every one of them had been shot by the way they were losing their minds. After a lake of tears and numerous angry threats, I had had enough!

"QUIET!" I screamed at the top of my lungs and a hush fell over the entire stage. When I had everyone's attention, I went on in my most commanding voice. "You're right, of course! I have no legal right to keep you all here. You're free to leave if you wish." There were nods of satisfaction and many turned away to go when I added, "BUT!" Then I pulled out my pocket watch and made a show of reading it. "By my calculations, you are all on the clock for the next two hours and twelve minutes! So, anyone who chooses to leave before we have finished, I will consider them as walking off the job and they will be stricken from the payroll." I let that sink into their dumbstruck sculls and added, "The only way you get paid is if you stay and cooperate."

As a whole, the mob didn't like that. Most of them thought they'd be down the street in a bar, now that the play was kaput. They also realized that they were lucky I was offering to pay them some wages just for sticking around. Time to seal the deal.

I cried out loudly, silencing the crowd and grabbing their attention. "For Pete's sake! Your friends and colleagues were slaughtered and maimed today! I know you're good people and you can sit tight for a bit until we figure this out." Then I gave them all a hard look, trying to look each of them in the eye as I scanned the room. "Unless, of course, you bear some responsibility for this mayhem! I imagine that person would rather just take their leave."

With that, I put my head down and pushed my way through the grumbling crowd.

"And those names will be the first I give the coppers," Salmon barked in our wake. "Now go find some place to sit and be quiet!"

I had a full head of steam when we reached the prop room. The door was open, and it was lit up, so I charged right in and found the culprit I was looking for. Bernard J. Brodnicki was a slight man, all elbows, knees and Adam's apple. His longish hair swayed with his almost bird like movements as he bustled around a long work bench set against one wall. He was examining one of the muskets, Salmon had gathered up, but set it down as I came up to him.

"Brodnicki!" I growled in my most menacing tone, "Tell me you didn't make the last mistake of your life!"

His eyes went wide with terror and he was trembling when he stuttered, "No... No...Sir! I loaded those muskets myself! There were no mistakes!"

I tilted my head and continued to glare at him in silence. After a minute, he composed himself and went on. "I don't understand it myself! I know I put blanks in all the guns!"

I stepped forward, making Bernard press his back against the table and with my belly up against his chest, screaming, "That carnage didn't come out of blanks, B.J.! There is a dead man out there and we'll be lucky if he's the only one! You had better have a good explanation, because if I find out this was your fault, I swear-."

B.J.'s face contorted with horror and his eyes welled with tears, "NO! No! I didn't-."

"Didn't what?" I cut him off. "Screw up?"

I didn't think it possible, but his eyes got even wider and the tears rolled down his face. "Lord no! I would never...I...I've known Mr. Gilmore for years and me and Munroe just went coyote hunting a few nights ago. I couldn't hurt any of them. They were my friends!" He looked past me and beseeched, "Kevin! Mr. Gillette! Tell him! Tell him I would never do something like that! I know my job. I would never endanger anyone! Whatever came out of those muskets, isn't what I put in them! I know the difference between a blank and a live round! Blanks are shorter and thicker! I have a new box right here. I... I don't even have any live rounds here!"

He spun around to the table and started going through the drawers like a drunk looking for his first snort of the day. He cried out in relief when he found what he was looking for and he slammed a box that rattled down on the tabletop.

"Here! Here they are! These are what I put in those rifles today! Blanks, by God! Fresh from a new box! Go ahead! Count them!" The tears were rolling down his face by then and I was afraid he might start foaming at the mouth, he was so upset. He kept up the gibberish in a low voice as he hugged himself with both arms.

317

I looked at William and he nodded slightly. Placing my hands on his shoulder, I gently straightened the poor man upright and said soothingly. "It's alright, B.J. I believe you." The tone of my words had a miraculous effect on him, and he immediately settled down and looked at me, wide eyed but in control.

"I swear on a stack of Bibles that I didn't want this to happen."

"I know. But I had to be sure." Unfortunately, though I was relieved that B.J. hadn't done anything intentionally wrong. Nor did I think in my heart that he made a mistake. I had the sinking feeling that William might just be right once again and this was going to turn from an unfortunate mishap into a quick Sherlock investigation. And it had better be quick.

"None the less," William finally spoke, "It has happened, Brodnicki, and we need to know how and before the rest of the cast and crew get wind that this was no accident!"

B.J. looked sheepish and mumbled, "A lot of people pointed fingers at me, and some were really mean about it. I told them I put blanks in those muskets, and they needed to talk to someone else about the live rounds."

William was chagrined. He even slapped the table for effect as he barked, "Damn it! Withholding that information could have given us a clear path to the solution!

"By now, I am sure that the entire cast and crew of this production know that there has been a foul deed committed today. This has made our task more difficult. We must move quickly before the culprits can cover their tracks."

"And we better find out before the cops get wind of it," Salmon put in, "or we're all in for a world of trouble!"

Our profession has always been a bit at odds with the law. A lifestyle of looser morals and lax attitude towards illegal substances in general is enough reason to shy away from the authorities. I don't condone it myself, but I've been around long enough to realize that creativity promotes a certain flamboyancy which flies in the face of every flat foot's sense of order.

"You're right Kevin. There's blood in the water and that's going to draw the sharks. Better have someone fetch our lawyer out here. I want some representation here when the Police arrive."

Salmon nodded and turned to carry out my instructions, William walked Salmon to the door, talking in a low voice. Salmon nodded again and left, closing the door firmly behind him. William turned slowly and surveyed the room, packing away every detail into his head, and then fixed his eyes back on B.J. Then slowly walked back to the prop manager and looked at a spot over B.J.'s head, saying in a grave voice, "I need to know your exact movements for the last two hours! Leave no detail out!" Then he steepled his fingers under his chin, closed his eyes until they were mere slits, and tuned out everything but B.J.'s narrative. I could see why William chose not to watch him. BJ was the nervous energetic type and his limbs were shaking. He was either hopping from foot to foot or throwing his arms around in a pseudo mime fashion. Even his voice echoed off various spots in the room as he shifted about.

"Well...uh...two hours ago is just about when I unlocked the weapons locker. I had already taken out all

319

the swords and daggers to wipe them down and assigned them, so I took out the rifles for the second act. Then-."

"When you say, 'assigned them' do you mean you assign a particular piece to each individual? Do you keep a written record?"

B.J. seemed almost offended at William's comment. "Of course!"

William ignored the jibe. "Fetch it."

B.J. hesitated just a second then he crossed the room to his desk and grabbed a ledger. He came back and handed it to William. BJ started to say something, but William buried his nose in the book and said curtly, "Continue."

"OK, OK...then I numbered them and laid them out on the table to wipe them down and loaded them. Then I proceeded to load the Flintlock pistol for the married man's dream scene. I put a little black powder, but no ball or wadding of course. Just enough powder in the pan to make a cloud of smoke but no real bang." He paused and looked up at William. Then Brendon and Jesse came in and I sent Jesse out with the silhouettes to lighting and Brendon took the gear over to Sound. Last, I wiped down the muskets and the flintlock pistol and loaded them." He paused and gave us a defiant look, "With Blanks! Well, except for the Pistol, that I just put a little powder in the pan. Nice pop and a lot of smoke."

"Why the pistol? Who had that?" I asked.

"Nobody in that scene," B.J. explained. "It was for the next scene, when my hero gets to shoot his ex-wife."

Even William smiled at that. B.J. was referring to the scene where Porthos executes the Countess De Winter after recovering the queen's jewels. I noticed William was starting to chafe again.

"Keep the train on the tracks B.J.," I admonished him before William carped again. "Then what'd you do?"

He shrugged, "It was fifteen minutes until the curtain, so I gathered everything up and took the bundle to the prop table."

William snapped his head around, "Which was located where?"

"Right center stage. There's a little alcove behind the backdrop wall. Want me to show you?"

"Shortly. Could anyone get at it?"

"Well... it isn't a locked room if that's what you're asking, but everyone knows to stay away from the prop table. If you muddle that up and it can throw the whole play off."

I shook my head, "Well somebody 'muddled' it you Saphead! Somebody had to switch those rounds,unless of course you really did-."

"I didn't!" he screeched, "I told you, I-."

"Enough!" William barked and gave us both a stern look. Nothing happened for a moment and I was about to gesture to William to get moving to the prop room now that Salmon arrived, but the door swung open and the bustling ginger walked in.

"Did you find him?" I asked.

"I sent one of the gillies. He's got a bicycle, but it is still an hour at best before the lawyer shows up."

"Have the police arrived?" William asked. Salmon shook his head. "Then let's move along gentlemen."

As usual, his long legs took him right out the door without a glance to see if we were following him. B.J. was right on his heels with Salmon and I behind. When we were out of the room, I could see William's standing profile about twenty feet ahead. He had that impatient look about him. When he was in character, delays were one of the many things he had little toleration for. This delay was B.J. as he slowly, with great flourish, locked the prop room behind him and buried the key in his pocket.

"See!" he proclaimed, "I'm always careful!"

William, still not looking directly at us, barked into the rafters, "Gentlemen! Time is of the essence!" He turned and resumed walking, leaving us to trail him like a pack of hounds.

PART NINE

The commotion had died down a bit and we made our way across the backstage. A few people tried to get our attention, but Salmon put them off reminding them that the more they pestered us the longer we'd all be stuck here.

Still, we didn't make it there right away. We were but a few feet away from our destination when Salmon suddenly froze and shouted, pointing off to our right, "YOU! Higgins! Where do you think you're going?"

We all stopped and followed his finger to a figure coming out of one of the dressing rooms. Jeremy Higgins was dressed in civilian clothes and stooped over, locking the door behind him. When he looked up and saw us, he gave the key a final twist. Higgins then straightened up, and tried to walk away, acting like he never saw us. Before anyone could say a word, Salmon growled and caught the man in a few steps and grabbed the man by his arm to swing him around. It was Artemis, the unscathed musketeer and he didn't look happy.

I couldn't make out what he snarled at Salmon, but that fiery red head reached into his jacket and produced the blackjack he took off the bouncer earlier.

"Sweet Jesus save us! "As soon I that blurted out, I looked to William. He made no comment except to tell B.J. to wait for us in the prop room and to touch nothing. I was afraid Salmon was going to bash in Jeremy's head and William must have too as he stepped over the scenery to find Salmon and Jeremy in a heated discussion.

"This play is finished, Salmon, so I don't work for you anymore and you can't keep me here against my will!" he said in a quivering voice. Jeremy looked at me as I stepped up. "You can keep my lousy pay! I just want to go back to my hotel and drink.

Salmon smacked the sap into the palm of his hand. "The only way you're walking out of here is with a good explanation or on a stretcher!"

Jeremy recoiled in fear as I asked "Salmon! What have you got against him?"

Salmon turned to me, "Don't you think it's a bit funny that eight men shoot at four and one is killed, two are wounded, and one is completely untouched?"

Jeremy bristled, "Are you accusing me of something because I was lucky enough not to get shot?"

"I don't believe in luck!"

"Then perhaps you should believe in providence." William said loudly, cutting off the argument. "Perhaps we should go into your dressing room Mr. Higgins. There are a few questions we need to ask." Jeremy looked as if he was about to be contrary again, but William gave him a level stern look. "I must insist!"

"Put away the thumper," I told Salmon quietly as Higgins hung his head and unlocked the door. "He's been through a lot, let's not spook him anymore."

Salmon just glanced at me as he stepped over to William and whispered. "He's hiding something. He's way too eager to get out of here!"

William never took his eyes from Jeremy and replied in a soft voice. "Perhaps, Salmon, but we are certainly not going to beat it out of him. Stay alert while I interview him."

We piled into the small room after him and Jeremy plopped himself in his dressing table's chair, hunched over with his elbows on his knees and his head buried in his hands. After a moment, his shoulders started to shake, and it was obvious he was crying. He raised his tear streaked face and looked to me.

"Please, Mr. Frohman, I just want to go home! It's all too much..." He buried his face again and William tapped his chest and jerked his head at the sobbing actor, gesturing to give him a drink. I didn't like sharing my private stock with the help, but these circumstances were extreme. I took out my flask and tapped it on the back of his hand. Jeremy opened his eyes then straightened up and eagerly took a swig.

After a moment, he stopped mewling and wiped his eyes. The hooch acted like liquid courage and he gathered himself enough to fix us with a glare. He glared at the three of us for a minute and we glared right back, but when Salmon reached into his coat for the blackjack, he threw up his hands in surrender.

"Alright! Alright! What do you want to know?"

"Anything that may shed some light on this matter. For example --why would I think you were 'Involved'?"

Jeremy opened his mouth to speak, but he must have thought better as he stayed silent while he gathered his thoughts.

"Everybody in this damn room knows that someone switched the bullets in those muskets. Hell, everyone in this theater knows it!

I...I don't know how or why, but if you think my being spared is reason to suspect me, you are wrong! Whoever did this is no friend of mine."

"Indeed," William replied. "Can you think of a reason why someone would wish to harm you?"

"No, I can't. I get along with pretty much everyone and I'm not on either end of any grudges."

"Then please forgive my being so forward, but are there any recent failed romances in your life? Money problems?"

Jeremy gave William a level look then snorted. "I see where you're going with this. Mr. Gillette, I am 28 years old, single, not deformed, have enough coin in the bank to live well, am doing what I love, surrounded by a bevy of beautiful and available girls. Am I even remotely a likely candidate for suicide?"

William considered that for a moment. "Then one of the others, or all three of your fellow actors were the targets, those who were struck by rounds."

Higgins stiffened at that. "You keep throwing that in my face! I don't have the foggiest notion why they missed me, but I assure you that if I knew those men were about to unload real bullet in my direction, I'd be humping the floorboards before they cocked their hammers!"

"That's the spirit!" Salmon muttered.

William ignored him, "Tell us what transpired from when the intermission started and the attempted murder."

Higgins mulled it over and shrugged, a haunted look in his eyes, "Nothing really. After the curtain came down, Paul went off to find his friend, Mary. Matt and I went back to his stall and... went over the next scene."

Salmon snorted, "With a bottle and not a script, I'll wager."

Higgins shrugged again, "One needs to be a little loose for a good fight scene."

"Where was Monroe?"

"Lewis? I can't say. He wandered off on his own as usual. Mooning over some gal, I'm sure. He's been mooning over the same one since rehearsals began."

"Which one?" I asked.

"We have no idea. At first, he made a lot of talk about the 'woman of his dreams', but then he must have got turned down because he would just mope and sigh and by the time dress rehearsals came up. Lewis was pissed off at the world. It got to be that we couldn't stand to be around him when we were off stage."

That surprised me a bit. "Really? You all seemed to work well together."

Higgins raised his eyebrows. "We're all professionals, Mr. Frohman. We work for you."

I ignored him. "Go on."

"Not much more to tell. Matt and I headed back about ten minutes before the curtain went up. Monroe was already in place. The idiot was off to one corner, lunging with his tin blade and moving his pistol from side to side in his belt after every thrust. Told us he was trying to find the right position, so it didn't fall out during the fight. Paul showed up right before the call boy came and we took our positions. The curtain went up and we entered...well, you know the rest.

"Paul didn't even get through the opening lines when they jumped their cue and...seven shots later, people are screaming and bleeding all around me and Matt... Matt..." He choked up and huge tears leaked from his eyes. His mouth moved silently for a minute and then he finally croaked, "Could I please go home now?"

Salmon shook his head and looked disgusted that a man should carry on so. I must admit, I had nothing but sympathy for the man. I didn't think he knew any more about what happened than we did.

William obviously didn't feel the same as I did. He shot to his feet and loomed over Higgins in his chair. No half-lidded looks, his eyes bored into Higgins like a drill went into wood.

"No! You may not go home, and you may never see your home for a long time indeed if you are not far more forthcoming, Higgins!"

Jeremy stopped sniveling as his eyes grew wide and fear replaced his grief.

"You are, if not lying outright, are withholding information that may be vital to this investigation!" he gestured downward with his finger and our eyes went to Jeremy's left hand that was clutching the left side pocket of his coat. "Could you be hiding something in the pocket? I noticed your hands strayed there a few times while you spoke."

Higgins shifted his weight in the chair, and I thought he might make a run for it, but we all were ready, so he sank back in the chair and dropped his head to his chest.

"I know I should have told you right off," he mumbled into his shirt as he reached into the pocket. He rooted around for a few seconds then pulled out a handful and dropped it on his table.

It was seven shiny brass shells with no slugs on the ends. The blanks.

Higgins looked up to William forlornly and asked, "How did you know?"

One corner of William's mouth twitched in a near smirk, "Your explanation?"

Gone were the crocodile tears and the panicked mannerisms. Higgins seemed relieved to answer. "After they checked me out, I came back to my stall to change out of my costume. When I put on my jacket, I found them in the pocket. There's no lock on the door and I left here before the play started and didn't return until a short time ago when I came to change clothes." Jeremy paused as he choked up a bit, "If Matt…were alive, he could verify everything I'm saying is true. Someone is trying to frame me. If your half as clever as they say, you would know that."

William didn't react to that, except to ask, "Why?"

Higgins looked William right in the eye, "I don't know. I've been racking my brain since I found the damn things.

Will just pouted his lips in a noncommittal manner and asked, "Where is your costume?"

Higgins was as surprised as us at the change in topics. He pointed to the door. "Hanging on that peg."

Without another word, William turned and carefully picked the white body leotard and held it up to the light. The other three of us just stared at him like he was a magician performing a trick, but he simply rehung it after a careful perusal and turned back to Jeremy.

"You may go now if you still wish."

Without another glance at us, he shot from his chair and walked to the door. He had it opened and was halfway out when William stopped him by saying, "Yet, Mr. Higgins, I would be sure to be at your lodgings if the police wish to speak with you. I assure you their treatment will be far harsher than mine."

"I'll be there, Sir. Drunk or passed out."

PART TEN

I had a lot of faith in my friend, but I couldn't see why he'd let that man walk away. But if I was confused, Salmon was outraged. I'd wager it took all his control not to rip into William, so I broached the subject.

"Do you really think that was wise to let him go, William?"

He shrugged. "There was nothing more to be gained by holding him here. I believe he knows less about what happened than we do."

"And what did checking his uniform for skid marks contribute?"

Salmon snickered at that, but William just gave me one of his long-suffering sighs and plucked one of the brass blank shells off the table. He tossed it to me. I caught it and looked at it closely. After a moment, I tossed it back to him, and then rubbed my fingers together. They were oily.

"Machine oil," William informed me. "The uniforms are silk and there would have been telltale stains if he had switched the bullets and brought them back to the room. Frohman, he's nothing but an intended patsy. An extremely lucky one, yet still a patsy."

William looked over at Salmon, who was hoping from foot to foot glaring at the ceiling. William must have thought it amusing too as he smirked and said, "Though Mr. Salmon does not agree with my actions, I fear."

Kevin's head snapped down and he glared at William. "No, Mr. Salmon does not! He had the dang blanks! That tells us something! He must know what happened! And you just let him waltz out of here! He's probably halfway to Mexico by now."

"Stop!" William ordered and Salmon's jaw snapped shut. "If you wish to contribute to these inquiries, think your comments through! Do not waste my time with conjecture, emotions, or innuendo! Do you honestly believe that Higgins talked all the guardsmen to fire live rounds and miss him deliberately?"

"No, I suppose not." Salmon replied sheepishly. He thought for a moment and shook his head, "I can't even see all the men playing the guardsmen working together. I've been thinking about it and they all have a different clique. The only time you see them together is at rehearsals." He was silent for a moment then shook his head again. "It doesn't make sense! Why would someone switch the bullets and then try to frame Higgins for it?"

I answered. "Whoever switched the bullets must have come out of the prop room and dumped them as fast as they could. This stall is as close as any."

"Ah! You are on the right track, Frohman, but answer this. How did our murderer know this stall was empty? Most of the cast go back to their rooms during intermission."

"That's right!" Salmon exclaimed. "Higgins said that Gilmore and Monroe went off while they headed to Barnes's room for whatever."

"Well, someone else must have seen them," I pointed out, "cuz out of those three, one's dead and the other two are shot up? I doubt Monroe, Barnes or Paul set themselves up to be peppered with lead."

"When all other possibilities have been eliminated, whatever remains…" William reminded me.

"-no matter how improbable," I picked up.

"Must be the solution!" We said together.

I'm not sure Salmon followed that reasoning, but he was having deep thoughts about the matter. "You know, it seems to me, and stop me Mr. Gillette if I'm wrong, that we need to figure out why someone switched the rounds. That would lead us to who did it."

"That is one possibility," William replied.

"That's if you don't think it's a conspiracy."

"I never said that, Salmon." William interjected. "I need to speak to the Cardinal's men. Have you gathered them up?"

"I put Winslow on it just after you arrived, so I imagine they're all in my office waiting for us."

"Let's check the prop room, and then get their side of the story." Without further discussion, he turned and headed for the door, leaving Salmon with his mouth open. "Come along Gentlemen. Time waits for no man."

William stepped briskly to the door but when he grasped the handle and pulled it open, a young man stumbled into the room. William stepped aside like a matador and if I hadn't stuck out my arm for him to catch, he would have kissed the floor!

The kid stood up right and looked back over his shoulder to see William staring at him for the inconvenient delay he was. He blinked a few times and looked around the room until he saw Salmon.

"Oh! There you are."

"What have you got Ty?"

"You wanted to know if there was any word from the hospital."

We all craned forward to hear the news of our friends. Even Sherlock by the door had a glint of humanity in his eyes.

"Give."

"Well Sir, Miss Corbet is back. I figured you'd want to hear it from her."

"Don't give me that guff, Ty! Spill"

"Mr. Gilmore is in bad shape. They're operating on him still and will be for a while. It doesn't look good. Miss Corbet is in rough shape too. She's holed up in her stall and hitting the jug pretty hard."

"How do you know all this?" I asked.

"Ty is my call boy. He's like one of those swamis. Hears all, sees all, and knows all." He winked at me, "King of the keyholes."

"Then tell me, King Ty," William said as he turned to face the call boy. "What did you observe right before the curtain went up for the second half?"

Ty looked to Salmon, who nodded, before he spoke. "I was just doing my job, ya know. I went over to the west wing to make sure the musketeers were ready. When I got there, Mr. Gilmore had just arrived, and the others were already in place. Costumes looked good except for Monroe, and Mr. Gilmore assured me that he'd take his cue when the curtain was all the way up, so I headed over to the east wing."

"What was wrong with Monroe's costume?" William interrupted.

"Nothing with his clothes. He just had his sword out. I went over to him and reminded him his sword was to be sheathed when he went on. He told me that his scabbard was broken, and his sword wouldn't go all the way in. I offered to try and get another one, but he said 'no'. So, I told him to at least keep it down." Ty hesitated and got a

333

bit red in the face. "Then he told me he would sheath it in my backside if I didn't bugger off, so I left. You know actors, bunch of spoiled brats, every one of them."

William kept a straight face, "Thank you, King Ty. That will be all."

"There's one more thing," Ty said, turning back to Salmon "The coppers showed up at the hospital just as she was heading out. Miss Corbet slipped out a side door, so she didn't have to answer any questions."

Salmon clutched his head, "You might have mentioned that first TY!"

"That tears it," I said. "we're out of time William. You can't possibly sort this all out before the police get here."

He raised his eyebrows and smirked, "There's always the chance you may be right, Frohman".
Then out the door he went.

PART ELEVEN

As I followed William, I realized that we had stepped from the frying pan into the fire. Across the way, at the mouth of the alcove where the prop table was, we could see thrashing movements and a caterwaul that sounded like a bloody murder was occurring. As my eyes adjusted, I could see what appeared to be a woman absolutely drubbing B.J. with a parasol! Poor B.J. was crying his innocence, but it was falling on deaf ears.

William sped up and jumped over some scenery props as Salmon sped past me. By the time I had gone around the props, William had Christine Corbet in a bear hug, while Salmon was helping B.J. to his feet. Miss Corbet, though restrained physically kept verbally assaulting at full volume, shaking her parasol. With Paul's blood still all over the front of her dress, she looked like a madwoman as she ranted, "You little vermin! Or are you an idiot! How could you be so stupid! I should shoot you, you son of a …"

It was obvious the call boy's report was accurate as she was three sheets to the wind. She struggled a moment longer, then snarled over her shoulder at William, "Unhand me you Brute!"

It was almost comical until she broke her arm free and raised her weapon of choice to lay into William. Salmon quickly stepped over and snatched the stick out of her hand and tossed it away. Grabbing her by both shoulders, he shook her like a rag doll. When her eyes focused again, he said firmly, "Stop this Christine! This was not B.J.'s fault. Someone else switched the rounds in the muskets."

Her eyes went wide, and she shook her head. "What? That's crazy. Why would someone do something that mean? For what reason?"

Kevin opened his mouth to reply but William talked over him. "Now is neither the time nor place for this discussion. I suggest you take Miss Corbet back to her dressing room. Frohman and I will pick you up there on the way to our last stop."

"And hide her bottle," I suggested before I took a pull on my own flask.

William rolled his eyes at me and turned his attention to B.J. "Are you alright? Do you need medical attention?"

I hadn't realized how hard she had laid into him until I saw him in better light. His face had quite a few red welts and as he unbuttoned his shirt sleeve and peeled it back, his forearm was covered with more welts. He touched them tenderly, winced then put his arm down.

"I'll live, I guess. I'm just glad you got here when you did. Papa raised me to never strike a girl, but I was about to!"

William flashed the briefest of smiles, "Indeed, we feared for her safety. Now, quickly describe how this prop station is operated."

The prop station was set in a small alcove where the scenery walls met, in the rear center of the stage. Only a thick piece of old curtain separated it from the walkway we were on and when B.J. flipped the cloth back, there was really nothing to see.

A long pine table was set against the back wall. At the time there was only a single box on the table which was to be used to hold the Queen's stolen jewelry for the third act. After thirty seconds I had seen it all.

"There's nothing here, William. Why are we wasting time?"

William ignored me, as usual, "May I assume you left the muskets here for the Cardinal's men to retrieve?"

"Yes. I put the rifles and the pistol and the box here."

"Did you assign anyone to watch the room?"

"No. Not that I would have necessarily, I just didn't have the men to waste standing guard over them. Not on opening night! There were fires to put out everywhere! You know how it is! Besides, there wasn't much in here. Everyone signs out for whatever they need for a show like this."

"Were you aware that Monroe's scabbard was broken?"

Changing directions like that confused B.J. for a moment, but after thinking it over, he replied, "Broken how? It was fine when he signed out with it! You want to see his signature to that effect?"

William didn't answer. He just stood rock still staring into the room like there was a vison of the lord on the wall. I could almost see his scalp light up from all the activity going on in his head. I was used to these bouts of sudden meditation, but the clock was ticking. I took another swig to give him a moment. William still didn't move, so I opened my mouth.

"William? What are we doing? There's nothing in here but that stupid box!"

Suddenly, his eyes lit up and his face looked like it did when he made his curtain call. That giddy smugness only he could portray.

"That's it precisely, Frohman!"

337

And again, he turned a started walking away, "Come along, Frohman. It is time to put your theory to the test!"

I had to almost run to catch up to him as he strode with purpose across the stage. "Where are we going now?"

"We shall have a word with our Miss Corbet, retrieve Salmon, and then we are onto the Cardinal's men." He looked down at me and winked. "We are still one step ahead of the local constabulary if we are quick enough."

"What did you mean, back in the prop station, when you said-"

I never got to finish the question because a man suddenly stepped in my path, bringing me up short. It was the director, Benjamin Buckley. And I could tell with one look, he was drunk.

"There you are, Frohman!" he snapped, "I have been looking for you all over this stage! I ham dishpleashed with this entire producshun! First, I'm dragged out here into the wilderness, then saddled with so called 'actors', who can neither learn their lines or their proper movements with a prop." His voice went up a notch, "I won't even bother to menshun the guns and blood! That was in total disregard for my expert instrucshuns! I will NOT work under these condishuns!"

He stood there, looking at me in drunken defiance with that glassy eyed righteousness only the truly inebriated can grasp. I reached up with my left hand and put the palm of my hand over his mouth and nosed and dug my fingers into his cheek before taking a step forward and put all my weight into my left arm to shove him backwards. Then I just kept walking.

He back pedaled ten feet before he tripped and landed on his fat bottom. I won't tolerate a drunk, and especially not an obnoxious one.

William caught up with me this time and gave me his patented smirk.

"What?" I asked.

He stopped smiling and looked serious again, "I am pleased you did not shoot him."

PART TWELVE

Salmon stepped out of Christine's dressing room, just as we walked up. He must have been on the lookout for us. He gently closed the door behind him, looking a little sheepish.

"Miss Corbet is inside, is she not?" William asked.

"Yes, but she got ahold of the bottle before I could find it. She's damn near useless now."

"You couldn't take a bottle away from a wisp of a girl like that? Did she pull a gun on you?"

"It was a hair pin. A long, sharp hair pin and she promised she'd stick it where it matters the most to me!"

William snorted and reached past him to rap on the door. "Miss Corbet? May we have a word with you?"

The was a slight hesitation then a voice called out loudly from inside, "Bring it in, Sonny!" It was followed by a peal of laughter.

Salmon shook his head, opened the door, and ushered us in. Miss Corbet was splayed out on her side upon a couch with a water glass filled with amber fluid in one hand, cigarette in the other. The bloody dress was draped over her dressing chair and though she was clad from head to toe in layers of underclothes from the period in history, it did little to hide her lovely form. Especially with the bodice unlaced to her navel.

"OH Charlie," she wailed "What am I going to do? I have nothing left."

I wasn't quite sure how to answer that. I sat down on a chair across from her and joked, "Don't worry darlin. We won't let you starve."

But my attempt at wit just seemed to set her off. Her eyes narrowed as she threw her cigarette into a large ashtray on the low table between us and she sat up quickly. She might have spilled some of the bourbon if she hadn't managed to take a healthy swig off the top as she moved.

"You think I'm fooling, Buster? I spent every last penny I saved to buy the right clothes and travel out here." Tears welled in her eyes as she swayed slightly. The girl wasn't long for this day, I thought to myself. "And now what have I got?"

William took one look at her and his face turned to stone. I'm not sure if he was offended by her drunkenness or that she loosened the laces on her costume all the way down to her navel. Either way, he took up a position behind the couch and left me to deal with her as he tried not to stare.

She stretched out her free hand to me, great tears filling "Please, Charlie, don't cast me aside like fate has. Surly you'll have something for me. Don't abandon me out here." Her voice trailed off as her eye lids began to droop. I had to speed this up.

"Of course, Christine. Don't you worry your pretty little head about that." That caught her interest and she seemed to come back a little.

"So, tell us how Paul is. What did the Doctors say?"

She shook her head, "Paul can't help me anymore. He's all shot up. Six…he got shot six times! The worst in his knee. The old Doc said he would most likely have to take the bottom half of his leg off. Which makes this his last opening night."

341

At that point, I just wanted to slap the little gold digger, but she was our only source of information for now. "Will he live?"

She shrugged, "They wouldn't say." Then she looked around the room and leaned forward as if to tell me a secret.

"But I don't think the doctors think he's gonna live."

"Damn," was all I could say.

She took a long pull on the drink. "You said it brother!" Then she took another pull and giggled. After a moment she whispered, "I guess I should have stuck with Lewis...." She laughed again, "He only got shot once!"

"How's Monroe doing?" I asked, hoping she could stay with us long enough to answer. She did, if just barely.

Looking slightly confused, she replied, "I dunno. I never asked." That was her last coherent statement, though she kept mumbling as she started going limp. "Where's your handsome friend? ... bit of a stuffed shirt...but he's... single." She pointed out before she slumped over and began to snore softly.

Salmon waggled his eyes at William, but he kept his mouth shut. I had no such restrictions and the look of distaste on his face prompted a comment.

"Well, here you go William. The future Mrs. Gillette on a platter."

He totally ignored my jibe and his reaction threw me off.

"Excellent Frohman! You managed to keep her conscious until we had gleaned the information we needed. No small feat considering the amount of bourbon she drank." He came out from around the couch and headed for the door. I stood to follow him, pleased that I could contribute to the investigation.

"Of course," He threw over his shoulder. "You speak the language."

PART THIRTEEN

Kevin's office was on the opposite side of the stage. We were still twenty or thirty yards from our destination when I grabbed William by the arm and stopped him.

"Will, maybe we should step back and consider this for a moment. We're running out of time and we're no closer as far as I can see. There is no way we can question all nine of those guys, one by one, before the Cops get here. And when they do, I doubt they will appreciate us doing their job. We're theater people from out of town. We'll probably be lucky if they don't arrest us for something."

William didn't respond right away. I thought, for sure, he would kybosh the notion and bull ahead as he always did. Yet, for once, he seemed to be giving the idea some serious thought and the longer he remained silent the more hopeful I became.

"I believe you are right, Frohman," he said in that dreamy way when he was concentrating. "We shall question them all together. That way they can corroborate each other or not."

Then the damn fool just kept walking. Salmon shook his head and shrugged before he stepped off and scooted around in front of William, pulling out his keys for the door. We heard no noise as Salmon unlocked the door, but when it opened, you'd have thought a cannon went off. All ten men in the room leapt from where they were sitting or standing and nine of them converged on

Salmon. William and I were ignored, aside from a few glances. I realized then that these guys were 'stock' actors and probably didn't know William or I. William, at least, seemed pleased by the anonymity as he focused on the group.

With everyone talking at once, you couldn't hear individual statements, but the tones were across the spectrum of emotions. Some angry, some groveling, and more than a few sounded regretful. Salmon was trying to calm them down, but they just kept talking over him, each man crying their innocence. The scene was quickly turning into pandemonium, until one of the ten man, and the biggest, stepped in front of Kevin, brandishing the old familiar sapp.

"PIPE DOWN YOU LOT!" Winston bellowed." They fell silent and he held their complete attention. "now sit down and shut your traps or I'll put you down." A few ominous thuds of the weapon on his palm later and they all found a place to perch.

William, Salmon and I just stared at the group for a moment. Salmon gave them a hard look, most likely to keep them on edge and I'm sure William was gleaning every detail he could from their appearance and their movements. They tended to look down or away from our eyes, not exactly sure of what coming next.

One of the men, who was sitting apart from the rest of the group, couldn't bear the silence any longer. "Mr. Salmon, if-."

"Quiet!" William barked, thrusting a forefinger straight up in the air not even looking directly at him. "You will get your chance to speak." It was then I recognized him as the Captain of the Cardinal's men. He was the one who missed the cue and ordered the crew to shoot. When I looked back over to the rest of the men, I

345

could see varying degrees of contempt on their faces. They obviously blamed him for their troubles.

William noticed the animosity and pounced on it. "Gentlemen, you must realize that your anger is misplaced."

"Are you a cop?" One of the bolder men in front demanded. "I don't think you are, so why are you here?"

All six foot-four, Winston exploded into action. He took two long strides and picked the man off his seat by the front of his shirt. Standing, the man still did not come to Winston's chin and he spoke over the top of his head, addressing all the actors.

"The man asking the questions is William Gillette. The man with him is your employer, Mr. Charles Frohman. Got that?" There were quite a few wide-eyed mutterings from the guardsmen. "Now I don't know if you're patsies or killers, and I don't much care. You WILL answer their questions with a civil tongue and show proper respect!" He dropped the man back in his chair. "Got that?"

He turned to William and nodded, "Go on, sir."

William nodded, almost seeming amused. He took off his hat and placed it on a table next to him. Stepping forward, he addressed the assembly in a stern, but grave voice.

"Gentlemen. Unfortunately, today's events cannot be ascribed to an accident or misfortune. We have learned that the ammunition in your weapons was deliberately switched for live bullets and the result.... was horrific." He let that sink in for a moment. "Moreover, the police will arrive shortly, and I am afraid that they may take the simplest view of the situation. You pulled the trigger and men were shot."

"No! No!" one of the men cried out. You could see he was near to breaking in his panic. "They won't charge me...us with murder, will they? Can they? You said you knew that we didn't know!" Tears were starting to leak from his eyes.

William stepped over to him and said with more compassion that his character usually showed, "You shot Porthos."

The man's jaw dropped, and his eyes exploded out of their sockets and torrents of tears flowed down his cheeks. He looked like he might deny it for just a second, but he broke and sobbed, "YES! God damn me to hell! I was aiming at him! Was I the only one?"

He looked around the room in desperation, but everyone just stared back in silence. "I aimed right for his heart you know...I was caught up in the moment. I wanted to do my best. Play my part right." He looked right at me, his eyes pleading. "Isn't that what you pay us for? We did it a bunch of times in rehearsal, didn't we? How'd I know this time would be different?" He sighed and stared off into space before going on, "But it was. When I heard the order, I pulled the trigger but this time the recoil nearly took off my shoulder! Matt's chest rippled and then the blood spouted. He dropped before I even realized he was truly shot." His head dropped between his knees and he laced his fingers behind his neck. He put himself in a personal stockade.

In the silence afterwards, one voice murmured softly from the back of the room, "Nice shot, Annie Oakley."

There were quite a few titters at the remark and I myself had to stifle a laugh. It is one of the uglier traits of human nature to use humor when it is the most inappropriate. Irreverent was always king in my book.

William though admonished the rest of the men.

"Gentlemen! Before you go casting any more stones, I will point out that, besides Barnes, Monroe was also wounded and D'Artagnan, Gilmore, was shot six times! That is eight shots! Every one of you shot someone!"

The joker jumped up from his seat and pointed at the Captain, who sat to my right. "Because he gave us the wrong cue! That jackass flubbed his only line and caused this whole mess!" The rest of the men chimed in all at once and the volume rose to a din.

"Thank you, Gentlemen," William barked in aggravation. "You may go now." He turned and gestured to the captain. "You shall stay. We will discuss your faux paux." The man gulped and sat back in his seat.

William turned to the rest of the men, "Once more I shall say this so take heed. You were all deceived, including your Captain. I warn you against setting the blame on one individual and would remind you that any malicious accusations against one of you will reflect poorly on all of you. Now, you may go."

The others started to object, but William was firm. "You are dismissed! I suggest you make yourselves available when the local authorities arrive. Any man they have to hunt down will more than likely suffer the consequences."

Winslow took no time to clear the room, brandishing his Sapp, "You heard the man, Gents! Out you go!" They fled like chickens, all except the man who shot Barnes who just sat, rocking back and forth. He walked over and tapped the man on the shoulder, "You too, sure shot." Then he hooked one of his massive hands under the man's armpit and held him upright as he walked him out the door.

When he returned and shut the door behind him, William grabbed a chair and placed it directly in front of the Cardinal's Captain. William sat in the chair, arranged his coat, and crossed his legs with a flourish. His eyes bored into the man. "Your name?"

"Timmie', Sir. Timmie' Jackson"

"According to the script, Mr. Jackson, when the curtain rose, the musketeers were to enter stage left and you were to lead your crew from stage right. Upon seeing each other, D'Artagnan was supposed to say a line, to which you were to reply with a challenge. Then D'Artagnan was to hurl his challenge, at which you were to order your men to fire. So, tell me, Jackson, what transpired that you so monumentally flubbed your lines. Please be concise." William paused as we heard loud whistles from outside the room that could only mean one thing. "and expedient."

Jackson gathered his thoughts for a second then answered, "Well sir, I was quite nervous, and I'll admit that as this was my first speaking part. I knew when I was supposed to give the order. When the curtain rose, as soon as I saw Paul, I also saw a sword drawn. Then I was confused and didn't know what happened to the other lines, but I did as I was told a thousand times a thousand ways. When I saw the sword' I was to give the order. So, I did. Exactly like it was beaten into my head!"

"Beaten? How so?" William asked.

"I can answer that, William," Kevin put in, "Benny, our drunken ex-director was annoying to the point of madness with his little diddys and rhymes he pushed on the cast, especially the novices and stock members. He's always saying, 'From the leads, I want emote--- from the stock, I want rote.'"

William looked back to Jackson, "Such as?"

349

"Gee, there was a bunch of them. 'When the blade is high, let them fly!' 'When you see steel, make it real! And my all-time favorite, 'When the sword is out- give your shout!' He nearly drove me bonkers with it! So, all that is going through my mind and when I saw a sword flash, I just lost my head and instinct took over." He hung his head in shame, "I gave the order."

William was a bit relentless on the man, "Yet, Gilmore never drew his sword! I am certain of this as I watched the act unfold."

"I know. I know," the man groaned. "But I did see a sword! I'm certain I did and now that I have had time to think about it, I'm sure it was Porthos, Monroe, who was behind Mr. Gilmore that was holding a sword."

William stared at the man for a minute, but I knew he really wasn't looking at Jackson. His look told me that his vision was turned inward as he sorted and extrapolated every word he had heard. With a large, graceful flourish, he spun from the chair and got to his feet.

"Thank you," he said to Jackson, and then pointed with his hand palm up, at the door and lowered his head. Jackson saw that he was off the hook and he scrambled out the door." When he went out, I caught a glimpse of blue police uniforms herding my protesting cast and crew. We'd be in the hot seat soon.

As soon as the door shut Salmon spoke up, "Mister Gillette, I think you may want to know something. Before Barnes and Higgins were, er,...great friends, Teddy Flint and Barnes were together."

William didn't comment. He just cocked his head and waited.

"Teddy Flint is the chap who shot Barnes."

"HOLY" burst out of me but William whipped his gaze at me so I changed what I would have said, "MOLY! Are you sure?"

Winslow grinned and shrugged, "It's the way I heard it. Everyone knew Barnes threw Teddy over for Higgins."

A lover's quarrel! I thought this would change everything but before I could even ask, once again to my chagrin, William dismissed it.

"Come along Frohman. We must make our way to the hospital before the authorities detain us." He snatched a script off of Salmon's desk and turned to my new junior partner.

"Salmon, can I count on you to give us enough time to slip away and delay them until we return?"

Kevin winked and gave him a wicked grin, "I can do that, but please don't leave me hanging in the breeze too long."

William turned to Winslow, "Can you get us out of here unseen?"

"Piece of cake. Just let me make sure the coast is clear." He cracked open the door and stuck his head out and then back in and turned to Salmon. "You should go out first and distract them, Sir. They're getting close."

Salmon nodded and headed for the door, only to pause in front of William, "Could I have just a clue as to what's so important at the hospital? My curiosity is killing me!"

"I need to speak with Monroe if it is possible."

"Why Monroe?" I asked, as surprised as Kevin.

William smirked, "As our director would surely say. "Because Monroe was the man with a sword in his hand!""

We had to leave it at that as we heard someone shout 'Police!' not too far outside the door. Salmon rushed out into the fray and a second later Winslow gestured for us to follow him. We stepped lively through the crowd, pulling our collars up and keeping our heads down until Winslow led us behind a couple of large pieces of scenery against the back wall. Just before I rounded the corner, I looked back to see a man poking Salmon in the chest and asking snidely, "Why is it we heard about this from the hospital and members of your audience, but we haven't heard a peep out of you?" All I could do for now was cross my fingers, and have another snort as soon as we stopped moving!

There was a doorway hidden back there and Winslow opened it and fumbled about for the light switch. "At the bottom of the steps, just keep walking until you see another set of stairs. Take them up and you can get out of the building. Should be an easy time of night to find a cab to the hospital!"

As we walked down the steps, William said over his shoulder, "Are you not glad that you had the forbearance not to dismiss that man now, Frohman?"

I didn't answer, but, in my mind's eye, I could see the condescending smirk on William's face.

"Oh, I'm ecstatic, William! I just love, after an afternoon of bloodshed, sneaking away from the police on some wild goose chase! Do you have any idea what really happened today?"

William stopped dead and replied, "I was well passed the 'idea' stage over an hour ago, Frohman. Now I need to prove it."

And without another word, he resumed his hurried pace. To my surprise, the second set of stairs led to the apothecary shop. An older gentleman was just hanging up a 'closed' sign when William and I barreled up behind him. The man jumped and stared wide eyed at the two men who suddenly appeared in his empty shop.

William, however, didn't miss a step. "Thank you for your hospitality." he said pleasantly, with a big smile, "We shall leave you to attend to your supper now." He nodded at the doorknob. The old man opened the door without a word, and we stepped out onto the side walk and quickly hailed a cab.

PART FOURTEEN

I angrily finished off my flask on the ride over to the hospital. I was out of sorts because I had a lot of questions and, as usual, no answers. In fact, I was told to shut up so he could think. To be fair, he did phrase it in keeping with his role.

"Please refrain from anymore conversation, Frohman. I dearly need to concentrate."

I was fuming by that point. I wanted nothing more than to throttle William for an answer to why Monroe's sword was important; enough for a sneak away to the hospital while the police were swarming all over my production and crew. I was not about to give him the satisfaction of side stepping the question with an admonishment! As usual, this whole mess was a quagmire of half-facts and missing information, yet, he expected me to see it all as clearly as him!

He didn't pull his nose out of the script until we almost reached the main entrance.

"Find what you're looking for?" I asked in my nastiest tone.

He just looked at me and sighed. "Just checking the facts, Frohman. I already know what's at the root of this."

Before I could jump on that, the cab jostled to a halt. William opened the door and looked at me. "I hope that flask is empty." Then he winked. "You are getting to be quite the curmudgeon."

"Oh Yeah?" I shot back as we climbed out, "Well you should try being around you and stay sober."

I had no time to question him further as he raced up to the reception desk and sweet talked the girl into telling us what floor Monroe and Gilmore were on. I had to rustle up two flights of stairs after him before we finally stopped at the Nurses' station. The woman who was manning the station was a pretty thing, filling out her gleaming white outfit nicely. William and I both leaned over the counter to get her attention, but all we saw was her funny little hat, kind of like a little bowler with enormous wings that was pinned into her hairdo. She never stopped writing notations in her logbook.

"I am heartened to see that this facility has the good sense to employ nurses who were trained at the famous ST. Iverson's."

The girl's head snapped up and she looked at us in surprise, which is all we wanted, but I just couldn't keep my mouth shut. "Now how the hell did you know that William?"

"Why, her lovely Chappal, Frohman. Most nurses where the caps of the schools they graduate from." He beamed his beat smile at her. "You wear yours proudly, Madame."

Now that I could see her face clearly, it was a match for her figure. Then again, maybe her beauty came from anger. She did not look happy.

"Gentlemen, I'm far too busy for smooth talking now. State your business please." Her voice trailed off as her eyes widened and her jaw dropped. I recognized the look -- she just realized who she was talking to.

"You're...are you?"

We didn't have all day to blather, so I stepped in. "I am Charles Frohman, and this is indeed Mister William Gillette, the toast of Broadway and beyond!"

William gave a warning look and focused on the girl. "And you are?"

"Oh, I'm Lisa. Lisa Bailey. Pleased to meet you." She snapped out of it suddenly and looked serious again. She took a deep breath and said, "I suppose you're here to see Mr. Gilmore and Mr. Monroe."

William beamed, "You are as clever as you are accomplished, Lisa bailey. Would it be possible to see them?"

She shook her head, "I'm sorry, but that's not possible."

William gave her the puppy dog eyes, "Not even for a moment? I assure you that it is vitally important."

"I'm sorry but they can have no visitors now. Gilmore is still in surgery and I'm afraid Mr. Monroe is not doing well at all. I'm sorry, but I think the doctors believe they will lose him."

"Why?" I asked. "He only had a wound to his hand!"

"So, it seemed, but he is still failing fast." She looked around then lowered her voice, "I believe the doctors are stumped! There is no infection to his wound, yet he seems to continue to fade quickly!"

"What are his symptoms?" William demanded, with all the authority his voice could hold. The poor girl was answering before the echo died.

"Fever. Distressed respiratory and blurring vison seem to be the front three."

William stepped back suddenly and opened the half door to the station. "Quickly now, Lisa bailey! You need to tell the doctors to look for poisoning! Perhaps arsenic or some other insecticide."

She looked at William like he had three heads. "Why would he have…"

"Go!" William barked and go she did. She hustled past us, looking more than annoyed and muttering something about us 'keeping our shirts on' as she raced off.

Of course, annoying the staff was not enough for my friend. When the nurse had gotten halfway down the long hall, he looked around quickly and stepped right into the Nurse's station! He immediately saw what he was looking for and crouched down to retrieve it. I leaned over the counter, both wondering what he was doing and feeling embarrassment at his total disregard for etiquette. He gave a satisfied grunt and brought his prize into the light.

It was a scabbard. Most likely Monroe's because I remembered the others were accounted for. Still, I had to ask.

"Monroe's?"

"Precisely Frohman!" He held it upside down over his head and squinted into it's opening, and then held it low under the bright lights. "AAAHH!"

He swiveled his head rapidly then locked onto something in our surroundings. He took a few steps up the hall, to where a metal cart was shoved against the wall. Along the top tier, gleaming, were a variety of instruments laid out, obviously ready for some procedure. Without consideration or shame, William plucked a foot-long set of pinchers from its place.

They were gently curved at one end, with fine teeth for grasping and twin metal loops at the other to slip your fingers into. Before I could admonish him, he slid the instrument into the scabbard's aperture, up to his knuckles and began to slide it around. After a moment, he stopped, and his knuckles went white with exertion.

357

He slowly drew the pinchers out and peered at what he discovered. I'm not sure if it was the bright lights, my age, or the fact that I was toting an empty flask, but I couldn't focus on the object.

"What the hell is that?"

"Hold out your hand."

I did as he asked, and he dropped a small metal object into my palm. I practically had to put my nose on my wrist, but I finally saw it clearly.

It was one of the missing musket blank. I just stared at the brass in my hand for a minute before that ray of sunshine broke through the clouds in my head.

"This is why Monroe had his sword partially out, the musket blank was blocking his sword?"

"Remember Frohman, Bernicki told us that the blanks were slightly larger than the real BULLETS." He held the scabbard up to my face, "Smell the inside."

I did and found the unmistakable odor of gun oil.

"I believe Monroe smuggled the ammo to the prop station inside the scabbard, but the first one got stuck when he tried to take the blanks out the same way."

"So, you're saying that Monroe is behind all this? That doesn't make sense. Why? He's lying on death's door himself and if you're inferring this was some kind of elaborate suicide, I don't buy it. I talked to him right after he got shot and he was plenty mad about it then!"

He plucked the blank off my hand and held it up to my face. "Frohman, no matter what you may think or what you may believe, this is a real fact! There is only one explanation for this blank to be in Monroe's scabbard. The scabbard was on him the entire time and you yourself saw him wearing it when they brought him here."

"Maybe someone put it there after he got here!"

William sighed. "Do you really think someone planted seven of the blanks in Higgins room then made his way over to this hospital, located his personal effects, and proceeded past Nurse Bailey to jam the last one into the scabbard?"

"When all other possibilities…"

"I know, I know all that." I groused, yet I could see he was right. No matter how I tried to debunk his theory, it all made sense. If that blank was stuck in his scabbard, then that explained why he had his sword out when it should have been sheathed, which in turn caused the captain to order his men to fire, causing all the mayhem. But who did Monroe want to kill or maim, and why? And why put himself in the line of fire? Unless… *That son of a gun was planning on ducking or hiding! But the Cardinal's man jumped the lines and he got caught with his pants down!"*

William raised his arms and face upwards and shook his hands, "Let the light shine down, for now he sees!"

I ignored his sarcasm, because the only thing I was really seeing then was red! One man dead and my dear friend Paul shot to pieces and all because that snake had some nefarious plot. I couldn't even imagine what he was trying to accomplish, but I was going to choke it out of him and soon as I could find him.

Fists clenched and face in fury; I took off down the hallway, where Nurse Bailey had gone. This time William had to catch up to me. The hallway ended but there was some commotion on the right, about four doors down. I caught a glimpse of the nurse walking towards a bed with a sheet in her arms. Despite William trying to restrain me with his hand on my arm, I barreled into the room.

The bearded man, a doctor, who was writing on a clip board jumped back. The focus of my anger lay on the bed they stood next to. She gave us a hard look as she shook the sheet out.

"Monroe! You...." What came out of my mouth then wasn't fit for an army campfire. William tried to shush me, but I just let the whole day's wrongness flow out in a stream of verbal sewage. Monroe didn't even bother to lift his head, but Bailey sure gave me the evil eye as she flipped the sheet out over Monroe and let it settle over him. She was still glaring when I realized it covered his face too.

"Gentlemen. Please! Show a little respect! The poor man has just passed!" the doctor chided us. Who are you anyways? This area is off limits to visitors and how dare you barge in here while I'm treating a patient!"

"Seeing how he was a murderer," I quipped, "You treated him just fine it seems."

The doctor's nostril flared and before he could retort, William cut him off. "Doctor, was the cause of death poisoning?"

The Doc's eye grew wide and he looked towards Nurse Baily.

"Lisa? Is this the gentleman who..." he let the question trail off.

"Yes Doctor." She turned her glare back on, "These gentlemen came to the station asking about Mr. Gilmore and Mr. Monroe. When I gave them a general overview of their conditions, the tall one sent me to you with the message."

"You were right, sir. Some compound like arsenic, I think. I'll have to do an examination of his blood to be sure. His wound, though serious was not life threatening. He was failing when they brought him in, and we could not stop the process. We assume the cause of his condition was from his wound. The symptoms were similar to shock but much more severe. It wasn't until Lisa gave me your message that I realized it was something else altogether."

"But he was fine before he got shot." I pointed out. "Why wasn't he affected then?"

William chimed in brilliantly, "Some chemicals can lie dormant in your system, or even build up with no visible symptoms, Frohman, and will manifest themselves in a time of stress, then the body's poison absorbing rate will accelerate greatly. Monroe's shock, the adrenaline from the pain, and the loss of blood could easily have raised the chemicals to a lethal dosage."

I really wasn't tracking that entirely, but the medical people in the room looked mighty impressed with William's explanation.

"But how did you know he was poisoned, sir?" the doctor asked him. Suddenly his brows furrowed, "Perhaps the police would like to ask you the same questions."

William gave him a bored look. "Did you notice the scratches on Monroe's left hand, wrist, and forearm?"

"Of course, I did!" the doctor replied indignantly.

"Perhaps in the future you will examine a patient rather than his specific ailment. Hopefully, it will lead you to a deeper understanding in the art of diagnostics so you can treat your patients in a more complete fashion. Good day to you, sir."

With that, William tipped his hat to Nurse Bailey and we turned for the door, however there was a man dressed in blue standing there.

"Did I hear someone say Police? Cuz that would be me."

PART FIFTEEN

He stepped into the room. "You must be Gillette," he stated, pointing at William. "Seen your face on many a Play Bills."

Then he pointed to me, "So that would make you Frohman."

"And you are?" I asked with trepidation. I think I would have rather faced a reporter.

He turned the lapel of his out and revealed a shining brass star. "Deputy Inspector Machaud. The Chief sent me over to fetch the two of you." Then he looked at me closely, with a glint in his eye, "Did I hear you say 'murderer'?"

I jerked a thumb at the bed. "There's your man, Inspector. Though I doubt you'll need to cuff him."

He furrowed his brows, not quite sure if we were pulling his leg, but William stepped in to mollify him.

"I will be happy to offer up an explanation to whoever oversees the investigation and accept your offer of an escort." Then he stepped up and handed the blank to the officer and said "Evidence."

Right on cue, William didn't wait for a reply and started heading out the door. I didn't want to be holding the bag, so I followed on his heels. Behind me I heard the confused policeman say, "Hold on! This is a blank! How do you murder someone with a blank?"

The trip back to the theater was a bit awkward. I wanted to grill William more as I couldn't see how he pinned Monroe for the crime. But, all of my questions faded from my mind as we reached the sidewalk and the Deputy Inspectorsteered us towards a bulky box wagon painted black.

Our mode of transportation was a paddy wagon. Locked in the windowless back with the deputy, we sat on hard uneven wood benches in the gloomy interior. Machaud made it clear that he wasn't an honor guard and we were lucky we weren't in cuffs! We were being brought in for questioning, and possible charges. I could see William stiffen, as he was used to better treatment, both in and out of character. After a few moments to let that sink in, he took a notebook.

Licking his pencil, he looked at William, "So, what happened today? That was a lot of carnage for a play."

William didn't answer right away, but finally replied in his patrician tone, "If I answer that question, do you have the authority to release Mr. Frohman and I."

"Oh no," he assured us shaking his head. "The chief wants you standing in front of him. He was plenty mad the two of you snuck out just as we got there. Everyone says you're the man with all the answers," he added.

"Answers I am not required to provide, Deputy Inspector, and will depend on whether Mr. Frohman and I are treated with the respect we are due!"

The Deputy got a bit cross. "Here now! It's the duty of every good citizen to aid the Police when called upon!"

"No," I pointed out. "It's our duty to pay the taxes from which you draw a salary to do your job. I'm sure our lawyer will explain what degrees of revelations are mandatory to your chief."

"Hear, hear, Frohman." William chimed in.

He didn't have a reply to that, so we spent the rest of the trip in silence. William glaring at the wall across from him, the deputy tossing the musket blank up and down in his hands and me wishing I had something left in my flask.

The scene had changed greatly in our absence. The police had everyone seated and quiet. Every flat foot who lauded over our employees had a pistol hung from their belt and carried a Billy club. My beautiful new theater looked like a prisoner of war camp. A lot of hopeful eyes turned to us as we were walked through to Salmon's office. William just stared straight ahead, fuming that the men escorting us would keep hands on us like we were under arrest.

"Wait here," Machaud instructed us when we reached the closed door. "The chief don't like surprises." He rapped on the wood, "Chief? It's me, Dave. I got Gillette and Frohman with me."

A muffled voice ordered us inside. Our tails had hardly cleared the threshold before the door shut behind us. Machaud brought William and I to an immediate halt and gestured with a finger to his lips for us to remain silent. I thought William might bust a gut.

Machaud walked over to the desk where the Chief was sitting. In fact, he was tilting back in Kevin's office chair with one leg tossed over the corner of the desk. He was a big man with a weathered face and longish graying hair that had the distinct hat marks from the enormous ten-gallon hat on the desk. With his worn cowboy boots and full goatee, he fit the consummate western lawman.

He didn't move a muscle as the deputy gave his report quietly, so only he could hear. He never even twitched until Machaud handed him the blank. Then he slowly turned his head to us. "Dave says that you know who the killer is…but are less than inclined to share with us."

365

William gave him a haughty look that I was sure would lead us to the hoosegow. "Your underling was informed of our conditions for co-operation. Yet he continued to manhandle us in a most unseemly manner."

The Chief glanced at Machaud who shrugged, "I didn't whack'em, and you did tell me to fetch'em."

The Chief looked at him for a moment, and then glanced at us. "Why don't you give me a minute with these Gentlemen, Dave?"

Without a word, the disgruntled Inspector headed for the door and William and I stepped apart to let him pass, which he did without a glance at either of us. When the door shut, we turned our attention back to the chief. He sat the same way and studied the blank in his hand, rolling it through his fingers like a man who has handled ammo his whole life. Finally, he spoke.

"Even out here in the west, I've heard of you Mr. Gillette and, of course I am familiar with your stage work. All that said, I will grant you that you probably know what we are all about. If my Deputy was rude to you in anyway, it was how he interpreted my instructions and that's on me. I am sorry if you were offended."

That was the last thing I expected to hear out of this rugged frontiersman! Even William seemed somewhat mollified and that was hard when he was in character. William gave a little shrug, but his features softened. "Your man was not abusive. Perhaps I was a bit too sensitive."

The Chief nodded sagely. "I have been a lawman for nearly forty years, Mr. Gillette. I've gotten pretty good at it. Horse thieves, cattle rustlers, card cheats and jealous lovers. I've led all kinds to the hangman. But that sort of criminal activity is straight forward. You know who the bad guy is and all you have to do is be stronger or faster or smarter to catch them."

He paused for effect and I realized that this man was in way over his head. He didn't have a clue where to start with this affair. William must have sensed it too because I saw the trademark smirk of his start to creep across lips again.

The chief started again. "Your manager tells me that someone switched the blanks in eight rifles for real bullets, but nobody knows who or why. Now, Dave tells me that you know who switched the ammo." He held the musket blank up between forefinger and thumb, "and one of the men shot, but he died from poisoning! Now, you're not a voting resident or someone under my command, so I will freely admit to you that I can't make hide or hair out of this mess! What can I do to get your cooperation?"

"First thing you can do," I said as I walked up to the desk, "Is to take your feet off the desk." The chief smiled and gave me a slight nod as he swung his boots to the floor. I reached over and open the drawer that was blocked by his calf. As I hoped, there was a bottle of good Irish whiskey lying on its side. Bless that red headed boy!

The chief's eyebrows shot up, "Got two glasses in there?"

I routed around but came up empty. "Not even one," I said as I twisted off the cap and took a good pull right from the neck. "Damn Irish barbarian!"

The Chief took the bottle from me and wiped off the top with the cuff off his shirt. "Heathens! Every one of them!" Then he took a swig. Just like that, we were pals.

"If the two of you would rather bond at the bottom of that bottle, I would be happy to go back to the hotel and get some much needed rest." William said a tad snidely, but with sarcastic humor.

"No. No." the chief protested, "Justice trumps libation in my book."

William nodded and stepped up to the desk. Taking a steno pad and pencil off the top, he jotted a short list of names and handed it to the chief.

"Have your man round up these people and bring them in here. I suggest he collect Kevin Salmon first. That should speed things up." He crossed over to the table and sat. Crossing his legs, he folded his hands across his lap.

The chief stood and looked a bit sheepishly at my friend, "I usually use Dave for my leg work, but I can get another if he rankles you."

William smiled and shook his head. "That is all behind us. I shall organize my thoughts while I wait for our little gathering."

The chief stepped out the door and came back in quickly. He looked as though he was going to address William again, but I gave him a little shake of my head and the bottle instead.

"Got cha," he whispered and winked. "Some men need quiet for the deep thinking."

"Brother, you don't know the half of it." I said.

William remained motionless, staring up at the ceiling as if God was going to let him in on a secret. I knew he was putting together one hell of a narration to lay a dramatic conclusion to this sordid affair. By this point, I was ready to spill everything I knew to the chief just so I could go and get some supper. The day's drinking was taking a toll on my empty stomach.

"Hey William!" I said loudly, "I don't suppose you'd just fill the chief in, so we could make some dinner reservations, Huh?"

William lowered his gaze to me and sighed. "I hope you have the decency to save some of that whiskey for its true owner."

The chief looked a bit sheepish corking the bottle up and slipped it back into the drawer.

I didn't have time to get a decent exchange going as the door swung open and Salmon strode in, leading a small parade. There was B.J., the call boy, Mary, Higgins, and the Captain of the Cardinal's men. Deputy Inspector Machaud brought up the rear and shut the door.

William remained motionless and silent until everyone had a seat. Except for Salmon, who went directly to his desk drawer and pulled out a less than full bottle. He gave me a look out of the corner of his eyes and then opened the drawer beneath it. He shook his head and muttered, "Animals," then pulled out three shot glasses.

He looked at me and shook his head sadly, "Didn't even put my baby in the cradle!" By the time he had poured us a tot, everyone was seated, and William looked ready to start. The low murmur of conversation in the room went dead as the Chief stood and announced,

"My name is Ed Stebbins. I'm the Chief Detective for the Phoenix Police Department. As we arrived late on the scene, I'm going to let Mr. Gillette explain the situation. Best that you know he speaks with my authority, so keep your answers honest and forthcoming or we can do this all back at the station, where you won't be half as comfortable."

He gestured to William and took his seat again, before putting his glass in the open drawer to pour another splash out of everyone's sight. I thought his speech was a bit melodramatic seeing how we already knew who the killer was.

William, on the other hand, had an audience now and was enjoying this immensely. He lived for a good soliloquy and he was every bit in a great Sherlock detective moment. At a slow pace, he began to move about the room. Like any great actor, he would let the tension build a little before he began. He stopped when he was dead center of everyone's sight and clasped his hands behind his back.

"Today we suffered the loss of two colleagues."

"TWO?" B.J. cried out. Mary was out of her chair just as fast, "Oh NO! Paul?"

I saw the flash of irritation on William's face as he hated to be interrupted, I smoothed it out. "B.J. sit down and keep quiet!" He did what he was told but Mary wasn't about to cooperate.

"Was it Paul?" she sobbed. When William didn't answer right away, I jumped in again. "No Miss Corbet, it was Monroe, though, Paul is in bad shape."

"Oh, Mother Mary save us!" she wailed and then her voice turned to a keening pitch, "First Athos and now Porthos! Why? What has happened here?" She carried on for a moment until she stood on the brink of hysteria. Clutching her ample bosom, with tears streaming down her face, her tirade was reduced to repeating 'Why?' over and over.

Thankfully, Salmon was the one to go to her and try and calm her while the rest of us rolled our eyes at each other in a common thought 'Women!'. Salmon managed to get her to focus again and sat her down gently, keeping an arm around her shoulders as he sidled next to her. She seemed to regain some strength from his presence.

William acted as if he were never interrupted. "And a third lies on the threshold between the light and the dark. All by design." He paused and looked around the room.

"These are the facts we know: First, B.J. loads the weapons in the prop room then places the eight muskets and a pistol at the prop station for use later in the play. Unseen by anyone in the opening night mayhem, someone entered the prop station and switched the blanks for live ammo. We know this because of the catastrophic results of this evening and the fact that we recovered seven of the blanks that were planted in Higgin's room."

"And we know that how?" The Chief Ed Stebbins asked.

"Because Higgins never went back to his dressing room after the start of the first act and the bullets were switched later," I replied for William.

"Excellent Frohman!" William said. "Though whether Higgins was a red herring, or his unlocked room was convenient, we will never know for sure."

Before he could go on, Christine looked up at Salmon and said, in a daze, "Why am I here?" Then she looked at William and asked again, "Why am I here? Why must I endure this? I have nothing to do with any of this."

"That, Madame, is not entirely true. In fact, you are the crux of this matter." Salmon slowly unwrapped his arm from around her and scooched over on the bench, away from her.

"If you had not so proudly displayed your gift of roses to us earlier in the day, I may not have made the proper connections. It was the thorns that led to our killer. Tell me, did you ever have a relationship with Lewis Monroe?"

The question caught us all off guard, but Mary managed to keep her wits about her. After a moment, she answered slowly. "He may have shown some interest in me back in New York. I always suspected he signed up for this gig so he could follow me out here with high hopes. I suppose we became friends on the trip out, but when I met Paul, sparks flew -- if you know what I mean. Still, what does that have to do with some cheap roses and a bit of bad poetry?"

"And I thought you said that someone had clipped them from the roses that were planted on the east wall?" I put in. A light burst in my head as I looked at William. "The scratches on Monroe's arms! You're saying that Monroe was the one who put the roses in her stall?"

"The evidence strongly suggests it, Frohman. I have pruned many a rose in my day and I recognize the marks the thorns leave on one's skin when they are drawn against the skin."

"Let's be clear on this," the chief cut in. "You're saying that this Monroe fellow switched the bullets because he was still carrying a torch for this young lady?"

"That's stupid!" B.J. snapped. "Why would he put real bullets in a bunch of rifles that were pointing at him? Just because he was mooning over this broad, that doesn't make him that big a fool! You are way off base if you think roses and a love note proves that!"

To my surprise, William gave him a look of compassion. "I know he was your friend B.J., but there is more." He turned to the call boy. "Tell us what happened when you came to collect the props, after the shooting. When you came to Monroe."

372

"Well, you were there, Sir. I already had his sword from when he dropped it, but when I asked for the pistol, he tried to knock my block off with it. I never did get his scabbard."

William just looked at B.J. and waited.

B.J. looked deep in thought for minute then his face drooped, and he heaved a mighty sigh.

"I'm afraid so." William said gently. "I believe he switched the ammo and then took the pistol for an alibi if anyone had seen him."

"So, this was some elaborate murder-suicide?" the chief asked. "Mad with love, he tries to off himself and he doesn't care who he takes with him?"

"The answer to that lies with our Captain of the Cardinal's guard." William gestured. "But I shall not make him give voice to his mistakes. The gist is that Monroe had his sword out in plain sight, which confused the actors and they fired prematurely. I would surmise that Monroe, having switched the bullets, was planning on ducking to one side or hiding behind a piece of scenery when Gilmore, as D'Artagnan, called his challenge and pulled his sword. But he was caught off guard when Mr. Jackson saw his sword and gave the order to fire too soon."

William pause for a moment then added, "This, I believe, is how the scenario unfolded. Monroe, having decided to exact revenge for unrequited love, figured switching the bullets would suit his purposes. If he was quick and careful, not only could he take out his rival for Mary, he may just move up a spot on the billing."

"So, the others were just fodder?" Salmon asked angrily.

William shrugged, "It appears he didn't care either way and it has no bearing on the outcome. One must

373

consider the costumes worn by the musketeers to understand why Monroe did what he did. The main article of clothing was a one piece, tightly fit, cotton Johnnie, covered by a simple tunic. Then there was a light floppy hat and cloth boots made to look like leather. There were no pockets pouches to carry anything in."

"I remember Paul complaining to me about that. I had to give him a cigarette and a light because he had no way to carry them." I put in.

"Yes, Frohman, and he was right. Only the sword belt and the scabbard. Thus, I believe that Monroe must have smuggled the real bullets into the prop station inside his scabbard. Eight bullets at the bottom of the sheath would still give him room to insert his sword.   But what Monroe did not account for was the larger size of the blanks."

"Blanks are bigger. I told you that before," B.J. said.

"Which is why," William replied, "That after Monroe switched the blanks with bullets, he discovered that he could not use the same method for taking the blanks out of the station. In fact, the first one he put in became stuck inside the scabbard and he was left holding the other seven musket blanks and he could not get his sword back in the scabbard."

"Which is why he carried the sword in his hand when the curtain went up for the second half!" I blurted out.

"Knowing that Higgins was spending the intermission in Barnes's stall, he slipped into Jeremy's room and put the other seven in his table," Salmon chimed in, shaking his head sadly, "Cheeky."

There was a stunned silence until Chief Stebbins cleared his throat and stood slowly. Hooking his thumbs in his gun belt, he spoke in a gruff, rumbling voice.

"That was a fair piece of figuring Mr. Gillette and I hate to be the fly in the gravy but there is one point you haven't addressed. You lay a great case against this Monroe fellow and I am satisfied, but I was told he died, not from his wound, but from poisoning!"

"Excellent. You have been paying attention." I almost slapped my forehead, but William plowed on before anyone lost their temper.

"Perhaps it would be more accurate to say it was a combination of two factors. When Monroe took the roses to put in Mary's dressing room, he was scratched up. Whenever one transplants a rose bush or bushes in this case, they are watered thoroughly and more often than not, sprayed with a powerful insecticide to give the plant a good chance to root itself. The dose of poison from multiple rose pickings built up in his body was probably not enough to kill him, but when he was shot, with the shock and the loss of blood, his heart pumped faster and the lethal toxin was released into his heart and he perished."

We all sat silently for a moment until William caught my eye and nodded slightly at the call boy, who had a quizzical look on his face and was shaking his head.

"Penny for your thoughts," I said to him.

All eyes turned on him and, with his eyes darting to Miss Corbet and back, he said slowly. "Gee, Sir. I don't know. It's just that, well, he went through all that sneaking and still ended up dead! Ain't love grand!"

Christine had the grace to blush and bury her head in Salmon's shoulder.

I took a gold piece from my vest and flipped it to the boy, who snatched it out of the air before it traveled two feet.

"You're all free to go," the Chief Stebbins announced. Everyone didn't need to hear that twice, and they left with the barest of acknowledgement to us. Salmon had to help Mary out of her seat, and he walked her out as she clutched him like a lifeline.

Deputy Inspector Machaud closed his notebook and the Chief stuck his hand out to me.

"Thanks for the drink, Mr. Frohman. I'm not sure I could have understood half of this without it!"

"I know exactly how you feel, Ed."

The Deputy put out his hand and I shook it, then they stepped over to William.

Chief Ed Stebbins drew himself up to his full height and looked William right in the eye. "I will admit I had my doubts, but I can assure you that I believe everything I have heard about you, Sir, including your handling of the Hermes Brothers just days ago." He stuck out his hand and William took it, "It has been and honor and a pleasure to watch you in action. And now I must attend to those details you mentioned earlier." He put his hat on his head and walked out the door.

Machaud stepped up. Wordlessly, he removed his hat and bowed his head to William.

William, of course, was grateful to accept his praise with little more than a slight twitch of the corners of his mouth. He was looking away when the deputy followed his boss.

I shook my head and poured another drink. "It's over now William. You can put Sherlock back in his closet."

I went to pick up my drink and found the tip of his cane lying across the top of it. "And you don't need another drink, Charlie! Not until we have dinner at least!"

"Then let's go get dinner, earlier I heard there is a great steak place just down the block."

EPILOGUE

I was standing on the train platform with William and Salmon, who had come to see us off. It was the main rail station in Phoenix, as we were taking a regularly scheduled locomotive for the ride back. I'd wanted nothing short of normal for this trip. Normal cars. Normal people. Normal drinks.

To be honest, I'm not sure we'd be welcome on Cooper's train again. Rae, my secretary, wired me with the new arrangements and hinted that was the case. Well, the hell with him, first class on the St. Louis line would be just fine with us!

The porters were just about to load our luggage, so it was time for final instructions and farewells.

"Kevin, I'll wire you as soon as I get back to the office and we'll figure out what you need to get the cast and crew back home. Until then, just continue to break it down and pack it up." I tried to be matter-of-fact, but inside my gut was churning over the bath I would take on this venture. "It's too bad, but there you have it. This whole fiasco has been a wash."

Salmon cocked his head, shut one eye, and held a finger up, then said, "The thing is, Charles, I've been thinking about staying here for a while. We still have the lease and Bernicki is willing to give it a go. Also, wardrobe, the lighting boys, the stage crew, and a decent percentage of the cast. And! I already have a beautiful and talented leading lady for the next production!" He

378

turned and waved to a woman, who to my surprise, turned out to be our own Miss Corbet. She waved back coquettishly. "It's going to be a Romantic Comedy. We'll set Phoenix on its ear!"

I loved his enthusiasm, but he seemed to be forgetting one of his biggest challenges.

"And just who is going to pay for all this Salmon? You may be a junior partner, but your first play never even made it to the final curtain."

He bridled a bit at that, "Perhaps, but that was no fault of ours! Besides, I have ways to raise my own capital."

"You're dreaming, Kev-."

"I have pledged my support, Charlie." William said quietly. He saw the look of utter surprise on my face and continued, "Kevin is an excellent manager and he deserves a chance. You know this, Charlie, that's why you made him a partner in the first place."

Kevin went on. "Many of the cast and crew have spent what money they saved to come out here for a fresh start. We can't fault their work or squash their dreams because of a lone love-sick madman. It's a good play and I'm sure we can find the investors to carry it off."

Now, they just didn't know who they were dealing with. I didn't get to where I am today by letting amateurs cut me out of a deal! And there were still all the original reasons why I wanted an outlet here in Phoenix. Time to set these two on the straight and narrow!

"The two of you should try swimming closer to the shore, where you can touch, because you're getting in over your heads here. May I remind you that I and I alone, hold the lease for this property, so, unless the drug store next door will let you set up some chairs and do your play there, you will have to deal with me. I decide whether the show goes on or not!" I let that soak in for a minute, and went on in a calmer tone, "So, you'll be a full partner. BUT the only one you'll get any money from is ME! I want a business plan on my desk by the time I get back to New York. Nothing too fancy, just an outline and some cost estimates." I shook a finger in his face and added "I had better not be throwing good money after bad Kevin…got me?"

He stuck out his hand and I took it. "I'll do you proud, Charles. In three years, Phoenix will be the Broadway of the west!"

"See that it is." I saw Mary casually walking closer, obviously dying to know what happened. "Now go tell the girl the good news."

He laughed and stuck out his hand to William, "Sir, if I live to be one hundred, I shall never see a performance like I did a few days ago. Thank you for everything."

When he said that last piece, I saw his eyes flick over to me and I knew I'd been had. Once again, William maneuvered me into doing the right thing. You are only truly had if you *admit* that you've been had, and I wasn't about to spill those beans. Ironically, I was tricked into a great investment!

William and I watched as Salmon took Miss Corbet by the shoulders and started talking excitedly. She dropped her parasol and threw her arms around my red-haired partner and kissed him soundly. After an embarrassing minute or two it was obvious that the kiss was more than celebratory. Salmon always did have bad judgement, when it came to women.

"Looks like our Miss Mary had decided to settle for the back of the house," William commented dryly.

I shrugged, "Beauty fades, and tastes change, but guys like Salmon and me will be around long after your stars have waned."

"Charlie, I plan to be playing Sherlock for a long, long time. You will keep making money.

"You just need some new material…"

Biography

James Michael Walker has been a professional chef for forty years proudly serving the residents and tourist around Mystic, CT.

His love of the New England coastline, local history, and mystery classics has inspired him to write many William Gillette Sherlock mysteries. Jim has been creating books set along the Connecticut shoreline since 1998, and lives in Mystic, Connecticut with his wife.

Books Published by J.M. Walker

The Case of the Flying Corpse

**Accounts of William Gillette
Five Mysteries**

JM Walker is on Facebook and Instagram. His books are available at:

Local Connecticut and Rhode Island Book Stores

Amazon.com